Noel Goreham is a budding middle-aged writer who only recently discovered storytelling and writing. By day he is surrounded by his cats, as he lovingly cares for his two children. His patient wife finances his lifestyle choices as he lives happily under the hot sunny rays of Dubai.

Edwige Narbey is now a temporary homemaker in Dubai, after fifteen years in the epic field of special needs education in France. With time on her hands and her appetite for fresh adventures, she wrote for the first time at forty, in English. She learns kite surfing occasionally.

Jarita C. Mitra believes that writing is that magical moment when thoughts floating in the universe meet her mind and they engage in a deep conversation. When she is not writing, Jarita enjoys a very fulfilling life as a mom to her teenage son, while balancing her multiple roles as an industry leader in healthcare logistics, cofounder of her free community library, and an NLP practitioner and mentor. Jarita sees her future self as a full-time author and motivational speaker.

Rashmi T. K. wears many 'hats' in her life like that of a mother, personal mastery coach, non-profit strategy consultant, and accidental nutritionist. Her newest hat is of a writer of stories: a shameless eavesdropper taking inspiration from her surroundings! She needs to tell the many stories that buzz in her head, gaining inspiration from her surroundings. After all, as they say, 'Truth is stranger than fiction'!

Fatima Ibrahim Faras is a young pharmacist. Along with her interest in science, she has always had a passion for writing, for as long as she can remember. She loves to write poetry and short stories, which help her to express her thoughts. She feels deeply inspired by the indescribable feeling when people tell her how her words move them.

Asma Khalid Yousuf Baker is an artist at Mawahib. She loves to draw and write about the world through a whole new light. She started writing when she was in her 9th grade and has kept writing ever since then. Crime fiction is Asma's favorite genre and she likes to write about mysteries.

Pam Jackson Murrell is an American living in Dubai. She is a creative soul, expressing herself as an author, entrepreneur, mother, and wife. As a long aspiring author, she has now finally taken action to begin a writing career. She believes deeply in the power and magic of words to inspire, impress, and ignite the hearts, minds, and actions of people everywhere.

Nudrat Majid is a preschool educator who is busy dancing to the tunes of her three teenagers when she isn't busy teaching toddlers. Nudrat also multi-tasks as a chef, cleaner, chauffeur, and a loving wife (not exactly in this order). But her secret avatar is that of a writer and she loves to read, along with spinning magnetic tales.

Ali Ihsan Cetiner is an Istanbulite living in Dubai. He is the proud father of two, an electrical engineer and the GM of a manufacturing company. He continues to scratch his head to solve the mystery of why he has this immense urge to write. The answer may be in the exciting ideas he harbors for the sci-fi stories he plans to write soon!

Rala Sabouni is a wife and a full-time mother. She has enjoyed raising her three kids in different countries around the world, wherever her husband's work has taken them. Due to her fascinating travels, she lived through, heard of, and saw many 'stories' that are worth sharing. Presently settled in the UAE, and with the kids having left the nest, Rala has more time on her hands to put all those stories on paper and pursue her passion to write.

Banu Alptekin is an HR professional with over twenty years of work experience. When she recently moved to Dubai with her family, she was happy to take on the role of a homemaker. Banu is Turkish, a mother of two kids, and happy to get out of her comfort zone. In fact, she has even started writing short stories in English!

L. Toma is an education consultant who believes that education is the superpower every child needs to change the world. L. Toma is passionate about learning, reading, visual communication, and discovering different cultures. L. Toma likes to explore writing, 'traveling' to different worlds of genres and characters.

Shetha Hijazi is an assistant manager at an amusement park entity. She is also a cancer survivor. At the age of nineteen, she was diagnosed with stage 4 oral cancer. She is currently working on her first memoir about her life with cancer, to give hope to other cancer patients out there who need strength.

Ruhie Jamshed

TRAVELERS' TALES

AUSTIN MACAULEY PUBLISHERS™

LONDON • CAMBRIDGE • NEW YORK • SHARJAH

ISBN – 9789948259190 – (Paperback)
ISBN – 9789948259275 – (E-Book)

Application Number: MC-10-01-6162086
Age Classification: E

First Published (2021)
AUSTIN MACAULEY PUBLISHERS FZE
Sharjah Publishing City
P.O Box [519201]
Sharjah, UAE
www.austinmacauley.ae
+971 655 95 202

Table of Contents

Foreword

Writing has a powerful purpose in our existence. Words tease our thoughts, change our opinions, and can even balm our souls. It is an art form that can transform the world. The pen, as they say, is after all, more powerful than the sword. Indeed, writers wield the power of change. For instance, many world leaders have poured their visions and opinions onto paper and revolutionized societies. The ability to be able to write well is a valuable skill and one that can be mastered.

It is quite interesting to me, then, as a 'crusader' of the written word, to discover that writing is also much-feared. For more than a decade as a writing coach and wordsmith myself, I have been fascinated to learn how picking up the pen and laying one's soul naked for the world to see on the bare blanket of paper can be a frightening ordeal for many. In more than a decade of trying to proliferate the love of writing in countries such as Australia, Singapore, and the United Arab Emirates, I have often had to climb a rather high mountain. I suppose writing is challenging not only because of the technical skills involved, but also because it requires digging into the depths of the human soul.

Children, of course, are much more receptive to penning their thoughts and stories than grown-ups are. Little ones tend to be far more creative and expressive with the written word. This probably stems from the fact that young children have not gone through the rigors of life and an educational system long enough to chain them into the prisons of a mold. Children are, in any case, naturally more predisposed to creativity, and fear encapsulates them less. The younger they are, the more easily their imagination soars on paper! However, I have realized that the task of getting adults to pen their stories is a much more arduous one.

Many adults fear being judged. They fear being vulnerable before the reader. It takes a lot for most to chip away the blocks of their consciousness and write with their hearts. Some of them might have previously believed an authority figure like a parent or a teacher who told them that they couldn't write. Others might be 'in-the-closet' writers who can never imagine letting anyone else read their work due to a lack of self-confidence. Yet, my experience as a writing coach has proved that after some egging on, many of the adult writers are capable of producing magic on paper.

My crusade, desire, and passion to spread the love of writing in society led me to design the Short Story Writing Workshop. During the workshop, a group of adult participants who made Dubai their home, got together to learn and be inspired to pen their very own collection of short stories. Many asked me why I chose to name this ambitious book project, *Travelers' Tales*. Put simply, Dubai is a vibrant city that serves as the meeting ground for people from various cultures. It is a melting pot that many people from all over the world call home for whatever time. Therefore, many in Dubai and the UAE at large, are the so-called travelers. However, this word, 'traveler,' need not only have a direct meaning – it can also be interpreted to refer to the traveling souls that all humans are.

If we think about it, each one of us is a traveling soul that goes through life and each one of us has a unique tale to tell. Indeed, the *Traveler's Tales* isn't just about actual traveling stories but stories about the human life experience. This collection of 14 stories written by first-time writers, who are all Dubai residents, consists of tales of pain, humor, mystery, traditions, the supernatural, and much more. As we embarked on this writing workshop to create this book, each participant was led to conjure up their unique tale that would resonate with their inner selves. I insisted that though there is a theme to follow, each one should pick their own story to tell which would have their distinct mark and style. This was, after all, their tale, one that was to be etched in the pages of this book forever!

The journey of eight weeks to pen each of their eight-thousand-word short stories was not an easy one. Lots of hurdles lay in the writers' unique paths. There were often protests of lack of time as many of these writers held grueling full-time jobs. They had to be inspired, encouraged, and 'pulled up' when they would slump into 'giving up' mode. Many did not take the criticism that came their way too positively. They had to whisk their unhappiness aside, bring objectivity into the picture, and persevere to rewrite their work. Tenacity and determination were a requirement, in addition to the good writing skills that many already possessed. Each participant in the workshop mastered the nuances of story writing like structure and descriptions, certainly ending up honing their craft overall and, I am sure, came out of the whole experience stronger and with a lot more confidence to write!

At the end of the 'race,' there were several 'winners' who are now a part of this beautiful book. Indeed, many of these writers have learned what an uphill task (even though a fulfilling one) is to write and I am sure they will agree that they have begun to appreciate writing and writers more. I, for one, cannot possibly ever forget the look of excitement and sheer joy that sprawled across each one of their faces when their stories were finally approved for publication.

Where I am concerned, I am truly happy that I started and finished this journey. Honestly, although this was a vision very close to my heart, I had to see how things would map out and if this dream would eventually materialize. Today, I can proudly say that it is indeed a wonderful feeling to realize a vision and contribute to making the dreams of many aspiring writers come true! I don't know if 'finished' is the right word, though. Does such a literary journey laced with passion and purpose ever end? Perhaps, having this book in our hands is just the beginning!

This book is my baby, but fourteen wonderful, inspiring individuals have helped to 'mold' this child. I leave you, the reader, now to experience the joy and amazement of reading these fourteen stories penned by fourteen unique individuals from all over the world – fourteen individuals who met in one place called Dubai to create this book through the Short Story Workshop. Their stories, I am sure, will inspire you, touch you, motivate you, and even entertain you! I have to reiterate here to emphasize that these are first-time writers who never quite thought that they would be able to write the eight thousand words that they did!

As you read through their tales, I hope you get inspired to write too. To spread the love of writing and propel would-be writers to pick up the pen is the mission of this book. I hope you enjoy the labor of love that the travelers in and of Dubai have so lovingly penned.

Ruhie Jamshed (M. Ed)

Writer, Editor, and Writing Coach

Without A Home

By Noel Goreham

The wind raged from across the North Sea to the Thames Estuary. Even half a mile inland, Emma couldn't be sheltered from these howling gales. She pulled her sleeping bag closer to her body in the hope that it would cocoon her from the elements. Her trusted flattened cardboard box had done exceptionally well to last a full week, especially considering the amount of inclement weather the town had experienced recently.

The rain had lashed from the heavens continuously for the past 24 hours, and the shelter she got from the organic soap shop doorway was inadequate at best. Nevertheless, she had no choice but to sleep another night with cardboard propped up over her head.

From the other side of the street, all that could be seen of Emma were the whites of her dark eyes and her fingers gripping tightly to her bedding.

After living on the streets for three years, it had become easy for Emma to sleep in any condition and position, and she was a particularly heavy sleeper. Hence, a night like this was no different from any other – she slept like a baby.

She awoke to a fresh day. It was as if someone had taken to the roads with a power hose and washed away all the greyness of the town. A seagull stood beside her pecking at an old piece of chewing gum that was stuck to the pavement. There was a time she would have shooed it away without a thought, but after becoming homeless, she felt a connection with all vagabond creatures. She looked down and smiled.

It was very early and the high street was deserted. It was time to get up because the shop owner would be coming soon to move her on from the shop front. The shopkeeper was polite yet stern, she recalled.

It was too late. "Excuse me, if you are to use my doorway as a bed, please could you leave it as you found it?" The organic soap shop owner was approaching her quickly, seeming taller with each step.

Emma, now with great haste, gathered what few belongings she had and tried to make off in the opposite direction. *Wow, this woman moves fast*, thought Emma, as the shopkeeper stood in front of her, preventing her exit.

"Oh… it's you," the woman said in surprise.

Emma smiled for no more than a second.

"I think it must be difficult to find somewhere… good to sleep since all those other… people have arrived, but as I said, I'd appreciate it if you could keep my shop front nice and clean." She finished talking and motioned for Emma to move along.

With a bag in one hand and cardboard under her other arm, Emma sidled around the shop owner, heading towards one of the more popular locations in the hope to find a friendly face.

"Before you go," she heard the shopkeeper shout from behind her, "I'm helping out at the homeless shelter, so please stop by and I'll make sure you get a healthy portion of supper."

However, Emma didn't stop walking; she rarely wanted anything to do with 'normal' folk these days.

After five minutes of walking, she made it to one of the service alleyways off the high street, where she found Nazir hanging inside a large bin.

Like many of the new faces in town, Nazir had arrived from Syria via several other European countries. Being smuggled across land and sea, he had experienced perilous boat trips on near sinking ships, he'd walked for miles and miles through rain and sun, and he had sneaked onboard trucks until he reached Calais where, under the cover of night, he clambered on board a moving train as it darted in the Channel Tunnel from France to England.

"Morning, Naz, what you found?" she shouted into the bin. His gruff voice reverberated around the metal sides of the rubbish container. She didn't have a clue what he said. Not that he didn't speak English, but he was half-buried in black rubbish sacks whilst chewing on a recently discovered sandwich, so Emma could barely hear him. Nazir half rolled back out of the bin, landing on his feet, clutching onto four packaged ham-and-tomato sandwiches.

"You've hit the jackpot," said Emma with a thumbs up. Taking a second to compose himself, he stared into Emma's eyes and handed one of the sandwiches to her.

They sat down together on a dry patch and propped themselves up with the alleyway wall. After eating their breakfast in silence, Emma swallowed her last mouthful and asked Nazir where Ola was.

"We fought," Nazir replied. "She said I want to take her things and pull her and shake her," he continued.

"And did you?" asked Emma.

His eyes lit up with disgust as he replied, "I would never do such a thing. I love her."

Emma nodded in agreement and dropped her eyes to the gray pavement, hoping that would be apology enough for such an accusation.

In many ways Ola reminded her of the sister she had lost all those years ago; her eyes were full of joy and as bright as the first days of spring, and she had a smile that brought warmth and humor like a secret joke that no one else would understand. Emma's sister, who she shared every birthday with and experienced various milestones with, was taken away by cancer. It was half of Emma that no loving husband or needy child could ever replace.

Her thoughts began to drift and several minutes of silence passed, broken only by the occasional cough.

"Any news on Adnan?" Emma finally asked.

"Maybe he found a better spot in a better town. Maybe he is with more Syrians. Maybe he has a job," Nazir said hopefully. Adnan was yet another homeless vagabond who had arrived on the streets within the last few months. After escaping the detention center he was put in when he arrived, Nazir and Ola had taken him under their wing. He spoke no English, so they taught him some basic words like 'Please,' 'Food,' 'Water,' 'Work.' He was a quick learner, and in no time, started stringing short sentences together. On top of that, he was a good forager, able to get his skinny body into all sorts of nooks and stretch his long arms into the deepest of bins. He had been their savior on the hungriest of days when no morsel of food could be found and the soup kitchen was closed. If you could find Adnan, then you were almost guaranteed to eat something.

He had gone missing the previous week, and no one had seen or heard anything from him since. He often worked alone and liked his own space, but would still generally meet up with the rest of the community at the end of a day. Homeless people going missing was nothing unusual – sometimes they would be picked up by the police or local authorities, and other times they would be taken into hospital. Nevertheless, they would mostly return. Occasionally, people would be found dead on the streets for any number of reasons including alcohol and drug overdoses, hyperthermia, or other health problems. But for a homeless man in his mid-twenties, Adnan was relatively healthy and he wasn't into drugs.

"The sun is shining today," Emma mentioned, breaking another five minutes of silence. "Perhaps Ola is down at the beach?"

Nazir shrugged both shoulders.

Emma interpreted this as, "I don't know, I don't care, and I have little motivation right now, so please leave me alone."

With the help of the wall, she got herself to her feet. Walking away from Nazir, she headed towards the high street. Just before turning the corner, she looked back to check. He had his head in his hands, staring down onto the pavement. Depressed, he was the most miserable she had seen him. She had also been a frequent sufferer over the times living rough. She hoped that finding Ola would cheer him up.

Nazir had come here for a better life and at the moment any life would be better than the one he was living. He wanted to work, not only for the money but to keep him sane. He wanted to provide – to prove that all the sacrifice, all these travels, all this humiliation, was worth it.

Emma spotted her, the wind tugging at her dark green headscarf. A wisp of dark brown hair danced about in the gusts, covering her pale forehead.

Ola was sitting amongst the pebbles on the beach, sorting through her favorite shells. She liked to collect the most pearlescent ones and make jewelry – sometimes she could even sell them for money. The lustrous inside of the shells reminded her of how skin once looked when she was a girl, not the dull gray lifeless stuff that covered her body now.

As she grew closer, Emma called out to her. Ola looked up and beamed once she recognized her friend. She patted the pebbles beside her for Emma to join her.

They sat on the beach all day using the old fishing tackle to hook the seashells together, creating necklaces and bracelets, hoping they could sell them in the forthcoming days.

Emma was at her happiest when with Ola, forgetting all her worries. Somehow, she felt as if her late sister was with her when she was with Ola. After an hour of chatting, Ola and Emma soon began to feel the pangs of hunger. They looked around to see if there were any morsels of food around when they remembered that the doors of the neighborhood Soup Kitchen should already be open.

The Soup Kitchen of St Benedict's was the saving grace for many homeless people in town. It was open every evening except for Sundays when the church's facilities were normally at full stretch from the worshippers attending the various ceremonies.

On this particular Friday evening, Ola and Emma soon joined the queue, still busily chatting as if they had not had any trouble in the world. Looking like old friends all excited, perhaps lining up to check into a flight to exotic destinations, or waiting to be sat at the opera.

The splat of the soup into the bowl brought them back to reality and they stopped mid-sentence.

"Thank you very much," Emma looked up and smiled at the owner of the organic soap shop.

"Now let me make sure you are both well-fed," and plopped another half ladle of brown meaty soup into her bowl.

Only now did Emma realize what a friendly face she had and felt bad for ignoring the woman earlier in the day. "It smells very nice," she remarked.

The organic soap shop woman gave a warm smile followed by a "You're welcome."

Soon, taking their full soup bowls along merrily, they sat on a round table which an old lady had just finished wiping down. It had seating for six people but only one seat was taken.

"Hello Hassan," Emma said to the older man.

His confused and heavily bearded face finally gave way to a toothless smile. He never made eye contact – instead, he attempted to inconspicuously duck his head below the table to take a swig of something from a paper bag.

"Isn't Nazir usually here?" Emma asked Ola.

"Maybe he is still angry with me."

"Did you think it was he who attacked you? I know the streets can change your brain but…" Emma replied, pointing to her head. Ola shook her head. "No, I do not think he did this. Somebody woke me, and I was scared. Nazir was next to me but thought he had too much vodka to remember to do anything."

"You mean someone else tried to attack you?"

"Yes. Maybe to steal my things."

Soon, the holy man came over to the table. He was a walking cliché of a priest; Father O'Brien was an Irish man in his mid-50s, head bald on top with short gray curls at the side. He wore tiny wire-framed spectacles and a large smile.

"How are you ladies this evening? Oh, and… Hassan?" Ola gave a nod to the priest as he looked at her for confirmation. Meanwhile, Hassan had passed out, head down, snoring away with a pool of dribble now building up under his chin.

The priest's attention returned to the two friends.

"How are you enjoying the hot meal tonight? You can thank the butcher for the extra meat this week. He had an abundance of venison I think, so we have a very hearty soup this evening. Good, don't you think?"

Emma had to admit this was one of the best meals she'd had in a very long time.

Father O'Brien wasn't a man who waited for answers. He was already looking around, trying to make eye contact with some other visitors to his church.

"Before you go, Father, have you seen Nazir today?" Emma asked.

"Hmm, I'm afraid not, but if I see him, I'll pass a message on." With that, he moved on to his next target, a reformed drug user. After finishing their bowls of food and warming their bodies from the church's radiators, Emma and Ola left church from the top of the high street walking back down toward the beach. The clear night's sky brought with it a coldness to the air, a coldness that would enliven the very fullest of bellies and sleepiest of heads.

For the first time in a long while, Emma was able to take in and appreciate her surroundings: the gothic church at the top of the high street, the narrow road once wide enough for single lane traffic had now been pedestrianized, a street as straight as an arrow that swept off to a right angle in an Easterly direction toward the shingle that covered the beach.

Much like the tides that creep up on the shores each day, the town's fortunes had drifted in and out. Once a small fishing hamlet, the Victorian era was a boom time bringing weekend holiday-makers and tourism. Much of the shops built during that time were the most pleasing to the eye and still in the prime location.

Unfortunately, the town stagnated after this period with many years of depression in the region due to migration away from the coast and wars in Europe. Not until the 1960s did people begin coming back to the seaside. The buildings of this time are more noticeable further away from the ocean in the less desirable parts of town.

Ever since she had been living here, the changes to the town have been very visible. Tea rooms had been replaced with betting shops, clothes stores replaced by charity shops, souvenir shops closed and boarded up, and the hotel was now a very popular squat.

She knew many blamed the influx of refugees on the town's demise. The government could not handle the number of people smuggling themselves through the tunnel from France. If they surrendered themselves to the local authorities, they would be put in detention centers waiting for files to be processed. Once they had been processed, they would often be sent back to where they came, perhaps not a war

torn country but as close to that as possible and as far away from this one.

So, these people instead opted to live on the street, stay with friends, and hopefully, some work would come along where they could live under the official radar.

The police had scarce resources to deal with the problem which some had branded as an epidemic. By and large, they would occasionally round up some troublesome individuals from one town and drop them back into another. The issue was that some towns had more than their fair share of homeless people with no facilities to address the situation.

Emma and Ola were now beginning to get worried about Nazir. They looked in his usual haunts. The bins behind Wimpy Burger, the doorway of the abandoned hotel, the chalets on the beach. It was not until they arrived back in an alleyway off the high street did they find some evidence of his being: Nazir's beanie hat – a blue one with a dirty bobble on top.

Ola swooped it up off the ground, holding it close to her chest like a mother protecting a newborn. She brought it to her face to inhale the familiar scent of her love.

"This is his hat, but where is he?" she said. "I hope I didn't make him run away."

"I'm sure he is around somewhere. He must have dropped it whilst sleeping." Emma hoped these words were enough to console her friend.

Why do bad things always happen on Sundays? she thought to herself.

She hated Sundays; her sister had died on a Sunday, and Emma's own doctor's appointment was scheduled for a Sunday. She knew she had a high risk of developing the same type of cancer as her twin, so telling her family she had attended the check-up at the hospital was a complete lie. Emma had no intention of finding out if she had the disease or how long they would give her. She certainly was not going to be a burden for her teenage daughter and her busy husband. Sunday was the day she walked out of her family home.

Days had passed and still, no one knew the whereabouts of him. Emma had spent most of the daylight hours in Ola's company filling the void that Nazir's departure had left. The police, although not unfriendly, did not appear overly concerned or helpful either. They noted the details of his disappearance and his identifying features – unfortunately, a photograph didn't exist to help them – but Emma knew a homeless person would never be a top priority.

On yet another day, after another large meal at the soup kitchen, the pair asked Father O'Brien for his assistance. He was his usual busy minded self, twitching like a meerkat and checking for any newcomers to his door, making sure to welcome all with a firm handshake. He promised to ask all of those who entered the church that evening about Nazir.

The priest also quickly mentioned he had heard of the disappearance of another homeless person, though he had little details. Before they could ask him any more questions, he quickly excused himself and gave them his blessings. Emma doubted the priest's prayers would do little in finding Nazir, but she thanked him all the same.

After a dry week, the heavens suddenly opened up that evening and rain fell as they walked back down from the church. Rain quickly turned heavy like the spit of a thousand unforgiving passers-by into their cupped begging hands. Then began the hailstones, the hard globules of ice felt like the spit had turned into stones bouncing with a sting onto their hats, shoulders, and backs. *This is truly weather created by a God*, thought Emma. Perhaps the prayers have been answered and Nazir would be washed out from wherever he has been hiding. Emma and Ola took shelter under a nearby bus stop where they joined a group of pensioners who were waiting for a bus to take them back home from a day out at the seaside. The elderly ladies shuffled en masse two feet backward like a slice of lemmings avoiding the jaws of a jackal. We have just avoided the touch of these hobos, Emma could feel them thinking.

The homeless pair turned their backs on them, leaving their dry haven once the weather had calmed down.

They had settled down somewhere together that evening, huddled up sharing a duvet, laying on a very thin and damp sheet of cardboard. "How are you feeling?" Emma asked as she squeezed Ola's hand. The lights had gone out in her eyes and her smile had eroded into sorrow.

"Now others are missing? Where is he and where are the others?" More and more homeless people had gone missing in their town and it was quite puzzling. Emma did not know the answers but felt her friend's pain.

If there was a connection between the disappearance of these street people then Emma vowed to herself she would find out. "We will find him, Ola, first thing tomorrow we will find him." Nightmares were all she had for the first six months of walking out of the family house in London. Something within her had made her take that drastic step and that thing was fear. She feared death and the misery it would cause her loved ones. She knew she had to leave... to run away. At that time, it seemed to be the only solution to inevitable illness and death. But dreams would also not leave her – dreams of her beautiful daughter, of her dear husband, but mainly of her twin sister. The guilt she suffered since leaving her family had since faded, knowing her husband's wealth and influence would keep her family safe. She had read the news stories of how she, a politician's wife, had just disappeared from a seemingly idyllic lifestyle. Emma got on with her life, focusing on living one day at a time and preparing herself for when she would be hit with illness.

That night, the nightmares returned. Vivid dreams, scarlet in color, colors of terror dripping like a gash through an artery. Deathly screams of fear sent shivers all along until it hit the base of her spine. Familiar faces with hollowed eyes and gaunt features surrounded her, poking her with malnourished skeletal fingers. Emma trembled and felt bile rise to her throat.

Then she was floating in a peaceful cool haze of aqua blues, a force lifting her well above head height and then further up over the rooftops, disturbing the seagulls nesting amongst the eaves. Now twenty feet above where she once sat huddled, looking down, she noticed the litter that encircled her. Empty crisp packets, discarded drink bottles, and torn rubbish sacks with more garbage strewn out from the tears. Used diapers, rotting food, plastic containers of microwave meals for one. It was endless.

The stench of the street was thinning and cool fresh air hit the back of her throat. She could breathe again, huge lungfuls of beautiful air. Looking down the town seemed a mere speck on the peninsula jutting out into the sea, like one tiny plankton on the tongue of a blue whale.

With a thud, reality returned. Rolling like a wheel of kebab meat on wet tarmac, a face full of dirty puddle water fully aroused her from the slumber. Tires screeched, and then a voice, *perhaps a man or woman or both*, she thought. Her vision was a blur, rubbing her eyes she did not know where she was exactly but it was not exactly unfamiliar either.

"Help!" she cried at the top of her lungs. Her throat felt as if she had spent the night chain-smoking through boxes of cigarettes. Something was happening to her – someone was trying to kidnap her!

With the slam of a car door and more tire screeching, an accelerating engine, Emma felt like she was on the starting grid of a Grand Prix. The sound of the engine rocketed away from her, fading and fading until she was left in silence, encircled by the smell of burning rubber and exhaust fumes.

She sat frozen with fright until her sight had regained. She worked out she was sitting half off the curb and on the road out of town. Turning to her left, checking if anyone was around, a pain shot up her neck. As she regained her composure, her hands felt the back of her sore head where she found a bump the size of a golf ball. Her hands were also hurt, and so were many other parts of her, she guessed, though her clothes hid the total damage. She had been attacked, but why? She was puzzled and unable to make sense of what was going on.

With one hand on the curb, she pushed herself to her worn knees. Emma held her breath, grimacing. With a long exhale, she got to her feet. Gripping hold of a nearby lamppost, she struggled to get to her feet like a foal learning to walk for the first time, wobbly legs looking to fall any moment. Eventually, she stood up and looked around. Where was she?

On a road, she thought. *Houses*. She began to study the area. Although it was still dark, she squinted her eyes due to a mixture of pain and poor sight. Cars, playground, school – she shuffled in a clockwise direction, still maintaining contact with the lamppost. She noticed the moon, a full moon that had escaped the cover of the clouds for the moment. Then she saw something ahead of her on the street, glistening like a silvery treasure. The shiny light was sitting on top of or attached to something else.

It was her shoe. "My shoe!" she cried out, only wearing a wet cold sock on her right foot. Feeling brave, she left the stability of the lamppost and shuffled like a zombie toward her footwear.

The moon's reflection disappeared when the clouds once more covered the lunar light. With it, the treasure on her shoe transformed into just a piece of metal, and as she slowly crouched down beside it. It became apparent that her shoe had a hook embedded into it. A hook with sharp points on either end, S-shaped and strong – *something that would be easy to pick up in any DIY shop*, she thought.

With some effort, she pulled out the hook from the sole of her shoe, and being careful not to cut her hand, she put it into a pocket. She could do without any more injuries today. And as she sat slipping her shoe back on her foot, she tried to picture together what had happened to her.

"So, you didn't see anyone? Do you think it was a van? And your friend Ola may be missing?" confirmed the policeman.

"Correct," Emma said. "And I haven't had a chance to look for her, but she was asleep beside me before… before the attempted abduction I suppose…" she trailed off looking up at the policeman from the hospital bed.

"Yes," he said nodding his square head whilst scribbling something down in his notepad.

She had met this policeman a few times before. A seemingly kind-natured man but most of their run-ins had involved moving her on to another doorway or waking her to see if she was still alive.

It had been the first time Emma had ever called the emergency services. She had always been the type to keep any problems to herself; she often felt there would be others who needed help more than she did.

The rare sight of a phone box was what made her dial 999. She remembered using a public payphone last when she was a schoolchild, calling up a boy she liked, enjoying the privacy of a dirty old red phone box, worth every one of those twenty pence pieces for a conversation that wasn't eavesdropped upon. Even to this day, with a desensitized nose, the stench of those telephone cubicles made her feel sick. *A pity they are used more for urinating than making phone calls*, she thought to herself.

The police officer cleared his throat to break the silence the daydream had caused.

"Well, madam, I will take a look down at the usual spots later today, and ask around, I'll also pay a visit to the church hall."

"But as I've said it's not just her, other people have gone missing too recently, and if you don't…" Emma said, making sure he hadn't forgotten.

"Yes, I have the details noted down," the officer said as he stood to quickly finish the discussion.

"Do you think it's gangs, or something else?" She was beginning to find it difficult to talk.

She started coughing. Interspersed with each cough the policeman collected his hat, nodded goodbye, and finally said, "I'll be in touch." With that, he was gone, disappearing through a curtain. He was replaced immediately by a doctor, almost like a tag team of wrestlers taking turns to keep a watchful eye over her.

She wasn't in good shape, they told her. She knew that already; she wouldn't be there if she was. The x-ray of her chest had picked up something, the need for further tests was the best course of action. She rolled her eyes and mumbled something that not even she could understand. She knew if her legs could have summoned up the power, she would have walked out right then.

As the doctor carried on talking, her eyelids became heavy. It became ever more difficult to stop them from shutting. She didn't mean to be rude, but her body (and the drugs) were telling her to turn off.

She awoke in the same bed but with a different view. *Nicer curtains*, she thought.

Her sole focus now was on finding Ola. She ached all over and, not knowing how long she had been in bed, she blamed her pain on lying on the bed for so long.

She discovered discharging herself from the hospital to be pretty straight forward, possibly because it was a Sunday morning and only a handful of staff were around, or maybe it was because she made a big fuss, telling the nurse where she could make a report. She left fake contact details to go with her fake name if anyone needed to follow up with her.

And that was it, she was out. She was standing at the entrance of the inpatients' department, one hand on her hip and another holding a plastic bag containing her clothes. *Not the best idea to go outside in a hospital gown*, she thought. Finding a nearby toilet, she changed back into her clothes. Putting her hands into her pocket, she was surprised to find the metal hook still there. Holding tightly onto it, she very gingerly walked back into town.

She headed straight to the church, where Sunday mass was in full flow. Peering through the window at the rear of the chapel, she could see Father O'Brien's hands facing the heavens. It was a small congregation, so it was easy to spot all the soup kitchen volunteers. Emma had a knack for identifying people from the backs of their heads. The round black- haired head of the butcher, the tall blonde soap shop owner, the candy floss white ones of Old Lady One and Two, and the shaven pale head of the former-drug-user-done-good.

The creaky old church door meant Emma couldn't sneak inside unnoticed. Nearly all eyes glanced round to see the newcomer at the ceremony. Her own eyes went immediately to the floor; head bowed, she slunk into the furthermost pew from the altar. She waited through two more hymns, stood, sat, and knelt with difficulty as the other churchgoers did.

When the prayers had finished, the flock of worshippers followed the priest down the aisle and out the creaky doors. As they did so, Emma could feel the eyes staring into her with each passing member. She stayed on and sat on the back row until the final person had left. She was sitting and waiting, not sure whether to follow the herd. Before she had to decide whether to stand or stay, Father O'Brien returned to the church.

"How may I help you, my child?" the priest asked as he placed a hand on Emma's shoulder.

After flinching from the pain of his contact, Emma let out a high-pitched gasp. The priest's hand retreated.

"Whatever is the matter?" he asked.

"You haven't heard, then?" Emma responded.

The priest frowned. "About what?"

"The policeman said he would visit you, speak to you about people going missing from the street, about someone trying to take me the other night."

"I'm sorry... I didn't hear about this. You must be–"

Emma cut him off. "Never mind me, what about the others? Have you heard anything about Ola, Nazir, Adnan?" She stared at him and waited for an answer.

"Again, I'm sorry but I do not know anything about their whereabouts."

Head in her hands, she sat staring into oblivion. She knew it well, spending hours of days, weeks, and months, waiting for money, gazing, being forgotten about. She would not forget about the homeless people who disappeared.

"Who is taking these people away? Where are they being taken to? Are they coming back? Do you even care?" she asked, raising her voice at the priest but keeping her focus on oblivion.

"I'll have another word with the police and speak to some of the volunteers who may know."

"Haven't you already done that! My God, I thought you were supposed to help or support at least."

She decided it was time to leave, the futility had exhausted her to her limits.

"Well, David in particular always seems so concerned about people in need of feeding."

"Who is David?" Emma asked, just before slipping into oblivion seemed the only option.

"The local butcher, I thought everyone knew him," he replied. "Could you please drive me? I'm not sure I have the energy to walk," Emma pleaded.

The priest knocked gently on the door.

"Perhaps he hasn't returned yet," Father O'Brien said.

"Knock harder...please," Emma said from behind him. The door eventually swung open. The butcher's wide frame almost encompassed the doorway of the shop.

"Ah, Father, what is it? I've only just returned from church," the butcher said.

"Sorry to disturb you, but one of our members of the homeless community would like to ask you some questions," said the priest. "Well, we are both off to the gym. Can we do this later?" the butcher asked.

Emma edged past the priest. "No, this is a matter of urgency. If you know or have seen anything, you must come forward with information," she blurted out. "Someone has tried to abduct me, and I believe has been taking other homeless people from the street. Have you heard or seen anything?" Her crazed eyes wide, seemingly larger than they had been before, stared at the butcher for answers.

"That does sound awful. I hope you are alright?" The butcher said in a mildly condescending tone. "I'm no detective myself but perhaps the police would be better help?" He locked the door as they entered the shop.

Emma explained that she felt they had not taken her seriously, most probably because she was homeless, a nobody.

The priest joined in the conversation but now gazed around the room. Emma had switched off.

The stench of blood and disinfectant lingered in the shop. She had never been in an empty butcher shop before. There was no sign of meat or any food, just cleansed shiny metallic surfaces. It brought back memories of death, and her sister lying flat shut-eyed in a mortuary under a thin white sheet.

Now, daylight shone in from the shop window spilling light into the dark butcher's store. It refracted off the glass-fronted display cabinet, where select cuts of meat were usually on display, beams of light glinting onto a long steel rod where about ten hooks hung.

Immediately, she darted her hand into her pocket. The hook was still there, its sides cold and ends sharp. The hook from her shoe the other night…could it be the same as those hanging above now?

She clenched her fist tightly around her hook, but worried about the attention it would cause, so she decided to keep it hidden in her pocket. "Excuse me, Father, I think we should leave now," she said in an overly loud voice.

"Wait, my child, David mentioned that he noticed a drop in homeless folk too, but that he saw many more amassing in neighboring towns. Perhaps that is where your friends are," Father O'Brien said, trying to sound upbeat.

"Yes, but we should go, I'm so tired and hungry," said Emma through gritted teeth.

"David!" a voice came from a distance.

"Be back in a moment, but please come in and sit down." The butcher gestured to a small living room through a door behind the shop front and then bounded up the stairs to the source of the shouting.

Once they were alone, Emma sidled up close to Father O'Brien and withdrew the hook from her pocket.

"The other night when I was abducted, I pulled this out of my shoe," she said in a hushed voice showing the priest her metal treasure. "It must have got caught when I fell out the back of the van somehow."

The priest took it in and turned it around in his hands, whilst Emma pulled another hook from the pole. It was identical.

A puzzled expression formed on the priests, "OK," he said, trying to comprehend what was being said to him.

"It's the butcher, he abducted me!" she cried out. "Don't you see?"

"I'm no detective, but I think you'll need more evidence than that," said the priest. "But the main thing is that I know this man and he has a good soul, and, as you know, volunteers his spare time at the church."

"I bet he drives a van, too," she said indignantly. "Probably the van I fell out of!"

Emma could see she was losing the patience of the priest. "I may be homeless but I am not crazy, Father," she said, now raising her voice. "This did happen to me."

The priest handed the hook back to Emma.

"Let's not jump to any hasty conclusions now," he said, "I'm sure there is a perfectly good explanation."

"I'm sorry about that," the butcher said, returning from upstairs. "An explanation for what, Father?"

"Oh, nothing to worry about," the priest said. "But before you head off to the gym, would you be so kind as to show us around your van. It would put Emma's mind at ease. Since the other night, she's been very jittery, as you can imagine."

The butcher looked at them both with suspicious eyes.

"I'm sure it won't take a minute and then we can all go on our merry way," Father O'Brien said.

Emma stayed close to the priest, but also maintained an eye on the front door in case she needed to make a quick exit.

Now, the organic soap shop woman descended the narrow staircase. Colorful running shoes and long legs came down first, followed by an athletic torso and a smiling face.

Emma was slightly shocked to see her here. She never imagined this pair together. Her face didn't hide her surprise particularly well. "I think you know my girlfriend, Kate," the butcher said to Emma. "I'm just taking them out to the van," he continued looking up at the soap shop woman.

Kate got to the bottom of the stairs and with a bright smile, said, "I hope you've kept it clean."

"Come on, this way," the butcher said, leading them out of the small living room through a wooden door that led them towards an enclosed yard of a garden. Emma stopped to look around, thinking that there didn't seem much space to run from such a cramped space.

"Where do you keep all the... you know... meat?" she asked.

"I've got a warehouse on the industrial estate where I can keep it all in cold stores. Now come on, my van's parked just round here," the butcher gestured to the gate.

The van unlocked with a press of a key fob. The lights flashed and the butcher opened the back doors.

Emma was hoping for a flashback from the previous night, her falling and rolling on the tarmac. There was no moment of clarity. Was it because she was too unconscious, too out of it, perhaps it wasn't this van? The thoughts whirled around her head.

"These hooks, David," Father O'Brien asked, discovering another one. "Are they a standard size or can anyone buy them?" "Those hooks are top quality, strong too; only can be purchased from certain suppliers," replied the butcher "Now, are we all done here?" "Where were you..." Emma had lost track of the days. "Friday... no, Thursday night?"

Checking his watch, "I'm a man of routine. After work, I go to the gym and then help out at the homeless shelter," the butcher replied. "And then?" Emma asked.

"Why all the questions?" An impatient glare formed on his large face.

Emma noticed a hint of worry on the priest's face.

"Thank you for your time, David, I think it's time we left you on your way," Father O'Brien said, taking Emma by the hand, leading her back through the yard to exit the shop from the front where they came in.

As they entered the darkened living room, the back door shut behind them making it suddenly darker. A figure pulled the priest back, a hand hovering over his mouth. She heard muffled screams and a little struggle. He fell to the ground.

Not knowing where to run, Emma attempted a weak cry for help, but the figure in the dark grabbed and held her as a strong-smelling cloth covered her mouth and nose. She looked down and the last thing she remembered was a pair of luminous green shoes.

"I can't believe we're doing this," the butcher said.

"They were asking too many questions. Snooping around, trying to set you up," the soap shop owner, Kate, said.

Emma awoke bound and gagged in between a heavyset stocky butcher to her right and a slim yet muscular goddess to the left. She was unsure that a homeless runaway was the filling they hoped for in this particular sandwich.

They sat in the front seats of the van together in a row, whizzing off out of town.

Her throat and nose felt stripped of a layer of skin.

"Where are we going? Where is the priest?" she tried to say but the cloth muffled her mouth.

"Hold her still, we're almost there," the butcher said as he turned the final corner into the industrial park.

It was the last unit in the corner that they stopped outside of. A warehouse with no branding or name on the front.

The butcher turned off the engine and jumped out of the driver's seat. Pulling another set of keys from his pocket, he unbolted several locks and opened a shutter, Emma heard the sounds echo off the front of the opposite warehouses. No one else was around, being a Sunday, it was deadly quiet as everyone was at home spending time with their loved ones.

The butcher returned to the van helping himself to the passenger door. With ease, Emma was pulled from her seat and carried into the factory, then plonked onto a plastic chair inside.

"So sorry about this, Emma," Kate said in a surprisingly sincere tone. The butcher started back in the direction of the van.

"Don't bother about the priest, he had a heavy dose. He'll be out for a good while yet so leave him in the back of the van," Kate said. He stopped in his tracks. "Be a darling and do shut the door," she continued.

"We need to work out what we have to do with them both." "I'm still unsure why we are doing this and how do you know how to gag people," said the butcher.

"You know I was brought up on a farm so learned many tricks… Anyway, the main thing is that they were nosing around, wanting to get the police involved unnecessarily. And that won't do," Kate said looking over at Emma tied up and wriggling on the chair.

The butcher followed her eyes, "I'm confused. The police…? We have nothing to do with the missing homeless people and attempted abductions," he said dismissively.

An eerie silence fell in the warehouse.

"Kate, is there something I need to know?" asked the butcher. The smile had dropped from his face.

"Well, I have been borrowing your van in the evening, you see."

"Okay…"

"And you know how much I detest this homeless problem the town has, all these immigrants coming over here, clogging up our streets. Hardly anyone visits my shop these days, not even your shop. Trade is down nearly fifty percent in the past few years. We had to share this space for both our businesses," she said, pointing around the warehouse.

Half of the factory was devoted to oils, scents with vats of liquid, whereas the other half had sharp knives, metal surfaces, and two large refrigerator doors.

"The council doesn't sort it out and, as we've seen from our friend here, the police don't care." She shot a glare at Emma. "So, I took matters into my own hands and removed these eyesores from the street."

Emma squirmed and wriggled more aggressively in her chair. "Oh, do quieten down, dear," Kate said.

"So where did you take them?" The butcher said in shock. "Did you drop them to another town, left them out in a field somewhere?"

"Not quite. I had to dispose of them another way," she said, raising her eyebrows with a guilty expression on her face. "This is where a joint warehouse came in very handy, David."

The butcher looked around the industrial unit. There wasn't much to it concerning storage.

He pulled one of the fridge doors open. A light pinged on to reveal a frozen room with rows and rows of chicken breasts, pork chops, and cuts of steaks. Then he tried the next door, which opened to a cooler world of hung pigs hooked up by their trotters.

"You won't find anything in there, my love. The evidence is gone."

"You've killed them!? And burnt the bodies? You're crazy!"

"Not burnt them, that would be too obvious... Well, the clothes I burnt but... you know. Meat and bones, I passed onto my nearest and dearest," she said gesturing toward him.

"That's disgusting... You told me it was livestock meat. You got it from your cousin. Something to do with having too much capacity and European Union quotas?" He was rubbing his temples trying to work out if any of this was real.

"Sorry I had to make something up, and you believe most things I tell you anyway."

Emma was frantically moving her legs and arms in the hope she could break free of these ropes. Her legs were firmly bound, but the ropes tied around her wrists seemed a little looser. She tugged and tugged and eventually fell off the chair.

"We used that meat for the soup and pies at the shelter...!" "Yep. We've been feeding the homeless to themselves. Beautifully poetic don't you think?"

The butcher had no words left.

"Who are you?"

"Ground up bones are perfect for dogs and human fat makes the best soaps. Although I may have to remove the word "organic" from my merchandise now, I'm not quite sure what they've been eating... Well, yes, I do. Each other."

With that, she let out a loud hearty laugh.

Emma felt sick to the core. She had to break free. *This woman is becoming more horrific with each breath*, she thought.

The butcher was screaming at her, "You are a maniac! I want nothing else to do with you! I'm calling the police!"

He pulled his phone out and was about to dial 999 when it was snatched out of his hands.

Kate stood beside him holding a large metal pole.

"I had a feeling you'd react in this way. It's a pity," she said. She swung and hit him first in the stomach. The butcher bent over in pain, and without a thought, she swung again. With a crack on the head, he fell to the floor.

Emma moved with fear like an injured caterpillar across the ground away from them, taking shelter in a corner.

"It's a shame it had to end this way," said Kate, looking down at his unconscious body.

"As for you, Mrs. Emma Pearson," Kate said now walking toward her, "I know your story. Running away from your perfect family after your sister dies. I read the papers, I read them all.

"Turning up in my town, outside my shop, you thought no one noticed you but I did," Kate said as she crouched down in front of her, pointing a finger in her face.

"Back then you were just one of a few street bums, going through the rubbish of an evening, I didn't mind as much. I was going to leave you as were, in your misery."

Tears streamed down Emma's face, her hands fighting with the ropes.

"But you need not worry now. You'll be off the streets too soon, and in soup with this handsome devil," Kate said as stood back up looking at the butcher.

Emma felt a chill run down her spine.

"Of course, the taste of those immigrants will be nothing compared to our local meat but you know too much, Emma Pearson. You landed yourself in hot water for sure," Kate guffawed.

Emma's heart began to pound like a symphony of a million drums. She knew she had to do something before Kate would kill her too. Just then, Emma broke her hands-free of the binding, took a hook from her pocket, and with as much might as she could muster buried it into Kate's lower leg, pulling it hard against her calf muscle. Kate dropped the pole and hopped around in agony, blood spewing out from her yoga pants, Emma found new strength to hop to her feet to pull the other hook out.

Kate jumped at her and tackled Emma from behind. Both of them smashed against the wall, Emma getting a face full, sending metal containers crashing all around.

Luckily, she managed to keep hold of the hook and when Kate pushed her back to the ground, she swung at her with enough furious strength that she slashed her arm and face.

Emma knew the face was the tipping point. Kate dabbed her hand onto her bloodied cheek and rage was now firing in her eyes. She looked over at a locked box on the wall and then to her keys which were left on the side.

Emma couldn't stand, couldn't scream, couldn't run.

Opening the box revealed a selection of butcher knives. Sharp, large, and shiny.

Emma shut her eyes once more, thinking of her daughter. Wishing well for her husband. Remembering her sister.

"Kate put the knife down. What on earth are you doing?" It was the priest, he'd awoken and contacted the police.

"This is my town. I need to clean up the streets. I will not let her stop me!" a crazed Kate hollered as Father O'Brien stood in shock. The police from the hospital came forward. "Madam, please drop the knife, no one wants to see any more blood now."

Kate eyed the policeman, then the taser gun in his hands, and then Emma laying shivering on the floor. She swung the knife up over her head.

To Emma, it sounded like a large mosquito that had been stuck in an electric fly killer. Then the sound of a metal blade hitting the ground, followed by the thud of the organic soap shop owner.

What An Orange Tree Can Do

By Edwige Narbey

"Hello? Paul? Can you hear me?" I said into the phone pressed against my perspiring cheek.

"Marie, how are you? How was your flight?" her husband asked. "I'm good, I'm in Tana! The plane had to make a stop in Mahajanga for some reason. We landed on a short runaway before resuming the journey towards the capital city. It was frightening, but one good thing was the beautiful sunrise..." I answered dreamily.

"I'm sure it was gorgeous. Promise me you'll take care of yourself there!" Paul said, a smile in his voice.

"I will!" I looked around at passengers hurrying by in pairs or as a group toward the glass doors leading toward an exit. "If only you were with me..."

"Marie, we're not going through this again."

I frowned and tucked a curl escaping from the blonde braid behind my ear. I didn't want to start one of those recurrent and painful conversations on fertility treatments versus adoption. I didn't want to think about the fact that I failed to convince Paul to come with me to finalize the adoption of Isaac, our son-to-be. "Don't worry, I'm fine," I replied, breath stuck in my throat.

"Good. I've got to go to work – I have three meetings today and I need to run this crazy program for a new client. I hope everything will go okay for you there," he replied.

"I still can't believe that the next time we'll see each other, Isaac will be with us!" I said excitedly. After the heartbreaking news that Paul and I couldn't conceive a child, Paul was willing to try any treatment but he hadn't shared my views about adoption. For him raising a child seemed already a difficult task so, comparatively, adopting was certainly a challenge. Although my husband had finally approved of my decision, deep inside I knew it was my own unfulfilled desire to be a mother and his love towards me that had resulted in the adoption. I recalled a time when I had implored Paul to adopt a cat.

"Okay, I'll pay for the food and the vet, but you're going to feed and clean it," he had said. I had never asked again.

"I can't wait to see you back safe and to meet…my son. I love you, Marie. I have to go now, but have a safe trip." With that, Paul ended the call.

"I love you, too! Bye!" I put my phone into my pocket and walked briskly toward the doors.

Comfortably settled in the rear seat of a silver Toyota, I started to relax after my ten-hour flight from Paris. I admired the lake Anosy and its frame of tall jacaranda trees. In front of a house, I noticed a traditional embroidered tablecloth on a washing line. I tried to identify the tiny, colorful characters on the white cotton fabric – they were usually farmers – and recognized a woman carrying a basket on her head, a man with a straw-hat planting rice crops, and another pounding grains. As the view opened on the Highlands, we left the road for the track – a straight, elevated red line of soil cutting through the greenery of extensive rice fields under an azure sky that was almost too blue to be real. When I arrived at the village, I was astonished to discover three houses made of orange bricks and thatched roofs, a rectangular white building which was probably the school, and nothing else. A funny thought of the Big Bad Wolf blowing one of the Little Pigs' houses, which were located in a village much like the one I was in now, entered my mind.

Finally, the car stopped. I gathered my things, opened the door, and stood on the dirt as I watched the car leave in a cloud of heavy orange dust. I abandoned my leather suitcase to follow an abrupt path leading to a plantation. There, I easily spotted a lady in leopard-patterned trousers and a raspberry-colored long-sleeved top among the lush, shiny leaves of banana trees. Coming eagerly to greet me, she introduced herself as Miss Voahangy, the directress of the school I came here for. Her face, a few shades lighter than the voluminous hair piled up into a bun on her head, breathed warmth, intelligence, and kindness. Admittedly, she wasn't exactly the image of a strict middle-aged school teacher with rimmed glasses I had in mind – even the bun was loose and not overly tight and rigid. I instantly categorized Miss Voahangy as the kind of person who could offer their hand, their smile, their laugh, and their heart all at the first encounter.

After greeting each other, we walked toward her house, the closest place to the school, and stopped in the courtyard to meet her sons. They both had lean bodies, short curly hair, and wore jeans and green t-shirts. The oldest was pounding rice in the shadow of the shed and the youngest was carrying sticks and dried leaves. I repressed the urge to pick up my phone to take photos. With their honey-colored skin, dark eyes, and bright smiles, they looked stunning. I secretly wished for Isaac, my son-to-be, to become a teenager as handsome as Miss Voahangy's sons one day.

We all had supper at candlelight, in the mundane, almost completely bare living room, eating piles of red rice served copiously by Miss Voahangy and laughing generously at our first attempts to communicate in French. Later, she led me to my bedroom, where I froze in front of a giant turtle with a shell reaching my knees. I had never seen this gentle animal from my childhood's stories in such a monstrous form. Terrified, I immediately called Miss Voahangy to the rescue. As she laughed hysterically, I learned that the three old turtles living in the house wouldn't bite me nor climb into my bed. When Miss Voahangy left, I moved the candle in all directions, using its golden glow to carefully observe each corner. The room was only occupied by one bed made of branches and an odorant straw mattress and a dark wooden table with a chair in front of the window. I started to unpack my suitcase. I first took out a dozen of white candles, half a dozen toilet paper rolls, a box of diapers, a can of powdered milk, two glass bottles, and then a great number of tiny clothes – all expensive gifts from family, friends, and colleagues from the hospital where I worked. I ran my fingers over the soft fur of two toys. I couldn't decide which one Isaac would love the most between a classic teddy bear and a white bunny. I finally pulled out my sleeping bag and clothes. Lying down in the dark, I stayed awake, thinking about Isaac. It would be a long trip for a baby and a new life for Paul and me.

When I woke up, the morning was hot and radiant. Too excited to sleep further, I was changing out of my pajamas when I suddenly felt a feathery tingle on my left shoulder. I turned my head and spotted a spider the size of two Euro coins taking a morning walk on my bare skin. Oh my God! I yelled in my head. I was either going to die of a heart attack or lose my mind. Resisting the impulse to scream, I quickly brushed the threatening insect away with a neat sweep of my right hand. Recovering from the initial fright and feeling very proud of myself, I opened the door and saw Miss Voahangy holding a breakfast tray. I smiled at the view of steaming white rice.

"Thank you for bringing my food. I could have eaten with you if you had woken me up," I said, smiling.

"My sons are already in the fields after their usual breakfast of rice. I did not want them to see the bread," she replied, looking out of the window and then pulling the cotton napkin off an oval-shaped bread that was smaller than my hand.

I was horrified that I hadn't thought of the difficulty of attaining bread.

"Please let me buy some bread for everyone tomorrow!" I implored, embarrassed.

"Thank you for the offer, but no. My sons are already used to not having bread and may want more," said Miss Voahangy, in a voice that called for no argument.

When she left, I had my first meal of the day alone in my room as a guest of privilege enjoying a peaceful morning while the children of the house were working the land and their mother was teaching little girls.

After a few hours, Miss Voahangy returned. "Time to go!" she shouted from the courtyard, hurrying back from a day at school. I went outside in a long, powdered pink cotton dress, blinking under the puissant sunlight, sunglasses in one hand, handbag in the other. "Are you okay with going there alone?" worried Miss Voahangy, holding a bicycle in the shade.

"Yes... I need to be on my own for this. I'll come back before sunset," I told her reassuringly.

"Good luck, Marie. I'll pray for you." The teacher handed me the bicycle.

I let her words caress my heart as I wrapped myself in a soft, warm blanket. Miss Voahangy was, after all, a mother. She knew what this encounter was going to feel like, probably better than me. After a grateful smile, I took the bike, set my tote bag on the rack, and rode on the track. I pedaled as fast as I could as I tried to avoid the treacherous potholes. It was the middle of the day, so farmers were either working in the fields or resting under a tree. I made a halt to catch my breath. I drank long gulps from my gourd to quench my thirst. I mounted the bike again, and I could feel myself getting closer to Isaac. As I rode on the bicycle, I pictured my new life, a life that would be filled with an innocent child's happy gurgles.

Finally, I stopped pedaling as I grew closer to my destination. I extracted a folder to check, for the last time, that the adoption papers were correctly signed by Paul. Seeing his handwriting pinched my heart, highlighting his absence. I also took out my pocket mirror. Good, my braid was still in place. I lingered on my eyes, which, according to Paul, were the color of the ocean after a raging storm. My lips were painted in deep red, which matched my manicured hands. I peered in disdain at my nose, which I found to be a bit too large for my thin face. What would Isaac think of me? Do I look like a mother? Oh, don't be silly, he's just a baby!

I closed the round mirror with a clap, fidgeted a little more with my handbag. I began walking towards the premises, which looked similar to the teacher's house, making my pulse accelerate with excitement. When I reached the entrance, however, I realized that it was closed. As I turned the corner, I stopped abruptly in my tracks when I saw four toddlers sitting in the shadow of the eastern wall. They had short hair and wore dirty underpants and stained tee-shirts. I searched for an adult but there was none. Of course, they were orphans, I thought, repressing a nervous laugh.

37

I knew Isaac wasn't one of them, because he was a baby. The children didn't look at me, nor were they looking at each other, either. Two were staring down at the dust. The others were staring at the space on my right side. They weren't smiling, crying, or making any sounds. One had his face covered with snot. Another one scratched his right leg, which was already full of tiny marks that looked like insect bites. I wouldn't say they were malnourished, but they did not have the round cheeks or plump bodies I was accustomed to seeing in my medical practice. What I was seeing shocked me. *How could people leave young children in such a state and by themselves?* I wondered as I started to feel upset. Suddenly, the door of the building opened with a bang and a young nurse wearing a beige uniform appeared.

"Hello, are you Marie?" she asked me.

"Hi, yes I am," I replied, not at ease.

"You came for Isaac, right?"

"Yes. May I see him, please?" I asked, suddenly feeling jittery. Isaac's name felt like an electric shock. I straightened my shoulders and moved towards the nurse.

"Follow me inside, he's having a nap," invited the nurse, turning back after a glance at the quiet orphans. We walked through the dark corridor and talked softly about the resting child, who was just a door away from us.

When I entered the cool room, a stench of straw and wet diapers hit me. On the yellowish wall stood a simple wooden cross surrounded by stains and the recognizable remains of dead insects, almost giving me the morbid appearance of a cemetery. I couldn't believe that in this cradle, hidden and protected by a mosquito net, Isaac was waiting for me. Walking softly, with a pounding heart and a racing mind, I gently pulled back the curtain on the most graceful thing on Earth: my baby. He was breathing calmly as he laid on his back, legs bent, his dark hair framed by his tiny arms and closed fists. Still a total stranger, but yet so close to my soul, this human being represented what I had always wanted. Almost my whole life, from my teenage years to my most recent days, my dreams had been filled by my baby. I had craved for this moment so much that it turned into a gnawing, physical ache.

Even though the nurse told me to wake him up, I didn't want to disturb the little angel. Gratitude was filling my heart as tears welled in my eyes. Isaac was my baby. He was going to be mine for the rest of my life. I took Isaac in my arms and cuddled him, gently stroking his soft hair. I inhaled the milky smell of his warm neck as he started to stir and move his perfect hands towards his face. Holding my baby made me feel calm and complete like I had never felt before. I didn't have the same soothing effect on Isaac, however, who started to cry, clenching his fists and straightening his whole body so hard that I was afraid of letting him fall. I held him tighter and he cried louder in response. He was probably hungry, or maybe he had wet himself. As a family doctor, I was used to carrying and caring for babies all the time as well as comforting worried mothers. Now I realized that taking care of my child would be another story and that I would have to deal with the constant doubts of motherhood. After having changed and fed Isaac, the nurse went through all the details of the adoption as I handed her the papers. She insisted on the fact that my husband and I would need some time to adjust to Isaac and our new life as a family. I listened to her but at that moment the only thing I worried about was to take Isaac away from this place as fast as I could. I finally wrapped him carefully in a large scarf so I could cycle with him to the village. The young nurse helped me to adjust the colorful fabric on my shoulders. Isaac was sound asleep once more, tightly curled around my chest. The way back went by in a blur, my mind focused on the track, my mood swinging from euphoria to anxiety at the realization I was carrying such a precious bundle.

The rest of the day flew by. Miss Voahangy put the cradle that had served her boys next to my bed after she boiled water for Isaac's bottle. I was following her everywhere while carrying my baby, rocking him and talking to him. As soon as Isaac was settled for the night, I retired to my bed feeling exhausted and overwhelmed by the emotions of the day.

The next morning, I woke up with an urge to scramble out of my sleeping bag. My legs were itching severely. I examined the dozen red spots on my leg. Fleas? What else could it be? I checked on Isaac who was still asleep, sucking his thumb and breathing evenly. I still couldn't believe he was my baby. I resisted the urge to pinch myself – instead, I gently stroked his hair. I didn't want to wake him up, so I went outside to shake my sleeping bag. I badly needed a shower. Miss Voahangy had shown me a plastic bucket on the ground in the corner of the courtyard wall, a spot half hidden by the shed where the boys used to pound rice and stock tools to use while showering. I had no clue where to put my clothes and my towel. Eventually, I folded my belongings in a small pile and left them on a flat stone. I enjoyed splashing water on myself, feeling warmth and wind on my whole body. Gradually running out of the water, I realized that I had to shorten this novel experience. The moment I wanted to dry my feet, I understood that the big stone had another purpose, to stand on it during the shower and avoid the muddy ground. I managed to put my clothes on without too much damage and went back inside. Miss Voahangy was getting ready to meet someone and she invited me to accompany her to visit her friend. I accepted, enthusiastic at the idea to meet more Malagasy people and to show Isaac around. After all, I chose to spend a few days in the village with Isaac to ease the transition for him, to discover the Malagasy people, and learn about their culture, so I would understand where Isaac was coming from and teach him about his roots. Paul, on the other hand, was opposed to this plan, as he felt that once we adopted Isaac, Isaac was ours and our culture was his culture. I shuddered as I remembered our ugly argument, with Paul accusing me of wanting to be noble as I screamed that it would be cheating – almost like stealing a child – and that I could never do such a thing.

Cycling with Miss Voahangy, Isaac comfortably swaddled against my back, we passed along a brick factory right on the side of the track. Some workers dug endlessly into red, sticky mud. Others were shaping blocks into rectangular wooden molds. Smoke volutes escaped from the small oven made of the same bricks that it produced. Hundreds of red clay rectangular solids were drying on the ground, stocked in piles or charged, and transported on carts pulled by sweaty men or black zebus. Further down the road, we crossed a river. Women were washing colorful clothes, using their hands and a piece of soap too minuscule to be seen. Children were splashing noisily in the water, swimming and cleaning themselves. At the top of the hill, we stopped in the refreshing shade of the sweet-smelling eucalyptus trees. We finally arrived at an isolated farm, at the end of a small path with only dried land around. The base of the house, made of clay, supported wooden walls covered by a thatch roof. It was half a hut. In the field, a woman in a yellow-and-green, flowery cotton dress was pickaxing the red soil, bent as she did her chore under a burning sun. We approached her and Miss Voahangy called out to her.

"Rindra!" she exclaimed.

Rindra stopped and turned, revealing a heavy belly. She looked like a round ball to me with her face, eyes, arms, belly, and even her bare feet looking like two brown buns! Edema of pregnancy, something I would never have, I thought, half-jealous, half-relieved. After a long, friendly chat with Rindra, we left, promising to meet again soon. We then went back home. Miss Voahangy explained that her friend would work the land until the day she would give birth and probably the day after if everything went right – this was the farmer's life in Madagascar. If ever the harvest wasn't good enough, Rindra may even have to abandon her baby, having already four children to feed. Right now they were helping their father to transport and sell vegetables in the neighboring village. I was crushed, feeling suddenly out of place with my newly-adopted son resting peacefully next to me. Isaac's parents were poor farmers, killing themselves at work yet unable to feed their family. I simply believed I was doing the right thing, offering a better life to an innocent baby. So focused on my expectation to become a mother, I hadn't realized there were other children just like Isaac and there would be many more to come. Rindra seemed a healthy and happy young woman. She spoke of her future baby like any other pregnant girlfriend I had, with hope and growing love. However, she could be forced to abandon her child one day. How could life be so unfair? As confusion and anger filled my heart, I opened it to Miss Voahangy. Patiently she explained that farmers didn't have enough land to cultivate and that the problem became worse when a son got married. His father had to share a piece of rice paddies with the new family. Then they had children on their own. It was even more complicated. Farmers needed arms to work the land and to take care of their old days. And they never knew how many of their children would survive because of illnesses and accidents. I nodded and remained silent for a few minutes, mulling over what she had said. What was happening to me? I should have been over the moon, enjoying my first moments with my son, in a hurry to go back home to present Isaac to Paul and my relatives. Instead, my mind was constantly disturbed by the farmers' situation that I couldn't ignore anymore.

The next morning, I spent time with Isaac, lying on my bed and trying to bond with the baby I hardly knew. My thoughts and emotions were disjointed. One moment I was ecstatic and confident, in awe of his active body and his beautiful eyes already following me. An instant later, I wasn't connecting with him, doubts assailing me. I didn't feel myself being a good person doing the right thing anymore. Guilt and sadness were taking over the joy of having Isaac with me. I gently picked my baby up, kissed him on his head, and went outside for a change. I walked towards the school with Isaac sitting in my arms. I waited for the last pupil to leave the class to join Miss Voahangy. Cleaning the blackboard, the only thing that hung on the white chipped walls, the teacher looked tired. The furniture consisted of ten wooden tables with the bench attached. How could all the children fit in? No books, no notebooks, no pencils, no instruments, no maps, no puzzles, no cushions, no flowers in this classroom. Miss Voahangy seemed surprised to see us, but she welcomed me and said a few words in Malagasy to Isaac. We talked about the morning lessons. Boys were in the other room, reciting the French alphabet in a chorus, "A, B, C, D…" Learning French in primary school was still part of the National Program. The teachers had been trained, thanks to a local organization. Last year, a volunteer had come from France to help for three months. I told her that I had counted at least forty girls rushing out to go home. Miss Voahangy explained that the village was bigger than the few houses surrounding the school. Farms were dispersed on the Highlands, some of them very isolated, like Rindra's. Children walked every day, sometimes up to ten kilometers, often on empty stomachs. We went outside and watched dozens of boys, aged between six to twelve, who were laughing, and pushing each other to be first at the door. A thin, tall boy in dirty clothes and bare feet shouted something in Malagasy and walked straight towards Isaac. He held my baby's hand and smiled broadly at him. I felt the ground opening under my feet, an icy current running up and down my spine. A string broke in my heart that would never be repaired. The boy left quietly, walking on the path to the Highlands without looking back. I was shaking and must have gone paler as Miss Voahangy was calling my name and pushing me with a soft hand on my back towards her house. Isaac started to cry. She took him from my arms, rocked him, singing in Malagasy, then, as he was calm, she put him in the cradle. I observed her unable to speak or to move, my body feeling like a giant puppet without anyone to pull its strings. She looked at me with concern, probably waiting for me to talk, but I didn't want to. I only wanted to be with Isaac and Paul in our cozy flat as a perfectly happy family, far away from this village and its people and poverty. I broke down, sobbing uncontrollably. Miss Voahangy hugged me tightly and spoke softly. The boy was Isaac's brother. He had recognized his youngest sibling and had called him by his Malagasy name 'Faralahy,' the last born. When I finally managed to stop crying, all I could mutter was, "I can't."

She told me that adoption was a very emotional process, especially when the biological parents were still alive. It suddenly became clearer in my mind. I wanted to give a family to a child. I didn't want to tear a child from his family. I was a doctor and my first oath was to not harm anyone. There must have been another way in which Isaac could stay with them, in his country, his home. I had enough money to sponsor Isaac and his whole family. I could also finance his education. This was part of the solution, but I needed to do more. If I had my waiting room full of sick patients, would I just pick one and treat him with the best care I could, leaving all the others suffering? Nonsense! I wanted to do something to help all the children in this village.

I promised myself I would put my thoughts into action. I talked to Miss Voahangy for hours. She mostly listened to me, only asking for some details sometimes. She ended our emotional conversation by advising me to sleep on it and to decide on my decision the next morning, on which I agreed. I spent one of the worst nights of my life, my mind full of the many children walking for hours along dirt tracks, the four orphans sitting outside the orphanage in dirty clothes, Miss Voahangy's boys busy in some domestic chore. Isaac's tiny face was blurring and I realized with pure horror that I was already losing him. I was going to give back my adopted baby! I breathed with difficulty. I felt feverish and my head hurt as if it was going to explode. Silent tears ran down my cheeks, my nose, and my chin as I realized the enormity of what I would be losing. How unconditionally I would have loved him! How delicately I would have taken care of his growing body! How well I would have fed him! I would have nurtured his curious mind, reading him tons of stories, singing plenty of rhymes even though I was really bad at singing. I would have held his hand until he was ready to let go. I would have told him again and again how the world is huge and full of adventures, how life can be hard but beautiful too. I would have showered him with words of encouragement. "You can do it! I accept you just as you are. You're amazing! You know how to make me laugh. Try again! It's okay to make mistakes. I'm proud of you." He could have kept these gems of love close to his heart, a secret treasure for his whole life. I would have taught him to ride a bike, to swim, and to ski, to catch a ball, to bake cupcakes and brownies, to blow his nose and his candles on his birthday cake, to climb a rock and a tree, to tie his shoes, to fly a kite, to play cards, and to count his blessings at the end of the day.

With much exhaustion, I eventually slept late into the morning. At the knock on my door, I stood up and opened my door in slow motion. Miss Voahangy told me to take more time but I knew that the longer I would stay with Isaac, the harder it would be to let him go. I had made up my mind, thinking only of Isaac's well-being.

My hands were shaking as I handed all the baby stuff to Miss Voahangy who put it in a bag. I wrapped Isaac in the scarf and helped Miss Voahangy to secure him on her back. My mouth was dry and my feet glued to the ground. Touching his hair, I inhaled the scent of his neck one last time, feeling his soft skin. I stared into his eyes and, swallowing the knot in my throat, I whispered, "I love you, Isaac. I wish you a beautiful life." I was desperate to impress an incredible memory of Isaac on me, and me on him. As soon as they left I crashed on my bed, sobbing into my pillow. I felt so drained that I blacked out for hours.

The following day, Miss Voahangy reported that she had heard me crying in my sleep and calling Isaac's name.

After having renounced the adoption, I was more determined than ever to help the children of the village. It was vital for me, the only way to keep me going, to keep me alive. I needed to stop thinking of Isaac all the time. Following the teacher's advice, I was cycling to a neighboring village to meet Léon, the president of an NGO involved with the school. He would be at the market and had heard about me by the word of mouth, the fastest way to communicate in the countryside. I wasn't alone – Mahandry, Miss Voahangy's oldest son, was sitting on the rack, holding the saddle, legs wide apart off the back wheel. He had to pick up his first confirmation suit at the tailor's and would come back on foot to help his mother in supper preparations. Those were orders from his mom, to be obeyed without argument. At the entrance of the village, I could feel people watching us. Luckily, I wasn't sitting at the back and the teenager pedaled as we did a few kilometers before, taking turns in the effort. People would have feared that the time of French colonization was back.

After leaving Mahandry, I put the bike against a wall and tried to make my way into the crowd. I didn't expect so many people, mostly men, all alike yet all unique in their shade of brown and their color of clothes. "How am I going to find him?" I murmured, looking everywhere. I hadn't reached the first stalls when I heard my name. A tall, large, confident man, gray-haired, wearing a black suit and a blue shirt, offered his strong wrinkled hand. Relieved, I took it without hesitation.

"Nice to meet you. You must be Léon. I'm glad you saw me!" I exclaimed.

Léon squeezed my hand, letting a good honest laugh escape from his throat.

"Marie, you are the only white person for kilometers around. I couldn't miss you," he laughed.

I joined in his amused laughter, but for the first time, I had a strange feeling of being different and viewed differently just because of the color of my skin.

Léon ordered sweet sugar cane juice and delicious Mofo Gasy, small pancakes made of sweetened rice flour. We sat in front of the narrow makeshift shop with rusty, corrugated walls, in a rather noisy place where chicken, children, and farmers clucked, cried, shouted, and laughed in a splendid cacophony.

Straining to be heard over this noise, I raised my voice, "I came here to adopt Isaac – I mean, Faralahy. When I left home, I was told by my agent that I would be adopting a baby from the orphanage. They are not orphans; their parents are alive, but they are so poor that they cannot feed their children, however hard they may work. I could not separate a baby from his real parents and siblings. I also realized that even if I was helping a child, there were many like him and would be many more." I tried not to cry, my knuckles white from pressing hard on a folded paper napkin.

Léon looked at me then said, "You probably know this proverb: give a man a fish and you feed him for a day. Teach a man to fish and you will feed him for a lifetime." I nodded and started to relax, relieved that I felt understood.

"How can I help? How can I best use the money I have for the betterment of the village children? I want to help the children remain here with their parents, with their family, where they belong. They should not be made to travel to other parts of the world to a family, however loving, that is not theirs," I said, my voice filled with urgency.

"Marie, there are many ways to help. Our organization works to get the whole village to become the motor of its development. You would have seen that we need furniture for the school, but our priority is to provide free meals for students at lunchtime by creating a farmer's operation. We want this project to become sustainable over time – however, we suffer from a lack of funds to start. This would make a big difference to the families who wouldn't have to abandon one of theirs. Children would get nutritious food once a day and they would come to school to receive an education."

"Why not grow rice on the land in front of the school? It's flat and quite big," I proposed.

"That wouldn't work. It's the highest part of the village, far too dry for rice paddies," Leon replied.

"What about cows? They could provide milk and meat for the children!"

The middle-aged man raised one of his gray bushy eyebrows. I saw a faint amusement sparkling in his eyes.

I went on. "Yesterday afternoon, I went to see Miss Voahangy's colleague, Mr. Auguste. As she told me he was always hungry, I brought him some biscuits and photos from my grandparents' village so we could have a chat in French. He just loved the cow, even called it a 'dream cow.'"

I perfectly recalled Mr. Auguste's face going from surprise to wonder. As soon as I had opened the picture of a dairy cow on my phone, the young, skinny teacher had expressed his admiration through many compliments. The cow was 'beautiful,' 'fat like he had never seen before,' it's body 'silky and shiny.' He had asked for the French name of the color 'brown' and as he was unable to pronounce 'brun' correctly, I had taught him the equivalent, 'marron.' And the grass on the photo was 'so green' and 'thick' and 'unbelievable.' He had wanted to know everything about the female, what she ate, why she had a bell attached to her neck. Amazed to learn that she could provide many liters of milk every day, he had almost choked on his pear when he had learned about cheese-making and beauty contests for cows. Could you fall in love with a cow? Mr. Auguste certainly did.

"Marie, have you observed zebus here? They certainly don't look like French cows. I know that they've tried breeding in Andriamabalany but they've decided to switch for chicken farming, less expensive to finance, not so risky." The president rubbed his calloused hands.

I saw a handful of horned animals, with only skin on bones highlighting their bump, wandering along the track, seeking invisible grass. Then I tried to picture a bunch of hens and a few roosters in the school. It would be very noisy and they would leave feathers and dirt everywhere.

Léon interrupted me in my thoughts.

"I think we should look more for something to grow that doesn't need a lot of care and will give a good yield," he proposed. "Something to grow…" I repeated slowly. The place, now almost empty, went quiet. Léon left me with the promise to keep in touch in the next few days, hoping to find the best option for the operative. I went back on the track, cycling alone as the sun was already low. When I arrived at my destination, Miss Voahangy was waiting for me at the door, worried that I wouldn't make it before sunset, and her children were making zebus miniatures out of clay. As night fell, people, chicken, and turtles were all shut in together, the overpopulated house becoming a fortress against carnivores and thieves – mostly thieves, according to Miss Voahangy. We had an animated supper. I reported the details of my meeting with Léon.

Later in my room, when I blew out the candle that gave light to my shadowy room, my mind was still filled with images of the boys sculpting small zebus in the golden sunset light. For the first time since my arrival, I had seen Miss Voahangy's sons doing something that was not working. They seemed to have such a different childhood from mine. I wasn't familiar with poverty, raised as a spoiled single child by two full-time dentists and a Welsh au-pair. After qualifying as a doctor, I started as an intern at the fancy hospital in the neighborhood where I grew up and then I was married to a brilliant financial adviser. Money was plentiful and our lives were opulent. We often went on glamorous vacations to beautiful places – the Maldives, Seychelles, Bora Bora. I belonged to the luckiest of the lucky ones who always had more than enough to eat.

Suddenly, I remembered my beloved grandma. The old lady used to tell me how she had to cycle to another village to work in a bakery, raising two small children in a house occupied by German officers while her husband was a prisoner on a farm on the other side of the border. During the three last Christmases of the war, all she managed to offer her boys was an orange each. When her husband returned from the war, they had two more children and they started a small business with two of their neighbors, sharing a small piece of land, their tools, and skills to grow orange trees. Their hard work paid off, and they were soon comfortable. My grandparents had enjoyed a very comfortable retirement, but they had never forgotten their struggles to make ends meet. My mother had gotten plenty of oranges during her childhood provided by the plantation owned by her father. I loved listening to these stories as I suckled on succulent oranges, the juice dripping down my fingers.

I inhaled deeply, almost smelling the citrus fruit when I remembered something else – my walks in the orange orchard with my grandparents, listening to them talk about the yield of the trees and how the fruit had helped many a farmer to survive after the war. The idea grew in my mind until, all of a sudden, I was filled with glee.

"Oranges! We're going to plant orange trees!" I exclaimed. The next morning, I cycled to the market village then took an overcrowded taxi-brousse with women and farmers holding children or chicken on their lap. After a noisy and bumpy journey, I arrived in Ambohimanga, a gifted village with historical burials of royal families and electricity. I went to the post office to use a computer offering internet services. I first sent an email to Paul asking him if there was any chance that his company would provide financial support to a Malagasy village and its local cooperative. When it came to money and funds, Paul would knock at the right door and brilliantly present the project to get what we needed and even more. He answered quickly, connected permanently to his mailbox like he always was. I often teased him, sending him the message 'dinner is ready' even though we were in the same room.

He said he would talk to his associate director today to make sure the money could be transferred rapidly. Then, we would finalize the presentation of the project together before the annual charity meeting next month. He asked me about Isaac and how it felt to be a mother. I felt tears well in my eyes. Would he judge me for what I did? The decision to give Isaac back to his family was entirely my responsibility. I had to deal with my change of heart and I would have to explain it to my husband. Just not now, I wasn't ready yet. I wrote back vaguely that it wasn't going the way I thought it would and that I would tell him all about it soon. In the next email, addressed to Léon, I took more time and carefully chose my words, explaining how an orange tree plantation supported by a French company for its start would give a future to each child in the village. In my last sentence, I simply begged him to at least consider my idea. He thanked me warmly for my message and promised to give the idea a good look as soon as possible. I was disappointed; I had expected much more. After a couple of days, Léon drove a small truck to the village with the precious loading of grafted orange plants. I watched him from the porch of the school, recalling the moment Miss Voahangy, coming back from the market village, had broken the news that Léon had accepted my proposition. I had jumped around her, surprised to feel happiness again. On the adjacent land, farmers were already at work, digging holes at regular distances.

"Marie, I have completed my research and you are right! During a single season, a well-looked-after orange tree can produce between five hundred and seven hundred fruits. One kilogram can be sold for more than 4000 Ariary (1,30 US Dollars) on the market. The weather here is also conducive to its growth. Your idea is indeed brilliant. I contacted your husband's company and as soon as I received their funds, I bought the seedlings and sent you a message." He shook my hand warmly and sat next to me.

"That's good, really good. I'm so happy it's going to work out," I answered.

"The small shop on the track could even sell orange juice by the glass. One squeezed orange mixed with water and a spoon of sugar will do the trick and still be affordable for customers." Léon stood up with enthusiasm.

I looked up at the old man for a long time. I couldn't think of who would buy a glass of orange juice, but if he believed this idea would work, it would work. Léon was certainly a discreet and peaceful person, but I had confidence this man could move mountains if needed.

We soon started to unload the truck and put ourselves at work. By funding the farmers' cooperative, I was offering a possible future to the village and hope for the children. By planting orange trees, I was helping Isaac to put down his roots here, in his magnificent country, instead of robbing him of his origins. Each time I placed a seedling in a hole, leaving the bud, where the orange tree is grafted onto the rootstock, just above the surface, I was giving something back to Isaac: the red soil, the eucalyptus smell, the local goodbye 'veloma,' the 'mountains of rice,' the teacher's broad smile, the zebus made of clay, the bicycles on the track, and much more I wasn't aware of. The farmers and Léon finished their chore by watering the land and joined me for the last tree. I hadn't been as quick as the men, but I had certainly worked my best. I felt contentment filling my whole body. Maybe for the first time in my life, I had found my true place in the world.

The joyful team sat in the shadow of the school's porch and Miss Voahangy brought us fresh water. They spoke in their language and I relaxed, rubbing my hands to remove dried soil. Rocked by a sweet melody of foreign words, my mind drifted away. Isaac belonged to his Red Island, to his complex yet generous Malagasy culture. I wouldn't be there to accompany him on his way to adulthood and I wouldn't see him growing up, but I would make sure he would stay here. I would make sure the village would be able to support its children, feed them, and educate them.

On my last day, I finally packed my clothes in my almost empty suitcase. Empty was how I felt now, terribly missing a child I would never get to know, at the exception of this tiny little seed of hope germinating somewhere deep in my heart, mostly at the idea of a possible change for the village children. I hugged Miss Voahangy for a long moment, not knowing if I would ever see her again. I was grateful to her for having opened my eyes with honesty and for accompanying me on this difficult journey. Léon drove me back to Tana. When we reached the outskirts of the capital, I took a final glance at the red track and the Highlands I was leaving behind me. Above, there were only blue skies – no trees, no houses – just wild animals and a handful of Malagasy men walking, cycling, and pushing carts. We separated at the airport with the promise that we would keep in touch about any development regarding the cooperative. As soon as I passed the entrance door, I rushed towards a free plug on the wall where I put my dead phone to charge. Then, I took a deep breath and called Paul.

The Distance Between Us

By Jarita C. Mitra

Part I: The Letter

April 2017, London

Joanna opened the book. There, stuck inside with glue, was a neatly folded letter. The edges of the paper had worn out, a sign that it had been read many times before, perhaps by the one to whom it was addressed. Its brittle crispness bore testimony to the years that had passed between the hands that wrote it and hers as she held it now. She carefully unfolded the letter for the umpteenth time since it had come into her hands that afternoon. An easy breeze blew between the pages of the book as if to bring the letter to life. The grass beneath her bare feet caressed her as she sunk into the depth of the words that had faded in ink, but were still witness to timeless love. Its emotions were raw in its freshness as if the letter had just been written:

"May 24, 1993
What happened between us last night was wrong. Yet, I don't know why it felt so right...
In your arms, I felt complete, as though I belonged there with you. My soul felt a calm that I have never felt before and all my pain was erased – suddenly, the rest of the world didn't matter anymore. But I cannot forget that I am of this world, and that life has chosen a path for me that can never include you. That is why I need to leave. I am a mother. I should be strong... But your love is making me weak. That's why I must ask you to go as far away as you can from my life. Your light shall be my guide in every path that I take, and you will remain in the deepest depths of my heart for as long as I shall breathe.
Yours,
O"

While looking for a gift today for her fiancé on their first engagement anniversary, she had found this worn-out book displayed at the window of her regular corner book store. A note on the book's cover had caught her attention.

"THIS BOOK IS PRECIOUS. IT CONTAINS A SPECIAL HANDWRITTEN LETTER THAT NO LOVER WOULD LIKE TO MISS."

The pages of the book had become yellow with age, but even so, she had been happy to pay a hefty 150 British pounds to acquire it. As she now closed her eyes to seep in the love that the letter aroused inside her, she tried visualizing the nameless, faceless lovers who seemed to have briefly united only to be separated, pondering what circumstances would have compelled them to sacrifice their love, wondering if this letter was the end of that love story or whether the lovers had found each other again.

As she carefully wrapped it in the gift paper she had purchased at the adjacent stationery shop and stuck her little love note on top, a voice inside told her this book would be her alchemist in finding her way back to her fiancé Om's heart. She longed to see his dark eyes full of love for her again, something she had missed terribly in the past year.

April 2013, Paris

For Joanna Miller, Paris was the most intimate essence of love. When she had visited here eight years ago with her college friends, she had instantly fallen in love with the beauty of the city and had returned every year to experience a little more of its innateness. It didn't matter that the city had lost its elegance in the wake of its sufferings throughout history, most recently succumbing to an economic downturn; Paris had continued to hold its charm in her romantic heart.

As she stood at the top floor of the Eiffel Tower, a ritual she had maintained on every visit, she once again felt the nudging sense that it would be here that she would meet her love. And once again, she felt a deep sense of disappointment.

Like always, she had patiently waited in the long queue for the elevator that had brought her here and had spent more than an hour wondering if she would meet the person of her dreams this time around as several groups of visitors had come and gone. However, not one person had appealed to her senses as the possible answer to her inner calling.

A fresh elevator of people now made their way to the top and Joanna made her way back to leave. As she walked back to the elevator, her right heel gave away and she toppled and fell.

She was awkwardly sprawled across the floor, her face flushed and eyes lowered in severe embarrassment as a crowd started gathering.

Making matters worse, her skirt hung uncouthly high above her knees and the contents of her purse lay sprawled across the floor. With the broken shoe in one hand, she struggled to get up, mild pain in her right knee slowing down her endeavor. In the chaos she failed to notice a dark-skinned tall young man who was now intently watching her from his spot, his eyes fixated on her golden hair.

Om had walked up to Joanna and said, "Let me help you." As Joanna looked up, her heart missed a beat. The man's eyes were dark and his long lashes lent an effeminate touch to an otherwise masculine frame. His dark curls were neatly folded into a ponytail and made him look somewhere between a rockstar and a dark Greek God. As she held out her hand to the stranger, her feet felt weaker now with double onslaught: first from the fall and now from this man's presence. His eyes continued to explore her face, making her blush heavily. Om had made her exit from the building prompt and as painless as possible. After ensuring an efficient administration of first aid at the site, Om had made his offer to her for a coffee. Joanna had accepted without a second thought. They had settled themselves in a café by the River Seine and hours had passed as they had sat and chatted, neither having the intention to leave. Unable to let each other go when the café was finally closing for the night, they landed up in her hotel room. By the next morning, she felt like she knew him for a lifetime. In the following few days, they had been inseparable. They discovered each other in nooks and corners of Paris, as well as in an ignited passion where the body met the soul.

When Om finally bade Joanna goodbye at the airport, the two young people were in love.

February 2014 To April 2017, London

She moved to London to be with Om within a year. Her law firm was looking for someone to start in their newly-opened London office and she had jumped at the opportunity. In the next two years, they had become what storybooks would call "two bodies, one soul". Whenever they were not working, they spent time together, sometimes walking through the London streets aimlessly hand in hand, watching a movie or a soccer game, and occasionally in Om's house when his mom cooked up a lavish meal to pamper "her two children" as she liked calling them.

Om's mom was a famous writer and she had passed on her genes to her son, whose two books had already made it to London's bestselling list while a third was on its way for publishing. Om's mother had helped Joanna settled down in the new city when she had first arrived, and between the two women, they shared a deep sense of respect for each other as well as an undying love for Om.

Then, on their third-year anniversary since they had met, Om had taken Joanna back to Paris. There at the top of the Eiffel Tower, he had gone down on his knees and asked her to marry him.

Without hesitation, Joanna had said "Yes!" pulling Om up to her and kissing him deeply, cheered on by an applauding crowd that stood witness to this blissful moment.

However, their celebration was short-lived. Within two weeks of their return, Om and Joanna had gotten busy with his mom who had recently been suffering from some unexplained weight loss. One evening, she collapsed just after Om had returned from Joanna's apartment. The reports came in confirming the fear that had lurked on each of their hearts: she was dying of cancer. The slaughter had been rapid and, within five months, she had succumbed to death.

But the suddenness of it all had deeply affected Om. His mother had been his mentor and his greatest inspiration throughout life; she had stood by him like his pillar of strength. Now, he felt a pressing guilt of having been so busy with his love life that he failed to notice his mom's fraying health. Therefore, as if in penance for a sin he had committed, Om decided to slow down his love life.

As months passed, Joanna felt Om slowly pulling away from her. Gone was his passion and his insensible need to be with her. He spent most of his time writing, often ignoring her calls and canceling plans she made. Any complaint from her ended in bitter arguments, with her spending sleepless nights alone in her bed crying, but unlike before, he never came to wipe away any hurt he caused.

A year had passed since Om had proposed and her engagement ring still sat patiently on her hand, feeling heavy on her finger as a reminder of the never-ending silence and growing distance that now sat between them.

April 2017, London, The Engagement Anniversary

Pleased with her choice of gift for Om, and hopeful of its power to mend their relationship, Joanna went home and changed into a low-cut blue dress. She liked what she saw in the mirror and hoped Om would too.

As Om opened his door to let Joanna in, she saw a flicker of admiration sweep through his eyes. As she was placing her handbag on the table, Om silently came up and tightly hugged her from behind, digging his face deep into the crook of her neck. His warmth and touch after a long gap immediately wilted her crumbling heart and she broke down in tears. He slowly turned her around and kissed away the tears from her face, murmuring "I am so sorry" repeatedly in her ears. They then finally gave in to a soft symphony of finding one another again after a long separation.

Later, he surprised her with a pair of 5-carat solitaire earrings which he had purchased with the royalty from his first book. Joanna took her gift out and laid it consciously on Om's lap.

Om read her little note that said,

"I love you, my God's best sent gift
– Joanna"

He smiled and kissed Joanna's lips again. Her heart bloomed at his touch.

In a playful voice he said, "I love you, too, my sweet little eternal bliss. Be mine forever!"

All the pain of the past year forgotten, they quickly found themselves in each other's arms again. Hours passed as they lay blissfully in one another's fold before Joanna nudged Om to open his gift.

Still lying in Joanna's arms, Om unwrapped his gift and looked confused as a rugged book presented itself. In a deep bass and a theatrical voice, copying in ditto the display note at the shop she said, *"Monsieur, this book is precious. It contains a special handwritten letter that no lover would like to miss."*

Om suppressed a smile at the dramatic effect she had tried to create. *With not much success, though – she is too sweet to be funny*, he thought fondly. He opened the book, unfolded the letter, and started reading.

As Joanna watched him in anticipation and excitement, she saw the tightening of Om's muscles, and a building of stress in his body. Untangling himself from her, he got up and walked to the window and stood there with his bare back facing her, the trace of strain in his broad shoulders unmistakable.

Unsure, she walked up to him and held him from behind. He stood there, shoulders taut and back slightly drooped, eliciting a sense of dejection that Joanna had never seen in Om before. It unnerved her. She knew something about the letter was bothering him, and concerned she asked, "Darling, what happened?"

Without turning, Om said, his voice cold, "That is my mom's handwriting."

There was finality in his voice that made Joanna shudder. She took a step back and in an attempt to pacify him she said in defense of the woman she had respected tremendously, "Mom? Om, this must be a mistake!"

"I know her writing too well, Joanna. I have at least 100 notes written by Mom to me throughout the years. She used to date each and every letter. She wanted her letters to bear a mark of history. This is her style.

And see she has even initialed this one! I wish this was a mistake, Joanna, but this is not. It's her."

Pausing, he added with a sarcastic laughter, "And looking at the date, she had not written it to my father!"

Joanna heard a sigh leave Om's throat as the last words came out. Om's parents had been a most devoted couple until his dad had passed away seven years ago. He had told her that when she was meeting Mom for the first time. This letter was shattering the happy marriage myth he had held, revealing a possible secret love affair his mother had had with another man while being married to his father...for in 1993 Om was already two years old!

She watched him as he sat down desolately on the narrow stool behind him, his head nestled in his hands covering his eyes. His head swayed from side to side as if in disbelief of the situation. His breathing became heavier as he tried to force away the realization of his current reality.

As Joanna searched desperately for something to say that could bring back some normalcy to the abnormally-charged ambience, Om spoke, almost to himself. A sorrowful bitterness lined his voice as he said, "I cannot believe Mom was so dishonest her entire life with my father, with me!"

Then with a deep breath that seemed to choke his voice he let out, "And to think..." He left the last words hanging but Joanna knew Om was questioning the years of his unadulterated adulation for his mother.

She wanted to say, "But Om, if the letter is true, your mom actually sacrificed her love to be with your father. That shows her commitment towards him and YOU!"

But she kept silent, knowing it wouldn't help alleviate the pain he was experiencing at the disintegration of his lifelong perception of his perfect mother. She recognized the signs too well.

As a 14-year-old, her perfect family had been torn apart when her dad had left Mom for another woman, and in despair her mom had given in to alcohol and multitude of one-night stands, seeking relief for her own grief, completely unconcerned of the trauma Joanna and her little sister faced in the process; left to their insecurities and instability the sisters had learnt to make themselves emotionally immune and independent of their parents' choices.

Right now, Om's perfect world was being snatched away and even though his parents were both dead, it was throwing him in the same state of insecurity she had overcome long ago as a teenager.

She wanted to say, "It will all be okay, Om!"

Instead she walked up to Om and kissed him lightly on his cheek, hoping her love would take away some of his pain.

Turning towards her, his eyes ice cold and his voice devoid of any love of the previous hours, Om said, "Joanna, I want you to leave me alone."

A chill ran down Joanna's spine. In his own pain, Om was oblivious to the tears that welled up in her eyes at the harshness of his dejection. She moved away and picking up her handbag quickly left the house. Om had already turned his back to her.

Back in her apartment, she had spent the first few hours trying to sleep and then given up and instead had watched three movies in a row…that way she could force her mind to think of something other than the possible aftermath of Om's last words.

At the first signs of dawn, she forced herself to get dressed and go back to Om's house, hoping his dismissal of her the previous night was only a temporary outburst.

But when she reached his house, the front door was locked. She opened the door with her keys and stepped inside his house to find that everything was still in the exact same state as it had been when she had left the house last evening. Om's bed had not been slept in, the sofa was a crumbled remnant of their last embrace, and the book still sat at the side table. There was no sign of Om.

Torn between fear and concern, she called his cellphone countless times but it remained switched off, immune to her frantic state. Unable to control the sudden shaking of her body, she lay down on the floor curling up like an embryo, soaking in the warmth of Mother Earth against the coldness of the situation that was now tearing her heart apart, howling her pain out. At some point between the tears and tiredness she slept.

When she woke up, she felt calmer. She reached out for the book and read the letter again. This time, she could place Mom's face and she could almost hear Mom's voice reading out to her.

Joanna had been born with very strong intuition – several bits of evidence had supported that since her childhood. When she had picked up the letter that day, something had told her this was her back way to Om's heart. Her intuition seemed misplaced now that this letter had created a wider separation between them than ever before. But she believed there had to be a reason for the letter written by Om's mom to have landed in her hands. It had to be more than mere coincidence…what if Mom was reaching out through her? What was Mom trying to tell her? She had to find out.

Suddenly her logical mind and legal training took over her hurt, and forgetting about Om for the time being, she walked into Mom's empty room.

Nearly seven hours later Joanna had scourged through every single journal, writing draft, story outline, and photo album in Mom's room. Not a single photo gave any clue that she could link to the man she was searching but each of the books she had written in her life had one common denominator; their protagonists all had names starting with the alphabet 'J.'

Knowing somewhere in those protagonists' names hid the real identity of her secret lover, Joanna diligently noted all names in her notebook: Jason, Jacob, Jad, Jaden, Jai, Jayden, Jazal, Jeet, Jishnu, Jordan, and Joshua.

Determined now to find out the truth behind the letter, and more to answer the question of why the letter had been brought to her, Joanna made one last failed attempt to contact Om before she left his house. In slow steps she made her way home allowing her thoughts to shuffle between the next steps she would need to take with those eleven names, and whether Om and her relationship had now reached its finale.

Part II: Where We Belong

Varanasi, December 2017

Joanna had spent the next few weeks reviewing many Facebook profiles. Then by permutation and combination, she eliminated all who had been born after 1997 – she didn't think Mom's lover could be younger than 20 years of age. The final list had narrowed down to 440 profiles.

She had then sent out a message to each of them, with a brief note and a picture of the book cover that said, "I have found this book. If this belongs to you, please send me a message."

In the last eight months, she had received several responses by way of casual flirtations and numerous friend requests, but no one had come forward to claim the book.

On the other hand, her relationship with Om had normalized – in fact, it had improved. Alleviating any fear she had held of losing him, Om had sent her a text after two days of his leaving home saying "Joanna, I really need some time to myself. Don't worry about me. And please forgive me for that night. I love you."

After three weeks away, spent trekking in Kilimanjaro and volunteering with a Children's District Hospital in Nairobi, Om had returned home. On their first meeting since their anniversary, he had kissed Joanna until he had closed his eyes to sleep making a promise never to hurt her again.

Om's promises were made to be kept. She had learnt earlier on that Mom had always ensured any promise that was made in their family, no matter how trivial or how significant, had to be kept at no matter what the cost. It was their core.

But in all the love that Om now showered on her, Joanna could sense emptiness within him – his luscious eyes which had drawn her to him seemed devoid of its earlier vibrancy, and it felt like a deep wound inside him was refusing to heal itself. Somewhere between her and Om's complete happiness, Mom's dark secret continued to loom.

More than ever now she knew that the truth had to be revealed. But her earlier attempt had led to failure. Disappointed, and not giving up, she proposed to Om that she wanted to see his birthplace, and wanted to learn more of his roots, his culture, assuring it meant a lot for her. Though Om himself had no memory of India, having moved to London when he was three years of age, he found a trip there to be a good getaway from the mundanity of London and a welcome change after the last few months of torment their relationship had endured.

During her planning process, between intelligent probing and attentive listening, she had figured out that Om had been born in a city called Varanasi and during 1993, his family had still lived there. Convinced that the truth or some significant part of Mom's secret letter and her lover rested there, she had planned their itinerary in a manner that they could stay the last one week of their holiday in Varanasi.

Now traveling in India, between Goa and Kolkata, Agra and Delhi, Bangalore and Jammu, Om and Joanna had come to enjoy the thickly populated country in all its diverse flavors, alternating between modern and old, sophistication and naivety, luxury and poverty, and had felt at home at the warmth her people had bestowed on them.

As the plane now touched down on the soil of the holiest city in the world, Joanna prayed for the place to deliver a miracle. After they had deposited their luggage in the Nadesar Palace Hotel and stepped out to explore the city which dated back to around 11th century BC, her first thoughts echoed Mark Twain's words, "Benaras is older than history, older than tradition, older even than legend and looks twice as old as all of them put together."

Wherever they went, the city in its innate ancientness was a curious contrast of soulful sacredness and colorful spectacle with surprises greeting them abound in every corner. Temples, mosques, and monasteries shared the mysticism of the land in secular unison. Narrow alleyways with centuries old houses opened out into wide Ghats

stretching miles across the city before meeting at the foot of the Holy Ganges. The living came to wash off their sins in her sacred waters and the dead took their last journey from here onto infinity. Numerous priests chanted Sanskrit mantras in a choreographed daily evening prayer dedicated to the river revered as a Goddess, as the sounds of bells, drums, and cymbals resonated through every nerve of its audience and thousands of night lamps lit up the entire surrounding in an orchestrated splendor.

An eternal combination of physical, metaphysical, and the supernatural, every spot in Varanasi carried its own mythical history. Within the first couple of days, the entire culture of the city had blown them away in fascinated charm.

But Joanna didn't forget her main purpose for being here. Everywhere they went, she kept her ears open for any name that sounded familiar and eyes observant to anything relevant that could lead her to the man she came in search of. Even though by the end of their fifth day she had met a Jai, a Jeet and a Jordan, sadly none of whom had ever known Mom.

Aware that a casual observation would not help in finding one man in a city of a million people, she decided to take deliberate action. When Om offered to stay back in the hotel to enjoy its amenities during their last couple days, she immediately jumped to his offer and proposed to explore the city on her own, reasoning that she was not yet done with her infatuation with this ancient city.

Hiring a *tuk tuk* for the entire day, she then moved around shops and alleys interviewing countless people and shop owners, showing everyone the book she carried and asking people if they had any connection to or memory of Om's family. In her earlier discussions with Om, she had tried to find out about any friends or relations he had in Varanasi, but Om had left from there very young and had no recollection. Joanna still loitered around the vicinity of Om's old neighborhood and tried to gather some recognition, but no one seemed to be cognizant of the famed British author and no one carried any memory of Om's family. At the end of her last day in Varanasi, not a single clue had led her any nearer to the truth she had hoped to unveil.

Exhausted and desolate Joanna finally gave in, her intuition and her faith defeated in the despotic deliverance of facts.

Their suitcases were now packed, and Om slept peacefully on the comfortable hotel bed, ready to return home after a fulfilled vacation. But Joanna's heart remained restless, dispirited about her vanquished hopes, the knowledge of having failed Mom, and the consciousness of having left Om's wound unhealed.

As she lay awake in Om's arms, suddenly she felt her stomach churn mildly. She ignored the pain at first believing the discomfort inside of her was an expression of her inner emotional distress. But as time went by the churning grew wilder and a slicing pain cut through her inside like a piercing knife. It was so painful that she finally sat up and groaned uncontrollably.

Waking up to her painful state, Om at first panicked. Then, after putting her to an immediate relief with a strong painkiller, he called the hotel manager who efficiently made arrangements for them to visit a medical practitioner in the immediate vicinity of the hotel. He also rearranged their flight schedule to a day later.

When the hotel manager had mentioned Dr. Woodsworth, the name had certainly rung alien in this land of mystique. The tall, slender gentleman who presented himself at the doorway of his chamber stood out distinctly as non-Indian by origin. His once blond hair now showed streaks of mild gray. His eyes partially covered by glasses revealed a pair of dark grayish pupils, the first sign of wrinkles failing to hide a once taut face line of a very handsome man.

"Dr. Woodsworth?" Joanna asked in formal acknowledgement. The doctor smiled at Joanna and said, "And you must be Ms. Miller?"

Joanna nodded.

Dr. Woodsworth then shifted his glance to Om who was sitting by her side holding her hands. His expression suddenly changed and a look of uncertain disbelief spread in his eyes.

"Om?" He asked mildly, his eyes now transfixed at Om's face, as if he had seen some apparition.

Om frowned mildly, trying to decipher how the doctor knew his name... as far as he was aware, the hotel manager had registered Joanna as the patient!

He replied, confusion now running in his mind, "Yes, but how do you know my name?"

"You are Oeshi's son," the doctor said with a sudden decisiveness, the look of confusion now completely vanished from his face and a tender expression now settled in his eyes.

Realizing that he had treaded an unexpected zone by the expression in the young couple's faces, something that bordered between surprise and shock, he added, "You don't remember me, do you, Om?"

As if struck by a sudden bolt of lightning, Joanna leapt from her sofa and almost shrieked, "Mom's letter...did she write it to YOU?" It was Dr. Woodsworth's turn to frown.

But before he could react to her words, Joanna quickly reached out inside her purse and pulled out the book. It was for this impossible probability she had been carrying the book all along. But before she could do or say anything further, as if by some force of gravitation that worked parallel to the Earth, Joanna found the book pulled away from her and nestled in Dr. Woodsworth's chest protected by his two wide palms.

Losing all sense of his surroundings, the doctor's eyes danced in joy as he said with the vulnerability of a child who had found his favorite lost toy, "Where did you find this book? This...this was the last touch of Oeshi I had!"

After a brief shocked silence that ensued, Dr. Woodsworth added quietly, "My name is Jaden."

Om had thus far been trying to comprehend the drama that was unfolding in front of his eyes. Now, all of a sudden everything came together in perfect clarity. He felt a strong weight pulling heavily at his heart just like the night when Joanna had gifted him this ill-fated book...all the pain, the betrayal he had felt then now resurfaced in its fullest intensity as this stranger stood ominously between his absolute veneration and melancholic denunciation of his mom.

He whispered in an uncanny calm that betrayed the inner storm now raring to break out, "So you are the man who my mother cheated my dad for! You are the man who slept…!"

Jaden's glare pierced through Om's eyes, stopping him dead in his tracks.

A moan diverted both men's attention from each other to Joanna who was now lying crouched on the sofa holding her stomach. Her face cringed in unbearable pain. The stomach ache had returned.

The two men promptly ran to Joanna, Om holding her face and hands in trying to ease her discomfort, the doctor deftly moving his fingers through her stomach in medical precision. A minute earlier the two men had been tied in a fist-less battle over one woman, and this minute they had united over another.

"There's nothing to worry about. It must be something she's eaten," Dr. Woodsworth said. "It's common here. I'll give her medicine, and I will write her a prescription."

As the two men sat quietly for long, waiting for Joanna's recovery, the air of friction between them gradually dissipated, calming Jaden down. Knowing Oeshi, he recognized Om would have been kept completely blind to his mom's deep secret. He would have liked to protect her need for secrecy, but Om deserved to know the whole truth about his mother, something that her letter wouldn't tell.

When Joanna felt better and she sat up, Jaden said softly, "Om, your mother was as pure as the River Ganges who could wash all impurities off any impurity she touched. You should know that."

The word 'pure' has a sense of sanctity in itself, a healing that touched the son's heart. What his fragile heart craved, an assurance of his mom's chastity, the stranger's words delivered with conviction.

And when Jaden asked, "Om, will you allow me to tell your mother's story, my story?"

Om silently nodded his agreement.

Jaden began. His voice distant, he almost spoke to himself. Jaden's life had come to a standstill the day he had lost his only child. She had been swimming when losing balance she had sunk in and by the time the lifeguard had come to her rescue, his little girl's lungs had filled with too much water. He couldn't bring her back to breathing despite all his medical training. In mourning the young parents had allowed their marriage to crumble. And his wife, unable to forgive him for what he felt was his fault, had left him.

Having grown up at a foster home never knowing his parents, he had married very early and had made his young family his identity. With them now gone from his life, there was nothing to tie him anymore to London. He had first resigned from his hospital, and then, selling off everything he owned, he had given away his all to a charity.

He had moved east, desperately seeking spiritual healing, bringing with him only one rucksack of basic necessities and no plans to return. He had first visited Tibet and then moved to Nepal and stayed there for a few months before landing in Kolkata at Mother Teresa's home, working there for the next few. His final destination was Varanasi, where he had been told every person had healed.

He had boarded the train at Kolkata (Howrah) station and taken his allotted seat. He found a woman seated there already. Thinking that she had mistaken her seat number, he had remained silent, politely waiting for the ticket master to guide her to the correct seat. When the ticket master finally arrived many stations later, he was told to get off the train. It was Jaden who had boarded the wrong train.

The woman had come to his rescue and negotiated with the ticket master to allow him to share her space. Her charm was discerning and the gentleman had relented.

Overwhelmed with gratitude, which was when he had looked at her for the first time.

She was the prettiest Indian woman he had seen by far, but it was not her beauty that drew Jaden towards her. She had a magnetic charm about her, a grace directly from the divine infinite, as if she had been to God and back. In the dimly-lit compartment and the warmth of the humid air, her dark hair had formed curls around her forehead, her pale skin glistened, and her eyes dove-shaped, small and of a dark brown color, guarded by huge lashes were like a secret lake determined to protect her inner world from the world outside her in complete confidentiality. Her divine presence had forced a craving in Jaden to unravel her mystery. But he couldn't. Her guard was too high for him to dare tread. Instead, he had bared his entire pain to her. From his orphanage to his broken marriage, he spoke up about his entire life story. Like she was the only one who'd understand. She never spoke. She listened silently until Jaden's lips realized that too long had passed.

When he had stopped, she got up, grabbed her water cooler, and poured him a glass.

"Here, drink this," she had said, her voice soft and understanding.

They didn't speak a word after that. As the night became lighter, Jaden had moved a little closer and touched her hands. It had seemed the most natural thing to do.

He knew it was wrong, for she belonged to another man, but he wasn't touching her as a man would a woman; he was seeking her divinity to seep into him and heal him.

She didn't object. Hours had passed without his noticing, until when the first signs of dawn pinned its narrow streaks through the frosty windows, and people began shifting in their sleeping bunks, that she finally shifted and very slowly let her hand free.

An hour later as the train whistled into the Varanasi railway platform, and she alighted, ready to leave with a porter carrying her luggage, Jaden suddenly realized he had not asked her name.

"Oeshi Chatterjee," she had said, a shy pink brushing her cheeks, her full smile shaming the brilliance of the beautiful sunny morning. Gathering more courage he had then asked for her contact details to which she had calmly responded, "Last night in your presence I felt a light touching me. I don't know what it meant, but I trust its presence. And I will let that light guide us to meet again if it is meant to be. If not, this is where our acquaintance must end. I truly wish you leave Varanasi a man purified of your past."

With that she walked away. The sight of her back fading in the crowd gripped Jaden in a numb paralysis, a sense of loss he couldn't explain.

Her light, whatever it was, guided him back to Oeshi again…in an odd play of circumstances.

Jaden had traveled to India without a return ticket and an intent to stay until Varanasi had delivered on its promise. To be economically sustainable, he had stayed in a cheap boarding house. The food there tasted terrible, the room smelled and was infested with mosquitos, but nonetheless he quite enjoyed the change from his luxurious life back home. The fulfillment of basic needs became so vital that it served to divert him from any thoughts of the life he had left behind.

But after the third week had passed, he returned one evening after a long day to find the boarding shut down. The owner was in heavy debt and had decided to fade into obscurity. His rucksack along with other boarders' belongings had been kept in the custody of a side store, after removing the last penny. Thankfully there were a few rupees and dollar bills on him, just enough for a few meals.

To clear his mind and make some sense of what was next; he had walked to the ghaat[1] and sat on the stairs trying to calm his mind in the cool breeze of the calming river and the beauty of the candles that lit up the whole place in a festive celebration of the faith of its devotees. Breathing heavily as if he could feel Oeshi's presence right then and there, Jaden said, "And there in the play of the dark and the light I saw Oeshi again. That was also when I first met you."

He paused and smiled fondly at Om. Om smiled back, a little shy. He didn't remember a thing, but he somehow felt nice at the thought of being witness to that meeting.

Om's memory of his mother was of a most practical, elegant, and eloquent woman. The image of the woman that Jaden was painting now seemed far-fetched from the mother he had known. But he carried some vague memories of his mom in their old house and he could sense how his mom was now looking in Jaden's eyes as he reminisced that moment when he met her the second time…in her bright beautiful cotton saree, curly long hair flowing in the evening breeze, her petite face orange in the flames of the surrounding candles.

That's how beautiful Joanna had looked when they sat at the ghat to watch the evening prayers and lamp lightings, her blonde hair had shone like gold, her white skin a hue of soft orange that had made her look like she was of some heavenly abode. Om moved close to Joanna and encircled her in his arms.

Jaden resumed his story.

That evening, ignoring several eyes that watched the unfamiliar scene of a man walking up to a married woman (as her red vermillion and the little boy in her lap clearly pointed), Jaden sat down beside her.

Smiling uneasily but visibly happy to see him again, she asked how he had been. And when he blurted out his sorry story she took him home with her and offered him to stay in the extra room in the attic until he could arrange some funds to afford a place. Om's father had also been kind and welcoming.

As days passed, Oeshi's demeanor towards him started changing as she started treating him as a parent would a child. He was a few years younger than her, but no less a man, and the more she made him feel a child, the more his compulsive obsession to prove his manhood to Oeshi grew.

One afternoon, he spotted her standing at the inner ledge of the roof with her hands outstretched, her eyes closed and head tilted slightly backwards. Thinking Oeshi was about to jump, he had run frantically to her and grabbed her from behind. Taken by shock she had shrieked and then slapped him hard.

When sense followed her action, she became visibly agitated that Jaden had even thought she could consider taking her life, and he had to tell his 'sorries' several times before she finally calmed down. She explained this had been her ritual whenever the dictates of life left her overwhelmed.

Then in deliberate caution, Oeshi revealed her story. After completing her bachelor's degree in Kolkata, Oeshi's dream had been of pursuing

Masters in English Literature and then becoming a Journalist. Having grown up in a household filled with books, writing had seemed a natural path to follow.

But decisions about her life had been made without seeking her permission. Her father had married her off fearing societal pressures to a man who was well-educated and financially stable, but much older: Dheer. Her husband was a kind man but of a traditional bearing. In serious pursuit of his career to fend for his family and in complete oblivion of her dreams and desires, he had unknowingly diminished her to serve only a single purpose, that to nurture a family. Over the years, an essential part of her being had gone missing in her existential limitedness, sometimes threatening her exterior calm. In such moments of despair, she sought liberation in the banks of the Ganges where his fate had brought him to meet her, or at the rooftop.

As Oeshi slowly let her barriers down allowing her vulnerability to surface, Jaden could see in her eyes an unspoken sadness he had not noticed earlier.

And in that defining moment of their relationship, in Oeshi's eyes Jaden had transcended from a seeker to a giver, from the protected to the protector, from a child to a man.

In the five months that followed their friendship had evolved and so had their deep understanding of one another. They shared an indefinable nexus of spirit that left them both with a profound sense of oneness in one another and with the Universe.

Jaden had gotten Oeshi a handcrafted diary coaxing her to start writing. And Oeshi had prepared one empty room as his chamber so he could resume his medical practice, almost forcing him into it saying that it was his responsibility towards humanity. But even though he was economically independent now, the question of his moving out never arose.

Then one night as he was preparing for bed, without forewarning Oeshi pushed open the door of his room and stepped in, her teary eyes smudged by her dark kohl. She had received a letter from Kolkata; her father was very sick and dying. He knew she had come to be calmed and he circled her lightly in his arms holding her there in silence. She stayed there until her tears finally stopped.

Their touch was devoid of any physical obsession, it was one of nurture, but perhaps nature has created an inherent fire that no man and woman can defy and suddenly the pureness of their embrace turned into a pressing desire to hold on. He pressed her hard into his chest. And she melted in him. Their breathing heavy, heartbeats loud in rhythmic unison, the longing deepened. Then without thinking Jaden planted a light kiss on her head. Suddenly Oeshi was back in her righteous self. And pulling herself away from him quietly, she left his room never looking at him and never looking back.

As he watched her back fade into the darkness of the night outside, he knew at that moment that he held no future with her, and that he held none without her.

That night was the last time Jaden would see Oeshi. After sleepless hours and a long morning walk to clear his mind from the emotional deluge, he had returned home to find Oeshi and Om gone back to Kolkata.

On his table she had left the book that now lay on the table beside him. Inside she had left a letter for him asking him to go far away from her life.

He had cried, caring nothing of his manhood that day, until his pain had been completely numbed and replaced by a dull emptiness; then, he had packed his bag and moved out.

For several days he had lurked around the place, hoping to catch a glimpse of Oeshi. However, Oeshi was careful never to bump into him, even though he knew she could see him from her place on the roof.

And then one day, a few months later, they were all gone. Jaden looked at Om and said, "I learned from your neighbors that your father had gotten a job in London."

He had stayed on, waiting for Oeshi to return someday. He had waited for 23 years, and he now knew with finality that she would never return.

As Joanna's eyes flooded uncontrollably and Om's heavy lashes remained moist, Jaden sat quietly for a few minutes, absorbing the ache that still pounded his heart.

Then, after a little while, he quietly walked up to a chest of drawers behind Joanna and Om and pulled out an envelope.

Five years ago, on a normal day like just any other, Jaden had just finished with his patients and had turned on the television. However, the day was not ordinary, for there she was, filling his screen, lighting up his life…his Oeshi.

The local news channel was covering a glimpse of her interview with British Television in a program called "Notable Global Indians of Varanasi."

Her long hair had been replaced with a short bob, her calm softness by a dignified confidence, and her bright cotton sarees by a dull formal trouser suit. She was still ravishingly beautiful, but very British. Her adapted moniker Oana C. also suited her looks very well.

But in her eyes, Jaden had seen the same desolation that he had glimpsed on the roof two decades ago…the pristine blue of the Thames wouldn't have offered her the solace that the serene spirit of the Holy Ganges had done when she would have needed it.

Realizing she was now widowed, he had written to Oeshi, with his forwarding address. And then again. No reply was received. Jaden had almost come to believe that distance and fame would have obliterated his memories from Oeshi's mind, until a little over a year ago, when he had received a letter from her.

Jaden handed over the envelope to Joanna. As Joanna pulled out a handwritten letter from inside, she immediately recognized Mom's writing. She read it out loud, letting Oeshi's last words fill the room as the morning sun started filling in with its soft warmth.

"August 27, 2016.
I have kept my word. You have remained in my deepest depths and in every breath I have taken.
But that was the only promise that I had in my power, for my life had been already vowed to Dheer before I met you. I am glad that for all the pain I have borne of my being away from you, I could remain true in my promise to him. My courage came from knowing that you were there for me.
When your letters came, God knows my heart craved to be with you, cradling your warmth, imagining silly fights with you over a sip of morning tea on who'd read the newspaper first, my greying hair and wrinkled face now clearly standing out from your still handsome youth and making me feel jealous of other beautiful younger women.
But I couldn't.
Perhaps I will, once I have completed my seven[2] lifetimes with Dheer, if you will be willing to wait, and after I have fulfilled my promise as a mother. I have remained strong for my son even in my weakest moments.
Om has grown up to be a good man, like his father and like you, and I really hope I can make him proud of his mom.
Your light has always guided me in my path, and your light is now fading as I prepare to leave this world. See you somewhere…
Yours ever,
Oeshi."

Knowing she was dying, Jaden had taken the first flight to London to be with Oeshi.

But when he knocked at the London door which was now Oeshi's home (its architecture so familiar yet so strange now after years of staying away), the expression that hung on the old lady's face who opened it told him clearly that he was too late. With a painful alacrity, he had quickly left without bothering to introduce himself and boarded the next flight out of London.

In his grief-stricken absentmindedness, Jaden had returned to Varanasi without Oeshi's book, having lost it somewhere. Life had remained hopelessly empty in the months that followed, and he had chosen to immerse himself in his hospital work.

Now, the book in his hand, his soul felt revived.

Slowly, he opened the book and unfolded the letter. He had read it thousands of times over the years, and every time, Oeshi's handwritten note had transported him back into that night as he held Oeshi again. Alive, loving. And in his mind, Oeshi never walked away. Instead, she stayed.

Jaden was suddenly aware of the young couple watching him closely. He stood up. He knew this letter had been a medium to bring Om to him. It was time to fulfil his final responsibility toward Oeshi. Jaden asked, "Om, would you like to visit your old house?" Surprised Om replied, "My house? Of course! Can you take us where Mom lived? I thought Dad had sold the house!"

"Yes he did, and I bought it."

Om remembered the tears Mom had shed trying to convince Dad over several weeks not to sell off the house. She had reasoned that it was sacred for her. But Dad didn't listen; he was a practical man and he didn't see a point in keeping an old house when they had no plans to return to it. When he finally sold it, Mom had remained silent for days; it had felt as if she had lost something. *She had lost a part of her, and it seems obvious she had no idea it had been bought by Jaden.*

And then, a few weeks later, she had chopped off her long tresses, completely changed her wardrobe, and became a new person. She had never worn a saree again.

It felt strange to him that Dad had seen Mom's change as welcome, happy that Mom had adapted to the British ways so seamlessly. Dad hadn't made the connection between the selling of the house and Mom's transformation, and neither had Om, until now.

But he realized now that it was Mom's silent revolt against Dad, against everything that life had taken away from her. Dad had unwittingly and unknowingly destroyed Mom.

Om silently offered a word of gratitude to Jaden for having brought in writing to her life, for in the words that flowed through her fingers, Om knew Mom had found her peace.

It felt even stranger that this man who had known Mom for such a short while, a man polar variant to Mom in so many ways from his origin to his culture and even his belief system, had sacrificed his own roots and his entire lifetime in wait for Mom, all the while fiercely protecting her roots.

He looked at Jaden and wished he had known about him earlier…he regretted that Mom and Jaden never had a chance at happiness, two people who lived for one another without each other.

He would not allow any such foolishness to separate him and Joanna. As soon as they got back home, he would complete his promise to Joanna and marry her.

Joanna slipped her warm hands in Om's as the three walked into the home Om had been born in. Om squeezed her hands and looked lovingly at her. All the pain that she had seen in Om's eyes in the last months had now relinquished itself. She knew with certainty that he was finally cured of his pain.

As she looked around, she felt a strong presence of Mom right there, standing somewhere very close to her. Even her German bearing could not dissuade her firm conviction that it was Mom who had taken her to the letter, that it was Mom who helped find her way back into Om's heart by leading them into discovering love in its most giving form.

She smiled in the direction she felt Mom stood and said silently, "Thank you, Mom!"

And as if mediating on behalf of Mom, she unwound her hand from Om's and went up to Jaden and hugged him. His innate warmth immediately embraced her, and as she let the kindness of his heart hold her, she felt a healing of the wounded child in her who had been abandoned by a careless father long ago. Joanna clung to him like a 14-year-old again. Jaden hugged her back with tender affection. Om suddenly said, "I remember you! You were my Jesus!" As an infant, Om couldn't pronounce Jaden. The name was too difficult for his brain to absorb that which was different from Indian names. But Om knew Jesus from picture books his mom had read to him, and with his then long brown curly hair, Jaden had fit the image of Jesus perfectly in Om's tiny world.

As if remembering the child in himself, Om also came up to Jaden and, albeit a little embarrassed, he gently rested his body against Jaden's. Jaden removed one arm from Joanna and reached out to place it on Om's shoulder, like a father would to a grown-up son.

After some time Jaden said, "I need to give you something." He released himself from the two young hearts, who took the opportunity to tangle themselves in each other's arms, and went up to the cupboard. From there, he drew out a bunch of keys. Handling them over to Om, he said, "These are yours." Realizing the implication of this gesture, Om said with determination "No, this is your house!"

Sensing Jaden's sudden withdrawal at Om's blatant refusal which sounded almost rude, Joanna stepped in to mitigate the situation. "Jaden, we will not live in this house and neither in this city. These are your memories of Mom. You should keep it."

Relaxing, Jaden responded, "I know Oeshi much more than any of you do. And if she is watching us right now, and I know she is, she would want you to keep this house. I was only guarding this until I could return it to her. And she lives within you."

Jaden recollected the very first entry Oeshi had made in the diary he had given her. It had a picture of Om holding his mother's hand with a note that said,

"Dedicated to my son:
I carry him inside my soul, and he carries mine within him."

Any further protest rendered useless, Om took the keys from Jaden and smiled gratefully at the man. A thought suddenly crept into his mind. Jaden was no longer a stranger. In one night he had become family. Om would love Jaden to hold and play with his children. He smiled at his farfetched thought and stole a loving glance at Joanna.

After an hour or so had gone by, when the initial discomfort of being new owners of the house had worn off, Joanna and Om had gotten busy exploring the house. Om was excitedly showing Joanna every part of the old house, his familiarity now restored along with his memory of it.

And they were busy pulling each other in their arms and planting little kisses as they moved around the house like two little children. It was time for Jaden to leave; Last night had been long, and his first patients would soon be arriving.

As he silently exited the house and closed the door behind him, careful not to disturb the lovers, Joanna and Om stood comfortably wound in each other's embrace, oblivious of their surroundings and of him.

As he made his way back to his house, the British doctor stood much taller than most people he passed, and he was fairer than them all. He was still very much an outsider in all his physical appearance, but in his heart, he was undeniably an integral element of this rustic land. In his long wait, Varanasi had grown on him and become home.

Jaden stopped momentarily and looked up at the sky, as if to feel Oeshi's presence. As he looked down and continued walking, he knew his wait was now finally over. Over the years, he had refused any attraction he had felt towards any other woman, and ignored any interest women had shown in him, for he had vowed his life to Oeshi. With Oeshi now gone, he was ready to settle down. That was what Oeshi would want him to do for her soul to rest. But, he was willing to do that only for this lifetime…for he would still like to keep his next lifetimes free, just in case Oeshi changed her mind.

1 Typically this is how the bank of a River is called in Varanasi.
2 A custom in Hindu marriages, where a bride and groom circumambulate the holy fire seven times in a sacred vow to spend seven lifetimes with one another.

A Surprise Inheritance

By Julia Marafie

One Sunday afternoon, Brigitte was standing at the window of her London flat and thinking about her future. She watched as the wind whipped the leaves from the trees. They fluttered softly onto the gray pavement, making a carpet of russet and gold. Soon those very leaves would be swept away as though they had never existed. *Everything is transient in this world, nothing of beauty ever lasts*, she thought sadly, picking up a photo frame from the windowsill.

A picture of her mother as a young woman of about 20 years old, vibrant and anxious to participate in life, smiled back at her. Tall and slender, wearing a pale green dress with tiny orange buttons, she was leaning against an old stone wall, the gray Atlantic behind her. Copper colored hair, thick and unruly, framed her gentle face. A broad smile lit up her pale blue eyes, momentarily hiding a lonely melancholy that had often lingered in them throughout her life; it was a look that had dimmed as she had aged, but had never truly disappeared. Brigitte sensed they held a secret buried deep within. Harrowing images began floating unbidden into her mind of the shriveled carcass that her mother had morphed into only a few short months ago, as she had lain motionless in a sterile hospital bed until the outstretched arms of death embraced her.

Brigitte had commented on the photograph several times, but her mother's vague answers and obvious discomfort at the mention of it made her think that perhaps it was something she would rather keep to herself. Oh, Mom! I wish you were still here to help me sort myself out. *You always knew the right thing to do*, she thought, putting the frame back onto the windowsill.

It seemed to Brigitte that recent circumstances had forced her to take a long, hard look at where her life was heading. The breakup of her marriage had left her feeling vulnerable and indecisive, followed closely by the sadness of her mother's death, and then, the shock of being made redundant at the age of 35. Was it perhaps a mixed blessing? Whatever had happened to the adventurous, freedom-loving person she had once been? Where was her creativity, her love of life? Brigitte flicked back her long copper-colored ponytail defiantly. *I'll get through this*, she thought. She wore chunky silver earrings and a thick sweater with a cowl neck. Her slender legs were encased in black jeans. She had a porcelain face with tiny freckles that started on the bridge of her nose and fanned out across her cheeks. *Even her clothes had become boring without her even noticing*, she thought.

A few weeks later out of the blue, she received a letter containing some amazing news. It was from a lawyer's office in Ireland informing her that she was to inherit fifty acres of land and a cottage in the west of Ireland, a place she knew nothing about; it was as remote to her as Timbuctoo. She had no idea why or who it could be. Brigitte wondered if this was perhaps yet another pointer goading her to make some changes in her life. It stated that the inheritance could be claimed only after she had lived in Ireland for one year, and it was this that had started the trouble with her best friend Mara.

Over a glass of wine next evening, she read the letter to her. Mara listened carefully and then began a torrent of questions. "My advice," Mara said eventually, "is to flog it as quickly as possible and pocket the money!"

"But it's not as simple as that! Remember, it stipulates I must live there for a year before it becomes fully mine."

"Well, that's insane. You must contest it! What sort of nutter would expect you to give up your life to go and bury yourself in some godforsaken hole for a whole year! Impossible!" Taking another gulp of wine, Mara ranted on, drawing attention to the fact that Brigitte would lose her job, miss her friends, her life in London, and her flat. Oh! It was all too ridiculous to even contemplate, and for what? Some daft benefactor who she had no notion of?

Mara hurried on with her objections, asking and answering her own questions, not giving Brigitte a chance to reply – but then, as she noticed a strange, defiant look on her friend's face, she stopped abruptly in mid-sentence.

"Tell me you are not serious!" she spluttered. "You can't be!" "I'm not saying I'm going," Brigitte paused, eeking out her words cautiously. "Just thinking about it. Nothing is decided yet." "It's bad enough to even let such a ridiculous idea enter your head!" Mara snapped, worried for her friend, unable to believe she'd be that crazy.

"It's just that ever since my breakup with Tom, Mom passing away, and now losing my job, there's not much to stay in London for," Brigitte explained sadly.

Mara was not inclined to listen and let her vivid imagination rip. "It is all very sinister," she said ominously.

She asked how this benefactor had even known that Brigitte was free to run off halfway across the world – how did they know she was not married, saddled with family responsibilities, with oodles of kids to look after, or aged parents she was unable to leave? These were all relevant questions and Brigitte had to agree that it was indeed strange.

Mara then suggested that it could well be a trap to kidnap her to get her inheritance, that she could be walking right into the hands of a drug cartel – she'd seen it on TV – and a rugged isolated cove off the West of Ireland would be an ideal venue for them to set up. Worse still, a gang of white slave traffickers might be operating in the area, and Brigitte would be a sitting duck, not knowing anyone or anything about the place. She advised her once again to forget about the whole business and left Brigitte's flat in a cloud of impatience at her best friend's foolhardiness, banging the front door behind her.

But Brigitte was not able to do that. Something was nagging at her inside, pulling her along into some unknown abyss, a place her intuition told her she needed to go, but why?

One morning some days later she awoke early. Her indecision had evaporated and she knew exactly what she had to do. She didn't know how she knew, just that she did. Lifting the telephone she booked her passage on the ferry, gave notice at her job, emailed her brother in Canada telling him of her intentions together with her new address. His prompt reply was cautionary, mentioning that he remembered their mother had once talked of someone she'd known in Ireland before he was born, but he knew no further details. She smiled at her little brother's concern. She contacted the solicitor in Ireland, a Mr. Oisin Murrin, and told him of her date of arrival. In return he offered to meet her at the property, enclosing a map for her journey.

Mara had been frosty since that evening and reaffirmed that she thought she was nuts, but if she was determined to continue on such a foolhardy escapade she must promise to keep her posted on her whereabouts at all times. Grudgingly, Mara then wished her luck. Brigitte agreed, joking at her friend's concern, reminding her it was only a few hundred miles away and that she had traveled extensively before marrying Tom. Discussing it later with her husband Johnnie, Mara said she was sure Brigitte was having some kind of breakdown, maybe a midlife crisis early, and they must both keep a keen eye on her. Johnnie had nodded, knowing better than to argue, but said she was a grown woman after all and had to lead her own life.

A month later, her old car packed and her goodbyes said, with Ruby, her elderly black cat, settled in his basket on the front seat, Brigitte threw caution to the wind. *This is what I've been missing in my life lately*, she thought as she pressed her foot down on the accelerator of her car.

The drive to the ferry port was long and tedious. Ruby registered her annoyance with constant meows. Brigitte switched on the radio and told herself that there was no turning back now. She'd had butterflies for days, but once her journey began, a strange calm had settled over her, as though she was being guided by some invisible force to a place she was meant to be.

Excited at the prospect of the unknown, she began to think of the things she might have time to do now that she wasn't working such long hours. Perhaps once again writing the poetry that had given her so much pleasure in the past, and maybe she would begin drawing once more after so long. If there was enough space she could take up beekeeping, something that had always fascinated her. New ideas and possibilities crowded into her head as she drove.

Arriving at the port in good time, she waited her turn in the queue, watching the juggernauts and cars enter the huge mouth of the ferry gaping open to receive its prey, reminding her of the childhood story of Jonah being swallowed up into the mouth of the whale. She maneuvered her car tentatively onto the shaky gangplank. Strange noises resounded from inside the ferry, as the crewmen used heavy metal chains to anchor things to the floor in case of rough seas. Strong whiffs of petrol fumes and oil mingled with the salty sea smells. All makes and sizes of cars, as well as campervans, caravans, and bicycles, were ushered into tight lanes.

Settling her cat with a bowl of water and reassuring words, Brigitte sidled out of her car and picked her way along the narrow gaps between the vehicles to join the passengers making their way towards a doorway. Four flights of metal stairs led up to the driver's lounge. Choosing a comfortable seat at the window, she bought a sandwich and a coffee from the bar and then settled herself for the four-hour crossing, exhausted from the long drive. The sea looked calm and docile from the port, but she'd been told that the crossing was notorious for being choppy, and the stewards were bringing around sick bags as a precaution.

A group of American tourists sitting opposite her introduced themselves, asking her where she was heading. Brigitte told them it was her first visit to Ireland as well as the reason for her journey.

"Oh," one of the women said surprised, "how interesting. I assumed you were Irish with all that beautiful red hair, and Brigit is an Irish name, isn't it?"

Replying that as far as she knew she had no connection with Ireland, and her name was spelled the French way in memory of her mother's dearest friend who'd lived in the South of France.

The Americans were heading for the records office in Dublin, to trace their ancestors who had emigrated from Ireland. There was only so far one could get on the computer, they said. They aimed to trace their family roots back to the time of the great famine when huge swaths of the population were driven from their land through hunger and pestilence onto ships leaving for The New World. They were known locally as the coffin ships, as few people ever reached America alive, the woman named Josie explained. She believed her family emigrated from Sligo in the far West of Ireland, and she intended to visit thereafter her trip to Dublin if time permitted. "Oh, that's a coincidence. That's near where I'm heading," said Brigitte.

"Oh, do you believe in coincidences?" asked Josie.

"Well, yes, I suppose so. I've never really thought that much about it."

"Well, I prefer to think of it as synchronicity myself," Josie continued.

"A message from the universe, meant to be and all that, fated, you know the kind of thing, being in the right place at the right time. It seems far more plausible to me."

Brigitte, puzzled, nodded, having no idea what the woman meant. Once the ferry had docked, she joined the stream of cars pouring off the gangplank. She checked her directions and then headed out along the motorway. She was struck by the vivid green of nature everywhere. The sky somehow seemed further away than in London, the air crystal clear and sharp. She breathed in deeply, pleased to be on dry land; the crossing had left her legs unsteady and shaky.

She drove through towns large and small, some gray and morbid, others painted in bright, garish colors. The main thoroughfares were always choked with traffic, and pedestrians pottering in and out of shops lined the main streets. Gaggles of school children walked along the pavements, heavy school bags on their backs, chatting or looking at their mobile phones. The church bell for the Angelus rang out at midday. A strong, heady smell permeated the air from the peat fires that burned in many houses. Cottages on the outskirts were guarded by dogs sitting patiently on front porches. Clothes on clotheslines billowed in the wind, housewives taking advantage of the fine weather whilst chickens rang freely around the yards pecking at scraps.

The scenery changed as towns gave way to a lush green vista. Acres of farmland were interspersed by narrow gray lanes that crisscrossed the land like thin ribbons. The sun sparkled across the calm, clear waters of the numerous loughs that were flanked by thick trees and bushes. Wooden picnic benches had been positioned to take advantage of the magnificent views. Brigitte noticed isolated cottages and bungalows dotted on the hillside, surprised at the amount of land each one had; it was such a contrast from the congested London streets, which were filled with hundreds of houses squashed together on top of one another, competing for air.

Further west, the landscape changed dramatically. The green vegetation gave way to a dramatic backdrop of mountains and open spaces. Large expanses of bogland, dark and brooding, where blankets of mist hung low over the land, created a sinister atmosphere of foreboding. There was not much sign of life, just an occasional car for company. The roads were little more than dirt tracks, narrow and twisting. Brigette couldn't see any signposts, unsure now if she was even headed in the right direction. The mist had confused her, and she felt unnerved. *What if the place I am going to is like this*, she thought, as she picked her way through the dense mist. Huge mountains that had been invisible when shrouded in the fog suddenly reappeared as the fog lifted, and she found herself on a narrow, rocky road skirting the coastline.

Turning inland, the road passed nearby fields edged with low stone walls. In the distance, the vast gray Atlantic ocean nibbled away at the rugged coastline. Now and again she'd see an old man riding a bicycle who waved in a friendly gesture as she passed. It was so different from London, where one could easily be mowed down for just standing still a moment too long. However, she was beginning to miss the screeching sirens, the deep throttle of buses stopping and starting, and the general noise and chaos of London. The mist had unsettled her and she was anxious to arrive to her destination.

"How much further is this bloody place," she muttered.

It was dusk by the time she reached the outpost that was to be her new home. The mist had cleared and the surrounding area looked green and lush from what she could see in the dwindling light. Outside, the cottage looked pleasant and well cared for, much like many others she had passed on her journey. Brigette sighed with relief. It was small and single-floored, with a brightly painted red wooden door in the center and a narrow, deep-set window on either side. The hinges on the wooden gate, which bore the name 'Myrtle Cottage' painted in elaborate lettering, squeaked as she opened it. She walked up the stone pathway to the front door, her heart pounding in her chest.

"This is it," she said aloud. "This is what I've come so far to discover."

She heard a chuckle behind her and jumped, thinking she was alone.

"Wow," she remarked under her breath as she turned around to see a man walk towards her. *He's gorgeous*, she thought.

"Are you talking to yourself already?" he teased.

Brigette looked down, embarrassed and hoping he hadn't heard her.

"Let me introduce myself," he said, offering her an outstretched hand. "I'm Oisin Murrin, the solicitor you've been in contact with."

"Oh," stumbled Brigette, trying desperately to mask her embarrassment. "Yes, pleased to meet you," she finally answered formally.

"I came here earlier and lit a fire in the cottage living room for you." His manner was casual and friendly. "The damp gets right into your bones this time of year."

"That's so thoughtful of you," smiled Brigette, staring into the softest pair of eyes she'd ever seen.

Oisin Murrin was about 35 years old, she guessed. He was slender and tall, with black curls trailing around his handsome face. He had high cheekbones and a generous mouth. He wore well-cut jeans with a casual sweater and tan leather boots.

"Would you like me to show you around, or would you prefer to be alone?" he asked. Relieved, Brigette accepted his offer gratefully, apprehensive to enter the cottage alone.

Lifting the door latch and stepping inside, she was overcome with the strangest sensation, for she could smell her mother's familiar perfume, the one she had always worn. Brigette remembered it even from childhood – the thick, powdery smell was very distinctive. She sniffed the air again – there was no mistake. She turned around to see if anyone was behind her. It was only Oisin, and surely he would not wear a woman's perfume. Feeling uneasy, she told herself it was due to all the traveling and her exhaustion was just playing tricks on her.

Myrtle Cottage had a generous-sized living room with a huge stone fireplace dominating the main wall. On the mantelshelf was an old clock, and to one side stood a tall metal candlestick. The fire Oisin had lit earlier cast shadows on the walls, housing wooden shelves, filled with books haphazardly placed in no particular order. There was a battered old sofa and a leather fireside chair to the left, pulled up close to take advantage of the heat from the fire and stave off the cold draught that whistled through the front door. Thick curtains hung at the window and a Persian rug was thrown across the gray flagstone floor. The room felt warm and cozy although it had been empty for some time. Various paintings were propped everywhere. Most were scenes of landscapes, and the sea, Brigette noticed.

"Whose paintings are these?"

"Oh, the guy who lived here," Oisin mumbled hurriedly.

"They're beautiful," Brigette gushed.

The small kitchen had a view of the sea from a tiny window and there were two bedrooms, one of which housed more canvases and had been used as a studio. Splotches of paint were splattered across the stone floor. An array of paintbrushes poked out from the top of old jam jars. A well-worn easel was propped against the far wall. More paintings were leaning against the wall, showing bright vivid scenes, a complete change of style from the ones in the living room.

In the bedroom, close to the brass bed, a battered leather suitcase lay open on the floor, half-filled with men's clothes. The sleeve of a shirt hung forlornly over the edge of the case. A pair of boots with red laces sat side by side, waiting to be packed, and a heavy black overcoat was strewn across the bed, a bright paisley scarf poking out of its pocket. A pair of horn-rimmed reading glasses lay on top of an open book of poetry on the bedside table.

"Looks as though someone left in a hurry," Brigette remarked.

The next morning, Oisin arrived to give her a tour of the outside. There had been a hard frost overnight, but that morning, the sky was a cloudless blue, the air still sharp, and very cold. Remnants of the frost cast a sparkle across the land. There was an untidy yard that housed an old bike and a few broken flowerpots.

The yard led to a large vegetable garden choked with brambles and neglect. A herb garden and a few straggly flower beds, all overgrown, gave way to open fields and farmland that seemed to stretch for miles towards the sea. A dirt track led into woods with a thin stream meandering through it. Hidden deep within the undergrowth of trees was a tiny wooden summerhouse overrun with long tendrils of ivy. It was full of half-empty paint pots and various art materials covered in cobwebs. *Any attempt to bring this place back to life was going to need a lot of help*, Brigette thought. She felt excited by the prospect. Perhaps this is just the challenge that I need.

A few days after her arrival, Oisin asked if she was ready to meet Clancy, the man who could tell her about her benefactor. Brigette excitedly agreed, and so it was arranged they would visit the following Saturday.

Clancy stood on the threshold, momentarily blocking out the dark indigo night flooding through the open door.

"Bless all within," he said, walking into the living room, introducing himself to Brigette and lowering his rotund form into the maroon leather chair by the fireside. He stretched forward rubbing his hands together over the roaring fire. She was struck by how sensitive his hands were, and stared at his long thin fingers that tapered at the ends. They seemed at odds with the rest of him, which was round and fleshy.

"'Tis a fine evening, so it is, though there's a cold nip in the air," he said in a friendly manner. "Sure, I can see the likeness in you." Then turning towards Oisin, he said coaxingly, "What about a drop of the hard stuff to warm us up?"

Brigette nodded consent as Oisin filled three glasses. Unused to drinking strong spirits, she felt the whiskey burning as it slipped down her throat.

Clancy wore a gray and black tweed jacket, a navy collarless shirt, jeans, and black cowboy boots. Around his neck hung a thin strand of tiny beads that looked like seeds.

"Those are unusual beads you're wearing," she said, making conversation, not wanting to launch straight into the reason for his visit.

"Ah yes, after my wife died a few years ago, I went back to India with your…" He stopped midsentence, realizing he'd made a huge blunder.

"Sure, Oisin, will you not throw some more peat on that fire?" he suggested, changing the subject quickly.

Now they were all settled around the fireside, Brigette could take a longer look at Clancy. She put his age to be about 70, but it was difficult to judge as his jovial manner gave him a youthful look, and he still had a shock of silver hair that hung to his shoulders in soft waves. A profusion of silver whiskers sprouted haphazardly around his mouth. He was of medium height with a round open face, and his eyes glowed amber in the firelight. Brigette thought he looked like a relic from the 1960s hippy era. Oisin had told her that Clancy was a great traveler and had never lived an orthodox life, steering clear of the rat race and the pursuit of money – instead, he had dedicated his life to his music. His wife had been a musician as well. Their only son had emigrated to America and now lived in Boston where he taught yoga. Clancy's mastery of the fiddle was legendary and he played various instruments from all over the world.

A good hour passed and Brigette, becoming impatient, began tapping her fingers on the arm of the sofa irritably. She decided that he may well be a man of many talents, but getting to the point was not one of them, for he was rambling on and on, and they were no nearer to getting the information she was waiting for than when he'd arrived. *It's going to be a very long evening*, she thought.

Brigette had imagined this meeting very differently back home in London when Oisin's email had first mentioned it. She had visualized a meeting across an office desk. A brisk official, coolly polite, in a jacket and tie, meticulously shuffling through the details outlined in the will, offering clear explanations of the formalities of her inheritance and the identity of her benefactor, concluding with a handshake and a vague offer of further assistance should it become necessary.

It seemed, however, that here in rural Ireland, business was conducted in a very laidback way and Brigette decided that people spoke in riddles, never really getting to the point, using ten words when one would suffice. She knew well that in the village, her present situation generated more than a ripple of interest.

Oisin interrupted Clancy's monologue the moment he stopped to draw breath.

"Can you tell Brigette about her benefactor please, Clancy, she's very curious to hear."

"Oh, yes, please, that would be great," Brigette added. "I am anxious to know everything you can tell me."

"Well, I hope you won't be upset," Clancy frowned.

"Why should I be upset? I just want to know the truth, and put an end to this mystery."

"Ah the truth," he cautioned. "Does one ever fully know the truth! For the truth is a moveable feast, is it not? And it depends on who is doing the telling. I suppose we could say it all began with Mrs. Flynn."

"Mrs. Flynn!" exclaimed Brigette. "Who is she? Is she my benefactor?"

"No, not a bit of it," said Clancy. "Wouldn't so much as give you the time of day, that one. Mrs. Flynn's two arms were always the one length, as we say here in Ireland!"

Brigette, not understanding what it meant, assumed it was some sort of joke, so ignored it, concerned he might ramble off the subject once again.

"Mrs. Flynn," continued Clancy, taking a sip of the whiskey, "was an odd sort of creature, cantankerous and quarrelsome. Fell out with all her children one by one! Well, didn't she take it into her head to come back to Ireland. Nothing anyone could say would pacify her 'til she returned to the place where she was born, to live out the rest of her days, as she put it. She was in her mid-80s by then and set up in a comfortable life in London – close to her children, by all accounts.

"Anyway, she landed back here complete with a wheelchair and a young woman to wheel her around! Between you and me, she was more than steady on her pins, until the day she dropped down dead on the floor of the public house years later, being near a 100 by then! The thing was she made out herself to be weaker than she was so that her long-suffering children would fork out the money for a companion to travel with her and settle her back down in Ireland.

"Completely unnecessary, of course – she had a clutch of relatives only too willing to step in and help, but that wasn't good enough for her. With all her airs and graces she saw herself as a cut above us all, having lived in London and the like. So there she was, being dutifully wheeled around the town each day by this young woman, always introduced as 'my companion', Mrs. Flynn togged out in all her finery with a dead animal slung round her neck. Her fur, she called it! Sure didn't the thing have a face and two glass eyes! Her wizened old fingers were laden down with large rings and on her head she wore a wide-brimmed hat, shading her greedy eyes that never missed a thing. Such fripperies!" He tutted, raising his eyes to the ceiling. "After 'the companion' went home, we never saw the wheelchair again, and Mrs. Flynn could be seen around the village walking as well as any of us.

"Anyway, lovely young girl she was, 'the companion.' I'd say not more than twenty years old. I remember the first time I saw her – she was wearing a pale green dress with orange buttons. It was the talk of the place, as we'd not seen styles like that around here in them days – 'course it's different today, the youngsters have access to all the trends now. I remember that she had copper-colored hair and a pale face, looked a lot like you but younger, of course," he said nonchalantly, hoping Brigette would take a hint.

"Really!" Brigette looked surprised.

Clancy realized this whole situation was shaping up to be a lot harder to discuss than he'd imagined, for how could he broach it without causing shock and grief to the young woman? Should he just come out and say it point-blank, or continue dropping hints? He decided on the latter, as he reasoned it would be the kinder way. He had hoped her mother would have told her a bit about the past, or at least hinted at it, but it seemed as though she had kept her word and never mentioned it.

I wish he'd get to the point, thought Brigette. He's rambling on again about all these irrelevant people and we are no nearer an explanation!

"Well, sure as luck would have it, Ned and I were walking along the main street one day when along comes Mrs. Flynn and 'her companion.' Then nothing would do 'til Ned was introduced to the young woman. He was smitten good and proper. Everyone said it was love at first sight, for they were inseparable from that moment on. Soulmates, they believed. Mrs. Flynn encouraged it, of course, anticipating the girl would stay long-term and continue her employment as companion. As it stood, she was only employed for three months and would be returning to England when her contract finished. It was rumored she had a fella at home waiting for her, to whom she was promised.

"Towards the end of the three months, Elizabeth, for that was her name, Lizzie for short..." Clancy stopped mid-sentence, and fidgeting uncomfortably in his seat, glanced over at Brigette, dismayed to realize that not so much as a flicker of recognition or understanding had yet crossed her face. "...was called back to London urgently. There was some sort of crisis at home to do with her father, and she had to leave, telling Ned she would return as soon as possible."

Brigette, unable to contain her impatience any longer, interrupted, asking who was this Ned and what did he have to do with her inheritance?

Her question was met with an embarrassed silence. Clancy and Oisin both looked at each other askance, unsure what to say.

"Wait, now," Clancy said at last, "let me finish my story and all will become clear." He hurried on.

"Ned was lost without her. He even talked of finding work in London to be with her, but things were difficult being an artist, money was short, and he had his beloved land to look after.

"Some weeks later he received a letter from her, 'course there were no emails or mobile phones in them days. When he read the contents he wanted to go immediately and fetch her back here with him, but she wouldn't come. That letter shocked him to the core and he was never the same man after that. She wrote that she'd changed her mind, and begged him to forgive her. She asked him never to contact her again and to forget about her, adding it was best for all of them and she hoped in time he would understand. It had been agreed that she marry the fella in England. Then she told him that if the baby was a girl she would name her Brigit in memory of Ned's grandmother whom she had become close to during her stay in Ireland."

No it couldn't be! Impossible! A coincidence these people had the same names, Brigette thought, trying to dismiss the idea that was creeping into her mind, but what if... All the color began to drain from her face and she felt as though a fist had mangled her stomach in a tight ball.

"Ned was distraught," Clancy continued, "beside himself with grief. How could he forget her just like that? He couldn't believe that he was to be a father to a child that he would never see! A child who would be brought up in a foreign country, and by a man who wasn't her real father, however kind he was. That poor child would never know its real heritage, never walk on the land of its ancestors.

"It destroyed him, so it did. He was my dearest friend and it broke my heart to see him turn into such a solitary figure, head bent, shoulders drooped, deep in thought, walking along the shore day after day. He never understood why she had left him. He sent the only photograph he had back to her with his final letter and kept his promise to never contact her again.

"He stopped painting for a long time and his poetry became dark and savage. No, 'tis only in recent years that he started again after our trip to India.

"When he heard through the grapevine that your mother had passed away, he decided it was time to find you to put matters straight, but as fate would have it, while packing his suitcase he took a stroke and landed up in hospital. Before he died, he asked me to find you and here we are!"

He watched Brigette's face in the firelight as a cold worm of understanding began to slither into her befuddled mind, though she had not fully absorbed all Clancy had been saying, as it seemed too impossible. *They'd mixed her up with someone else*, she thought, clinging onto the fact that her mother had never even been to Ireland. The very idea that she would have been in love with another man other than her father was ridiculous, and she would never believe it. Her mother had been devoted to her father all their married life and never even so much as looked at another man.

Reeling from the shock, Brigette vehemently lashed out at Clancy, her voice raised in anger, accusing him of not knowing what he was talking about, and indignantly emphasizing the fact she had a close relationship with her mother and she would surely have explained something about it to her!

Clancy remained silent for a long while, then looking down at his hands, embarrassed, said wistfully, "Well, my dear, you know sometimes in life things happen between two people that are not meant to be shared with anyone else. It gets locked away in their hearts and they move on with their lives through necessity. Maybe she thought it for the best, not wanting to hurt your father and all, and sure what good would it have done, the decision had been made long before you were born," Clancy soothed.

"Well, I would not have been living a bloody lie for a start," retorted Brigette, tears running down her burning cheeks. "I'm 35 years old and I don't know who the hell I am! And now it's too late and I'll never know the truth!"

"Sure, this must be a terrible shock for you to take in, but all will be well."

Everyone was silent for a long time, the atmosphere heavy with denial and confusion. Brigette broke the silence. Her voice was as cold as steel.

"I need to get this straight! You are telling me this cock and bull story and expect me to believe it! That this Lizzie girl was my mother!"

"Aye, that's correct," replied Clancy softly.

"And that she cheated on my father with some guy called Ned?" Brigette continued shaking her head in disbelief. "Then dumped him? It's absurd!" Her voice rising to a high-pitched shriek, "And on top of that I'm the kid! And I was a terrible mistake!"

"That is so," Clancy's reply barely audible.

"I won't believe it! I never will! It's a bloody nightmare and I'm gonna wake up in a minute!"

She sat by the dying embers of the fire. A chill had filled the room and she was alone, but Brigette hadn't noticed. She was still weeping, trying to understand, when dawn crept unheeded across the living room floor casting its cold light on the day ahead, making her shiver violently. She was stiff with cold as she bent to throw some kindling into the grate and set a match the fire. The more she thought, the more questions arose in her mind. Was I just a mistake? Unwanted, hidden away? Did my poor father know I was not his daughter? Did he ever really love me? When he looked at me, was he looking for telltale signs that I was his? Did he too live a lie? Or did my mother tell him the truth? Maybe he did know and yet still married her because he loved her and wanted to protect us from the blabbing tongues. She shivered at the thought. And what about poor Ned, how he must have suffered! Oh Mom, how could you have treated him so badly? Red hot emotions of anger and blame swum around Brigette's brain. She hated her mother at that moment.

Mara was very shocked on hearing the news and sympathized with Brigette's indignant anger, but quietly reminded her friend of how her mother had put Brigette before anything else in life, and therefore, she must have thought it was the best thing to do at the time.

"Remember," Mara reasoned, "times were very different then, and if an unmarried girl found herself pregnant, the baby would be taken away from her as soon as it was a few days adored. It would be adopted, its name changed, and the mother would never know what happened to it. Imagine the anguish and fear any girl would feel in such circumstances. Maybe your mother was scared that Ned would let her down at the last moment. Perhaps she made the safest choice she could for all of you. We can never know what it really cost her, can we? Ask yourself what you would do in that situation."

Brigette was far from having any empathy for her mother, obsessed with the fact that her whole life had been a lie. Who could she ever trust in this world? How, she argued, could she possibly accept this inheritance when her mother had been the cause of such unhappiness for this man, and to make matters worse, she now had to think of him as her biological father! Unbelievable! She moaned. It was all too painful for words!

She slept fitfully that night, and in the morning as the weather was bright, she took a long walk along the beach hoping to clear her mind. The wind blew her hair into a tangled mess, but she felt comforted by the waves that lashed against the cliffs. *Ned must have walked along this way, his heart heavy and confused, a victim, unable to do anything about the situation he found himself in. But then, she argued, if he cared so much, why didn't he ever contact me when I was an adult? How I wish I'd never been told all this, that I could rewind these last few months. Some inheritance*, she thought moodily.

Weeks passed, Mara was in constant contact, helping her to piece together her fractured thoughts. Once or twice she had told her it was time to stop wallowing in the situation and to pull herself together as the past could not be changed. The important thing now was to make the best of the future and value the gifts she had been left. Slowly Brigette reached some semblance of understanding, but forgiveness was still too difficult a concept to contemplate. Oisin called often and tried to reassure her that time would help.

She grew to love her daily walks along the rocky paths leading down to the sea, hearing the billowing waves, their force and power crashing hungrily against the black foreboding cliff face, spewing up a silver-blue mist high into the air. The rhythm of the land she had inherited was slowly connecting her with her ancestral roots, drawing her towards them, linking her to this place. Being in nature was good for her, and she felt content in an odd sort of way even though the knowledge of her past was painful and confusing, life seemed to be bringing her some meaning again. When she told Oisin this one afternoon, he grinned.

"Yes! This land does that to its people. It weaves dreams around them to coerce them home!"

One evening, Brigette was sitting by the fire with Ruby purring loudly on her lap, reading a book from Ned's collection, tired after a day in the local café where she worked part-time, when Clancy opened the door.

"Bless all within." Brigette smiled, pleased to see him. "Sure you'll be wondering why I'm here tonight."

"I'm sure you'll tell me, Clancy," she said as he took his usual seat by the fire.

"Well 'tis like this. Today it would have been Ned's birthday. I have something he wished me to give you."

Brigette looked up surprised, wary, too tired to talk about things again tonight. The numerous postmortems over the months since their first meeting had always left her more confused.

He drew from his pocket an envelope, dog-eared around the edges as though it had been in his pocket for some time. Her name was written on it in flowery handwriting.

"Should I open it now?" pouring Clancy his usual glass of whiskey.

"Sure, it would do no harm."

Brigette removed the letter from its envelope with shaking hands and began to read:

Dear Brigit,

I'm writing this letter now to set the record straight, as time has run out for me and sadly I now have to accept that we will never meet in this lifetime. You may like to know that you were named after your great-grandmother, Brigit Mary Kelly.

Brigit is the name of the Irish Goddess of wisdom, fire, and poetry. I wonder have you any of these qualities, my dearest daughter?

I used to dream that the day would come when you might seek me out, be curious to meet me, to learn about your family. But then reality would break in upon my daydreaming and remind me that you don't even know of my existence, so how would you ever come?

I will never know if my reason for not trying to find you sooner was because of the star-crossed love I held for your mother or my cowardice at the thought you might reject me.

I need you to know that I truly loved your mother. The short time we spent together were the happiest days of my life. If I had my time repeated I would not have let her go so easily, the three of us would have been together whatever the consequences.

You were conceived in love, and whatever you think of us, please don't judge us harshly. Maybe your heart is big enough to forgive us?

My sister Josie knows about you and has promised to contact you. She is married with two children and lives in America now. She is a historian and can tell you so much about our family history, your heritage, and the struggles your ancestors endured to maintain this land through the centuries of strife that our beloved country has experienced.

I hope one day you may decide to make your home here in Ireland. If you do, I know that you will grow to love and respect this beautiful land with all its complexities as much as I do. I now pass it to you with all the love and pent-up emotions I was unable to express to you in person.

Clancy was my greatest friend throughout my life, and he will help you in every way he can. It was his idea to ask you to spend a year in Ireland. We both hoped it would give you time to understand and forgive the past. Was he right, I wonder?

I will be near you always.

Your father,

(Ned.)

Edward Joseph Gallagher

Myrtle cottage

Co. Sligo

EIRE

Brigette folded up the letter tenderly, as though it was a precious jewel, holding back her tears, and thanked Clancy. She cherished the words that her father had written and reread the letter often as the past fell gradually into place for her.

One evening, walking to the local pub for supper with Oisin, she told him that Ned's letter had said she was named after her great-grandmother.

"It wasn't Mom's friend in France at all! She even misled me about that and I'm beginning to wonder if I ever knew her at all!" She hesitated turning towards him. "Do you think we ever truly know anyone?"

"The question is," he said, "do you think we ever really know ourselves, never mind know anyone else? Perhaps, in the end, it is who you alone believed your parents to be, that's important. None of us can change our past, but we can build on it to create our future. Life is full of challenges and it's how we deal with them that is the important thing."

"You know, Oisin, you have been such a good friend to me over these past months, always there for me, calm and unruffled, never judging me, listening to all my grumbling as I try to unravel my past. I must have been a real pain, only really thinking of myself. I don't know how I would have coped without you."

After they had finished supper he took her hand and looking deeply into her eyes said, "Brigette... Do you realize you have been here almost a year now? Let's take a walk along the beach. There's a new moon tonight, and I have something I've been waiting to ask you for ages."

The Woman In The Train

By Rahim T. K.

Manjula waited at the train station along with hundreds of other people, wishing that she was back in her small hometown, where she would whizz around on her two-wheeler and not depend on trains. This was not the life she had expected when she moved from the small town of Agra to the big bad city of Mumbai. The distances, the pace of the city, the rough language of the people, the constant noise of traffic! Her biggest grouse was the daily train travel from Andheri to Churchgate. She had never traveled on a local train before she moved to Mumbai.

Here, the trains were the lifeline of the teeming millions who commuted to their place of work or education every day. Given the traffic in the city, the trains were the only modes of transport that were reasonably fast and they were taken even by well-to-do businessmen. Unlike the modern trains of Europe, these trains are old-fashioned, open to the elements, and extremely crowded. It was not uncommon to see young lads perched on the roof of the compartments, as there would be no space inside. The local trains are Mumbai's lifeline. There were separate compartments for women, but a few of them were separated by netted windows and the men would ogle at the women, passing snide remarks and mouthing unmentionables. There were a couple of first-class compartments too, but Mumbaikars often joke that the price difference is for the difference in the sweat smell – the first-class passengers used expensive perfumes, so the air in the compartment was relatively easier to tolerate! Boarding a crowded compartment was an art by itself and many a non-Mumbaikar have been left standing on the platform, watching train after train depart without boarding them!

Luckily for Manjula, her mother's friend showed her the ropes for a few days, when Manjula moved into Mumbai. Manjula was awed at the sheer number of people who were waiting there to board the train and stood there politely waiting for her chance to board. She watched in awe as women tucked in their saree pallus, tied their dupattas, clutched their bags in the front of their bodies, and raced into the compartment in the few seconds that the train waited on the platform.

Manjula soon mastered the art of commuting in Mumbai. She even started enjoying the commute. The compartment was filled with women of different backgrounds, all working hard for a living. They woke up

93

impossibly early, ensured that food was prepared for their family, and hurried to the station, to their offices that were far away. Their lives were on the train and each had their friend circles and found solace in them. There were regular groups, one group that sang devotional songs; another discussing the storylines of the many soap operas; another group that seemed to be constantly complaining about one of their relatives. Manjula was a shameless eavesdropper to many stories of their lives, a child who topped his class, another who refused to study, a husband who wanted sex every day, another who would not touch his wife. She loved the morning commute to work; she almost felt as if she belonged! She was too shy to speak to anyone but developed nodding acquaintances with many. She was proud that she even had a seating space!

As the train started moving, she came back to the present, mentally taking attendance of the regulars. The members of the singing group cleared their throats and started singing "Jai Ganesh, Jai Ganesh!" The other group started talking over the cacophony. Another commute had begun! She saw the lady who was color blind, always dressed in sarees that clashed with her skin complexion; another woman who always looked as if she was a sack of potatoes, lumps of flesh sticking out from her tight kurta; and how could she not look at the androgynously-dressed twenty-something? In the corner, diagonally opposite her, sat a woman who looked so much like her aunt back home that she felt a sharp pang of homesickness. Feeling her eyes brimming over, she quickly looked down at her phone and stared at the screen as if her life depended on it! Just as her feelings threatened to overcome her, she heard a soft voice. "Excuse me!"

Startled out of her bout of self-pity, she glanced up to see a woman who she thought was sheer perfection! She had almost translucent skin, and in the crowded coupe of women who were not exactly well-dressed, stood out for her perfect dress sense. Her light-yellow kurta fitted her like a second skin, showing off the figure of a model, and her face was perfectly made-up, yet looked as fresh as a rose in the morning. Her hair was loosely tied into a soft bun and small gold earrings twinkled on both ears. Manjula looked enthralled at this vision of perfection and said "Who, me?"

"Yes! Sorry to intrude! My name is Malini. I have been seeing you since the last month or so and have always wanted to talk to you. You remind me so much of another friend I had!"

Manjula blushed and said shyly, "I am Manjula. I am sure if I had seen you earlier, I would remember such a vision of beauty! You are so beautiful!"

Malini looked amused at this innocent yet heartfelt compliment and said, "Goodness me! No one has ever told me that I am beautiful before! Thanks! So, Manjula, what do you do?"

"I work as Assistant Manager – Finance at DN Industries, my office is at Churchgate."

"Finance! You must be clever. I have no head for numbers. My father is a businessman and I am his only daughter. He had hoped that I would take over his business, but I just couldn't manage the finances. We had so many arguments, but thanks to my mother's intervention, I trained as a visual artist and got a job at an advertising agency." Malini's face was animated as she spoke about her job. She went on,

"Are you from Mumbai?"

"No, I am from Agra. I moved here for work. There are not many businesses in Agra and not one where I would be paid so much. Supposed to be saving up for my marriage."

"Wow! Congratulations! Who is the lucky guy?" Manjula blushed and swiftly shook her head.

"No, no. There is no guy yet. I come from a middle-class family and we don't have much money. You know how it is with us, we need to pay a fat dowry to get a qualified groom."

Malini looked at her with sympathy and silently nodded. She then asked, "So where do you live now?"

"I live in Andheri. I was lucky to get a safe guest accommodation near the station. I have a room to myself, and the rent does not include food, so I eat out all the time, generally from the street vendors. Everything is so expensive here! I had thought I could eat in a nice place, but what with paying the rent, sending money back, etc., I hardly have enough to spare."

"I know what you mean. Mumbai is an expensive city. It must also be quite lonely for you, but I am sure that you have many friends at work."

Manjula shook her head again. "Not really... the people at the office are nice, but not very friendly. I miss home so much! I miss my mother's cooking, my friends, even my youngest brother who is a brat and was the bane of my life." She wiped away a tear and smiled brightly to hide the fact that she was close to tears.

Malini looked away discreetly and after a few minutes said, "Well, you can no longer say that you don't have a friend in Mumbai. I am your friend!" She gave a dazzling smile and continued, "That is... if you want me as your friend."

Manjula's reply was almost a squeal. "Are you kidding? I would love to have you as a friend!"

The train screeched to a halt and both hurried out, promising to meet the next day.

They met almost every day on the train and were soon thick as thieves. Malini was soon privy to Manjula's innocent secrets. She learned about Manjula's secret addiction to romance, the Mills and Boons kind, where the tall, dark, and handsome hero gives up his wayward ways once he meets the innocent, beautiful heroine. Malini also learned that her young friend was a die-hard fan of Bollywood romances and believed that her Prince Charming existed somewhere. Manjula did not want an arranged marriage. All her cousins and her friends had arranged marriages, and none of them seemed to live happily ever after with their husbands. On the contrary, they lived in a state of constant friction, either with their husbands or with their mothers-in-law. None of them felt unduly perturbed by the fact that they lived a life that was less than perfect, nay – they did not even seem to be aware of it! Manjula had decided that her life would be different and from the minute she stepped into Mumbai, she was waiting for her prince.

Malini encouraged Manjula to tell her more stories and Manjula prattled on, never realizing that the conversations were one way and that she did not know much about Malini, except that she worked in advertising, she did not even know the name of the firm.

Months passed until finally, the monsoons began in Mumbai. Train commute was the messiest during this season. The trains did not have doors and were open to the elements. Many office goers resorted to keeping a change of clothes and footwear at the office in case of an emergency. The floods of 2006 had also raised the paranoia level of the Mumbaikars and they would peer suspiciously at the skies, wondering if it was going to be a deluge again. This was Manjula's first experience with Mumbai monsoons and she enjoyed it. She had never experienced rains like this before, and every Bollywood fan worth her salt knows that most heroes and heroines met during the monsoons, and generally would sing and dance in the rain.

In a compartment filled with disgruntled women reeking of damp clothes, Manjula sat with a dreamy smile on her face, her mind far away in an imaginary world. She had watched a movie last night where a young heroine was in love with a much older man and, after the perfunctory dissidence, the lovers were united. She wished that her love story could have a similar happy ending, for Manjula, who was all of 27 years old, had fallen in love with the 50-year-old Amit Gupta, Managing Director of DN Industries. She was bowled over by his looks the first time she met him during the employee orientation program. She was far too junior in the hierarchy to have any contact with him, but she would see him walk around the office often.

She would also eagerly wait for the monthly employee town hall meetings where Amit addressed all the employees. She would dress carefully that day and would gaze at Amit dreamily. In her saner moments, she was aware of the ludicrousness of the situation – the age gap, the difference in their status, the caste differences – but her romantic self would sweep away all these arguments and would remind her that true love finds its way. As she sat on the train, she was fantasizing about Amit declaring his love for her and both of them walking away into the sunset.

Malini, noticing the shy smile, asked her, "Kiddo, a penny for your thoughts!"

Manjula blushed and denied any reason, but, upon being coaxed by Malini, shyly revealed her thoughts.

Malini did not laugh at her, but looked at her thoughtfully and said,

"Manjula, you are truly in love with Amit! I have suspected this for some time now; all your conversations have a mention of Amit. I was hesitant to talk to you about this, but since it is out in the open, we should do something about it."

Manjula blushed, looking adorably confused. She was secretly happy that her friend did not seem to be shocked at her confession. Instead, Malini seemed to be genuinely happy for her. She felt a rush of gratitude for her friend, who accepted this unconventional situation without any judgment.

Malini continued, "Tomorrow is Saturday and I work only till 2 pm. I know that you have to be in the office till 4 pm. Let us meet at Churchgate station around 4.30 pm. We will walk along Marine Drive, sit on the wall bordering the sea, and, as we watch the huge waves, talk about the next step. No, I do not want any arguments. Remember, I am the one in advertising, not you! If it is about numbers, I will bow to your superior wisdom."

Manjula meekly acquiesced, secretly thrilled at Malini's interest, and hoped that she could indeed help Manjula in winning over Amit.

The next evening, the two women sat on the broad barrier, looking at the sea, munching on a cob of corn that was roasted and delicately spiced with salt and a dash of lime.

Malini started the conversation, "You are indeed a sly one! You have been in love with one of the most eligible men in town and you had kept it a secret even from me, your best friend! I'm hurt."

"Please, please don't say that! I was not sure of my feelings. I have never been in love before, except with Shahrukh Khan. And for me, Amit Gupta is as unattainable as Shahrukh Khan! I know that Amit is a widower and he is single now – but the age difference! He is just five years younger than my father and my mother is a year younger than him. What about the huge gap between us in terms of money? I come from a lower-middle-class family and Amit is one of India's well-known businessmen. I will be considered a fortune hunter. Do you think that I haven't considered every aspect? I have stayed awake countless nights debating with myself, every night promising myself that I will snap out of it, but when I see him, all my resolve goes down the drain and I am even more in love with him. I wish there was a way that I could fall out of love with him."

Manjula sobbed uncontrollably. Malini looked at her with sympathy and offered her a tissue. She said in a hearty voice, "Why are you crying? You are in love and the heart has its reason. One cannot fall in love rationally. Didn't you read about the woman who fell in love with a murderer and wanted to marry him? Or about the man who married a woman who is paralyzed for life? Love is just love, an emotion that is so pure that it elevates you and makes you do crazy things! Even I fell in love with a man who was not acceptable to my parents."

The last statement made Manjula look up sharply. "What? You never told me your love story! Who is he? Where is he? What happened?"

Malini smiled wryly and said, "That is a long story and to be told over wine!"

"You can't do that! That is so unfair. Please tell me a little bit at least!"

"Stubborn girl! Okay, just to get you off my hair, I will tell you. But you must promise not to ask for more details. I am still not over it and I find it difficult to talk about it."

"I promise!"

It was Malini's turn to look dreamy as she gazed out into the sea and started her story. "He worked at a client's office. I used to be very shy and would hardly talk to people, but he sought me out and would talk to me on flimsy pretexts. I slowly emerged from my shell and fell in love with him. When I announced my decision to marry him, my father was furious. My father was a wealthy industrialist and my lover was not very well-to-do, though he was well-educated. I rebelled and finally eloped!"

Manjula sat transfixed at this confession and said, "That was a bold step. What happened afterward?"

"That is a story for another day! You promised that you won't ask me any more questions!"

"But…"

"No buts! You will know the whole story one day, that is a promise!" Malini's voice was solemn and Manjula felt goosebumps all over her body and, as she looked at Malini, a thought occurred that Malini had never looked more beautiful, a mystical smile on her face, the evening light forming a halo around her face and giving her an unearthly appearance.

The spell was broken by the loud honking of a passing car and Malini said, "Let us now talk about your love story! It should not end up as one of those unrequited love stories. I like love stories with a happy ending!"

Manjula giggled and said, "I agree with you! I have frequently wished that I had a fairy godmother like Cinderella had, one who could, with a sweep of her wand, make me prettier and more appealing to my prince!"

"This is your lucky day! Behold, your fairy godmother at your service!"

Malini playfully curtsied and continued, "I do not have a magic wand, but I have many a trick up my sleeve. We will first get you a makeover: decent haircut, better clothes, lose a few pounds, get some confidence, discreet makeup, and as for the rest, just listen to what I say unquestioningly and I can guarantee that he will propose marriage within six months!"

In the following weeks, they went shopping and bought clothes and accessories. Manjula bought colors that she ordinarily never would have purchased, but was silenced by Malini's imperious "Trust me!" Malini took her to a beauty salon in Colaba, where Manjula's hair was cut and colored, her eyebrows were shaped, and her feet were pedicured. Manjula couldn't recognize herself in the mirror after the beauty experts had worked their magic on her. Manjula learned how to modulate her voice and speak in the right tone. She learned to walk gracefully and not clomp about. The small-town gauche girl was transformed into a chic, stylish, polished woman of today. Malini finally declared that Manjula was ready to start "Operation Amit."

Though Manjula had agreed with Malini, she still was not sure if she was doing the right thing. For a small-town girl brought up with the Indian middle-class sensibilities, the thought of actively pursuing a man was abhorring – only women of cheap virtue did it, not someone with a father who worked as a clerk in a government office and a mother who rarely stepped out of the house. She spent sleepless nights pondering over this and would voice her doubts to Malini, but Malini would silence all her arguments with "Malini knows best!" Manjula was under Malini's spell totally and was like putty in Malini's hands. Soon, Manjula kept her doubts to herself and threw herself enthusiastically into the plan.

What is the worst that could come of it? He may reject me, but if the plan succeeds, I would be married to the love of my life. Papa and Mummy will accept the marriage once they get to know him. He won't expect any dowry and if I get married to him, I can help Papa too. Poor Papa! He has three daughters to be married off! Once I am Mrs. Amit Gupta, I will be a part of high society and I can bring Deepa and Rekha to Mumbai – I can give them makeovers and then get them married off respectably. It would be such a load off Papa's shoulders. Once Dinesh and Rajesh finish their studies, I can help them get jobs in Mumbai, maybe even in DN Industries – after all, they would be the MD's brothers-in-law. I will have enough money to buy a house for Mommy and Papa. They have been living in that small rented house all their lives. I will also silence the mouths of all those busybodies who have bemoaned the fact that Papa's eldest child is a daughter, and how he would never get three daughters married off on his tiny salary. His salary is barely enough to feed all of us. Mommy's jewelry is long gone to meet the expenses of sudden illnesses, education, and to ensure that we have a roof over our head. I must look after my family.

Malini is right, these are the points I should use to convince Papa. When Papa sees that I am genuinely happy and am not sacrificing myself, he will give his blessings.

Manjula would frequently have variants of this conversation with herself and managed to convince herself that her romance would have a 'happily ever after' ending. Malini did prove to be an able strategist and she skillfully guided Manjula.

"The first step," she said to Manjula, "is to attract Amit's attention. You are a lowly-placed employee in his company and you do not even deal with him on a day-to-day basis. You need to be visible in the office. No more being the shy wallflower – you should talk to your colleagues and become a part of the various cliques in the office. You should also work harder and demand more responsibilities from your boss. Finance is an important department and you can ask for specific productivity projects that would allow you to showcase your abilities."

Accordingly, Manjula started interacting with her colleagues. She had rarely spoken to anyone so far and had resisted the polite attempts of a few at friendship. The Manjula, version 2.0, was different, however. She sought out the company of her colleagues, talking to them about movies, gossiping about office politics, joining them for lunch, bringing sweets or chocolates to the office, making movie plans with her colleagues, etc., and was soon popular in the office. Following Malini's advice, she developed a close relationship with Jenny, Amit's secretary, and fiercest protector. It was rumored that Jenny was in love with Amit, but he never considered her as anything but his secretary. Jenny was used to many people befriending her in the hope that they would get access to Amit and her suspicions were always raised. Manjula, however, never asked about Amit and would talk to Jenny only about Jenny's life. Even if Jenny mentioned Amit's name, Manjula would say, "Let us not talk about office. Given the position you are in, I don't want you thinking that I am friends with you for any ulterior motives."

Jenny, who did not have any real friends in the office, was suitably thrilled at this attention. Manjula would ask her regularly about her children and would even remember when her son Robert's music test was or when her daughter Angela's dental appointment was. She even stayed over at Jenny's house for a few days when both the children were down with the flu, helping Jenny in their care. Within a few weeks, Jenny was convinced that Manjula was a genuine person and a true friend.

Malini congratulated Manjula on the day Jenny invited Manjula over for dinner. Malini said, "Well done, kiddo! If you have managed to win over that dragon, you can now have access to Amit. Remember, do not mention a single word about Amit, and take expensive gifts for Jenny and those bratty children of hers!"

Parallelly, Manjula worked hard and frequented her boss's cabin with various doubts on work and with a few tentative suggestions. Her boss, Mr. Srinivasan, was soon impressed by the young girl's enthusiasm at work and her uncomplaining acceptance of last-minute work. She seemed to revel in taking more responsibilities and did not make excuses about why a deadline could not be met. He liked the fact that she worked long hours, staying at the office till 11 pm on quite a few occasions, and still turned up for work an hour before the official start time. Unlike the other people in the department, she did not want to run to her family or her friends. She did not giggle unnecessarily and waste time over endless cups of tea and idle chatter. He was especially impressed by her work in the last month and tried her mettle by giving her increasingly important projects, which she worked on with aplomb.

At the regular war council, Malini said, "That is step number two. Continue working this way and your boss would soon be highly dependent on you and will trust you with sensitive projects, which will give you access to Amit."

Malini's words proved to be prophetic. When Amit and Srinivasan were discussing a project for increasing productivity and choosing a project team from different departments, Srinivasan had no hesitation in recommending Manjula's name. His other colleagues demurred at the suggestion, voicing their thoughts that she was far too new, young, and junior for such an important project, but Srinivasan spoke convincingly about her abilities and cited examples where she had proven herself to be an astute finance professional. Amit's interest was piqued and he asked to see her resume. Jenny added her recommendation too and Manjula was chosen for the project. Working on the project meant weekly meetings with Amit and briefing him on the progress. Manjula's insightful comments and her thorough work impressed Amit, and he soon started to rely on her opinions more.

After one such successful meeting, Manjula met Malini, flushed with happiness, and squealed, "Malini! You would never guess what happened today!"

"How many guesses do I get?" Malini asked teasingly.

"As many as you want, but you will never guess!"

"Is that so? Well, let me try. Give me a few minutes to think! Don't say anything!"

Manjula hopped about impatiently as her friend took her time to think, and finally losing patience screamed, "MALINI!!!"

Malini laughed and said, "My first guess – your team members gave you a standing ovation at one of your recommendations and even Amit was impressed. Your suggestion would save the company tons of money and as a reward, Amit is throwing a party in your honor at the Hilton!"

Manjula looked at her open-mouthed and spluttered, "How... how did... how did you know? This was exactly what happened! It is almost as if you were there!"

"Little one! I am everywhere! Always following you, like a shadow. No, not even like a shadow, the shadow disappears in the night, so more like a ghost. An eerie presence just there. How else do you think you get access to so much information that is not easily available? How do you think that you made such huge progress in your career? Do you think you have suddenly become so smart?"

Manjula felt a shiver up her spine at Malini's words and tone; there was something eerie about the way she spoke and Manjula looked at her uncertainly, when Malini suddenly laughed and laughed till tears fell down her cheeks. Amidst the paroxysm of laughter, she said, "Oh! Look at your face! It is priceless! It is like you have seen a ghost! Yes, I am indeed a ghost. A ghost that travels by trains, that works for a living, that eats food with you. Little one, you have been watching too many movies! And even in movies, have you seen a ghost like me? Ghosts must wear white and walk around ghoulishly and appear only at midnight, not in bright sunlight!"

She continued to laugh, and the laughter was so infectious that Manjula joined in, laughing at her idiocy.

Once they stopped laughing, Malini said, "Let us go shopping and get you a smashing outfit for the party. After all, you are the guest of honor!"

After hours of trudging in and out of shops, they finally emerged victoriously. On Malini's insistence, Manjula went to a beauty salon for her makeup and hair and stepped out looking like a supermodel in a light blue chiffon saree that accentuated her figure, a single strand of pearls around her neck, pearl drops in her ears, and two thin gold bangles on her slender arms. Her hair was blow-dried to perfection and her makeup was understated, almost not there. When she walked into the ballroom of the Hilton, Amit could not take his eyes off her. Until now, he had seen her in a work environment wearing clothes that were well cut, but suitable for office wear. He had never really concentrated on her looks, he was more impressed with her work and had thought that she was one of the brightest employees he ever had. But seeing her today, as she floated into the room looking like that, something stirred inside him, something that he had thought was long dead. He had truly loved his wife, whom he had fallen in love with at first sight, and had never thought that he would feel the same about any other woman. He stood there transfixed as he watched Manjula meet other people, laugh at jokes, nod seriously at a comment, nibble daintily at a snack, and sip a glass of wine as if she was born to rule.

Looking back, he did not know what he did and said that evening. He was shocked at his behavior, a 50-year-old man behaving like a lovelorn teenager! Shame on me! I am old enough to be her father. She is my employee. How can I have such thoughts? I had sworn after Devika's death that I would never marry again, never fall in love, and yet here I am!

He decided to keep his distance from Manjula and have a strictly professional relationship with her. But fate, and Malini, were against him. On Malini's instructions, Manjula organized a party for her birthday and invited all her colleagues, who she claimed was her family. She invited Amit too, but he refused, and so Manjula did as Malini had advised.

"Sir, I know that it is impertinent of me to invite the MD. Believe me, I am not trying to win brownie points. I consider you a mentor and wanted you to be part of the celebration. This is the first time I am hosting a party of this kind. I come from a humble background and have seen these things only in movies. When I write to my family about all these things, they are so proud of my achievements. I invited you because you are the reason for all my success. If it were not for your kind encouragement, I would still just be toiling with daily accounts." Pausing for effect, she continued, "I understand why you wouldn't want to come. It is not right for the MD to come to such a low-level employee's party. Please forgive my effrontery. I cannot and will not force you to come," she ended with a woebegone smile that would have melted the stoniest of hearts.

Amit's heart melted and he quickly said, "No, no, no... you misunderstand me. I refused not because I did not want to come, but because I know that the presence of the big boss is a damper. It is a party for youngsters and you should enjoy it without fear of the boss."

Manjula smiled radiantly, "Sir, everyone wants you to come. You may be old, but you are such fun! People still talk about the way you behave in office picnics, just one of them, not like a big MD."

"Thanks for pointing out that I am old!"

Manjula blushed and stammered, "Sir… that's not what I meant!"

Amit smiled and said, "I know what you meant! Anyway, when and where is the party? I have to check with Jenny if it clashes with my travel plans."

"Sir, I have already checked with Jenny and arranged the party on a date when you are free."

"Smart girl! Well, look forward to the party. Now, scram and get back to work. I want to see the presentation before the end of the workday! I am one of you only outside – here, I am still the boss!"

Grinning at his sally, Manjula gave a mock salute and fled the room.

The party was a huge success. Thanks to Jenny's help, Manjula got a good rate on the venue and the food. On top of that, Aparna from marketing helped organize the games, Ali from Operations helped her get a great caterer, and Swapnil from IT helped her get the booze. On Malini's recommendation, she had made it into a theme party, the theme being Bollywood, and everyone dressed up as a Bollywood character. The only grouse was that Malini refused to attend the party; she claimed that she would be an outsider and hence would feel uncomfortable. Nothing that Manjula said could make her change her mind. This did not stop her from enjoying the party. She was a solicitous hostess, ensuring that everyone had a good time. She spoke to everyone in a friendly manner, seeing that they had enough to eat and drink. To Amit, she looked like a pretty butterfly flitting from flower to flower gracefully, reposing on each flower briefly and then flitting on to another. She would catch his eye occasionally and bestow on him one of her dazzling smiles, but to, his disappointment, she did not spend much time with him apart from the initial welcome and the occasional word.

He thought that she looked simply ethereal, dressed as Anarkali from the iconic movie Mughal-e-Azam. He had chosen a safe route, wearing a simple kurta and pajama that could be any hero's look from any movie, but, upon seeing her, he wished that he had dressed as Prince Salim from the same movie.

The party was the topic of office discussion for many days, everyone claiming that they had a great time and that Manjula knew how to entertain. It was amazing how, despite her increasing popularity, no one felt jealous of her – instead, all of them had a brotherly attitude towards her, bordering on paternal affection and concern. They helped her in her work and she kept getting better at it.

She was enjoying all this attention and her popularity in office, when Malini gently reminded her, "Kiddo, you seem to have forgotten your real goal. It is nice that you have other friends, but you need to focus on winning Amit over, not winning over his employees!"

Manjula was brought down to earth with a thud and she said in a small voice, "You are right, Malini. I have indeed lost focus. What do I do now?"

"Create opportunities for you to meet Amit. When you are in his cabin, working on something, ask for a cup of coffee, and while drinking the coffee, make small talk, initially on general topics and slowly move on to personal topics. Ask about his interest and claim that you have the same. Ask him for book recommendations. Tell him that you are thinking of pursuing an MBA and ask for his opinion on the same. Build a personal rapport with him."

Manjula did as she was told. Amit never realized that he was being manipulated, and he answered many questions and offered to help her with the MBA. He was falling for her slowly, but surely!

A couple of weeks later, Malini instructed, "Tomorrow, you will go to the office without any makeup and wear a drab set of clothes and look very woebegone. You will not smile as usual but instead, keep a serious face, and when you are with Amit, you will stick only to work-related topics and will not ask for coffee." She went on with further instructions and Manjula nodded her head like a well-trained puppet.

The next day, she behaved exactly as instructed. Amit kept glancing at her throughout their meeting but did not say anything. He waited for her to ask for coffee and was disappointed when she did not. He could see that something was very wrong and he asked her gently, "Manjula, what is wrong?"

"Wrong? Nothing, sir, nothing is wrong!"

"Manjula, look at me. I can see that your eyes are red, you have been crying. You are not your usual self. You made so many mistakes in your document and you look as if you are in deep mourning. Don't you think that I am close enough to share? Treat me as a friend and not as your boss. I know you have no family here, so please talk to me."

Manjula still did not say anything, so Amit said, "Is it boyfriend trouble?"

Even as he uttered those words, his heart sunk at the idea of her having a boyfriend. To his relief, Manjula vehemently shook her head.

"Sir, no, nothing like that!" Manjula said hurriedly.

"So, what is it?"

"I got a letter from my father. They have arranged for my marriage and he wants me to come to Agra for the engagement ceremony."

"Is it someone you know?"

"No, I have never met him. But in our family, girls do not have a say in their marriage."

"What nonsense! This is 2016, not 1816! An independent girl like you should not be forced into marriage."

Manjula smiled wanly and said, "Sir, that may be true in big cities, but life in small cities is very different. My father is a low-paid clerk and he has five children – three daughters and two sons. I am the eldest in the family. The proposal which has come is from a family that is willing to accept me without a dowry. My father feels that this is a golden opportunity and hence he has written to me."

"If that is the case, why don't you want to marry him?"

Manjula did not say a word, and stared at her toes, apparently hypnotized by something there. Amit again asked, "Manjula, why don't you want this marriage? Is there someone else?"

She nodded shyly and with a heavy heart he said, "But you just said that there is no boyfriend."

"Yes sir, he is not my boyfriend."

"Manjula, I am confused. Can you please explain clearly? Or wait, I have a better idea. Let us go to the coffee shop at the Taj and talk. This is not the place for such delicate confidences."

Soon, they were sitting at the coffee shop of the Taj and, after Amit ordered for refreshments, he said, "Now, you were telling me that there is someone else, but you don't have a boyfriend."

"Yes, sir. He does not know that I love him."

"What? Are you for real? Why haven't you told him? Is he married?"

"No, sir."

"What is the problem then?"

"Sir, I do not know how he will react."

"You will know only if you tell him. Again, this is 2016, and girls are allowed to propose."

"Sir, he is older than me!"

"So, most men are older than their wives."

"And he is richer than me, really rich, and I am not."

"Manjula, again, this is 2016 and these things don't matter. You are educated, have a good job, and you earn well. You are anyone's equal. What is your next argument?"

"Sir, he is a widower."

"Manjula, I am losing patience now. He is a widower, which means he is available. You are just making silly excuses. I can't wait to hear the next one."

"Sir, he is my boss."

Amit opened his mouth to react when he realized what she said and then burst out, "But Srinivasan is not a widower."

Manjula looked up at him with her doe-like eyes, fluttered her eyes, and looked down shyly without saying a word.

Amit exclaimed, "Do you mean me?"

Manjula bashfully agreed and Amit said, "Oh, my darling! But can't you see, this is impossible? I am twenty-five years older than you!"

"Sir, you just now said that most men are older than their wives!" "You little minx! Don't give me any sass! You know what I mean. This is not possible. I am sure that I am as old as your father."

"Sir, my father is five years older than you, but my mother is a year younger than you."

Amit groaned, "There you go! How do you think this is possible? Society will never accept it!"

"Sir, do you mean you accept my love?" Amit looked at her with so much intensity. She asked again, "Tell me, sir, do you?"

Amit said, "I do... but on one condition!"

"What is that?"

"Stop calling me Sir!"

Manjula blushed and said, "Amit, I love you!"

"Manjula! It is music to my ears! I have fallen for you too! You have no idea how I have longed to tell you this, but the age difference always stopped me. If I was 20 years younger, I would have proposed to you a long time back. Darling, I love you so much!"

"If you were twenty years younger, I would not have loved you! I love the way you are, with your salt and pepper hair, your tiny wrinkles along with your eyes, the laugh lines on the face. I have been in love with you for so long, but never could tell you, for the fear that you would think that I am a fortune-hunter!"

"A fortune-hunter and you, never! You are one of the most innocent and truest souls that I have ever known."

They went on in this vein for some more time, each professing their love in different words, not caring about the time and realizing the surroundings only when the waiter came to light the candle on their table, indicating that the sun had set. Shaken out of their romancing, they arrived on planet Earth with a thud. Manjula excused herself to go to the ladies' room and, as she was washing her hands, she felt someone tickle her ribs. Startled she turned around to see Malini grinning widely.

Surprised, Manjula said, "What are you doing here?"

"When you did not reply to my calls on your cell, I called up your office and asked for Amit, pretending to be someone's secretary, and I was told that he was at the Taj Hotel. I have been sitting at the coffee shop watching you lovebirds, and you did not even see me!" She danced around gleefully and said, "So, was I right? I told you that he would profess his love within six months! Sweetheart, never give Malini a challenge!"

Manjula laughed, "I agree! It is thanks to your grooming and coaching that this has happened! I can't thank you enough!"

"Reserve your thanks for post-marriage!" Malini's expression changed and she said in a serious tone, "We have to strike when the iron is hot. We cannot let him take too much time to court. When you get back, tell him that you checked your phone and your father wants you in Agra by the weekend. Force Amit's hand. Plead with him to come with you to Agra and meet your parents. Use all your feminine wiles. Make me proud!"

Manjula said doubtfully, "Isn't that a bit manipulative?"

"Kiddo, you are innocent. We live in a manipulative society. If we must succeed, we need to play the game. You are not cheating him – you do care for him deeply, and that is enough."

As always, Manjula was swayed by Malini's words and she agreed to do as she was told.

Malini then said, "And another thing, tell him that you have a phobia of flying and you want to travel by train."

"But I have no such phobia!"

"Idiot, I know that. I want to be with you when you meet your parents. I can travel in another compartment and meet you midway on the train; if we go by flight, I would not be able to hide. Amit would see me immediately."

Manjula's mind was in a whirl with the day's happenings; she did not listen to Malini's words carefully and just agreed to do what she said.

She left the room and joined Amit who was staring dreamily into space and, after a few exchanges of sweet nothings, manipulated Amit as per Malini's orders.

The following Saturday saw Amit and Manjula board the first-class, air-conditioned compartment of the Punjab Mail. Malini had assured Manjula that she would join them a couple of hours later and told her, "I have booked all the berths in your coupe with another name, so it will only be the three of us and we can chat on the way to Agra! What fun it would be! I will bring a lot of snacks and maybe even sneak in a bottle of wine! Unfortunately, you two lovebirds won't be left alone, but that is okay!"

Manjula sat on the berth happily; her dream had come true. She was eager to introduce Malini to Amit and she imagined that the three of them would be firm friends. As the train chugged along Amit said,

"We need to get your phobia cured soon. How else can I take you around the world? Train travel is not my favorite mode of transport."

Manjula blushed with shame, recollecting that she had read about Amit losing his first wife in a train accident. She said in an apologetic voice, "I am so sorry! I am so insensitive, I had heard that you had lost your first wife in a train accident, but I completely forgot about it in my hassled state. Please forgive me!"

Amit assured her that there was nothing to be forgiven and went on, with a catch in his voice, said, "Her name was Devika. I met her when I was around 27 years old working as a Marketing Manager in a company. Devika worked with our ad agency. She did not have to work; her father was a rich businessman. But Devika wanted to be independent and took up a job in another organization. She would say that she did not want to be known as the boss's daughter, but for her work."

He stopped as if lost in long-lost memories, and Manjula nudged him. "How did you two meet?"

"As I said, she was my colleague. I think I fell in love at first sight, but she was very aloof, always professional, and never over-friendly. She was not stunningly beautiful, but there was an aura about her that spelled class and dignity. Her entire demeanor, her gait, her soft, dulcet voice all made her stand out. You remind me of her quite a bit!"

Manjula smiled at this sudden compliment and Amit went on, "It took me over a year to woo her, but finally she was mine! Convincing her father was another matter altogether. I was the proverbial poor young man and she was the heiress of a business magnate. We couldn't convince him and finally, we had to elope."

Manjula felt a vague sense of unease on hearing this, it sounded so much like Malini's story! Can two people have similar stories? She put it aside to coincidence and said, "So, you had a happy marriage?"

"Happy? More like ecstatic! It was sheer bliss. We were so happy with each other. Her father wanted me to join his business, but I refused on principle. But Devika coaxed and cajoled telling me that there was no one else, and she had no interest in running the business and that she was happier being my wife and the future mother of my children."

"And you joined the business?"

"That started all the problem! I was brought in as a Vice President and I had to travel around so much to learn the business that I had no time to spend with Devika. To make up for my absence, I planned a romantic trip to the Taj Mahal on our second anniversary. Those were the times before flights were common in India and we took the train. We had so much fun at Agra; she was like a child, and I was so happy to see her face. Little did I know that I would lose her so soon. We were returning from Agra and I was fast asleep in my berth and when I woke up, she was missing. She had fallen somewhere on the way, in pitch darkness. To this day, I blame myself for the accident. If only I had not gone to sleep… if only I had not planned the Agra trip, if only… if only…" He was sobbing his heart out and Manjula composed him.

"It was not your fault! There, please compose yourself. Drink some water, you will feel better," she urged worriedly.

"I loved her more than I loved myself! It has been so many years since she died, but I have still not accepted that! I always think that it was a dream, and if I open my eyes, I will see her standing in front of me!" Theatrically he closed his eyes, sighed, opened them, and glanced at the coupe door.

His blood froze when he saw Devika standing there! He blinked his eyes a couple of times, but she was there, in flesh and blood, with a small suitcase.

He stood up, gobsmacked, and heard a shriek of delight from Manjula, "Malini! What a surprise!" Turning to Amit, Manjula introduced Malini as her dearest friend from Mumbai. Amit could not respond; the world seemed to spin in front of his eyes.

Who was this woman? Not only did she look like Devika, but even her voice, her touch, her smell… everything was Devika's. But how could that be? Devika was dead! Killed by his own hands, she must be a look-alike, a doppelgänger, if you please.

His mind raced back to the fateful day he had decided to kill Devika.

Amit was a ruthlessly ambitious man, and he desperately wanted to become rich. Marrying Devika was a stroke of luck. He genuinely loved her, but he wouldn't have married her if she did not come from money. His initial reluctance to join his father-in-law's business was an elaborate strategy to make him look like a saint. He started siphoning money from the company without anyone realizing it. He had borrowed heavily from a few unscrupulous characters to support his gambling habit and that was the reason he started siphoning off the funds. He had not repaid them yet and he knew that they would kill him if he didn't pay back the loan with interest.

Devika found out his duplicity by accident and threatened to tell her father if Amit did not change his ways. She was extremely angry when she realized that Amit was stealing from the employee's pension fund and building his wealth. She told Amit that if he did not mend his ways and return all the money, she would personally hand him over to the police. Amit was rattled on hearing this. He knew that Devika would indeed carry out her threat.

He was caught between the devil and the deep sea.

After much thought, he decided that there was no way out but to kill Devika and make it look like an accident.

According to his plan, he pretended to be apologetic and deeply remorseful. He spoke to her at length, apologizing and self-berating in turns till she was exhausted and agreed to give him another chance. Amit was pathetically grateful and promised her that he would never again give her the chance to complain about his behavior.

True to his words, his behavior was exemplary – he was the ideal husband! Devika bloomed under the showers of love and affection. Amit would surprise her with small gifts, impromptu outings, and, most importantly, his time. She truly believed that he had turned a new leaf and that her love had the power to change Amit. Amit was her first and only love, and she strongly believed that he was her soulmate.

He planned a romantic trip to the Taj Mahal for their second anniversary. They spent three days in Agra, visiting the Taj Mahal, the Agra Fort, and other areas of interest. It was with a heavy heart that Devika boarded the train back home.

Amit looked at her, sitting with a faraway look on her face, her beautiful face serious and he asked, "A penny for your thoughts?"

She said, "I was just thinking how lucky I am! I am glad that you realized your mistake and stopped all that bad work. We can now live in peace with our honestly earned money!"

Amit said, "Honey, I promise you that I will never repeat that mistake! Let us now forget about the past. Come, let us enjoy a smoke, as we watch the train go through these dark farmlands."

Devika and Amit went near the door and stood there smoking.

Little did she know, that it would be her last smoke! As she stood there, she suddenly felt a violent push. Her hands left the door railing and she fell, hitting her head against the rock that was near the tracks. As she lay there, bleeding, face-up, her last sight was that of the speeding train, and Amit craning his head to look at her – and what a vicious look that was!

The ruling was "death by accident."

After a couple of months, his father-in-law died in a massive heart attack, naming Amit as the sole heir for the business and all his wealth.

He was brought back to the present by Manjula calling,

"Amit! Amit!"

"Sorry! What were you saying? I must have been wool-gathering!"

Malini gave a mirthless laugh, "Or have you seen a ghost?"

Amit could feel the sweat beads gather on his forehead despite the air-conditioning the coupe. "Wha... what do you mean?" he stammered.

Malini said, "I was just joking! Come on, join me for a smoke!" She fished out a packet of Marlboro from her bag and beckoned Amit.

Manjula said in mock anger, "Both my best friends have this filthy habit! I refuse to inhale second-hand smoke! Both of you puff away to cancer!"

Amit followed Malini as if in a trance. He couldn't figure out who this was, this person who looked so much like Devika. He had regretted killing Devika, but he consoled himself by saying that he had no choice – it was either her death or his death, as the creditors would have killed him. He watched in morbid fascination as Devika – no, Malini – lit up and offered him a cigarette.

She said in a conversational tone, "Darling! I never thought that you were unintelligent!"

"What do you mean? This is the first time we are meeting!"

"How soon do you forget! Are you telling me that you do not recognize your wife? The woman whom you claimed was your world?"

Amit asked in a voice that sounded strange even to him, "Who are you?"

"How do names matter? Hasn't Shakespeare said that a rose by any other name would just smell as sweet?" She smiled sweetly and continued,

"But you do need a name...shall we call it nemesis?"

Suddenly, she pushed him from the train and watched with grim satisfaction as he fell, his face frozen with fear, his screams lost in the thundering of the train.

Days later, the verdict was announced as "accidental death."

A Journey To The South

By Fatima Ibrahim Faras

It was a chilly morning at a train station in New York City. The sun had still not risen high enough and there was a slight cold breeze. Besides the conductor's occasional shouts and trains' screeches, there were lots of people at the platform bustling and chattering about. I stood on the platform and waited for the train anxiously when the train conductor shouted, "Five minutes left until the train arrives!"

I looked up at the board that read "FINAL DESTINATION – GEORGIA" and a wave of both excitement and anxiety washed over me.

By that time, I had adjusted the barrette on my hair a dozen times. I never left my house without my barrette and I had owned it for as long as I could remember. I held a tight grip on my washed-out suitcase and I looked down at my hands that firmly grabbed the suitcase. I looked like a nervous little schoolgirl on her way to her first school day. I took a deep breath and slowly breathed out repeatedly, a futile attempt to calm my nerves. I was indeed nervous. It was a pleasant surprise that my boss had assigned me this task. I did not know what to expect, or what kind of man Mr. Miller was – all I knew about were his famous name and business.

Mr. Miller was a rich man who owned several plantations in the South and I was going to write an article on his success. I was excited to meet him, but I was even more excited to prove to my colleagues that I was more than the shy new graduate at the news agency office.

Writing had always been my passion. It had always been a way for me to express my feelings when I was too shy or afraid to speak up. I particularly remember how I, as a little girl, used to save my money to buy notebooks. My mother used to think that I was a unique and rather strange child since I never asked her for dolls or toys. Writing was therapeutic for me. When I was younger, I used to write about all the times I was teased at school for looking different; I was adopted, and being adopted was not common in those days. I never fit in. My hair was different than my adoptive mother's; Hers was thin and blonde, whereas my hair was the opposite – long, thick, curly, and dark brown. My hazel eyes and olive skin complexion differed from her pale skin.

On top of that, I did not know my adoptive father – all I knew was what my mother told me. He moved to New York a year before he married my mother. He later died from a heart attack when I was very young, and

I do not remember him. I guess I did not need a father since my mother already did everything for me; she loved me dearly and taught me to be strong. For that I was grateful, but it still did not fill the void of the sense of belonging I lacked. I wanted to know my origins and my story because I had no clue, but I was too afraid to find out, and my mother knew that. I always felt like a stranger in my family, at my school, and in my neighborhood.

However, my mother was a strong woman who taught me to never feed into people's negative comments about me. She always told me that I was beautiful and that I should be proud of my skin color. There were moments when I would believe her and brush aside my insecurities. However, as I grew older and bloomed into an adolescent, those feelings of lack of belonging would invade my mind again. I never felt like I belonged, and my only comfort was, therefore, writing about my feelings.

As I was immersed in my thoughts, the train finally arrived, and I entered the wagon.

After a few hours, I reached my destination and headed to my hotel. Tired from the long journey, I immediately fell asleep like a baby. As I drifted off to sleep, I wondered what the following day would entail. There was a feeling of great exhilaration that overcame me, but my lethargy got the better of me soon and I dozed off.

When I woke up the next day, I met Mr. Brown in the hotel lobby. He was going to be my assistant for the upcoming days at the Millers' in Georgia.

"Nice to meet you, Ms. Johnson," Mr. Brown said as he reached out his hand to shake mine.

Mr. Brown was a rather petite man, shorter and skinnier than me, with round glasses. The glasses were the same shape as his head. He emitted a nervous aura.

"Nice to meet you, too, and please, call me Rose," I said as I shook his hand and smiled at him. We had a long trip ahead of us, and I took a seat in the horse carriage.

As we arrived at the countryside where the Millers resided, the heat embraced me in its tight grip and I felt like I was suffocating. Sweat dripped incessantly down my temples as I peered up at the unforgiving sun. There was nothing but silence, except for the occasional neighing. My eyes moved to the enormous cotton field behind me that looked like a giant cloud on the ground. I peered at a bunch of people on the field with their backs bent, plucking cotton. I was startled when I heard a loud noise. A whipping noise. I caught sight of a man on a horse that whipped the people on the field while yelling at them. I was astonished at the scene in front of me. Although I knew slavery was very much alive in the Deep

South; I was still taken aback by the scene that I witnessed up close in front of my eyes.

"I understand that this is very strange to you, Miss Rose, but this is the South. Slavery is still legal here," Mr. Brown said as he saw the troubled look on my face.

"Uh, yes, of course," I said, as I cleared my throat. "Perhaps we should make our way to the house now," I said as I looked in the direction before us.

Soon, Mr. Brown and I stood outside the broad porch. The smell of the horses beside me was intertwined with the aroma of food seeping through the house. The smells were intensified by the heat, and the different aromas made my stomach growl. I could almost taste the food on my tongue.

I looked up at the mansion. The house was even more spectacular than I had expected a huge, ivory-white mansion surrounded by neatly trimmed bushes. Marble statues stood tall and mighty by the porch and I could not seem to take my eyes off the brilliant details carved on them.

Soon, Mr. Brown raised his hand to knock on the door, and someone quickly opened it. We were met by a tall, well-built man in his fifties. The man greeted us with a big grin on his face as he gestured with his hands for us to come inside. My eyes moved to his disheveled brown hair that was parted in the middle. His yellow teeth exposed a gold tooth that almost blinded me as the sun struck it.

"Ah, Ms. Johnson, welcome. A pleasure to meet you. Mr. Brown, pleasure. Please come in," he said.

"I assume you are Mr. Miller," I said as I entered and shook his hand.

"You are looking at him," he said with a smile spreading across his face as he spoke while pointing both of his thumbs towards him. I smiled at him as I took off my sweater to hang it on the clothes hanger.

"Oh no, wait. Loretta! Come on in here and help our guests," he said as he raised his hand to stop me. I stiffened with my sweater half on and half off.

In came an elderly black woman wearing a burgundy uniform. She walked in hastily while looking down the entire time. Her hands were folded together. Her gray hair was short and the wrinkles on her face were prominent and deep. The uniform was tightly hugging her large body.

"We have people to ease our tasks, Miss Johnson," Mr. Miller said. I discreetly moved my eyes to Mr. Brown, who looked at me casually and shrugged his shoulders.

Mr. Miller gestured for us to come into the living room. As I entered, I tried to keep myself from gazing with awe, but I could not. I saw that Mr. Brown had already lost that battle. He walked around in circles examining the room bit by bit, pressing the piano keyboards and running his hand along the walls. The mansion was spectacularly grand. The marble floor was glistening, and opulent stairways stood in the room climbing toward the upper level. The walls were painted a subtle brown and had intricate designs embedded in them. Grand paintings decorated the well-maintained walls. In the middle of the hallway was a fireplace with a crackling fire. An expensive-looking statue of an angel was placed near the firestone.

"You have a lovely home, Mr. Miller," I said, my eyes fixed on the huge crystal chandelier hanging from the ceiling.

Mr. Miller smiled with pride and followed my gaze with his eyes. "That one was imported from Italy, custom-made," he said. "My wife wanted it," he replied satisfactorily.

Soon after, Mrs. Miller came in. She was a young and fair red-haired woman in her thirties. Her dress looked extremely expensive and matched her red locks perfectly; it was a pleasant sight for the eyes. She made her way towards me and kissed me graciously on the cheeks. I noticed that she had a thick southern accent.

"Lovely to meet you, Ms. Johnson. My husband told me that you are here to write an article for a New York news agency about his success on the cotton field," she said proudly.

"Uh, yes, something along those lines," I affirmed.

Mrs. Miller's eyes darted towards my barrette. She looked at it with much interest as she said, "What a lovely barrette – it certainly matches your hazel eyes."

Later that evening, Mr. Miller invited me to his office. I sat in front of him with my hands folded, my notebook and pen in front of me on the desk. An awkward silence lingered upon us as I waited for him to start the conversation. I was very excited to finally interview one of the richest men in this country. My eyes wandered to Mr. Miller in his seat. His heavy body was slouched, his leg crossed over the other. He rocked back and forth on his chair while he clicked his pen and occasionally examined it carefully. Mr. Miller's office was bigger than my entire flat. The smell of cigarettes wafted all around, mixed with the strong scent of his cologne. I could feel my throat tighten. He was quite a well-known man and it was quite overwhelming to sit across him. My eyes nervously darted to his desk where he had stacks of papers. Next to the pile, I caught sight of a photograph of Mr. Miller outside his porch with a big grin, exposing the gold tooth.

I looked up and saw Mr. Miller pour a glass of whiskey. He looked up at me and asked if I would like to have some. I shook my head and nodded at my tea, signaling that I still had not finished with my drink.

"You Northerners are so uptight," he said and raised the glass to his lips. Surprisingly he finished it all in one gulp. I cleared my throat and quickly glanced down at the background notes about Mr. Miller that my boss had provided me with.

"So, Mr. Miller, from what I understand, you are an agriculturist and you own a cotton plantation with a little over eighty slaves. Among them are men, women, and children. Some of these slaves are house slaves, and the majority are laborers that work at the cotton field," I read out in a monotonous voice.

Mr. Miller nodded casually and attempted to sip the last drop of whiskey in his glass. I proceeded with my interview and asked him how he had become so successful.

He finally put down the glass, folded his hands together, and cleared his throat. Mr. Miller told me that his grandfather owned the land where the cotton field was and that he had invested the money that his father had left for him on slave trading and the cotton plantation.

"You see, Ms. Johnson, I figured the only way I could invest my money successfully would be on the cotton business, and you cannot have a cotton plantation without slaves. That is what my business consists of now," he said while shrugging his shoulders. He then proceeded to pour himself another glass of whiskey. I fervently wrote down everything he said.

After the long interview, I went to the room upstairs that I had been provided with during my stay. It had a huge mirror across the room, and I moved my way over there. My reflection perfectly described how I felt. I looked exhausted, even my eyebags had become bigger due to a lack of sleep. I tightly gripped my barrette and adjusted it with heavy eyes before I scrambled my way to bed and laid on my back. I dozed off while replaying the conversation with Mr. Miller in my head.

The next day, I woke up early to visit the cotton field with Mr. Brown. Now that I had interviewed Mr. Miller, I wanted to have a look at one of his businesses; the cotton field. I figured I would be able to describe it more vividly if I visited the plantation.

"Ms. Johnson, how did the interview with Mr. Miller go?" Mr. Brown asked.

"Well, it went great. Mr. Miller described his whole life and how he succeeded with his business. I am sure it will be a good story and hopefully, my boss will be impressed," I said, as I adjusted my hat and prepared to go out to the plantation in the heat.

The heat was unbearable, and the fan I had with me did not make much of a difference. I looked at Mr. Brown and his forehead was already dripping with sweat.

The field was so huge that we could hardly see where it ended. I caught sight of more than fifty people working, their backs bent. Across their shoulders, they all wore a tote bag. I saw men, women, and even a child. One of the little girls toiling in the field was not older than eight years old.

"Get up, boy! Thinking you can cause trouble here, huh? Get up, I tell ya!"

Mr. Brown and I jumped when we heard the noises coming next to the plantation. We followed the loud noises and our eyes fell upon the most dreadful scene I had ever witnessed.

One of the slaves, a young man, was tied with both his hands while being flogged by an overseer. My entire body stiffened and my knees shook. The hair on my back bristled. I breathed with difficulty and my hand clenched into a tight fist. My lips curved whenever the lash struck his back, his shrieks piercing through my soul, sending chills down my spine. I opened my mouth, but I could not utter a sound. My heart pounded in my chest and I felt a wave of helplessness rushing over me. I wanted to help him, but I could not move. My eyes moved intently to the plantation and I caught sight of a few heads stealing glances at the scene, but the majority were still bent down and busy plucking. As the pounding of my heart became louder and louder, the shrieks and the sound from the whips became muffled.

"Miss Johnson, Miss Johnson!" Mr. Brown called out to me.

I finally shook myself out of my stupor as Mr. Brown's voice gradually became louder. I quickly regained control of my senses. Mr. Brown and I briskly made our way to the scene.

The overseer stopped the whipping and tied a rope tightly around the young man's hands, which made it hard for him to find the balance to stand upright. He yelled at the slave to get up since he stumbled repeatedly. I finally caught sight of the young man's face and quickly studied him. Although he was a young man, the life at the plantation had left its marks on him; he was worn-out. My eyes traced his slender yet muscular figure. I looked at his back, where the wounds were still freshly carved in him as blood ran along his back. I shuddered with a horrible feeling enveloping me. He was dragged along as the overseer sat on his horse, tightly holding the rope. He fervently pulled the rope and the young slave man wriggled in agony without uttering a sound.

"Ms. Johnson, do you perhaps want to see the rest of the plantation?" Mr. Brown asked carefully as he looked at me. I was still stiff as a log.

"I would rather do that later," I said without looking at him. My chest was still pounding loudly, as I witnessed how the overseer dragged the young man away.

After watching the entire scene helplessly, I was led away by Mr. Brown to my room. There I felt sick to my stomach. I walked over to my bed and sat on the edge of it, slouching my back. I chewed nervously on my nails. I could not believe what I had just witnessed moments ago.

Thoughts ran in my mind with wild abandon. I recalled the scene with Lorett when she helped me with my sweater, the slaves that were flogged at the field, and, most recently, the whipping of the young man. I shuddered. I felt repulsed by the fact that other human beings were treated like animals because of the color of their skin. I could not understand how one person's value was greater than another's.

I was excited to meet Mr. Miller and write an interesting article on his success, but my mind could not stop thinking about the horridness I was encountering. Who was I kidding? I had to admit that I could not be detached as I should be as a journalist. My emotions were being triggered and perhaps I was getting too personal with my assignment... Perhaps this made me a bad journalist in a way. Maybe my boss chose the wrong journalist for this task. Maybe my colleagues were right. I was nothing but a city girl, a new graduate, one who had never witnessed such atrocities and wouldn't be able to handle the task like a professional. Self-admittedly, I could not help but feel bad for these people. I quickly grabbed my notebook and pen to write down these events when I was startled by a knock on the door.

"Miss, It's Loretta! I am here with your tea."

I hastened to open the door. "Good morning, Miss," Loretta said with a soft smile, her wrinkles appearing more prominently.

"Thank you so much, Loretta, you can just put it on the nightstand, thank you," I said and gestured with my hand. "Would you like to join me?" I asked with wide eyes.

Loretta made her way to the nightstand and her eyes lowered. Her body language reeked of discomfort. I could sense that she felt small and subservient before me. I was, after all, the honored guest of Mr. Miller and she was only a house slave who was to serve me fulfill all my whims.

"Why, I possibly could not, Miss!" A look of horror sprawled across her face.

I was struck by the strange injustice of it all. Was she not just another human being, after all? Why did she need to be encaged? I wanted to know how she felt about her situation. Gently, I looked at her and gestured for her to come and sit next to me. I explained to her that I came from the far north. I found the whole concept of slavery deeply repulsive and I looked at her as nothing more than a human being doing her job. Her eyes lightened up when she heard my opinions.

"Miss, you are a good soul. For so long, I have been accustomed to being looked upon as nothing more than a possession, a thing. I dare not sit next to you, Miss," she sighed apologetically.

"Okay Loretta," I smiled understandingly, "but I do hope you will allow me to ask you a few questions to quench my curiosity!"

Loretta's eyes widened and there was a tinge of fear, but she nodded nevertheless.

"Oh, your hair is so pretty, miss... What lovely curls," she said and tilted her head while her eyes lit up. I grabbed my comb from the nightstand and made my way to the chair in front of the mirror.

"Please Loretta, here," I said as I handed her the comb and loosened my curls from the hair tie. She looked very reluctant, but she carefully grabbed the comb and cautiously combed my hair, which had now turned frizzy from the heat. We did not say much until I decided to break the silence.

"When did you get here, Loretta? How long have you been working here? It seems to me that you manage a lot of things amongst the house slaves," I asked.

Loretta took a long pause and a tinge of nervousness spread across her face before she opened her mouth to speak.

"Well, I am the oldest and the most experienced. That's why the Master has made me the head house slave. Every day here is the same. I wake up early, prepare breakfast, do house chores, assign chores to the other house slaves, and do all other errands," she replied as she robotically rattled off her daily tasks. Simultaneously, as she spoke, she combed my hair.

Loretta told me about the time she was bought by Mr. Miller almost 20 years ago while working at a tobacco farm in Maryland. She said that Mr. Miller thought she was suited as a house slave after working many years at the cotton plantation. Loretta looked at me, curved her lower lip, and slightly shrugged her one shoulder.

"What do you think the future holds for you?" I asked with a soft smile.

Loretta laughed timidly at my question. "Oh, Miss, I am an old woman... The only thing I would want is to die as a free woman," she replied with a hopeful smile.

I smiled at her reflection in the mirror and felt sorry for her. Her eyes wandered to my hair again and her face sprawled with shock.

"Oh, miss, that looks rather similar," Loretta said pensively and pointed to my barrette. I touched my hair and reached for it. I turned my body towards her to face her.

"Oh, this? I've had this one for as long as I could remember, I never leave the house without it," I smiled.

"Well, who would have thought I would see that barrette again..." Loretta laughed nervously and shook her head in denial.

"This barrette?" I ask again, confused as I reached for my hair to untie it. Loretta was in a trance and snatched it from my hand and examined it carefully.

"Oh no, this cannot be," she mumbled to herself, "I did not know, I... I must be going mad!" She continued to whisper under her breath while occasionally looking at me with wide-open eyes. I kept looking at her, wondering what was going on.

"Um, Loretta, what's going on?" I asked carefully.

"Yes, Miss." She quickly looked up like a startled dear and snapped out of her trance. She hastily turned around and almost ran to the door. Loretta told me that she had to go as she avoided my eyes and slammed the door behind her, leaving me in a state of confusion.

The next day, I woke up to visit the plantation. While I was there, I replayed my conversation with Loretta at the back of my mind: *why was Loretta so shocked when she saw my barrette? I mean, it's just a barrette,* I thought to myself.

"Ms. Johnson, are you alright?" Mr. Brown asked and interrupted my thoughts. He looked at me with wide eyes.

I smiled back at him wearily and told him that I was fine. He did not look convinced but still managed to nod with a soft smile, proceeding to walk briskly beside me as we entered the Millers' house.

"I'll see you in the morning, Ms. Johnson," Mr. Brown said as we parted ways and I made my way upstairs. I took off my hat and massaged my temples to find relief from the headache I had all day. I could not wait to take off my boots, take a bath, and head straight to bed. Suddenly, I caught sight of a figure that briskly walked past me in the hall. I rushed to turn around and get a hold of her before she left.

"Loretta!" I grabbed her by her shoulder. She stopped and did not say a word.

I told her that we needed to talk about what had happened earlier in my room as I firmly gripped her shoulder. She managed to loosen herself from my grip.

"Oh no, Miss, I have to go and help prepare supper with the others," she said hurriedly.

"Loretta, please, I feel that you are hiding something from me, and I need to know what that is," I pleaded.

She sighed, passed by me, and quickly entered my room.

Loretta made her way to the window stand and looked outside into the pitch darkness as the moon shone luminously above. A few stars could be seen from afar.

"It was a day like this," she sighed. She still had not turned around. I could feel my palms sweat and my pulse quicken. I did not know what to expect to hear as I stood behind her.

"Remember when I told you that before I came here, that I was at the tobacco plantation in Maryland?" she asked. Although she could not see me, I nodded, while fiddling fretfully with my fingers. Loretta continued with her story. I could hear her voice crack slightly and fail her. She told me about a young lady whom she got to know at the plantation there. The woman was a beautiful, fair house slave who worked at the master's house there. The master's name was William. William was a tall, handsome man with the most sparkling blue eyes.

Loretta stopped briefly before she continued and raised her hand to her face. I believe that she wiped off her tears as I could hear her sniff slightly.

"Everyone knew that Master was fond of Shauna; she was a breath of fresh air, a beautiful, charming young lady who could sweep anyone off their feet. Now, I don't know if you could call that being fond of someone. I would rather call that rape. She used to bring me extra bread from the house, knowing that we, who worked at the plantation, did not get enough food. She was a kind soul," Loretta said dreamingly.

Loretta cleared her throat before she continued her story. She told me that one day Shauna came to her in the middle of the night as she cried in panic and told her that she was pregnant. "Loretta, I am pregnant, what do I do, what do I do?" I embraced her and patted her back as I felt sorry for her, but there was nothing I could do to ease her pain.

Loretta went on to mention how more than the pregnancy itself, Shauna was traumatized by the idea of bringing another child into this world who would be 'chained' to spend the rest of their life on these plantations as a slave. "Shauna kept telling me that she did not want her child to be a slave and grow up at the plantation. She wanted the child to be free." Loretta turned around with tears in her eyes and pointed to my hair. "She used to walk around with that barrette from the first day I saw her. The barrette was made by her grandmother and given to her as a gift. She carved in those letters at the smith a few days before the deal was sealed," Loretta continued.

What is Loretta talking about? I wondered to myself.

I could not quite understand how or why she was linking my barrette to this slave woman called Shauna. *Maybe Loretta is spinning a story to get some attention. Her story is so outrageous*, I thought to myself with a bit of annoyance.

My irritation was quite obvious, I think, as I told Loretta to abruptly leave as I was tired.

Loretta looked at me with wide eyes and with her chin down.

"Oh, Miss, I knew that this was a bad idea," she mumbled to herself, as she folded her hands nervously and her eyes watered up. I made my way to the door and gestured for her to leave. Loretta walked briskly past me without saying a word as she wiped the tears that fell on her cheeks. I closed the door behind her and stood still for a while. My thoughts began to whirl in my mind again. *Was there a connection between me and these slaves?* I brushed the thought quickly. Loretta was making up a tall tale probably to play with my emotions. Mr. Miller would often speak of how these slaves were an untrustworthy lot and should not be shown any compassion and pity.

The next morning, I had breakfast with Mr. Miller and Mr. Brown. The table was filled with all sorts of food. A young house slave beside me poured fresh orange juice for all of us. My eyes moved to what had been laid in front of us. There were cheeses of all sorts, and ham, as well as neatly-cut turkey. The fragrance of newly baked crumbs reached my nostrils.

"These darn slaves! Someone needs to show them how things are run here," Mr. Miller grunted after sipping his orange juice. He pointed at his glass.

"Loretta! Loretta!"

Mr. Brown and I jumped as Mr. Miller yelled like a stuck pig. We looked at each other perplexed. Loretta quickly entered the kitchen while she fiddled her fingers nervously as she asked Mr. Miller what she could do for him. Mr. Miller did not look at her and was still pointing at his glass. My eyes moved intently to the other maids that were standing in a line, with their heads bent down and hands folded together. It was as if they were awaiting Loretta's verdict in silence. I stole a glance at Loretta and I could tell that she was nervous from her body language. She gazed at Mr. Miller with startled, almost frightened eyes.

"How many times do I need to tell you that I want three spoons of sugar? This juice has no sugar in it. One of these niggers was stupid and did not put enough sugar in it," he yelled.

Loretta stuttered as she told Mr. Miller that she would bring him a new one. As she quickly reached over the table to grab the glass, Mr. Miller picked it up before her.

"Oh, no, wait. You think you can walk away from me that easily, huh?" he scoffed.

Loretta stiffened and looked down with wide eyes while she slowly shook her head as an answer. Before anyone of us reacted, Mr. Miller quickly splashed the orange juice on Loretta.

I jumped and gazed at Loretta with wide eyes as she jumped with surprise, panting. Her burgundy uniform was drenched in orange juice.

"If you don't humiliate them and hold them on a leash like this, they will never respect you," Mr. Miller said while looking at me. Suddenly, he calmed down and winked at me. Then he devoured a piece of biscuit as if nothing had happened. Mr. Miller told the other maids to bring him a new glass of orange juice and waved off Loretta with his hand without looking at her. Loretta had not said a word and briskly walked away from the dining room. I was still shocked and looked to Mr. Brown who was sipping his coffee unbothered. My pulse quickened, and my body stiffened as a log. This is horrendous! How could someone treat another human being in such a terrible way?

I excused myself and told them I was going to the bathroom. I quickly made my way out of the dining room. Just then, I caught sight of Loretta walking up the stairs and I hastened to follow her.

"Loretta! Are you all alright? I am so sorry. This is horrible. I cannot believe Mr. Miller did that to you," I said with shame and a heavy heart.

Loretta smiled vaguely, devoid of any emotions as she looked at me and said, "It's alright, miss. I am fine. Please, Miss, go downstairs and finish your breakfast." Although Loretta seemed normal, I sensed her sadness.

I stopped for a minute and hesitated before I continued.

"Loretta, I am sorry about yesterday. I should not have behaved in such an abrupt manner," I said before Loretta interrupted me. She told me that she had something for me and was going to come to my room later. Her eyes met mine and she immediately dropped her gaze.

After breakfast, I entered my room to work on my article when I was interrupted by a knock on my door. It must be Loretta. I quickly opened the door and asked her to come in.

"Miss, I have to go soon, I just wanted to give you this. I spent the whole afternoon yesterday looking for it amongst my things and I finally found it," she said and looked at me with wide-open eyes. Loretta told me that she wrote this letter for her since Shauna was illiterate. Shauna had asked Loretta to keep the letter with her so that the other house slaves would not find it in the house. I met her eyes with a confused look sprawled across my face.

Loretta's eyes started to water. "The next day, Shauna had been sold to work at a plantation in Virginia and I did not have a chance to give her the letter or to say goodbye."

She handed me the letter and I grabbed it with shaky hands. The yellow-toned letter was worn out and stained. As Loretta turned back to leave, I felt how my heart started to beat fervently and my palms started to sweat. I grabbed her hand firmly and asked her to stay with me while I read it. Loretta did not resist. I opened the letter to start to read and my heart started pounding faster as I did not know what to expect. I looked up at Loretta and she nervously looked at me with wide eyes.

Dear Rose,

I hope this letter finds you safe and in the best health. I am writing this letter to you in the hope that it will reach you. I hope you have a good life in New York. I don't know how much you know by now, but I just wanted to say that I only did what I did because I wanted the best for you. I wanted to grant you a free life. I wanted you to be in charge of your own life. I know I could not be there for you while you grew up, but I left you this barrette as a piece of me. I wanted to give you something that belonged to me. I hope one day we can meet, my dearest Rose.

Love, your mother.

I slowly reached for my hair and grabbed my barrette. My hand violently shook as I twisted it in my hand to try to find the letters that Loretta said a smith had carved in. "With love, S." I dropped the pin in shock. I could not speak as I felt how my tongue slowly became numb. My knees had already failed me, and I crumbled to the floor.

"Oh, miss!" cried Loretta as she hastily embraced me. "Your mother loved you so much that she gave you the most precious gift; your freedom. Something some of us still seek," Loretta said and rocked me slowly as my tears soaked her chest. I could not move, and I felt how my body was paralyzed. Suddenly, I felt that there was an aura of gray that surrounded me. Tears continuously rolled down my cheeks and I felt as if there was a giant hole in my heart. I was left in a state of confusion and pain.

The next morning, I was still lying in my bed. I had not gone downstairs to eat breakfast. The blanket felt heavy and I could not make myself leave the bed to get ready for the day. I replayed the letter Loretta had given me yesterday repeatedly in my mind. My dearest Rose. Love, your mother. I had been lied to my whole life. What angered me the most was that I was the product of the pure evilness – slavery. I was conceived by rape; my father a wealthy slave owner, and my mother was a young slave woman. I still could not wrap my head around it. How could my life take such a turn? If Shauna had not arranged for me to come to New York, I would be picking my hands bloody at a plantation by now. Or if I would have been somewhat lucky, I would have maybe ended up as a house slave just like Loretta. My dream of becoming a journalist would not have come true, even worse yet, I would have a life worth less than an animal's. Loretta was right, Shauna had given me a precious gift: my freedom. I thought about everything I had witnessed since I came down here; from the young man being flogged to Mr. Miller pouring the orange juice on Loretta. Who was I kidding? I felt ashamed of myself. I was excited to meet Mr. Miller and write a paper about him. I walked in here with excitement. I did not expect that my time here would unravel such atrocities. My thoughts began to fly. I felt a strange sense of responsibility towards these slaves. Almost as if I was now one of them. I had to do something. I had the power to write and I wanted to let the public know what was going on in this country. I sat at the edge of my bed with clenched jaws as tears rolled down my cheeks.

During the afternoon, Mr. Miller had asked me to join him for tea in his garden. Today was my last day at the Millers' and the next day, I was going to head back to New York. Mr. Miller and I had been served biscuits and crumbs with tea as we sat in the garden. My eyes caught sight of a young slave boy cutting the grass from afar.

"So, today is your last day?" he said and sipped his tea. "How do you find the Southern hospitality?" he asked with a broad smile.

"Splendid," I replied and raised the cup of tea to my lips to conceal my expression of repulsion. I hadn't been impressed by what I had seen, although I did not want to make my actual thoughts apparent to Mr. Miller.

Mr. Miller talked to me about my article and how far I had come in my writing. I thought that this would be a perfect opportunity to ask him about Master William in Maryland.

"William Jackson, a tobacco planter in Maryland, next to James River," Mr. Miller said thoughtfully. "Yes, I know about him. Very successful man. You see, he sold Loretta to me. However, I do not know how he is doing now. I just know that I would love to do business with him," Mr. Miller laughed.

William Jackson. In Maryland, James River, I repeated to myself.

New York felt cold, even though it was still summer here. I had missed the busy city life terribly. The story about Mr. Miller was a success. My boss loved it and so did the public. Although I had finished my task already, I decided I wanted to write and publish an article about slavery and the abolishment of slavery. I had to let the public know about Loretta and the others, I owed them that. I had so many emotions built up in me and I wanted to unleash them by writing.

The wind caressed my cheeks as I took deep breaths. It felt incredibly refreshing. As I kept walking, the smell of newly-baked pastries emanating from the nearby confectionery, and my nostrils caught the tantalizing scent. Loud noises from salesmen reverberated through the air. I was on my way to one of the biggest news agencies. I had to get my article published.

As I came home later that evening, I had already visited several news agencies. I was rejected by most straight away, but a few agreed to at least read my paper and later decide if they were going to publish it or not. I must admit that I knew it would be difficult to convince news agencies, but I had to at least give it a try. My thoughts wandered to the anti-slavery demonstration I was going to attend tomorrow. I did not know what to expect, I just knew that I needed to be a part of the antislavery movement and contribute with whatever I was capable of. Slavery was indeed an awful thing, and even worse when witnessing it up close.

As I slumped in bed; my thoughts began to fly. The abolishment of slavery needed to occur anytime soon. I thought about Loretta; she deserved to die a free woman. My thoughts wandered to my biological mother, Shauna, whom I was grateful to; for risking her life to grant me my freedom. I thought about the young man who was flogged at the plantation because he wanted to take the whips instead of that little girl. I thought about Shauna. I wondered what she was like, I wondered what she looked like. I felt some type of warmth when I thought about her. I finally knew who I was. The lack of identity that had plagued me my whole life had dissipated. Finally, I belonged.

My thoughts moved on to my mother; who took me in, sheltered me, and loved me for all those years. The life I had lived was a lie. I knew she only did me a favor by not telling me the truth, but I still would have wanted the truth. I was sure I was ready to hear it. I vaguely smiled at the fact that all this time I thought my adoptive father's name Steven was written on my barrette. I guess you believe anything to fill the void in your heart.

The next day, I made my way downtown. I held the flyer in my hand as I approached a huge crowd outside the entrance to the courthouse. THE UNION IS IN DANGER. Rally, Freemen, To the rescue! Grand Mass demonstration of the constitutional union party. On Thursday, September 6, 1860, the flyer read. The American Anti-Slavery Society was an abolitionist society and I had decided to join them in their antislavery movement. The crowd consisted of approximately 70 people and I caught sight of all types of people: black, brown, white, native, women, and men. All of them were gathered here for this cause.

The weather was quite hot, but it did not deter my need to fight for this very crucial cause. The sun peered through the clouds as it cast a spotlight on the various placards held by the people. I read them in awe.

FREEDOM IS EVERYONE'S RIGHT. STOP SLAVERY NOW. I was pushed into the crowd without knowing where to go. Strong smells of cologne, perfume, and sweat filled my nostrils.

"Here, hold this!" said a man's voice. I looked behind me and I saw a tall man with a scruffy beard and prominent cheekbones. He had a serious face and I felt intimidated by him. His hat was placed so low that I could barely see his eyes. He was holding various placards while distributing them to the demonstrators. I looked at them as he reached one out for me. I held it firmly and whispered a quiet thank you. The man walked off and I turned the placard around, 'NO UNION WITH SLAVERY,' it read. I raised the placard and joined the crowd with the slogans being said out loud when I felt that someone knocked on my back.

"Oh, you must be Rose?" she said and reached out her hand to me. "I recognized a new face here. I heard we were going to have a new member joining today," she said and smiled at me.

I turned around and saw Anna Murray-Douglass. She was an abolitionist and a civil rights activist who fought for the abolition of slavery. She was known as a strong woman who stood up for the rights of the oppressed. It felt surreal that she stood in front of me and reached out her hand to me. She wore a white dress with lace details around the neck. Her dark brown hair was parted in the middle and tied at the back in a low bun. Her mahogany skin glowed as the sun cast its light on it. Her rosy cheeks matched her bright red lips. I quickly shook her hand and could barely speak properly.

I told her that I was a journalist working at a news agency and that I wanted to raise awareness about slavery and join the anti-slavery movement pushing for the abolishment of slavery. She listened carefully to me, joy spreading across her face. Anna told me that she was happy that I had decided to join them and that I would be a great asset since I had the power of the pen. I felt content; I was making a difference.

"What an inspiring young woman you are," she said as she held her placard higher up and turned around as she shouted out slogans loudly with the demonstrators. Both of our voices drowned out in the huge mass's voices with slogans being yelled out loudly. I was amongst all kinds of people, fighting for justice and equality. I was not being stared at nor did I feel alienated. For the first time in my life, I felt like I belonged.

What was in store for me, then? I had shoved the thought for a while now. I knew I had to fill the void in my heart, and I knew how. Finally, I dared to do it.

I was back on the train, this time heading to Virginia. Only this time, I was not a nervous girl on her first mission. On the contrary, I had matured and life had left its miserable marks on me. It showed me how I could drown in my dark thoughts. Life also thought me how to heal after it had caused me to bleed. Who knew, maybe in the future I would have the courage to even travel to James River, Maryland, and meet Mr. Jackson. My involvement with the anti-slavery movement for the past year had taught me a lot. I knew I was capable of being part of something good. I fought for Loretta, Shauna, and everyone else. However, now was the time and I was ready to meet my fate. For the first time in my life, I felt like I finally belonged; that missing puzzle was finding its place. I just had to secure it, and I knew how.

I gazed at the trees as they quickly disappeared in the distance. I sat comfortably in my seat with my notebook and pen in hand as usual and adjusted my barrette. I did not know what to expect as I arrived in Virginia. All I knew was that it was now time to write down my own story.

A Case Unsolved

By Asma Khalid Yousuf Baker

On a street filled with sunshine, one house stood out. This house was once bright and full of smiles, but everything changed one fateful day. It soon transformed into a dark place filled with sorrow. The walls were full of dust, broken windows, cobwebbed stairs, and eerie rooms. The only room that was occupied was the basement. A 23-year-old man silently sat on a chair in the middle of the room. His name was Ahmed. He was a tall man with shaggy brown hair and curious eyes. Ahmed was very curious and had a way of making friends instantly. He was dressed in some old, torn-up jeans, a tattered shirt, and a thin jacket. He was staring at the dusty walls and the bloodstained floor.

The basement was full of memories, and not all of them were pleasant. One of those memories was what got him to his present state, where he was blankly staring at the dusty walls and the bloodstained floor. This was the place where his parents were murdered, and his life had transformed for the worst after that. However, the case of his parent's death was never solved; it was closed and forgotten.

Ahmed finally walked back upstairs, his eyes staring into space. He was looking for a way to avenge his parents, to find out the truth about their murder. He went to his garage and saw his father's old car. He started to make a plan on a piece of paper. He drew a blueprint of a time-traveling car with a speed that would surpass time and space to open up a wormhole to the past. He was going to fix everything and make them right. This was a plan that he knew would work. Ahmed and his brother's family would live the lives they always dreamed of.

Just then, he looked at a picture on the wall. It was a picture of a young man, a woman in his arms, and three boys; the couple was Ahmed's parents, and the three boys were Ahmed and his brothers Mustafa and Yasser.

Mustafa was 23 years old when he became a successful bank manager; Yasser, on the other hand, was 25 years old and had no job, money, or responsibility. Yasser hated his brothers and had no intention of counting on them for support. It was corruption and jealousy that got his family to this state. Mustafa left the family when Ahmed was 11 years old. Mustafa married right after; he had a beautiful wife named Alia. They moved out to a house which was a wedding gift from his parents. Ahmed was always visiting Mustafa and his family, and when Ahmed turned 13 years old, he met his brother's kids, Nader and Najeeb, Mustafa's twin sons. Three years later, the tragedy happened.

The next day, after actually creating the time-traveling car, Ahmed parked it outside his home. He went inside his house to get some things he needed and then got ready to head out. The car was built to look like a normal car. It was red and had a regular exterior, but something was different: there was a rocket booster at the back of the car, which was something Ahmed added to create the speed he needed. He built the rocket booster from things he found around the house. Ahmed managed to complete the rocket booster with a few trinkets from the kitchen in his house.

The next day, the neighbors were standing outside the house and watching him. They started to talk amongst themselves.

"Finally, little Ahmed came out of that old dusty house," one of them said. "He needed to move on. He was so occupied with his parents' deaths that he withdrew from reality and the good things in life."

Soon, Ahmed stepped out of the house, got himself ready, put the picture of his family beside him, and drove off. He got ready to speed up. He went faster and faster. He accelerated at supersonic speed. Soon, he clicked a button that opened the rocket booster.

Suddenly, the other-dimensional porthole opened up and he drove into it. The speed he was going at was incredible. He saw blurred lights and timelines of the past. The excitement he felt was growing, and the light in his eyes was showing the possibility of his life. He knew that the time would come when his plan would materialize. When he found the timeline that he wanted – his first day of high school – he passed through that particular time hole and stopped. He had finally reached the past; he had finally reached the time he wanted to be at. His car had worked and had transported him to the world of his past!

Now in the past, on the street he lived on, he recognized the area he was in. It was a place Ahmed recognized as his house, except that now, it was the house he remembered. The sun shone brightly in the clear sky. The grass was a vibrant shade of green the broken windows were gone.

He stopped his car on the other side of the street, hopped out of his car, and made his way to the basement. He hid in the darkness behind the shadow of a box and waited. As the basement door opened, he heard the sounds of people talking. He made out the sounds to be Yasser, his brother, and his parents, Sara and Jaber.

"But, Mom, I need the money urgently! What can I do without your help?" Yasser whined.

"We have your little brother to worry about, too. Start to work like your brother Mustafa and you might get some money," Sara said crisply. "We already gave you money last week."

"I have my own life now, too, but you are still my parents. You should provide for me, too. Not just Ahmed. Do you even care? Ever since Ahmed was born, you've just ignored me," Yasser argued.

"We do care, Yasser, but you have been asking for money a lot more now," Jaber said. "We are losing a lot more than we gain... your mother and I are doing all the work. What do you do?"

Yasser and his parents were always arguing about money. Every time Yasser would come to visit and see his parents, it was to confront them about his financial woes. He would keep insisting that he needed their money to help him. It was always the same argument, and Yasser finally got fed up. He was upset about his parents' indifference. He needed them to help him with money quickly, but they were not budging. Immense anger built inside of him one day. It was almost as if a demon had overtaken his mind. That's when Yasser had enough of his parents! He started to scream and moved forward with anger as his parents moved backward.

"Please Yasser, stop screaming," Sara pleaded.

"We'll try to help you any way we can," Jaber said.

The next thing Yasser knew, they were falling down the stairs and stopped moving. He stood there unable to move, then he walked down and started to shake them. He checked their pulse, they were gone. He fled the house and never came back.

Ahmed stood paralyzed in his spot. It felt as if his blood had turned to ice. *How could he have done that? How could he have done that to our parents?* Tears started running down his face.

Ahmed was shocked that the boy he once knew, Yasser, was gone; he had turned from a hero into a monster.

No evidence existed that could help the police find the suspect. Yasser escaped without any evidence that tied him to the accident which happened to his mom and dad; this would be the mistake that he did for the future.

Ahmed's eyes were tinged red as he watched the past; he didn't want to believe that his elder brother did this. Blood of his parents continued to pour on the basement floor; his parents were gone forever and there was nothing he could do. He could hear his heart beating thunderously in his chest. His brother was the one who did it and nothing that he would say would let him forget what he saw that day.

Ahmed's eyes were swollen with tears. All he could see was red; his heart was in pieces and his body rigid. He was at a loss for words.

Suddenly, he remembered to look at the time. It was 2:00, the time younger Ahmed would finish school and come back home.

As scenes from the past played on, a 16-year-old Ahmed was skipping down the road, whistling a tune. He reached home, opened the door, and put his bag down. Then he started to look for his parents.

"Are you guys playing hide and seek?" he asked playfully.

He looked everywhere, but he didn't find them. He wandered to the one place he was not supposed to enter: his father's basement. As he crept down the stairs, he saw two bodies on the floor. "Are you guys sleeping?" he asked as he kept going down the stairs. He went further and looked down. He saw the blood and screamed, his eyes almost shooting out of his head. Shocked, Ahmed froze in his tracks and slid down against the wall behind him. His shoulders were shaking violently.

He sobbed into his hands. Someone had left his parents to bleed to death. *But why?* He cried as he had never cried before. He experienced immense trauma seeing the scene of blood…and that too of his very own beloved parents.

He knew one thing for sure; his parents were not coming back. "How can this happen? Why did they leave me? I wish I didn't go to school, then I would have protected them from this tragedy." He started to blame himself. He ran upstairs and called the one person he could always depend on, his brother Mustafa.

Mustafa had just come back from work, greeted his family, and sat down for a little rest. Then the phone started ringing. He picked up the phone. "Hello," he said. On the other side of the phone, all he could make out was a muffled sound. He knew by then that there was something wrong. "Ahmed, talk to me, is something wrong? Did something happen to you in school? Where are Mom and Dad?" Mustafa then heard Ahmed cry, but it was no ordinary cry. Mustafa knew something was very wrong. "Stay right there. I'll be over there soon. Wait for me, okay." Mustafa hurriedly put the phone down, told his family he would be back soon and rushed out the door to his little brother's house.

Younger Ahmed waited for his brother to arrive. He sat in there in the dark, bloodstained basement. He didn't notice that his future self was there watching him, waiting for the right moment to run and plan what to say to Yasser.

The older 23-year-old Ahmed had no right to call Yasser his brother anymore. After what he did, he had no right to belong to the family. He betrayed not only his trust but his loyalty to him too. He continued to watch as his younger self's body was trembling. He had one thing in mind – to destroy his brother. He caused this to happen, and for what?

Money? *Money is poison, it's what drives this world to madness*, he thought.

Soon, the younger 16-year-old Ahmed heard the bell ring. He trudged up the stairs of the basement with a heavy heart and a foggy mind and opened the front door. He saw his brother Mustafa standing there with a worried expression on his face, Ahmed couldn't hold himself anymore. He jumped on his brother, hugged him, and took out all the pain and regret he held up inside, sobbing violently. Mustafa was shocked.

Mustafa should have run down to the basement immediately, but he didn't. He waited for his little brother to settle down and fall asleep from crying too much. Then, he walked down the stairs of the basement. As he saw his parents' bodies, he screamed on the top of his lungs.,

He knew that it was something more than just pushing his mom and dad down the stairs. He found no evidence as to who did this. He was sick to his stomach. He ran upstairs and went straight to the closest bathroom.

23-year-old 'older' Ahmed ran up the stairs, out the door, and to his time-traveling car. He finally knew who had caused all this misery in his life – not only to him but to Mustafa as well. If it wasn't for Yasser, they would be smiling and laughing. They would not be sleeping with a face full of tears, a sick feeling festering within their organs. Yasser was the cause, and he was going to do what he had to. No one would figure out that he was going to destroy his brother's future, and the case of his parents would finally be solved. But first, he had to go back to his house to gather some things he needed for his plan to work. Ahmed headed to his car and left.

16-year-old Ahmed woke up a couple of minutes later and found his brother, Mustafa, on the phone with the police. Ahmed looked like a wreck. His hair was sticking up, his face was all red from crying, and his body looked like someone had beaten him up.

"This is all a dream! Mom and Dad are not dead. When I wake up, this nightmare will be over, and everything will be back to normal," Ahmed whispered to himself. He groaned and started to walk to his brother. When he arrived in the living room, he wanted to see his dad having a conversation with his mom. Instead, he only saw his brother on the phone. He ran to the basement again, only to still see the bloodstained floor and the blankets covering his parents.

By then, Mustafa put down the phone and went to look for his little brother. "Ahmed, the police are coming. We need to explain what happens here, OK?" he said.

"OK," said Ahmed, "but all I know is that they were like that when I got back from school." Then his eyes started to water again; Ahmed had not cried that much in a while. The last time he had gotten this emotional was when Yasser left, leaving his family behind.

In the future, 23-year-old Ahmed continued with his plan in the house of his parents. He planned to give Yasser a feel of what he felt and make him plead guilty. He would scare Yasser by showing up at his house and show him that he knew what Yasser had done.

That will teach him a lesson. He'll learn to never again make a family suffer, or else he'll get what will come to him. I won't stop, even if he begs me to… Just like he did to Mom and Dad.

He was determined to do his part right, and then he and his brother Mustafa would not have to worry about anything. They would have a wonderful life – not like before, but still, they would be a family. They would not worry about someone coming after them and skipping town just to get away from a murderer. Yasser didn't care about Ahmed, but he still went after Mustafa and his family. He wanted to manipulate Ahmed into trusting him, then betray him and leave him alone. Ahmed wouldn't let that happen – he would change everything. He went back to his time-traveling car and left to go back to the past.

16-year-old Ahmed was interrogated by the police. He was asked questions that he didn't know how to answer. They were very eager to get to the bottom of this case and would stop at nothing to get what they needed. They needed to have a lead and then search for evidence. If they couldn't find anything, they would have to leave this case unsolved. Unfortunately, despite their efforts, they found nothing that could lead them to the culprit. It was almost as if a magic wand had been swirled and everything had been erased. With time, the police investigation ceased, leaving Ahmed to go on with his life. With his parents gone, he went to live with his brother. The case was closed since not even one piece of evidence showed up.

After that, Mustafa arrived home with Ahmed. He carried his sleeping brother up to the entrance of his house and rang the doorbell. Nader, his son, opened the door and called for his mother, and then he left. Alia came to the door and was shocked to see her husband standing by the door holding his little brother in his arms.

"What happened? Is everything all right? You rushed out in such a hurry. You got me worried," said Alia.

"Something happened to Mom and Dad. They were found dead in the basement," Mustafa explained, his voice shaking. "I brought Ahmed to live with us. I can't leave him in that house alone. He wouldn't be able to handle it, and I'll also call his school. I need to tell them that Ahmed won't be attending school for a while. He needs some time off," he continued.

23-year-old Ahmed arrived back to the timeline he wanted, ready to make his future right. He waited until he saw Yasser leave the house with a paper in his hands. He went closer to hear what his brother was saying.

"This will, it will not be found. I'll get everything, while the rest of my brothers will get nothing," Yasser said, "I will get everything and be rich, rich, RICH," he screamed joyously. "What do you think of me now, Mom and Dad? I am getting what I want in the end," he grinned like a Cheshire cat laughed, and then walked away.

Ahmed followed him, creeping behind him like a ghost. Ahmed was carrying a bag with a pen, a paper, and a sneaky plan in his mind. He was going to get the will, send it to his brother Mustafa's house, along with a confession note from Yasser. The note would explain why he did it and state that he was planning to drown himself in the river. Then, he would let his brother go to the police station and turn himself in while making sure nothing went wrong and his brother would get what he deserved. It was the perfect plan, and no one would be able to stop him.

16-year-old Ahmed woke up at noon, washed his face, and ran up the stairs. "Mom, Dad. I had the weirdest dream…" He said, then paused. "Hi, Mustafa, where are Mom and Dad, aren't they coming to visit?" Just then, the young Ahmed paused. His eyes were solemn. Reality had silently struck deep within his heart.

"No Ahmed, Mom, and Dad are not coming. They are dead, they were murdered and their case is closed. No one knows who did it," Mustafa said quietly. "You'll be staying with us from now on."

Ahmed knew then that his parents couldn't be with him, and that he had to stay strong for Mustafa and his family. He had to keep them safe from whoever did this and make sure the same thing didn't happen again.

23-year-old Ahmed watched Yasser go to his house and waited for the right moment to go in and confront his brother. He stayed in the abandoned house across the street. When the time would come, he was going to burst in and surprise Yasser with his future self and explain his whole situation.

"I got away with it. I can't believe how the police didn't figure out that I did it. Ahmed would be blamed as the perpetrator," said Yasser. "I never really liked him. He is the cause of all this happening to me. He is the reason for me ending up like this. He should never have been born."

16-year-old Ahmed woke up with a jolt, screaming. He was sweating and violently trembling. What he saw made him terrified; he had no way of sleeping. He just hoped he didn't wake anyone up. Then he heard running footsteps, and his door opened. He saw his brother standing by the door with his wife, staring at him with shocked expressions.

Eyes wide as golf balls, they rushed by his side. Ahmed had a nightmare about Yasser, and how he would find him murdered by the same killer who killed his parents. He was shaking. His whole body moving like a toy moving on its own. He couldn't control himself. The whole situation got him into a bundle of nerves. Even as he tried to speak, all he did was a shiver.

"I-I-I s-s-saw Y-Y-Yasser," Ahmed said, terrified. "H-h-he w-w-was –l-l-lying i-i-in a-a-a p-p-pool o-o-of h-h-his b-bl-blood." He started to cry again.

Mustafa hugged his little brother, soothed him, and put him back to bed. Mustafa was sure he had to visit Yasser the next day to make sure that his other brother was OK. Yasser and Mustafa had been close as kids; they would tell each other everything that was bothering them. And they would be very open to one another. But Yasser had changed with time. Maybe it was the bad company he had gotten himself into or his horrible wife with her lavish lifestyle. His big brother, Yasser, had grown uglier as a human being as the days passed, which had created a divide between Mustafa and Yasser. Nevertheless, Mustafa still cared for Yasser. Hearing Ahmed's words made him worried and he decided to check on his older brother after a long time.

The next day, Mustafa was getting ready to go to Yasser's house when Ahmed came down and saw him. "Ahmed, you stay here, I'll be back. I just need to make sure that Yasser is fine."

Ahmed went to Nader and Najeeb, his twin nephews. He agreed to babysit while Alia was at work and Mustafa was at Yasser's house. He loved the kids; they were the only ones who listened when he talked. It was wonderful to have someone to listen to you and not judge you. Ahmed knew that Mustafa and his wife listened to him, but some extent, they would still just tell him what to do. He needed someone to make him smile, not soothe him.

After Mustafa left Yasser's house, Ahmed knew that something was up. He knew that he was hiding something, but he couldn't point it out. Something was up, Yasser would never lie to him, so why now of all times? Mustafa was at a loss; he had to find out what happened in that house. The loss of their parents affected the brothers a lot, but mostly Ahmed. This made Mustafa worry. What had him confused was how Yasser was not affected at all.

23-year-old Ahmed went to Yasser's house that night. He sneaked through the backyard door. Yasser was starting to regret his decision to keep everything to himself. He loved his brother Mustafa, but he had Ahmed with him. Yasser deeply hated Ahmed. That meant that he had to alienate Mustafa.

"I can't help it if Ahmed is in his life. He is the reason Mom and Dad are dead. I know I'm the one that let them die, but it's still his fault," Yasser muttered to himself.

The 23-year-old Ahmed heard everything, and he felt the world collapse around him. Rage burned inside him like he was a volcano. His eyes were as red as coal, and his aurora was burning like fire. The fierce energy was showing all around him. He rushed in the same room Yasser was in. The door crashed behind him. Wood was everywhere, flying all around them.

"Ahmed...? It can't be!" Yasser stuttered. "You're older! How did you grow so fast?" confusion showing in his voice.

"I'm not from this time. You have done something for our family. You destroyed it by betraying us," Ahmed said.

A look of confusion sprawled across Yasser's face. Finally, Yasser found his voice and spoke. "I didn't mean to do it, it was an accident. Mom and Dad were ignoring me. All they cared about was you." Yasser continued, "I wish you weren't born," he said ominously.

Ahmed took out the paper and pen. Then, he looked at Yasser. "I want you to write a confession to Mustafa," he said, his voice dripping with poison. "Explain everything that happened, as well as why you did it. Then I want you to go to the police and turn yourself in. Tell them that you did it and that you escaped the scene."

Yasser stood there frozen. Thoughts whizzed in his mind. There was no way for him to run. Yasser had to find a way to calm Ahmed down. He decided to go ahead and pen the note just to appease Ahmed. He would tear up the note later. So, he took the pen and paper and started to write without a second thought; Yasser knew that one false move and Ahmed would not stop the rage in him. He'd be dead in no time at all, just like his parents. He was shivering and his bones started to ache. When he was finally done writing, he watched as Ahmed scanned through the words.

Dear Mustafa,

The words I'm about to write are the truth. I killed Mom and Dad. But it was an accident. I did it out of jealousy, and I decided to keep Ahmed away from everything. But I'm regretting it right now. Here is the will. I took it out of our parents' house after you and Ahmed left. Sorry for the lie. I'm not going to see you again after this note. I will be going to the police to confess and stop your suffering.

Take care.

Your Brother,
Yasser.

Ahmed snatched the paper as soon as Yasser was done writing. Yasser had no chance to tear up the paper and watched as Ahmed took the paper, made a copy, and put it in his pocket. When he noticed that no one was around, he looked at Yasser with burning eyes.

"You brought this upon yourself. You were going to betray me. See what happens when your future comes to get you," Ahmed said. "This is your punishment. Don't deny it!"

Yasser was scared. He wanted all this to stop. He started to fear for his life. He started to think he was going crazy. "Why?" Yasser screamed. "I did what you told me. I did everything… Please spare me," Yasser pleaded as tears glimmered in his eyes.

Ahmed told Yasser to follow him. He led Yasser to the car, started the engine, and drove to the police station. Ahmed watched as Yasser confessed to the police. He was put in handcuffs and taken away.

After that, he went to Mustafa's house and dropped the letter. He then went to his car and returned to the future.

16-year-old Ahmed woke up with a startle, went down for breakfast at his brother's house, and was surprised to see the police. The lawyer was there too.

"Yasser confessed to everything he had done." Mustafa was weeping silently. "We know," the police officer said, "He came to us and confessed. He will be put in jail with no one to bail him out. We have nothing to worry about since the killer confessed, you'll be fine," he continued.

They moved to their parents' house and cleaned everything. Finally, their life changed for the better.

23-year-old Ahmed's life was also changed; he had a job, lived in Mustafa's old house, and had his own family. He had a wife named Sara and a son named Jaber.

Since Mustafa moved to his parents' house, he gave Ahmed his house after he married. He grinned; a new picture was put up in the house, a picture of the new family. Mustafa, Ahmed, their wives, and kids. Life was great and Ahmed never forgot about his parents. His life had changed, but he was happy. His future had become better, but he still left one thing: the rocket booster, just in case he needed it later.

Pam at the Poolside

By Pam Jackson Murell

Friday

As she sat at the corner table in a tall orange leather seat, Pam felt somewhat hidden, visible but unnoticed amidst the bustling Friday morning brunch. This was her favorite corner at the Club Lounge, the restaurant she visited daily. There at the corner table was a direct view of everyone entering the place. She could watch the folks coming in to go to brunch and she could also see the pool and its surrounding deck area. It was such a quiet pleasure to watch the families and friends at brunch, those at the pool, and those moving between the two places. Pretending invisibility as she watched worked in her imagination, but probably not in reality. People noticed her when they came in, and when they did, she tossed out her brightest smile, mouthing the words good morning more often than she spoke them.

This time allowed her to enjoy the space and the freedom to move attention from what was in front of her eyes to what was behind them. Her thoughts danced between the people she saw with the lives she imagined they were living and the life she was living. The dance of her thoughts was offbeat and chaotic in the apartment, on the 9th floor of the residential hotel, which was where Dad was dying.

At the poolside, on the 29th floor, she could forget about him for a few minutes and enjoy thoughts that were soothing, elegant, and comfortable... or at the very least, distracting.

In the apartment was her dad, a strong, wise old soul who had been in and out of her life for her 40 years, sometimes in a good way, sometimes in a bad way. He was a loving, caring, and generous man who had been a big part of her life in a positive way for segments of it, though not the whole way through. The relationship had moved from loving and sweet to empty and non-existent, to chaotic and stressful, to distant and tolerant, and now back to intimate and sweet. And now here she was at its end, and it couldn't have been more painful, nor more disappointing. Now was not the time for him to go.

At his bedside, Pam's attention was always divided between him and the machines being used to keep him alive. He was terminally ill, and she knew he did not want to be kept alive. In America, he had signed all the proper documents stating that he did not want to be resuscitated. But they had traveled overseas for one last trip. He chose Dubai, a place he had dreamed of visiting for years, and he had fallen too ill to take the flight back to the States. Now, here in the United Arab Emirates, they did not allow for such medical directives and they did not honor those directives from abroad. She found herself not wanting to have to be the one to end his life, but now, at least she did not have to be the one to tell the medical staff to unplug the machines. He was suffering, and neither of them wanted that. The local law allowed for her father's machines to be turned off if three separate specialized doctors agreed that his life could not be saved. Two had already come and gone and it was Pam's choice to call the third one. She did not have to be one to tell them to turn off the ventilator, and yet, she had to be the one to make the call to the person who would say it. She had picked up the phone to dial that third specialist more than a hundred times and had hung up each time, afraid, unsure, and hating to have to be responsible. After three days of this, she left the apartment, allowing herself to be whisked away by the elevator to another floor, and, as far as she was concerned, another world... if only for a few minutes, or an hour.

At the poolside restaurant, she enjoyed being in the orange leather chair with its tall back. In the chair, she could pretend to have the sense of safety and comfort she used to find in her father's arms, but no longer. The chair had wheels, so she enjoyed turning a bit here and there to see what was going on. This was her safe place, and in that restaurant, besides the comfort of the chair, she enjoyed the comfort of the staff that knew her and her father. They had arrived from the States more than a week ago and she had not cooked a meal in all that time. Every staff member, chef, host, and attendant knew her and most had brought food to the room and knew of her father's condition. It was just the two of them in Dubai and they had received a lot of support when his illness worsened. They all seemed to be travelers on the journey to the end of his life.

But this day, this moment, with Pam in the orange chair, he still had life in him and was downstairs resting. In this spot, she took a break from thinking about him and enjoyed letting her imagination wander with the people she watched. There was the mother, who was apparently from France, with her husband and two daughters. She saw the mother and daughters every day, but never the husband. He was at work, according to the restaurant staff who gossiped to Pam. The two girls were young and lovely, probably ages five and seven, she guessed. One was whiny, though, and loud. So very annoying. The mother was nice and sweet and tolerant, but her eyes displayed the costs of all that niceness with their puffiness and dark circles underneath. Her thin skin did not look healthy vibrant. Her thin hair looked like it used to be luscious, rich, and full. As Pam watched from her orange chair, she noticed that she felt like the woman's hair looked... once vibrant, but now lost, mistreated, neglected, and disempowered. Pam wondered whether this woman didn't understand how to take care of her hair in this heat. Here in Dubai, it must have been very different as compared to France. Or perhaps she just did not spend energy managing it because her time and attention were elsewhere. She looked like she used to know how to manage hair care, but now, there was just depletion and exhaustion. Not nourished, not regenerated, not vibrant, not vital. Just like Pam.

The girls were a different story, full of energy and light; their hair was beautiful and long and thick and shiny, clothes clean and dainty. Pam soon learned that they weren't visitors traveling through on holiday. They moved here for his job, according to Mr. Anil, the waiter who always liked to whisper stories in Pam's ear to make her smile or at least lighten her mood. He knew he succeeded when her eyes would brighten. Mr. Anil always noticed Pam when she was in her orange chair though he could tell she preferred to go unnoticed. Pam felt so lucky that she could watch the people and feel like they were so oblivious to her. Did the beautiful, rich orange leather chair make her invisible, or was it who she was being, soft and vulnerable, isolated and alone, wanting to escape but not able to do so? While she dreamed of escaping her current circumstances, she did not want to go with these travelers; their lives did not look better than hers. Since she faced no better option, she chose to head back downstairs to her father. She liked being with him but not with the machines; their beeping, whooshing, whirring and blinking annoyed her.

Before she rose to leave the restaurant to return to her father's bedside, Pam reflected on how she'd gotten to this place. It had been a long road of trials and tribulations. As a young child, she grew up with Mom, Dad, a nice house, two cars, dog... Happy, carefree, and at ease. She was a spunky, feisty, curious child who asked tons of questions, explored all kinds of mysterious things, and loved sitting in her father's home office in the house. The place was dark, with cherry-wood-paneled walls, mahogany-colored carpet, windows draped with heavy curtains, and the smell of the tobacco from the pipe he smoked in there. It was here in the office that she rested her mind and body after her adventures, listening to her dad on the phone or talking to himself as he worked. She adored him and he adored her. He loved her bright, keen thinking and that she listened to the answers he gave to all the tons of questions she asked. She was beautiful inside and out, he always told her. Back then, Pam had believed him and felt strengthened and reinforced by his affection and appreciation of her. It gave her fuel to go be boisterous and rowdy at school, carefree and unwilling to tolerate boredom and mediocrity. Even if she was on the playground examining the gravel in a corner, her petite frame, bright brown eyes, and long pony-tailed hair were always vibrant and radiant. It was as though every part of her was excited by what she discovered, even when it was quite ordinary. She was a sponge ready to absorb every single exciting thing the universe offered her. She was a blessed child, free to think and act, and afraid of nothing. And, as Pam sat still in the rich supple orange leather of the chair, she marveled at that girl, wondering what she would have been like had she stayed around, and knowing exactly when and how that bouncy, bold, brave girl she was disappeared. A piece of that girl remained with Pam; she was curious and interested in the world and had spent years studying, training, and traveling to learn all kinds of things. The bounciness had been replaced with seriousness, though, and the need to collect knowledge came from a need for security as much as it did from a sense of curiosity.

Saturday

The day was a long one. She had not been able to make it upstairs for morning coffee because of the many visits by nursing and hospice staff to the apartment. Now, it was 8 pm and everyone had come and gone. They would not return until after the third specialist had come to assess her father. "Tomorrow, or the next day," they had said. Pam sat by the pool, on the wicker brown sofa this time, not the orange chair. It would only be tomorrow or the next day if she called the specialist. She had not. The night sky was cloudless, dark, and heavy, unusually so, which matched her mood perfectly… but not the mood in the pool. There, two fathers and their daughters were splashing around at the far end of the pool under the gentle glow of the soft orange lights being used to offset the night's darkness. Pam basked as much in the glow of the lanterns as she did in the joyful vibrations of the men's voices and the girls' laughter. The laughter, like the water, had a shimmery, vibrant, energizing quality, and danced in the night air. Pam could feel her heavy heart and dull spirit-lifting. Maybe, she thought, *I can make the call. This is about freeing my father, which frees me too.*

The men were brothers, in town from Cape Town, South Africa. She knew this from Mr. Anil, of course. The girls were ten and eleven years old and were competitive swimmers who were in the pool playing, rather than training, for the first time in months. They laughed and giggled and splashed around. The dads stood in the pool chatting with one another. *Frolic* was the word that came to Pam's mind as she watched all of them.

She had no memories of frolicking with her dad or even other girls her age and envied the ones she now watched. She had been a competitive swimmer too, from the age of five through to high school, and her dad was an assistant coach on the team for the first five of those years. Her memories were of him, poolside, with a whistle in his mouth or around his neck, demanding and commanding... No frolicking, no fun, and not much joy. Notably, the joy and intimacy she shared with her dad in his office at home were never shared by the poolside. After the 2hour daily practice, Pam was always ready to leave, but her dad wasn't.

"Pam, the worst thing in life you can be is a quitter! Get focused, get stronger, be better, and keep swimming," he'd insist. He wanted the best for her; he always did. Being of service was his way of loving her. It is what his dad had done for him and it was what he knew to do. His way was just the hard way, and though Pam understood it, she did not like it. Her reply was always, "Yes, Dad." What she wanted to say was, "Why can't you be nice to me or at least just leave me alone?" Unfortunately, her silent command was honored and, by her tenth birthday, her parents' marriage was failing. Soon after, her father moved away, indeed, he left her. And that was the place in life where the vibrant, bold, brave, boisterous little girl in love with the world died. The bouncy steps lost, the bright curiosity muted as the tons of questions evaporated, and her general interest in the world around her died a fast death. It would take a decade for some of that little girl to resurface in Pam.

As her attention returned to watching the two girls in the pool, Pam realized she had no memories of times like these with her half-sister. They did not grow up together and had only met when Pam was in her late-twenties. Lisa was the product of the next marriage, the one that helped maintain the distance between Pam and her father. The demands of the new wife and child served to keep his attention and resources during Pam's junior high and high school careers. It wasn't until she traveled from the Midwest to the East Coast to college that geography allowed reconciliation. *Initially, though, Dad was open to reconciliation and I was not,* Pam recalled for herself. It took many overtures, dinner invitations, gifts, and miles for her to warm to him and begin to rebuild their relationship. He was dedicated, dutiful, and committed, driving the 120 miles from Washington, DC, to Philadelphia to see her several times a month. She eventually reciprocated his care. She even took a job that required her to be in DC every Friday, so she could travel at her own expense, see her dad on Friday nights for dinner, and then head back on Saturdays. Over time, a phenomenal relationship of trust, camaraderie, love, affection, and partnership was created between them. It took several more years, though, before she was willing to meet his wife and their daughter. He was patient and gracious, but in time, there was no longer a wife to meet, only Lisa.

Pam and Lisa met at Lisa's mother's funeral. Lisa was in her mid-teens and the sweetest, loveliest girl. Not surprisingly, the two clicked right away. Pam had compassion for Lisa's loss and guilt at her stubbornness in not choosing to get involved with her father's second family sooner. They were opposites in personality but looked like they could be twins, if not for the decade-plus difference in age. Lisa was sad at her mother's passing but relieved that her mother was in peace. She had breast cancer which had been discovered way too late, in part due to a long battle with Lupus. She was too weak to take the chemo and, after one treatment, gave up and surrendered the fight before there was a battle. No one had to deal with her being on life support and having to decide to end her life. She was gone before it got that far. Lisa had said it all happened too fast for her to even understand what was happening and their dad was paralyzed with sorrow and shock. When he could express his feeling, he had told her, "I feel like I am drowning in mud... it is warm and comforting to my body but smothering me none-the-less. I am comforted by the knowledge that Lisa's mom is no longer suffering and, yet I am devastated to be left alone. How can I go on?" Pam, having no answer, found the only response she could provide was to stay. They lived in DC and she commuted back to Philadelphia to finish her last year of course work and take her qualifying exams for her doctoral program. After she became a candidate with fellowship money, she no longer needed to teach and thus did not have to be on campus. Pam stayed in DC and commuted to Philadelphia once or twice a month. The time was a blessing for all three of them. Her father worked and buried his grief in his service to clients. As a social worker and therapist for juveniles in the DC court system, he found himself in the presence of pain deeper and more profound than his own, and when he could be the one to help make it dissipate in others, a bit of his went with it. Pam was a great mentor, advisor, and presence for Lisa as she finished her high school career. As a dancer and scientist, Lisa used these outlets to invest her passions and pain with Pam, who provided an audience, a ride, a meal, or anything else Lisa needed to flourish. There was such a sweetness to the sisterhood because they were both so open and so raw. Their time was joyful and adventuresome even with the backdrop of sorrow that took a long time to disintegrate. Theirs was a remarkable time of love, attentiveness, and intimacy for all three, and as they grew their bond, so too did they grow their accomplishments. The girls graduated together, Pam with her doctoral degree in economics, Lisa with her bachelor's degree in psychology. By that time, the healing had been complete, and the family of three was restored to wholeness; each had the strength to go their own way.

Pam's dad became her shining star of joy and support when she got engaged to be married, so proudly escorting her down the aisle at the glorious and intimate wedding he helped her plan and finance. Then he became her rock and her salvation five years later when her husband died, suddenly and but not quite unexpectedly during one of his flights overseas to provide medical support to troops fighting in Afghanistan. Her father had gotten the news first and then, without telling her, accompanied her to the Army base so she could learn first-hand from her husband's commanding officer. She never made it back to the apartment she shared with her husband and stayed in her father's house and loving care for two years before she found the strength to be on her own again. It was his turn to restore her to wholeness.

Some years after that, now, her heart felt heavy as she reflected on her travels through time with her dad, and the hard truth that the traveling was at its end. Not only that, she was the one who would have to make the call to the person who would end his life. Today, the staff had confirmed that he was in comatose, that his level of brain activity was low, and he had reached the state called brain death. After 24 hours in that state, there was no reason to keep him on the ventilator. The specialist would confirm that and would be authorized to disconnect the machines. It was time to make the call, the nurses warned her with exasperation, barely showing hidden behind limited patience and generous understanding.

She knew her father did not want to be in this state, and there was no lack of clarity in all the legal and medical documents he had initiated weeks earlier when the news of the stage IV pancreatic cancer was delivered. Lesions, they said. Her dad had been complaining of shortness of breath, had endured a long-term battle with congenital heart disease, and both had assumed that it was time for medication adjustments. When the meeting was held to discuss the screenings, x- rays, and the series of examinations he had experienced in the prior week, she expressed that she did not understand what lesions had to do with her father's shortness of breath. Finally, they got to the place where the doctors could say all there was to say. Stage IV cancer, with tumors, also known as lesions, on or in his lungs, liver, pancreas, and stomach. It was as if a brick hit her in the head when she finally understood 'lesions.' She had been in the doctor's office with her dad, and Lisa was on speaker on the cell phone, more than 5,000 miles away. She sat, numb and speechless, limp even. At that moment, staring at her father who suddenly looked very far away and as if in a haze, she realized that she was the only one in the room being blindsided by the information. Cancer. Stage IV. They could do chemo, but it would not cure the cancer, just buy time; they'd found out about it too late. She sat still, frozen and stunned, hearing that people were still speaking, but not understanding anymore of the words. She was startled by the noise the phone made as it slipped from her hand, clattering as it hit the floor. It was unharmed and rang out with Lisa's voice yelling, "Hello? Are you still there?"

When Pam and her father had traveled to Dubai for her father's last wish to see the Middle East, Lisa could not arrange her schedule to join them until her semester was over in a few days. She taught neuropsychology and clinical psychology and was on faculty at two different universities in the U.S. *She is a psychologist. Those people know how to handle stuff like this. Lisa is the one that should be in the room, not me, the economist*, thought Pam at the time. Lisa was the person who acted calmly in the face of any circumstance, never frozen, always unstoppable. As Pam retrieved the phone from the floor, the doctors continued their discussion with Lisa, asking questions, collecting information, and making plans. Both Pam and her father were silent as she continued to absorb the reality that her father was neither shocked nor stunned. She would learn more about that later.

At the poolside, longing for her sister, Pam, rose from the sofa, knowing it was time to return to the apartment. She noted the girls had migrated to the chaise lounges with their big white cups of hot chocolate and the dads had remained in the pool, still chatting and laughing and enjoying one another's company. She hoped and prayed that her sister could get to Dubai soon. She wanted to enjoy her company and not feel alone and lost, untethered, afraid, and sorrowful. She wanted the time back, the time in DC when the three of them had become united in strength and courage and faith, recovering from the loss of another. She wanted to be on the chaise lounges with Lisa, two sisters chattering away with hot chocolate and the comfort of a dad close by, available, healthy, and ready to be of support and interest.

Sunday

As the sun rose on the day and peeked through the drawn curtains of her father's bedroom, Pam stirred quietly in the chair beside his bed. She had not slept, though she drifted a bit into a state of unconsciousness at a few points during the night. Her father had a high temperature, his body radiated heat, and he twitched and moved despite his comatose state. It was as if he had something going on, some sort of conversation or argument he was participating in with someone. Pam wondered if indeed her father was yelling at God. He had done so many times over the last few weeks of his life and he had even yelled at her about God, so much so that it seemed as though he would have a stroke and that, not cancer, would kill him. She wanted death for her dad, so he could have peace, and yet, she so did not want to lose him, and she did not want to be the one to pray for his death secretly. She felt like she had just found him again even though 'just' had been almost a decade. Stopping suddenly in her thoughts, she realized how much time had passed since her husband had died and how it was her dad sleeping in a chair by her bedside as she tossed and turned and cried out in the night, feeling robbed and cheated by God. Her husband had been the absolute love of her life, yet it had taken some time to figure out how to be married. By the time they had gotten it right, he was gone. She had cursed the Lord back then for taking her joy too soon and causing such a deadness to be born in her... The same deadness that had grown when her father went away when she was a girl. Was that deadness going to come again for a third strike?

More than anything in the world, Pam wanted to take away her dad's anger and she felt so very helpless at being unable to. Long before the discovery of the cancer, life was not going the way Dad wanted for himself and he was very open about it. Last January one of his clients, a twelve-year-old girl, Philomena, had killed her father and siblings, and Pam's dad felt responsible. For two years, the girl had been assigned to him by the District of Columbia Superior Court, a ward of the court, after being removed from her home because she was abusing her younger brothers. Dad had not felt like he was making a difference in counseling with the girl, and reported regularly to the court that alternative plans should be created. He was ignored. Even after 50 years of service as a therapist and 30 of them with that court system, he was saddened by their lack of responsiveness and frustrated at the lack of options. He had pursued a placement for Phil in a youth camp in rural Maryland, where she could be free of urban pressures and enjoy more of nature to heal her mind and soothe her soul. However, she had no willingness to go and he could not get the courts to mandate the move. They weren't paying attention and then it was too late. The call from the police in Ward 5 had come to Dad quite regularly because of Phil and so when the next one came, he thought little of it. His automatic response was to say, "I'll be right there," hop in his car with his loyal companion, Mr. Bones, his boxer, and drive over to the house. Phil did not live at home with her family, since her assignment to a group-home facility a few months ago, but visited them almost every day. When things got rough, after finishing with the police each time there wasn't an arrest (which was about every third call), Dad, Phil, and Mr. Bones would go for a walk so that Phil could talk and process her anger. They'd finish off at McDonald's, always with a

McFlurry, Big Mac, and large fries for Phil and a bowl of water for Mr. Bones. Dad never ate.

When he arrived, Dad was surprised by the ambulance and immediately knew. He couldn't even get out of the car. The police captain at the scene knew him, though; he knew his car and even knew Mr. Bones. He walked over to the car after noticing its driver was frozen at the wheel, staring at the scene. Phil was not in sight, already in the back of the police car, handcuffed and still raging, blind with the fury that came from the unknown place Dad had never been able to identify. The captain stood silently by the car, waiting to have Dad's attention. Fifteen minutes went by before Mr. Bones finally broke the silence with a loud growl and bark as he recognized Phil in the police car as it rolled past. *The details didn't matter*, the captain thought. He knew Dad felt that he failed and all was lost. Delivering the news, four dead on the scene, one adult male and three male youths, all by knife wounds, the captain paused, acknowledged to himself that no reaction would be forthcoming, and walked slowly towards his car, shoulders slack, head down, and body fatigued.

It took a week for Pam to learn what happened. The night of the killing, her father had eventually made his way to the jail and had a conversation with Phil, who was far from remorseful and unyielding in her righteousness. The universe violated her by allowing her mother to die at her birth and Phil was unwilling to ever find forgiveness in the heart. She blamed everyone and lived life as the adversary to all. Never had such a client been assigned to her father and the experience broke him. The police called Pam to come to get her father as they watched him sit immobilized behind the wheel of his car in the parking lot all night. By the time Pam arrived, knocked on the window of the car, and spoke to her father, he was willing to move, but not talk. She followed him home, let him get into the house, and took care of the dog out back. As she left her dad, she kissed his still unresponsive face, not knowing what else to say or do. Later that day, she headed back to her father's house and found him in the same chair with the same expression and the same lack of responsiveness. It took two more days before he would talk and, even then, only to his therapist. After a month, he started the processing of his feelings, refusing to see his other clients, most of whom had been reassigned after he missed the weekly court-appointed therapy sessions.

When he finally started engaging with people and returning to his routine, the physical symptoms of failing health became noticeable, and, surprisingly, he made it a point to get himself to the doctor's office. Several visits to specialists, MRIs, and other tests later another devastating blow landed for Pam's dad, none of which he shared with her, as she learned later, and much to her dismay. He had cancer. If he had taken action immediately, they might have been able to do some aggressive rounds of chemo and get it handled. He didn't get treatment early enough, though, because he had quit already. The same passionate, fierce, determined guy who yelled at his ten-year-old daughter to never quit, quit. The day Phil killed her father was the day he quit.

Hence, when the cancer news came, he was fine. *No, no chemo for me,* he had thought. What he told the doctors was "Sure, I'll schedule an appointment right away." But he didn't. A year later with the Stage IV diagnosis and Pam in the room, his reaction was in line with the confirmation that his plan to die as close to being executed. Suicide by cancer. Pam had found out by accident when she got the electronic medical record from the States after her father had fallen ill in Dubai. Her father had known about the lesions and the potential for cancer more than a year earlier and had taken no action. Pam understood it all intellectually, but not emotionally.

Still at the bedside, Pam rose knowing it was time to get upstairs. This day, a special one, she would not be alone at the restaurant. Sullie and Bob were coming to visit Dad and they wanted to meet with her first to find out what the latest news was. They had flown from San Francisco and Virginia respectively to visit after learning their best friend of 50 years from college would not be making it home to the States. Both men had been shocked to get the call from their friend nearly a month ago, with word of the illness, its terminality, and the intent to travel to Dubai for one last adventure before dying. They packed their things, made plans, and headed east as soon as they could, but were arriving too late to enjoy being with their friend, 'Jack Rabbit' as he had been called by them. Jackson had been a sprinter in college and somehow could manage to sprint longer distanced races, becoming known as Jack Rabbit for his undergraduate and graduate career. Much to his chagrin, these two never stopped calling him that even when they were in their 60s and far from able to sprint any distance at all.

Bob, Sullie, and Pam had lunch poolside as they enjoyed the photos of the time Pam and her father were able to see a bit of the city. They had only made it to the Jumeirah Beach Hotel, to Jamie Oliver's restaurant inside the hotel, and the beach. Dad was a supreme fan of food and was an experienced and talented cook. It was one of his creative expressions and he used food and cooking in his work with children and in caring for his family. Sunday dinner was always at Dad's and each week Pam would never know who she'd find around the table or what would be on it. Sometimes there was a seafood feast with shrimp prepared three or four different ways plus a smoked whitefish, steamed crab, or lobster, roasted scallops, or mussel. Whatever his mood, he cooked, and feast days sometimes included just Pam or Pam plus ten other people. The conversations were always lively and random because the people were, and the food always caused momentary lapses in the conversation when moaning could be heard, or lip-smacking at the least. Jack was known for pleasing people and that pleased him.

At Jamie Oliver's, Dad moaned and smacked his lips as he fell in love with the truffle tagliatelle with its finely shaved wild black truffles in butter, parmesan, and nutmeg sauce that was 'finger-licking good.' He'd had it two days in a row, making Pam profoundly grateful that he was eating. She had photos of him with the wide, thin, slippery pasta noodles dangling, first in front of his face on the fork, then half-eaten, hanging down his chin. Rather than lip-smacking, it was a slurpy sound that signaled his great satisfaction.

After each meal, they had sat for hours at the beach, the first day looking at the sunset behind the Burj Al Arab. It was a fantastic place to enjoy the fullest, fattest moments of the yellow sun turning orange and pink before disappearing along the horizon. The Burj provided a dramatic contrast to the skyline, standing all alone with its odd yet striking geometric shape. The curvy structure was one of the three tallest hotels in the world; at over 320 meters, it was an architectural marvel captured in the photos Pam shared. On the second day, after the meal, they spent time at the long wooden walking bridge that led to the Pier Chic Restaurant. Dad had spent four decades of his life as a carpenter in addition to his social work, and the bridge fascinated him with its rich dark cherry wood coloring preserved even in the blazing temperatures of Dubai. He sat for hours marveling at the construction and the coating and was oblivious to both the heat and the photos Pam took. She'd captured the oddest smile on his face, one that showed a deep sense of satisfaction and yet discomfort, all at the same time. It seemed to perfectly portray what she imagined was his experience, not just at the time of the photo but also more generally here at the end of his life.

The other photos that Pam had to share were of her father on the balcony of the room which had majestic views of the city. There were three different palaces within a kilometer or so of the hotel and visible from their side of the building, including the palace of one of the members of the royal family, Sheikh Hamdan bin Rashid Al Maktoum, the Deputy Ruler of Dubai and the Minister of Finance and Industry of the United Arab Emirates (UAE). Pam had a hard time understanding the lengthy names and barely followed the relationships, but the beauty of the palace, even from the distance, was notable for her. She had a photo of her dad with the bright lights of the palace in the distance behind his thin frail build. To the left, one of the largest mosques in the city, Zabeel Masjid, with a capacity for more than 5,000 prayers was within two blocks and the night time views of these remarkably designed buildings were glorious with lighting that seemed so soft and elegant, yet shining in such a bright way, accentuating the contours of the stark square of the building contrasted with its round domes and statuesque minarets. The minaret, Pam had learned on one of the tours her father could not make, was a tall, slender tower that was a significant feature of every mosque, and was one of the earliest characteristics of Islamic architecture. The dome was symbolic of the vault of heaven, a place her dad swore he was not going. The Zabeel mosque was so close that Pam had a somber photo of her dad at the balcony at dusk looking at the mosque with it visible and identifiable in the background. The gray sky and his posture captured the mood perfectly. Not quite resigned, but full of strength, courage, wisdom, and surrender. Rather than defeat, there was a sense of accomplishment. He would walk out of this life with his head held high and proud; consciously choosing death in the same way he consciously chose life after almost losing it twice before. Long before the cancer came, there was congestive heart failure, the high blood pressure, the triple bypass surgery – he had faced life-threatening illness before, done battle, and won. This time, he did not bother to battle. because he knew he would not win. His body would be killed by the chemo; he had known that a year ago.

Bob and Sullie were glad for the opportunity to connect with Jack, even if only digitally. They recalled the funniest stories from their college days, most of which Pam had heard at least once before, but was nonetheless grateful to experience again, especially the ones about her father when his cooking skills had not 'fully developed' as Bob liked to say. There was the time he set the kitchen on fire and smoke-damaged a 10-story apartment building, causing more than 150 students to have to run out into the cold, 25-degree Fahrenheit temperatures (or -3 Celsius as Pam was learning in the UAE) late in the night, for five hours. And the time when one of his first seafood fests had not been so wonderful and six of his dearest friends were in the hospital suffering from food poisoning and dehydration.

The more recent example that always kept them chuckling was that Dad cooked dinner twice every night, once for the dog and once for himself. His dedication was sweet and notable, though barely comprehendible as far as Pam and Bob were concerned. Sullie claimed to understand and appreciate the devotion.

Jack adopted dogs and typically chose boxers who often were abused by their first owner. The adoption process, typically because of a court-appointed guardian, in the case of dogs owned by drug dealers, was lengthy, well-supervised, and highly intensive. And Jack took the responsibility seriously, willingly participating in interviews and home visits before the dogs were placed in his care. He took to cooking their meals as a part of his commitment to show them love and generosity when he'd known it was foreign to them. His search for just the right day-old meats from the grocery stores for the dogs made him a big friend of the butchers who felt privileged to be in deep discussions about their products with Jack. They saved the best leftovers of each day's meats for him and he got great markdowns on the prices too. Pam always enjoyed the smells as her dad sautéed the meats, usually prepared in a hot wok, with steamed broccoli, and boiled potatoes. Despite the absence of seasonings, the meal always smelled good and caused a slight bit of envy on Pam's part as she watched the hot food get mixed with the 'regular' dog food and be served; Mr. Bones was the one who would always look at Dad first, lick his hand to say thanks, then start to eat. Max, Rudy, Che, and the Angel never bothered.

After lunch, Bob and Sullie headed downstairs to spend time with Jack and to say goodbye. They left Pam by the poolside with a letter that Jack had sent them in the event of this occasion. They'd mentioned the letter when the arrangements were being made for them to travel to Dubai, but Pam had since forgotten. Now she sat in her favorite corner, in the orange chair, wondering about her father's words. She assumed she knew. For sure he would be reiterating that he did not want to be kept alive on a machine and probably he'd reiterate that he would want Pam and Lisa to be of one accord. She hoped he'd say something that would motivate her to call the specialist. She had gotten to the point of dialing and waiting to hear the receptionist answer the line, and then she'd hang up. Whatever else the letter might say, she really could not imagine. Their last conversation had been just over a week ago and as far as she was concerned they had both said everything there was to say.

Dear Pam,
I am dying or dead by now. Sorry if this bothers you, but I am fine with it.

Pam thought to herself, and wanted to scream at him, *Yes, of course it bothers me!* Instead, she continued reading the letter.

I hope you know how much I am at peace with this end of my life. I do mind leaving you and your sister. You both are such wonderful and accomplished women. I am so proud of you and the adversity you have overcome to get where you are today. I am done with my contributions to the world and satisfied with the difference I have made for people. I failed

156

more often than I succeeded, and I did not reach all my goals, but I did give everything I had every day.

I will miss seeing who else you will become, but` I live satisfied with who I became. I am grateful that we had the life we lived including all the ups and the downs; the absenteeism and the forgiveness; the losses and the gains. I hope you know how much all of that makes life so worth living. It is that journey, not the destination, that matters, and I feel authoritative about this since I am at the final destination. I fought the good fights and the necessary fights... Some unnecessary ones too, more than should have been. I hope you fight the good fights and avoid the unnecessary ones. You have so much talent and joy to share with the world. I love you and I bless you and I thank you for your friendship, your faith, and your forever love.

Thank you for being with Lisa and for Lisa and may that always continue.

May your very best of today be the worst of all your tomorrows.

May you let yourself feel all the moments of joy and all the moments of sorrow.

May you cling to life and fight for living. And never stop being forgiving.

May your heart sing and dance and be filled with glee. And may you let everyone enjoy you being the way you be.

May your light shine forever brightly,

And may your steps be forever lightly,

As in heart and soul and mind, may you always be kind.

To yourself and every other one, I love you from the moon to the sun and back again.

With love,

Dad.

P.S. pull the plug.

P.P.S. By now you may have noticed that I knew about the cancer long before it was formally announced to us that day in the doctor's office with Lisa on the phone. I knew about it and did not tell you. Truth is that I am tired of living in this ugly world and I have seen enough of it. After Phil's death, my desire to fight was gone. No more fighting for the abused and mistreated, no more fighting to empower the downtrodden, no more fighting, not even the cancer. No more fighting for the angry children abusing themselves because of the abuse they received. No more fighting to protect the innocent child from that abuse of an angry parent. I knew I was done with the fighting. I had none left in me and no reason to go find it somewhere else. I wanted peace the only way I knew how.

Numb in her chair and cold from the shock on the page, Pam's tears wet it, smudging the ink. She ached for her dad and the resignation he felt… or had felt. She understood completely and wondered what difference she could have made had she known. Never one to spend time on what could have been, Pam's attention returned to the letter only to realize she was at its end.

I am ready to go, Pam. I hope I do soon.

Monday

The taxi that took Bob and Sullie back to the airport brought Lisa from it. As she arrived at the hotel and the front desk rang the apartment, Pam held the phone unsure of what to think or feel. In one set of thoughts, she was grateful for the companionship and to finally be not alone by the bedside. On the other, she wondered, *Will I have to debate this woman about Dad's wishes? Does she have any clue what I have been going through for the last month? How will she react when she sees him still comatose but actively twitching, feverish, and seemingly quite fitful?* Pam had such disbelief in the doctor's vow that the brain activity had ceased days ago when she watched the movement of her father's body. "Involuntary muscle action unrelated to or signaled by the brain, spinal reflexes," they had said. Reflex movements were common, as was something called the Lazarus sign, where the patients' arms moved as though reaching for someone. Luckily, she had not witnessed this in her dad's behavior.

Lisa's arrival was as uplifting as it was overflowing with her radiant energy that always filled any room creating a big presence in stark contrast to her petite figure. She gave Pam the biggest hug and kiss, did the same for her father, and turned back to Pam. "It seems as if his time has come, dear. Are you ready?" she asked. Pam stared, blankly.

Ready? Pam's face asked though no sound passed her lips.

Pam looked at her father, Lisa, at the floor, as he started to struggle with each breath. Pam could feel her veins constrict as she started to be acquainted with death so closely.

The low humming and whooshing sounds in the room ended as did her father's seemingly ceaseless involuntary spasms. Pam froze as she witnessed the moment. But why was Lisa so brave? Lisa stood there with not an ounce of emotion displayed. "We probably should say a prayer… Do you know one?" she whispered, seeming to not want to wake her father.

Pam automatically started reciting the Lord's Prayer while grabbing the bible by the bedside to find Psalm 23 and pass it to her sister. In the silence that followed, they sat still, close to the bed, with their hands resting on some part of their father, watching and waiting as he continued to breathe on his own. As his breathing slowed, more than a half-hour passed before it quickened noticeably, causing the girls to move closer, each holding one hand of their father and one of the other.

Instinctively they started talking to him.

"We love you, Dad."

"We'll miss you."

"Sweet dreams."

"Goodbye."

The breath ended and in the stillness another hour and then another went by before either girl moved.

It was at that moment when Pam howled in tears. Daddy was gone. Gone forever. The paramedics and doctors arrived soon after and attended to her father's body. Pam had lost all composure. Lisa knew that she needed to do something. She took Pam to the place that was her comfort.

At the poolside, finally with her sister, Pam, sat in her favorite orange chair watching Lisa learn how to swivel in the other one. No longer feeling alone and lost, Pam felt peaceful and even joyful, and she believed her father had felt. Free from the artificial life-preserving bondage, done with the fighting once and for all, Dad was in another place, one that was a good one, Pam hoped. Pam was happy for the camaraderie of her sister and thoughtful of the two girls who had been here at the pool just recently. Lisa seemed to be delighted to be there, enjoying the companionship of her sister. Lisa knew Pam had been suffering as much if not more than her father. She needed to be there for her sister and balm her sorrows.

"Lisa, I am so grateful to you. You are courageous and brave! I could never have been able to handle Daddy's death without you being here." Pam's gratitude was deep as her words rang out from a place deep in her body.

Lisa replied, "Pam, you did the hardest part. You were here, every day, by his side, through every breath, every tortured movement, and every conversation with the doctor. I did not come here to free Dad... I came here to free you."

Afia's Revenge

By Nudrat Majid

Afia lived in a small village in Pakistan called Chak Paar. The people of this small village were poor, hardworking, and humble. They lived together as a tight-knit community leading simple lives. Although it was the modern era, the only means of transport were bicycles and donkeys. They looked out for each other and solved each other's problems.

Afia was the youngest daughter of her parents, Younus and Maryam. She was 18 years old and lived alone with her elderly parents. At only 5'3", she was of small stature with a thin wiry frame. She was demure but had a steely determination and internal strength that belied her size. She dressed simply – her hair was always in a very practical style, one that was suited to the daily chores of village life.

Village life was simple – every morning, the soothing sound of the *azaan* woke Afia up before sunrise, when she would get ready to pray the *Fajr* prayers and start her day. That particular day, when Afia heard the azaan, the crisp cold air made her want to snuggle back up in her blanket and go back to sleep. However, she could not as she had a lot weighing on her mind. That day would be the last day of doing her chores in this house. Reluctantly and with a deep sigh, Afia got out of her *mangi*[1]. As she blindly felt around the cold dirt floor, she put on her slippers and quietly tiptoed out of the small dark room that she shared with her parents. Stepping outside of the hut, her head turned toward the dark shadow of a flowery bush. She paused for a moment, staring intensely as if anticipating someone's arrival from beyond the bush, but after a brief moment of fixation, she blinked and shook her head as if to wake her senses up.

The smell of the fresh morning dew was clean and aromatic. The chill in the air made her wrap her scarf around her head and shoulders tightly. After prayers, she walked to the stream with the other girls from the village to collect water. There was no piped water supply to her home or her village, unlike the modern city homes where there was an endless supply of water. Every day, these village girls would make their arduous journeys to and from the stream, chatting away, but Afia always kept quiet, preoccupied with her thoughts.

---

[1] Mangi – A handmade bed.

Afia knelt and scooped the water into the pots from the tinsel. She then took a drink of the water and felt refreshed, full of energy, and ready to continue her daily chores. Walking steadily down the pebbled path towards her home, she balanced one pot on her head and one in between her arm as she tried her best not to spill any water. Afia could see her small mud home from a short distance. It had a mini wall built around the mud home and bordered the property that belonged to them.

Afia started to think back to her daily chores. She had been doing them as long as she could remember, but she knew that they were coming to an end and it filled her heart with an unexpected sadness.

In one corner would sit *Ummi* [2] busy cooking away next to the '*chulha* [3],' the clay stove open fire. The stove was burning buffalo dung as fuel as *Ummi* would make *parathas*. Baba would bring the *mangi* out from inside and would sit wrapping his turban around his head preparing himself for the long hard day's work on the fields. During the day, the *mangis* would be brought outside of the house and used as sofas. In the evening, the *mangis* were taken back inside and used as beds.

After an exhausting day from numerous journeys back and forth to the stream where she was washing clothes by hand and collecting water, Afia was finally finished. Afia had tended to the domestic animals and helped Ummi with the food preparation. The back-aching part was the constant crouching down and sweeping the floor, which she would do with a straw brush, unlike the long brooms used in modern houses. Afia's body felt shattered and she was ready to retire to bed.

She looked at the flowery bush again and walked calmly toward it. Afia would come to the bush regularly; buried under the bush was her sister's grave.

Afia's sister's name was Alia and she was three years older than Afia. The love between the two sisters was more like a mother and daughter's love. Ummi and Baba were too occupied with their everyday chores and did not pay any attention to the girls. Alia would bathe her little sister, as well as brush and plait her hair. She was given the responsibility of looking after Afia from the tender age of five. The sisters grew up happy within their own company. They would do everything together. Alia would do most of the work – afterward, they would sit by the stream at end of the long day and tell each other what they dreamt for their future. They did not miss the lack of love and attention from Ummi and Baba.

Sadly, Alia had passed away in an unfortunate accidental death... or so it seemed.

---

[2] Ummi – Mother
[3] Chulha – clay stove

Every day before sunset, Afia would go and sit by Alia's grave, and she would return home just after sunset. The only place where she could think was by her sister's grave. She thought about how her death had shaken her from inside; how her heart bled for her dead sister. It was as though she was under a dark, clouded sky.

Afia sat there, closed her eyes, and prayed for her dead sister. After a while, the sun began to fall behind the horizon as the sky began to adorn itself with brilliant colors of oranges and reds. A gentle breeze made the leaves rustle and the silhouettes of birds were seen flying home. It was getting dark, signaling that it was time for her to return home.

Stay by my side and give me courage, Afia thought, praying she would have the strength to go through the exchange. She gently stroked the soil on the grave with a feeling of emptiness in her mind and body. Finally, she stood and began walking back home. She was ready for vengeance.

Afia got up as usual when she heard the *Fajr* prayers, taking in every sight, sound, and feeling as she thought that this would be her last *Fajr* in this village. Afia went to the stream to collect the water and returned slowly, her mind on the impending activities.

"Ummi, the water is here," she said, placing the water pot on the ground carefully next to her, ensuring not a single precious drop was spilled.

"Afia," her mother called her.

"Yes, Ummi?"

"You are to do no more work today, as it is your last day here. The girls from the village will help me."

Ummi gave a warm loving look at Afia's rosy cheeks and said, "You get ready, for the people will be here soon."

Her tired, empty eyes were beginning to fill with tears. She quickly looked away and continued rolling out the dough. It was a strange sight for Afia to see Ummi like this, especially as her mother had never shown her any type of emotion before. The daughters in these villages were typically raised without any affection so that they would be prepared for the hard life they might endure after marriage.

"Ummi, don't worry, I'm not like Alia. I will not let them hurt me. I will punish them for her death," Afia said defiantly.

"Now, now, child, do not speak or think like that. Stop thinking that your sister was killed. Her time had come. This was God's will, my child. You are now meant to make that home beautiful. You have to look after yourself and don't do anything that will endanger yourself." Ummi stared at Afia deeply and slowly grabbed a large kitchen knife and handed it to Afia. "You make sure you keep this knife under your pillow. If anyone

163

tries to hurt you… you… you…" Ummi words were beginning to stumble out of her trembling mouth, "You protect yourself, my sweet child."

Afia couldn't understand how her mother could advise her to marry into this house while secretly fearing for her. Perhaps the mother's instinct made Ummi want to protect her, just in case.

Afia knew exactly what Ummi meant. She wished things were different in their village. *Why did daughters have to be passed off like things to be discarded, one after another?*

Lost in a mix of anger and hurt, Afia finally spoke, "But why does Baba not end this horrible tradition? Why does he have to sell his daughter in exchange for money? Why? And why to the same man that was married to his older daughter? Just for the offer of money they were making?" There was anger in her voice. She took the knife from her mom and began to sob loudly as she ran inside the dark room.

A feeling of distress overcame Afia. Her mind was feeling heavy with pain and she could not think straight. The time seemed to pass very slowly. Afia's mind wandered back to how it all began.

Afia's exchange had been planned a year ago. Afia's father had naively fallen prey to the bride hunters. She was sold! Some girls were sold for a little amount of money, but some were sold for two or three goats. She was not sure how much or what she was sold for, but from the look on her father's face, he seemed pretty satisfied with what he had received. And it was the same family that Alia was married into, who 'bought' her for their widowed son. She would be marrying her brother-in-law and Afia felt awful about it. Her father had succumbed to the deal as a burden was lifted when he did not have to give dowry.

Afia's sister, Alia, was sold four years ago at the tender age of 15. Alia was like a mother and best friend to Afia. She always kept her close to her and made sure she did all the hard work while her little sister played. Their mother paid no attention to them; she showed little love or affection to them. Their father just treated them like they did not exist. He would seldom speak to them, not even giving them a glance of gratitude when they served him food. It was alright, though, because the sisters had each other; they would not even talk much to the other village girls.

A year later, Alia returned to the village – in a coffin. Afia could not believe this and was in shock for months. Alia's husband told Afia that the gas cylinder had burst in the heat of Alia's new home and Alia was unfortunate enough to be in the kitchen at the time. Afia did not believe a thing that evil, insensitive man said about her death. Alia had given her hints of his brutality and the ill-treatment he meted out to her.

The man had given her father some blood money as goodwill and acted like he was genuinely saddened by her death. He vowed to return for Afia with a promise of another lump sum of cash – and stupidly and greedily, her father agreed.

"They killed her!" Afia protested but her claims fell on deaf ears. Everyone thought that this just was the reaction of a grieving sister.

But Afia believed this cruel family murdered Alia. She had a deeply intuitive connection with her sister. On the rare occasion when she met Alia after her marriage, she had felt the negative change in her sister. She seemed worn-out and depressed. Afia even had dreams where she would see Alia crying and begging for help.

Afia told her Baba about the time Alia had asked the family driver to secretly drive her down to her parents' house and how she only stayed for a little while, scared the family would find out that she was missing.

"Alia promised me that she would return again and that she only came to see my face and hug me, she said next time she would stay for longer, but… but…" her lips were trembling, she was struggling to find the words to tell her Baba. "Alia told me… she was always scared of the evil people in that family, especially the evil man… she… she… she told me they would shout at her and hit her…"

Tears were streaming down Afia's cheek as she spoke of Alia's ordeal and remembered the frightened look in her sister's eyes. She could not forget the bruises she saw on her body. It was as if she had especially come down to meet her and say her final goodbyes. *Why did I let her go back?*

Afia's father, even while knowing the truth, was in denial.

"This is how her death was written," he said and made her speak no more of the matter. From that day on, Afia had given up protesting, but she was mentally and physically preparing herself for revenge. She was determined to find the real reason as to why her sister died. Her every moment was haunted by the scene of her sister's burnt corpse. Deep inside, she knew the poor, innocent girl did not die accidentally but was probably tortured or set alight. But who could Afia complain to? After all, she had no income and the police would not have believed a word she said. They would not even glance at the case because these types of cases happened so often.

Now, four years later, it was Afia's turn. Her father wanted to get rid of the responsibility of marrying her off; to avoid giving dowry, he agreed to sell her, not caring about the outcome.

Afia was to be married to the same evil man that day. Afia got herself ready in her room and sat there waiting for her groom, all the while playing through her mind how she was going to exact revenge on the man's entire family; how she was going to make them feel the same pain that she had felt and imagined that Alia had felt whilst with them.

There was a kind of eerie, motionless feeling as Afia sat in her room. She sat rigidly on the hard handmade *mangi*, anxiously wringing her hands. Her scarf was so low over her head that she had no option but to gaze down uneasily at the dirt floor. She felt invisible in the small, dark room. She could hear the sound of people arriving at her house and exchanging pleasantries. Afia knew it was now time for the wedding ceremony and she was preparing herself. Dressed in oversized red bridal attire, which hung loosely on her slim frame, her long, lustrous hair was tied back into a bun as a heavily embroidered scarf covered her head and half of her face. The wedding ceremony had been performed in Afia's poorly lit room in front of the father, the imam, and two witnesses from the village. It was a quick and quiet procedure with only her immediate family and the two witnesses, just like Alia's wedding.

After the ceremony, the witnesses, father, and *Imaam* left the room.

The time for *rukhsati* – the departure – arrived and her mother hugged Afia tight. She had never shown any affection towards her before – maybe she had not experienced it herself or maybe she did not want to get too close to her, as she knew the day was soon to arrive when she would eventually have to let her go. As she hugged her goodbye, tears began to flow out of her sorrowful eyes. Afia held her tighter and was overcome with such emotion that she could not control her crying. 16 years of motherly love were made up for in a mere few minutes.

Her mother wept brokenheartedly. Afia did not want to let go of her, for she knew she would never see her again nor would she feel this moment again. At that heart-aching moment, they were pulled apart; her father grabbed her arm and dragged her out of the room. Her legs felt lifeless as they were forced to walk out of the dark room with him. Reaching out with her other hand, she tried to pull herself free but his grip was too strong. The words could barely come out of her trembling mouth as she cried, "Baba, wait a few more minutes! Baba, please!"

He ignored her pleas and dragged her out of the room and escorted her outside to the car. Afia was struggling, yearning to run back to her mother for one more last embrace. As tears streamed down her cheeks, she looked up pleadingly at his cold, merciless eyes. Her father's eyes had turned puffy, bloodshot, and filled with tears. Only then she realized how hard this must be for him, too. Afia felt weakened and surrendered.

Now, she had resigned herself to the fact that this was going to happen no matter what. She felt like a sheep being dragged down to the slaughterhouse by the ears, knowing it would never return.

Her new husband and another person were already in the car. Slumping in the back seat of the car, she took one long final look at her home, hoping to see her mother's face one more time. However, there was no sign of her and her father had turned his back as he walked away from the car. Rocks and dirt clots clanged against the car as it drove away.

There was a strong whiff of cigarettes mixed with aftershave and sweat coming from the front of the car, where she heard the voices of two men. Afia's head was still and stayed low; she was scared of looking up. Now she felt frightened – who was this person she was married to? What was he like? Not knowing what destiny had in store for her, she closed her sore eyes and prayed to God – *Oh Allah, guide me* and *give me strength*. Eventually, she fell asleep.

Afia awoke from her slumber, blinking rapidly as she realized she had slept through the whole journey and that day had morphed into night. She looked around and there was not a single person in sight – even the front passengers could not be seen. After a few moments, something blunt poked her shoulder.

"Eh, get up!" a low husky voice ordered.

Rubbing her eyes, she glanced up at the shadow of the man who was standing by the side of the car waiting for her to step out. The dim streetlights shone down on the figure of a tall, overweight man who had a cigarette in his fat hand, which was adorned with gold rings and bracelets. A thin line of smoke could be seen wafting of the cigarette as he took a last long, slow drag from the cigarette. The man threw the cigarette butt on the floor and crushed it with his foot. He had thick black hair which was slicked back with oil. He was not wearing the traditional *salwar kameez* – instead, he was dressed in jeans and a shirt with a gold chain hanging from his hairy chest and a large ear stud in his left ear. Afia felt intimidated by this man and could feel her whole body shaking with fear.

"Out," said the man in a harsher tone. With a lot of trepidation, she nervously stepped out of the car. The cold seeped through the thin sole of her slippers. She wrapped her scarf around her shoulders tight and stared at the large villa that stood before her.

"Come!" shouted the man as he turned and began to walk briskly up towards the front of the villa. Afia felt apprehensive as she followed the man up the pebbled pathway leading to their open wooden door. He stood by the door and waited for her to enter first. The stench from the man was making her feel nauseous, so she held her breath and walked past him. She paused for a second and looked up at his beady eyes, staring up and down at her with a menacing grin on his face. An uncomfortable feeling of fear pervaded her senses.

Afia was guided into a small room on the first floor, which had bare, gray walls with two beds – one in each corner with a small window partitioning them both. There were two small drawers parallel to the beds. The room was slightly bigger than her previous one and she was glad to see a window even though it was small. She wondered what the view from it would be like.

Soon, there was a faint knock. A woman suddenly entered the room. She was rolling down her sleeves as if she had just finished washing dishes. Her wrinkled, calloused hands showed she was a hard worker.

She must be the maid of the house, Afia thought curiously. She sat down on one of the beds and looked at Afia with a warm, sympathetic look as if she was her long-lost relative. There was a motherly type of warmth about her. She gave Afia a welcoming smile.

"That one is yours," she said, pointing to the other bed. "What's your name, child?"

"Afia," she whispered.

"Ah, pretty name, just like your face. I'm Nasreen," the woman said.

Afia had so many questions and they all raced through her mind at the same time. Afia did not want to waste time exchanging pleasantries and wanted to know what happened to her sister.

Afia sat down on the other bed and paused. "Nasreen, did you know my sister, Alia?"

"Ah, the poor child…" she sighed as a faint sign of pain flashed across her face before she quickly composed herself. Nasreen smiled at Afia and continued by saying, "You know… you have the same beautiful big eyes and sweet dimples as your sister when you smile."

"What happened to her?" asked Afia, eyebrows high, head leaning forward. She yearned to hear some news about her sister's death. "How did she die?"

"Eh, don't ask too many questions," Nasreen began shaking her head and lowered her eyes. She sighed again. "Oh, did you meet Afzal?"

"Huh, who?"

"The boy who was driving the car is named Afzal. He's my son," Nasreen explained. "Well, I shall call him," she continued. She took out a mobile phone from under her pillow. Afia watched curiously at what she was holding.

"What is that?" she asked.

"It's a phone," Nasreen replied.

"Oh, we had one in our village. We all shared it. I remember I spoke to Alia once – she told me she was scared, but that's all," her voice went quieter. "Nasreen, was she…" Afia was interrupted by the door swinging open.

It was the same man from the car. He looked at Nasreen first and then at Afia. Once again, his demonic glare sent shivers down Afia's spine.

"Come, Madam wants to see you." Before he turned to walk out, he gave a sinister smile to Afia.

"Nasreen, who was that scary man?" asked Afia after he left, feeling her throat go dry.

"That was Salim, Sir's younger brother. He does not have good motives, so be careful of him," Nasreen warned Afia. Coming closer to her and staring at her in the eyes, she said sternly, "They have bought you here from your parents' house as a bride, but really, they just bought another maid. Sir will have nothing to do with you. He will not even look at you. It is Sir's brother you have to be careful of. Stay close to me, do as I say, and you will be fine."

Afia was expecting that things would not be ideal here in her new home. She looked around, still in awe at how big the house was compared to her little mud house. Despite the lavishness, she knew she would not find any love here... like the way her sister hadn't. There were tall ceilings, shiny walls, luxurious silk cream-colored curtains, and large sofas.

As Afia looked around, she saw, sitting on the cream-colored lavish sofa, a smartly-dressed woman. She had a stern look on her beautiful face. The lady looked like she was in her early 40s – however, she looked good for her age. The lady had an air of authority and seemed to be someone who liked the finer things in life, judging by her clothes and jewelry.

The lady looked Afia up and down twice, gesturing toward her to come and sit next to her on the sofa. Afia felt as though this woman was seeing deep into her soul and it left Afia feeling very cold and anxious.

"Do you know who I am?" menacingly whispered the lady when Afia sat down beside her. "I am the boss of this house and everything in it, including you. You will call me 'Madam.' You are only here because I willed it – your 'husband' is actually my husband," the lady said. Afia's eyes widened. She was now the second wife of a man she hated. Afia wondered why her sister, Alia, had never mentioned anything about her husband's first wife. Hadn't her father known about this? Or had he?

Afia's mind began to whirl. Why had she allowed her husband to take on a second wife? Almost as if the madam had heard her thoughts, she answered her, "Don't think you are the lady of this house. That title only belongs to me – your status here is nothing more than a maid to your husband. Don't you ever try to charm him into being yours. Just do your work, you understand?"

Raising her eyebrows and looking sternly at Afia, Madam whispered, "If you disobey or cause us any trouble, you will be dealt with just like your sister. Is that clear?"

Afia could not believe what she was hearing or seeing. Lots of thoughts zoomed in her mind and she tried to connect the dots. *What did this lady mean when she said, 'dealt with like your sister?' Is she the person responsible for Alia's death? Why did Alia not tell me of this woman when she came to meet me? She just spoke of how she feared the evil man. No, this woman must also be responsible. They did something to my sister...*

Soon, anger rose in Afia's chest. She clenched her fists and thought of hurting the lady in some way. It was a herculean effort to keep Afia from actually doing or saying something that would end up getting her in trouble. Afia knew she had to bid her time and wait for the right moment.

"Yes, madam, you will not get any trouble from me," Afia said timidly through clenched teeth.

"Good, now go back to your room and get changed. Then, report into the kitchen where you can begin your chores," the woman ordered.

Afia ran quickly from the room and headed straight for her room. She ran in and slammed the door shut. Leaning against the closed door, Afia breathed heavily as sweat dripped from her head. She now had a face to match against her enemy and she would never forget this face. Afia had a renewed strength and vengeance was making her strong again, her eyes lit up as if they were on fire and a scary smile appeared across her face.

"Your days are numbered, madam. You will pay for what you did to Alia and the pain you have caused me," Afia murmured to herself in a quiet, determined voice.

Minutes later, Nasreen banged on the door. Afia composed herself and opened the door. Nasreen looked at Afia and could see that she was up to something.

"Whatever you are planning, now is not the time; you must be good if you want to stay safe in this house. Just follow me and do what I do. Don't get any crazy ideas about running away or harming anyone here. It will end badly for you," warned Nasreen. "Your last job for tonight is to serve tea and sweep the floor. Now hurry up and get changed."

Nasreen showed Afia where the extra clothes were. The madam had instructed Nasreen to ensure that Afia only wore simple, worn-out clothes. She wanted to make sure that Afia would not appear attractive in front of her husband. Nasreen waited outside whilst Afia got changed. They both headed down to the kitchen, Afia following a few steps behind Nasreen, keeping her eyes on the ground.

They had arrived in the kitchen and Afia looked around, taking in every detail. *This is where they killed Alia*, she kept thinking, imagining where and how they did it, getting angrier and angrier inside yet remaining calm on the outside. All of this was feeding the rage inside of her and Afia knew she would need this rage to carry out the mission she came for.

Afia's first chore was to make tea and snacks for Madam, Sir, and Salim. Afia gathered the necessary cutlery and cups and laid them on a tray, along with snacks like biscuits. The strong scent of cardamom wafted through the kitchen as the tea came to boil.

Afia grabbed the teapot that contained the freshly made tea and entered the drawing-room where Madam and Sir were sitting, laughing, and whispering to each other. They suddenly stopped when they heard Afia approaching and stared at her as she approached them.

"Leave these here and go and take a cup up to Salim in his room," ordered Madam with a look of contempt for Afia. The madam did not want Afia to stand in front of her husband – she wanted to make sure that although her husband had taken on a younger, prettier wife, she would continue to stay as a divide between them.

Afia did not like the sound of this and looked nervously towards Nasreen, who was still in the kitchen.

"Yes, Madam, right away, Madam," stuttered Afia, thinking that nothing good could come of going alone to Salim's room.

Afia picked up a cup of tea and headed back to the kitchen, where she approached Nasreen. "Madam wants me to take this tea to Salim. Where is his room?"

"His room is on the first floor directly opposite our room. You be careful and do not look him in the eye. Put the cup down and hurry back to the kitchen," advised Nasreen with a very worried look across her face.

Afia walked up the stairs slowly and silently, trying to make as little noise as possible; she did not want to give Salim any warning that she was coming. She eventually made it up the stairs to his room. She stood outside the room, nervous and breathing heavily. With a deep breath, she knocked on the door, opened it, and entered the room.

Salim was laying on his bed, shirtless. When he caught sight of Afia, he flashed a leery smile at her.

He gestured with his hand for Afia to put the cup down on the drawer next to his bed. Afia had hundreds of thoughts running through her head. Digging deep and channeling the fire in her soul, she confidently walked up to the bedside drawer and put the cup down. No sooner had the cup been placed on the table, Salim jumped up from his bed and stood behind Afia, walking toward her and forcing her into a corner.

"What else do you have for me, eh?" sneered Salim as he rubbed his hands together whilst continuing to walk toward Afia.

He lunged forward and tried to grab her by the shoulders. However, Afia was too quick – she ducked and ran out of the room and straight down into the kitchen.

Afia knew that she would not be so lucky next time and that she would have to put into action her planned revenge much sooner than she had anticipated. She would attack the first opportunity that she got. Afia imagined Salim doing the same shameful act with her sister Alia… or much worse. *How must my wonderful, quiet sister felt in this house all alone? She must have felt terrified… so lonely… so helpless*, tears began to well in her eyes as Afia thought about the situation her sister had suffered for months.

Afia quickly ran to her room. She went through her belongings. She only ever had a few belongings, so it was easy for her to pack when she left the village. Her small bag contained the few garments of clothes that she owned, as well as some of her favorite photos, especially those of Alia. The bag also contained the knife that was given to Afia by her mother. Afia pulled it out of the bag and stared at the glistening blade. Why did her mother give her this blade? *If she knew I was going to a bad place, then why did she let me go – why did she not stop this from happening?* Tears welled up in Afia's eyes as she pondered why her family was so unlucky and what she and her sister had done so wrong as to deserve this fate. Afia wiped away her tears and put the knife away under her pillow. She knew she would need it soon.

It was late evening now and Afia was busy clearing up the garden, sweeping away all of the dust and rubbish that had gathered there. Afia felt safe out there as she could see people walking along the street outside.

Soon, a man walked through the gate of the house and up to Afia. This was a young man, handsome and well-built with thick black hair styled like an old Bollywood film actor. He looked at Afia and smiled, but Afia turned away and continued her work. The man walked up to Afia and said, "Salam, I am Afzal, who are you?"

Afia immediately felt calm when she heard that it was Afzal – although she had never met him, she felt that he was a good person as he was Nasreen's son.

"I am Afia," she said quietly.

"Very nice to meet you. I am Nasreen's son. Please do let me know if there is anything I can help you with," he replied.

Afia smiled genuinely for the first time in a long while. "Very nice to meet you, Afzal."

Afzal finally disappeared along the side of the house and Afia continued her work. She heard madam calling her from inside, so she collected her broom and ran inside the house.

"Look at the state of you, girl! Why are you bringing all of this mess into my house?" shouted madam. She ran up to Afia and slapped her across the face. "Go and clean this up quickly!"

Afia stood there defiantly, refusing to cry, and then started clearing up the mess. "Soon you will see who is going to be dealt with," muttered Afia under her breath.

Afia looked around the house and could not see or hear sir or Salim, so she went off into the kitchen to put away the cleaning equipment. She noticed Nasreen putting away clean pots and pans.

"Where are Salim and Sir?" inquired Afia, as she wanted to make sure that she was nowhere near where they were. *How did Alia cope with this, hiding and trying to avoid people in this house?*

"Every week Sir and Salim go down to the town, play cards, and get drunk. They are vile when they get drunk, so you had better beware of them. Do not go near them," warned Nasreen.

It was late and the housework had finally been completed. Afia went up to her room and got herself ready for bed. As she was laying there, all she could think of was poor Alia, how she had spent a year here with these horrible people, and how she was going to get revenge. *Why didn't sir talk to me? If Baba knew that his daughters were going to be slaves, not wives, then Baba would not have sold us to him. I wonder if Salim was the evil man Alia was talking about.* Afia waited for Nasreen as she had many questions about Madam, Sir, Salim, and Alia.

It must have only been a few hours before Afia was woken up by loud sounds coming from outside. It sounded like two people arguing and fighting. It sounded like Salim and Sir were fighting while they were drunk. Afia shot upright and strained to hear what was going on outside. She heard the sound of a car door opening then slamming shut, while another sound came of someone coming into the house and slamming the front door. The shuffling footsteps got louder and louder and seemed to be coming toward Afia's room. Adrenaline surged through Afia's body as she looked around the dark room, desperately trying to see Nasreen. However, she was nowhere to be found. Afia looked around for somewhere to hide, but the room was not big enough to hide, so she readied herself for trouble.

Afia shuddered at the sounds of footsteps coming toward the door. Along with the sounds, she saw a shadow approaching closer with the hand reaching out to push the door open. An uncomfortable premonition of fear pervaded her senses. Her heart began to pound rapidly. She breathed in and out quickly but found the air struggling to enter into her lungs. She tried to scream but it felt as though her throat had gone dry. Her legs had turned into jelly as the fear was paralyzing her.

"Oh no," she whispered under her breath. Her lips trembled with fear. Just then, she remembered the knife that she had hidden under her pillow.

Now, the moment for her to utilize the knife had finally arrived.

It was Salim who entered the room. His eyes were bloodshot and he smelled like alcohol. He was slowly walking toward her. His evil eyes, red with intoxication, were fixed on her. His demonic glare was sending shivers down her spine. Her heart wanted to hammer its way out of her chest. She suddenly lunged toward the bed and desperately searched for the knife under her pillow.

"Go away!" she cried, tears flowing down her cheeks.

He grinned, showing no remorse, and grabbed her leg. She reached for the pillow and threw it at him. However, it missed him completely, making him smirk.

"You're are a feisty one, aren't you," he hissed. "Your sister was more willing."

Those words felt like fire burning through Afia's eardrums. Suddenly, she felt adrenaline flow through her veins as she pointed her knife toward him. Now, the moment that she had been waiting for had come; she had to stand up to him and bring justice for her sister.

His hands were now on her body. They felt like the claws of a hungry wolf.

With a scream, she turned with all the strength that she had within her and stabbed the knife into his chest. The flesh felt soft and pudgy. She twisted the blade and then jerked it inside until the shiny metal had disappeared. Salim let out an agonizing roar. It was a satisfying sound to Afia's ears. She took the knife out quickly and stabbed it into him again and again, feeling possessed, like something had taken over her body and given her the courage to make the fatal attack.

"Die, bastard," she screamed.

Afia looked down at her bloodied, trembling hands, and then at him as he lay there on the bed as blood flowed from his chest. *What have I done? What Am I going to do now?* These thoughts were going through her head when she looked up and saw Nasreen standing by the door.

"I–I–I–had to... He–he–he... he was going to attack me!" Afia said defensively.

"You did the right thing," replied Nasreen. "Now, quickly, we must do something about the madam."

"But... But..." Afia couldn't think straight. She was in shock. She had murdered Salim. She had finally exacted revenge.

Afia's hands were still shaking and bloody. She got up and took the knife out of him. She stared at the corpse with a grim and shuddering fascination.

"Now for Madam – we need to move fast!" said Nasreen, grabbing Afia's arm and pulling her toward the door. "We need to kill her and then take the keys from her drawer, open the safe, and take all the money and gold. Then, we will be safe."

"But, how do you know?" Afia asked, still holding the knife.

"That's not important. I'm calling Afzal – we need to leave tonight!" she replied.

They hurried through the house silently, driven by shuddering fear. The candle was shining a dim light toward madam's room. They paused outside the room. Nasreen looked at Afia.

"Don't think about it," she said. "Just attack!"

Afia couldn't think straight. "I can't," she whispered.

"Yes, you can. She showed no remorse when she set alight your sister, so why are you afraid?"

"But…"

"No buts!" Nasreen said, glaring at her. "Just think – we will be free and you'll go back home!"

With shaking legs, Afia opened the door and entered the room. She began walking toward the bed, expecting the madam to be there, but she wasn't. All of a sudden, she felt someone lunge towards her and stab her with something sharp. Shocked, Afia turned around and saw Madam's bloodshot eyes staring straight at her. A knife, dripping with blood, was in her hand. Before madam could stab Afia again, Nasreen sprung forward and hit Madam on the head with a large brick. Madam collapsed onto the floor – now a soulless corpse – as blood dripped from the wound on her head.

"Oh dear, Afia, are you OK?" Nasreen said. Panicking, she came running to Afia and wrapped her scarf around her stomach to stop the bleeding. "Leave the knife in and apply pressure to it – whatever you do, keep the knife inside!"

Nasreen jumped up from the ground, frantically searching inside the room until she found the keys that would lead to the safe. Nasreen then grabbed a bag from the wardrobe and walked to the hidden safe behind the painting. She took down the painting carefully, opened the safe, and quickly placed all the gold and jewelry inside the bag.

Rushing to Afia, she helped her up. "Come, you wait by the back door. Afzal will be here soon."

Nasreen helped Afia walk to the back door. She opened it and Afzal stood there. "I came as quickly as I could!"

Together, Nasreen and Afzal helped Afia into the car. They then turned and began to walk away from the car.

"Where are you going?" Afia asked them.

"We need to set the house on fire so that no evidence is left," Afzal said.

While Nasreen went inside to her room to grab a few of her belongings, Afzal spread petrol everywhere, ready to set the house alight.

175

Afia sat in the car thinking about what just happened. The adrenaline had worn off and the pain was kicking in now.

"We will go to the hospital. I have money for your treatment," Nasreen replied, tears flowing from her eyes.

"Nasreen, please, I beg you, take me home. If you take me to the hospital, then the police will get involved and you will be caught. Plus, I know I won't survive. I'm losing too much blood. I need to see my sister's grave. Please take me home," Afia begged Nasreen with sorrowful eyes. Nasreen could not refuse her last request.

The journey back home felt like days. The pain came in waves. Afia's vision blurred as she felt herself close to fainting.

"We are here," Afzal exclaimed as he drove through the narrow dirt road leading to Afia's house.

"Call Ummi outside," begged Afia, her voice getting fainter and fainter due to the loss of blood.

Afzal banged on the door and Baba opened it. They stood there for a few seconds while Afzal hastily explained to him what had happened. Baba ran back inside and back again – this time Ummi came running out with him. They ran towards the car.

Tears were streaming down *Ummi's* face. "Afia my child, my sweet child, what have you done?" Ummi cried.

The *Fajr azaan*, the morning call for prayer, could be heard from the mosque, signaling the beginning of another day in the village.

With her last breaths, Afia whispered to Afzal, "Take me to my sister's grave, please."

Baba and *Ummi* led the way as Afzal carried Afia to her sister's grave. As she lay there, she looked around at the surroundings of her village. For the first time in her life, she could see and appreciate the beauty of the place. The rising sun, the singing birds, and the smell of fresh flowers brought a smile to her face.

"I have avenged your death. The people who hurt you will hurt no one else again," she whispered to her sister's grave. Finally, she put all of those thoughts and feelings of revenge to rest. Finally, she felt at peace.

Troubled

By Ali Ihsan Cetiner

A Good Morning

I slowly opened my eyes in my bedroom, lazily wishing for more sleep. I was alone in my bed. I guessed that my wife was already in the kitchen, preparing breakfast for us. Sunlight filtered in through the window. I always liked the rays of sunshine seeping through the blinds. They heralded the coming of a beautiful day and filled me with peace. My dear family and I would be ready to meet the day.

With a yawn and stretch, I got out of bed. I took a moment to sit on the bed, silently thanking God for the promise of another beautiful day. Stepping out of the bedroom into the corridor, I was greeted by a wonderful smell wafting from the kitchen: *Sojouk* and eggs. I went into the bathroom to complete my daily routine, and later, with the exuberance of a happy man, I announced to my family that the father was in the house.

"Mustafa, come catch this little mouse that's stealing our food!" I heard my wife teasing our daughter as our beloved baby giggled and ran around with the swift steps of a ten-year-old.

Soon, my belly began rumbling and I was eager to bite into the sumptuous breakfast my wife had prepared for us. With a grin splitting my face in two, I entered the kitchen. After chasing my daughter and finally catching her, I planted kisses on her cheeks.

"Daddy, stop it! You're gonna eat the breakfast, not me!" she squealed.

"Oh, I don't know about that. I thought you were my breakfast! Those cheeks are surely by far the most delicious things in this room!" I said, which made my daughter giggle even more.

Only then did I realize that my wife had not uttered a single word since I entered the room. When I looked at her, I saw her beautiful hazel eyes watching us. I could get lost in those eyes even then, after so many years of our marriage. I felt the warmth of her smile, almost like a physical, tangible thing, gathering my daughter and me in, wrapping us in layers of love. At times like these, I wondered what I had done to deserve such a wife and child. I felt profound gratitude and offered a silent prayer to God for the peace and love he had granted me. What more could a man ask for?

The weekend breakfast was one of our favorite times together. It was the deep breath we took rising out of the sea after a long dive. It was when I would start replenishing my energy. My wife would unravel the knots of tension in my soul; my daughter, an endless source of joy, would seep into my cells, lending me enough of her energy to last me the whole coming week. I lived for them. My life was complete with their presence.

As I discovered at breakfast, my daughter had another successful week at school. She chattered away the entire breakfast about what she had done the whole week. Her piano lessons were going very well, of course. She was chosen for the class debate team and, much to my excitement, their team had won the debate against the neighboring class' team. And, she had done so well that her teacher had congratulated her in front of the whole class! My little chatterbox certainly deserved a reward!

"Uh-huh! So that's what my little monster was coming at!" I said, pinching her nose. "You little trickster! You have been steering us towards the topic of this reward, eh?"

"Noooo, Dad," she laughed. "But I always wanted to see the new zoo. Would it not be nice to visit the zoo? Please, Daddy, can we go there today?"

It was settled then. We would be going to the zoo after breakfast.

End Of Weekend

It had been a gorgeous day. My daughter thoroughly enjoyed the zoo. My wife and I trotted along after her while our daughter ran from one animal to the other. It was one of the best things in life, seeing a child – our child – amazed at life, filled with wonder and laughter.

It was with a weary body but an uplifted spirit that we went back home that evening. After quickly freshening up, we sat at the table for a quick dinner. The aroma of the hot, creamy tomato soup revived us and soon I was wiping my bowl clean with a piece of bread. I was thinking about the chatter of my daughter again when I realized my wife asking me:

"Darling, are you alright? You look a bit troubled."

I was starting to feel troubled. However, I had not realized that it was reflected on my face. Normally I was careful not to let minor things out and bother my beloved family. I must have been too tired to hide my anxiety this time, however.

"It must be all this crazy darting around in the zoo, love. I'm having this strange numbness in my legs. Nothing painful, yet kind of annoying, you know," I replied.

"Alright then, why don't you," she said, "slip into your pajamas and retreat to our bed? A good sleep should help you shake it off."

I nodded my acquiescence, kissed the top of my little monster's head, and went to bed.

Sleep was not coming anytime soon, though.

Tired as I was, the numbness had turned into a tingling sensation across my upper legs, though it was still not painful. I would not describe myself as someone to experience anxiety at the first sign of trouble, however, that was the first time I felt such a weird sensation. I got up from the bed, swung my legs around, made a few rounds in the room, and went into the bathroom.

Red eyes stared back at me from the mirror, bloodshot with weariness. The muffled laughter of my daughter and wife reached my ears through the closed bedroom door, alleviating my mood at that moment. Well, I was just tired and would feel fine after a long night's sleep, so I figured I needed to sleep as soon as possible. I opened the medicine box, popped a sleeping pill, and swallowed it. After returning to bed, this time sleep found its way to my body: the last thing I remember was smiling inwardly at yet another joyful shriek from beyond the door.

Doctors

The thin long arm of the clock ticked away incessantly, without tiring, without stopping to see if anyone was following. It seemed oblivious to its environment. Moment after moment, it moved. It seemed to be insignificant by itself, going around in circles for eternity. Yet, when it moved, the whole world moved. Seconds ticked into minutes, into hours, into days. People were born, grew up, and died by its movement. Whatever was happening in my body, it was probably small, very small to avoid detection. It was happening at a molecular level, yet, it was having this effect of putting my whole life under a new uncertainty, one that I was not yet equipped to deal with. How could anyone deal with something that he does not understand?

The softly sound of approaching steps pulled me out of my pensive state and I looked toward the sound.

"The doctor will see you now," said the nurse.

The past couple of weeks had seen my wife and me at a series of doctor visits. The tingling in my legs had turned into a sort of sharp pain shortly after that first night. It was not too sharp nor was it continuous; it came and went at seemingly random intervals. When it became obvious to my wife and me that the intermittent pain was not going away, we decided to seek medical help. The first person to announce to us that there was nothing wrong with me was the internal medicine specialist. However, I still had doubts due to the way I was feeling. Then thinking that maybe

180

something was wrong with my back, we saw an orthopedist. However, again, we were told that there was nothing to worry about and that my spine was in good shape – there was no disc out where it should not be, no worn vertebral facets. Yet, I still harbored a nagging doubt. Therefore, not trusting one doctor, I visited another, but in vain.

With each visit to a doctor or diagnostic lab, and failure to conclude what ailed me, the churning thoughts in my mind gained more momentum and slowly turned into a maelstrom. The dinners at home passed with a bit more silence than what was usual for us. The irrepressible exuberance of our daughter helped me ignore my undiagnosed condition, albeit for limited periods. Nevertheless, I made sure that I never forgot to offer my thanks to the Almighty for the boons He had granted my family and prayed for quick relief from my situation. However, in the end, no matter how I tried, I could not entirely shake off my sullen mood.

"Thanks," I said to the nurse, without bothering to look at her eyes, and stood up. My wife held my hand softly as we walked toward the doctor's cabin. The bright white walls of the corridor leading to the doctor's room did not help the mood in the hospital. Few patients seated along the corridor could not blend into the environment; the stark white of the walls contrasted with their existence and brought out every painful look, every line of worry on their faces, every hunch of desire to just curl up and embrace their poor selves. Light-headed, with butterflies in my stomach, I moved through this exhibit of human misery. Part of me wanted to get in that room and hopefully learn the truth about my illness to finally put an end to this torment. But the other part of me screamed silently and wanted to turn and flee, dreading the moment when this doctor, too, would proclaim that there was nothing wrong with me. I paused when we reached the door. After a few seconds, my wife squeezed my hand and when I looked up, her gaze held mine, as if lending her soul into mine, giving me the courage I needed. I took a deep breath and turned the door handle slowly.

Even for normal illnesses, a patient entering a doctor's room is always filled with shyness, as if afraid to misstep and lose the doctor's good graces. On can't help but think, "Stay on the good side of the doctor and maybe your illness will not be that bad." So I trod lightly and respectfully. In my state, I was not sure how to act. So we stood there, slowly closed the door, and waited. The butterflies in my stomach had gone on a riot now; if I opened my mouth then, I believed some of them would make a run for it. Some of them were waiting at the back of my throat, ready to gush out.

"Mr. Mustafa, please come in, take a seat."

Mercifully, my wife led me to the seat in front of the doctor's desk and we sat down. I could only bring myself to look up at the doctor then. After a few words of pleasantries from the doctor and myself trying to reply as civilly as I could, he moved on to the topic:

"Mr. Mustafa, I have looked at your lab reports."

What followed was a detailed description of what they had done for diagnosis. He was talking, yes, but words were coming to me muffled as if being spoken underwater. Against a backdrop of a mouthful of EEGs, EMGs, CT-scans, my breath coming shorter with each passing second, I waited patiently for the final words. My gaze fixed to a spot on the floor in front of me, I waited helplessly, afraid to cut his speech short and offend him. Finally, he said:

"And as far as we can see, you are perfectly healthy, Mr. Mustafa."

I started hearing a rhythmic thudding of which I could not locate the source. Damn air, it had become too hot. I tried to breathe in more air but nothing was coming. This was a waste of time, I wanted to tell my wife that we should leave. I lifted my eyes to hers, only to see her lips already moving. She, too, was now talking as if underwater. Her forehead creased with worry, her eyes open wider than normal, I barely heard her asking:

"Mustafa, honey, are you alright?"

I wanted to tell her that I was fine – all the doctors said so! – that this was all just a waste of time and that we should just leave and go back to our home. All I wanted to do was lie down and rest. The thudding had grown heavier, and no matter how I tried, I could not get enough air in my lungs.

"Please take me home, love," I managed to say. I started rising from my chair and then everything went black.

Waking Up

I came to my senses.

I had no recollection of what I was before, but seemingly in an abrupt way, I became self-aware. I could feel the air filling my lungs and then leaving. But it was dark. Why was it dark? A beep penetrated the silence and I heard, again abruptly. My awareness extended to the outside world. I could hear the muffled sounds from outside, now the periodic beeping of some device. I could feel a warm spot on my arm; sunlight?

I opened my eyes to a white ceiling. Too bright that my eyes hurt, so I closed them again. Slowly, gradually I opened them again, all the while my senses getting restored more and more, dispersing my disorientation. There was probably nothing that could have prepared me for what I saw and felt after that moment. I was apparently in a hospital room, bedridden and to my horror, all kinds of wires were attached to my body, with a tube going deep into my nose and another into my mouth. My pulse started racing and my heart beating violently in my chest. I could feel it thumping against my ribs like a beast banging against its cage. *Where was I? What was all of this? Where was everyone?* Panic gripped my body, the air became thicker, more difficult to breathe. A gag reflex constricted my throat but I managed to let out a cry:

"Gaaaahh!"

I started pulling all the cables from my body. *Oh my God, how long is this tube in my nose?* My movements became frantic as I pushed myself off the bed, only to fall face-first to the floor. Air gushed out of my lungs with the impact. My vision started to turn black at the edges. Just as I saw, from my skewed perspective on the floor, the room's door bang open and nurses rushed in.

I must have lost my consciousness momentarily as when I came back to my senses, I was again lying on the bed, but with the nurses around me this time, and with no recollection of how I was lifted back onto the bed. Gratefully, this time, none of the tubes violated my body. The company of the nurses eased my sense of panic so that I could muster enough breath to ask:

"Where am I?"

One of the nurses turned to me and smiled.

"Hello, sir. So good to see you wake up. You are in a hospital. Don't worry, you are safe," she said. "Your vitals are looking good, you seem to have stabilized and recovered pretty well."

If that was an attempt to give me some assurance and make me feel comfortable, it had failed tremendously. *Recovering? From what? Was I not stable before? What do you mean? What happened to me?!!!* The thoughts were racing through my mind but I was feeling so weak that I just lay there for a little while before I could ask:

"What happened to me?"

She did not answer me straight away. She ostentatiously made herself busy reading some screens, scribbling something on her notepad.

Then she fumbled around tidying my bed, tapping a few more buttons, and finally said:

"Can you tell me your name please, sir?"

"Mustafa."

"How old are you? Where do you live?"

"I'm 45. I live in Brookesberry. What's the meaning of all these questions?"

"OK, thank you, Mustafa. Please try to get some rest now. The doctor will be in very soon and he will answer all your questions, I'm sure. Just relax now."

I wanted to demand answers. I wanted to get up and look for someone who could provide me those answers. It was so obvious the nurse was evading my questions and I knew something was wrong, however, I was so enveloped in a shroud of weakness, with barely enough energy to cling to consciousness, that I simply kept my mouth shut. I stubbornly resolved not to drift to sleep before this doctor came to me. I consoled myself focusing on one thing: staying awake until then. Seeing that no more questions were coming from me, the nurses both nodded their heads, wished me a peaceful rest, and left the room.

Deafening silence descended on the room, fueling my unease once again. Apart from the periodic beep of the life support system, the only noise I heard was that of my thoughts, turning endlessly in a loop, demanding to know at that instant what had happened to me.

I had no idea how long I waited in that state. It could have been minutes or mere moments. Then the door opened with a swish and an elderly man stepped in. He looked to be in his late fifties, with a thinning hairline, and a fair complexion. Large spectacles encircled his eyes, which seemed to hold no malice. He looked like a man you could trust. Seeing I was awake, he broke into a disarming smile.

"Mustafa, welcome back to the world! When the nurses told me the good news, I was so happy for you. You are a fighter, Mustafa. You've come through a serious deal but look at you, you're doing great."

I certainly did not feel as if I had achieved any victory at all. "Doctor, please tell me what happened to me. Why am I here?" Then, he told me.

I had been in a car accident. It had been a nasty one, as per his description. The news had come out mentioning that my car had digressed from the lane and crashed into the truck coming from the opposite direction. Police had deduced that probably I had slept – time being so late at night – and, having ruled out that I was not drunk and there had been no trace of alcohol in my blood – of course, there would not be, I never drank alcohol. My car was destroyed and I was lucky to be alive.

But that was a story that I could listen to with some detachment. I had no memory of the accident, or even where I had been coming from, driving that late at night. It sounded as if I was listening to someone else's story. The first blow, however, that tipped my mind into disarray, was when he told me that I had been comatose for almost two months now.

Comatose? For two months?!

It was not something that you could believe with the mere mention of it. My mind rebelled at the thought of such a drastic thing happening to me. It could not be real! Surely I would remember if I had been in an accident! My thoughts raced, trying to recollect the last memories I had. Yes! I remembered my family then. Strange as it was; it had not occurred to me until that moment to ask where my family was.

"Listen to me, doctor! Tell me where my family is. Where is my wife? Where is my daughter?"

"Mr. Mustafa, please calm down. All will be explained in due time. For now, we need to focus on your recovery and rehabilitation. Now if you calm down, I will continue telling you about your prognosis."

Afraid that I had angered him, I shut my mouth. Trying to control my breathing, I closed my eyes for some time. My memories were getting more distinct. We were at the doctor's, with my wife. And I was given the same diagnosis, yet again, about my legs. My legs! Yes, I had had this periodic pain in them and that's why I was at the doctor. And I remembered asking my wife to take us home, and then… And then, nothing. Try as I might, I could not remember anything after that – it was utter blackness. So I opened my eyes and told the doctor:

"I had been having this pain in my legs so we were seeing a doctor, my wife and I. Then I must have fainted because that's the last memory I have. Then, I woke up here. I don't remember an accident."

He looked at me quizzically for a moment and kept his silence. Then his lips pursed and eyes squinting with a sad look on his whole face, he broke to me the really bad news.

"Alright, I'm not saying that you are wrong. But we have looked for records of you when you were brought to the emergency room, and nothing showed up in any police or hospital records about any prior complications in your health, Mustafa. We might be wrong about it and we can probably check once again. However, this will not change what I am going to tell you next."

He gave a pause as if it was too difficult to get on with his speech. I could not say that it helped my unease at all. What could be worse than being comatose for two months?

"Mustafa, the traffic accident you went through was a severe one. We did not think your chances of survival were high. Your car had been trampled upon completely and apparently, your legs got stuck. I'm sorry to say this, but we could not save your legs. They had to be amputated to save the rest of your body."

I froze with my mouth agape at what I had just heard. My mind was a blur for a moment. I couldn't believe my ears. Surely this was a cruel joke.

It could not be real, simply because I still felt my legs, my feet. There, when I lifted the blanket, I would see them and prove him wrong.

Except that it was the bitter truth awaiting me under the blanket. I was petrified, staring at an empty bedsheet, with nothing extending from my body where my legs were supposed to be.

The sheer horror of what I had seen was too much for me. Shock, outrage, sorrow, and denial beset me from all sides. I was overwhelmed by the ferocity of these emotions, and could not utter a word, could not even think. I lay in the bed, disabled.

Fate chose that moment to act. The door slowly opened and a little figure peered inside. She was what saved me at that moment. My daughter was the most beautiful thing in the world that could ever happen to me in such a situation. She rushed to my bed crying "Daddy!" and leaped onto my embrace. The rest of the world ceased to exist at that time. I enveloped the most precious thing in life in my arms, buried my head into her hair, and cried my eyes out, sobbing loudly.

Revelation And Despair

In the following days, I became a sullen, pouting man. I could not shake off the feeling that the doctors had not done their best trying to save my legs. In the modern world where all these advancements were achieved in medical science, I refused to accept that there could be nothing they could have done. To hell with the hesitancy against the doctors. I had nothing to lose now: I had already lost everything, so I cared none at all if I would anger a doctor or not. So unlike my old self, I shouted at the doctor for not doing his job well. I blamed him for my condition. I blamed the nurses for their incompetent ER procedures. I had become a bitter wretch, angry at anything and everything.

I lay most of the time in my bed, staring emptily at the two stumps that were supposed to be my legs. I was weak from days of sleeping in the coma, my muscles showing signs of atrophy. Like a baby learning to eat, they fed me gravy most of the time. "To go soft on your gastrointestinal system," the doctors said. My skin was regaining some of its warmth, slowly recovering from the whiteness of death. The cadaverous face I had seen during the only time I had requested to see myself in a mirror, told me how much I had lost. I do not remember ever being someone with vanity, but that face in the mirror had me cringe in horror.

But that was not the worst of it. I had to live through, quite possibly, even a bigger shock: As I kept inquiring about my wife and my daughter, the doctor revealed to me the bitter reality: all those memories I remembered from my life before the accident? They had all been part of a dream! I had been in a coma triggered dream all that time!

My loving wife, our happy family, the feeling of all that bliss, the wonderful life I thought I had were nothing but the cruelest of jokes. It had all been a dream. I had never had those precious things that had filled my heart brimming with happiness. My wife's eyes had never engulfed me with her love, we were never the joyful family that was in my dreams.

We became divorced a couple of years back and my wife had custody of our daughter. I was living alone in my one-bedroom apartment.

Doctors said it was probably a self-preservation effort of my mind, urging my body to cling to life by synthetic memories of a good life, a life that I was deep down missing greatly.

Speech was possible with some effort. Not that I wanted to speak much. I still could not reconcile my thoughts to lead any meaningful conversation; so I kept my mouth shut when I was not busy throwing barbs at the hospital staff.

I could not accept the reality that was so brutally, so unfairly pushed onto me. I knew I was a cripple now, but my mind kept wandering back to the joyful days in my dream. Maybe this was the dream and I should wake up. Like those dreams that you know, something is off but you cannot wake up. My soul cried out to the heavens, demanding to know why. I had to know. I did not deserve this. I could not bear the look of pity in my daughter's eyes. I could not seem to find the right words to say, to offer her comfort that her daddy is still there. At times, I would catch a hint of fear in her eyes. I could tell she was afraid of something she saw on my face.

She was my sole consolation in this farce of existence. She visited me sometimes in my room, as well as at other times when the nurses took me out to the hospital's garden to get some fresh air. When I was in the worse mood, which was all the time, she would refrain from speaking but put her tiny, warm hand on mine and sit next to my bed or walk beside my wheelchair. They seemed to have given my daughter a free run of the hospital. She was able to go in and out whenever she wanted to. I guess I was thankful to my ex-wife for at least bringing our daughter to visit me, although she never came to visit me herself.

As days passed, I felt myself succumbing more and more to the idea of being a pitiful, disabled man. My pink dreams during the coma had probably helped me with the positive aura they created for my soul to cling to hope, cling to life. But now, the memory of those dreams had quite the opposite effect: it reminded me of my loss. I would never be able to live a life like that anymore. Who would want a cripple in their life?

One night, sleep did not come as early as it should. My mind started traveling astride my bitterness. *I am never going to be able to walk again. I am a pitiful cripple. I have always been a faithful and practicing believer. Oh God, what have I done wrong that you punish me so? How am I going to live now? What is left there for me to do? How can I live when I am not even able to move around?*

A blanket of despair descended on me, smothering, unyielding. I could not even try thinking positive, try envisioning a life that could be lived as a cripple. I could no longer work in my past line of work. I would not be a man who would take pride in earning the bread for his family, who would be the mountain they could rely on, who would be the shelter when they needed one. All I could ever be now was one thing: A burden. A difficulty. A complication in the otherwise happy life of others. On a deeper level, this self-pity was feeding the flames of contempt at myself, disgusted at what I had become.

As my thoughts got heavier, they became a bottomless pit sucking my energy. It was as if the weariness of all those days enveloped me finally. I felt a deep lethargy descending over me as if injected into my bones. I tried to remember my past life, tried to catch glimpses of the happiness that I had so easily taken for granted. Even the good memories were denied to me. *Am I not even allowed to dream of good days past? Have I fallen into such a deep well of darkness?* Life had never looked so meaningless, so dead. I drifted into a black unconsciousness. The utter lack of feelings in that place was welcomed by my tired soul. Perhaps death, if it was akin to this nothingness, could be the end of my pain? What was left there to live for me anyway? Whatever lines left holding my soul bound to this wretched shell of a body were getting snapped one by one. I lay there in my bed, my stare fixed to the ceiling. As the last line holding my soul in place snapped, I felt myself being pulled into the depths of a black pit where nothing existed. Darkness swallowed the edges of my vision as the ceiling narrowed down to a small white spot. Finally, I let go, willing myself to just stop existing.

Recovery

"I love you, Daddy. I miss you so much," were the first words that got through my foggy mind. The warm tiny fingers holding my hand twitched when I croaked through my parched lips:

"I'm here, sweetie."

"Oh, Dad! Thank God!" my daughter exclaimed, eyes glistening, voice shaking.

Seeing my daughter next to my bed somehow reinforced my grip on reality and I fully came around. I was still in my room at the hospital. Plain green painted walls, lit softly by the diffused light from the half-open window shades. So I learned that a man could not will himself to death just like that.

My eyes fell on the pitcher at the wall across my bed. With a deep sigh, I pointed at the pitcher.

"Can you get me that water over there, honey?" I asked. "How long have I been sleeping?"

The slight hesitation before her reply should have steeled me.

"It's been two days, Dad," said a trembling little voice.

I guessed that was normal. They had been feeding me sedatives to dull the pain of my missing legs, and more, I thought, for dulling my suicidal mood. The almost constant drowsiness had put me in a twilight zone where time and feeling had lost their meaning. So when my daughter informed me that I was out for two days, it was probably a good thing that my system still had residues of the sedatives. Or maybe I had stopped caring at all.

"It is OK, sweetie, I am back now," I said after a brief silence. The thirst was severe and my throat was hurting from trying to speak. "Can you get me that water over there, honey?"

Right at that moment, the door opened and a doctor stepped in, followed by a nurse. I did not recognize the doctor or the nurse. Had I seen them before? Were they the ones who treated me all that time? Was he the one who amputated my legs? How could a human being do that to another? In a flash of thoughts, my bitterness rose, the imagined horror of a merciless doctor sawing through my legs overwhelming my senses.

"No! No! Please, no! How could you?" I cried. I felt myself hyperventilating.

"It's OK, Mustafa, calm down. We are here to help you." I heard the nurse, holding my shoulder firmly but not unkindly. "Just look at me, and try to breathe normally. I am here with you."

What calmed me down finally was the touch of my little daughter. Her small, warm hands had become a tether to peace among the turmoil I was going through. Her hands allowed me to focus on her, to shut out all my fears and anxiety. My instincts as a father would kick in, reminding myself that I had to be strong for her. My little brave daughter was helping me in ways she could not even begin to understand yet, with her sweet heart.

Seeing that I had once again returned to normal, the nurse checked my vitals, took notes on the patient records at the foot of my bed, all the while the doctor watching me from afar. He had probably realized that his presence was what put me in a panic attack in the first place. The nurse finally offered me the water I was craving.

"You got us worried, Mustafa, sleeping so long. But apparently, you needed that rest. You must be hungry now. I'll have some food brought to you and after you eat, let's take you out for a stroll. We will leave now but I will be available outside. Just push this button if you need me," she said and with that, they left. My daughter and I were left alone in the room, greeted by a sudden silence.

Just as I was going to return to my brooding, I felt my daughter's eyes on me. She would always watch me… yes, but this time it felt different. When I lifted my eyes to hers, I was surprised by the intensity of her gaze. Gone were a child's innocent and clueless looks, replaced by this questioning probe, piercing straight to my heart. She held my gaze for some time and then shocked me with a question:

"Why do you want to die, Daddy?"

To say I was surprised would be an understatement. That was not a topic I would want to discuss with a child, let alone my daughter. I was dumbstruck, unable to utter a word. So she repeated the question, stressing each word slowly, with a pause between them.

"Why… do… you… want… to die?"

"I… I… I do not want to die, sweetie."

"Then why don't you get better and leave the hospital, Daddy? It looks like you just don't want to live and you are waiting to die here."

The directness of the questions and the fact that they were coming from the mouth of my ten-year-old left me speechless once again.

When had she gained such wisdom to see through me and grasp what was in my heart, even when I had not admitted it to myself before?

"My baby. I don't know anymore what is left for me in this life. I don't know what to live for and how to live, even."

"But Daddy, why is that? What changed? Were you living for your legs before? Is that why you lived?"

"I… of course not… but… it is not that!" I protested.

"Then what is it? I'm seeing you every day here, just sitting and doing nothing. Doctors say your wound is now healed. There is nothing more they can do for you in the hospital, Daddy. So why don't you come home? Please, Daddy. I want to see you live again. I need you. You used to call me 'my little tiny,' you are not calling me that anymore, Daddy. Why? You don't love me anymore? Please, Daddy, I missed you, I need you to live for me and be my father again!"

With that, she burst into sobs and ran out of the room, without even looking at me. I held out my hand after her as if trying to grasp and bring her back but no words left my sealed lips. I don't remember how long I stayed like that, looking at the space my daughter had just occupied. This was the first emotional outbreak from her of such magnitude, and it triggered something inside me. For the first time since I had woken up in the hospital, I truly felt the connection with my daughter' she needed her father. *A father who had so selfishly made this all about himself, not even stopping to think what it would mean for his child.* It came crashing down on me then: How scared she must have felt. How desperately she would cling to me all those times when I woke up to find her holding my hand with her tiny fingers as if scared that I would die the minute she let my hand go. And for the first time since many days ago, I felt something other than anger and depression: shame. I was ashamed of myself for failing my duties as a father, failing to comfort my child. I was also ashamed of failing at the first real test of my faith. True, I had shed now a broken shell. But deep down, it was still me. My physical body should not have defined my character. My broken body should not have translated into a broken soul. I had always prided myself in not being a material man, in being a man of faith, and believed that tenets of this life were more immaterial than what we saw. This was the first test of my faith, and I had failed miserably.

I cried again. But this time, it was not filled with self-pity and degradation. I cried for forgiveness. As my tears streamed down my cheeks, they washed away the dirt on my soul. My silent sobs shook me, trying to wake me up from the slumber that was eroding my life away. With every exhalation of my tired breath, I felt my spirit uplifting, floating up out of the dark pit it had descended into. A tiny spark of resolution lit inside me then. I clung to that spark that would save me. That little spark was named "my daughter."

Discharge

The next day onward, my daughter came to see me every day. She was again the small package of joy that I remembered from before. As I recovered more and more from my depression, I chatted with my daughter, talking about the fun we had in the past and more importantly what more fun we would have once I was out of the hospital. When the nurses took me out to the gardens, my daughter would hop and skip alongside. Then the nurses would park my wheelchair under the great oak tree at the small hilltop and leave me to enjoy the fresh air. I would watch my little daughter, with her endless source of energy, run around cheerfully. One moment she would dive behind the bushes, hiding from eyesight, another moment she would be rolling down from the hilltop like a human barrel. And when she came to hug me from time to time, I would inhale the earthen fragrance clinging to her from the grass and the flowers she had crushed.

I let all of this in, allowing myself, this time, to be healed. This was the therapy for my soul I had so badly needed. There was peace in the world, and I had to only decide to find it in what I had, not what I had lost.

The hospital staff noticed my spiritual recovery, too. Within a week of first informing me that soon they could discharge me, my doctor came to my room with a group of nurses. Everybody was beaming when, with a grin splitting his face in two, the doctor announced:

"Mustafa, the psychiatrist has given you a clean chit and confirmed that you have improved. I am so glad to inform you that we can release you from the hospital."

So it was time. The past few weeks in the hospital felt like a lifetime. I could not say that I was fully eager to leave but I was resolved. It would be the beginning of a new life, after all, and I felt a mixture of anxiety and hope. Despite the odds, my daughter had given me the courage to hope for the future and I would not let her down this time.

"Thank you, doctor. I guess it was past the time already. I've been enough of trouble for you all."

"Do not worry about that, Mustafa. I am happy for you that you were able to overcome this all by yourself. As I've said before, you are a fighter. You deserve to have happiness in this life, as much as anybody."

"So when can I be off?"

"All is accounted for, your insurance has completed the formalities and we are ready to say goodbye when you are ready."

"You mean, I can go what, like now?"

"Yes, sir! If that's what you want!"

A slight shiver of excitement crossed my body and I took in a deep breath with anticipation. I had overcome possibly the most difficult ordeal of my life. I wanted my daughter, my most precious being, to be by my side, living it with me when I left the hospital.

"Alright, I believe I can leave in the afternoon. But may I please ask that you call my ex-wife and ask her to send my daughter to meet me? I would love to be with my daughter when I do this."

The little chit-chat of the nurses, the wide grin of the doctor, it all suddenly stopped. Nurses started looking at each other, as if uncertain how to answer that. The sheer sign of happiness on the doctor's face just a moment ago turned into unease first but then his eyes betrayed apprehension and even fear. Worry creased his forehead. Very slowly, carefully, he asked:

"Mustafa, what do you mean really? Do you want your ex-wife to come and pick you up? I can ask her to do that, yes."

"No, no," I replied, "not my wife. I honestly don't think she would do that for me. I just need her to bring my daughter to me, just as she kept bringing her all these past days."

The worry in their eyes turned into incredulous stares, as if unable to trust their ears about what they were hearing. Unease also crept into my face, I squinted and squeezed my jaw. I was unable to think of anything that could bring out this reaction from them.

"What's wrong, Doctor? Why are you looking at me like that? I simply asked for my daughter, what is the problem?"

All the nurses were hushed, staring at their toes, then. It was as if they were frozen, afraid to make a move. The doctor took off his spectacles, wiped them with the skirt of his white coat, and slowly put them back on, all the while staring at the floor. Then, he took a deep breath and gave out a sigh. Just as I was opening my mouth to demand an answer, his answer froze me in my bed:

"Mustafa, that night you had the accident… your daughter was with you in the car. And I am sorry, but your daughter did not survive the crash."

Chris

By Rala Sabouni

Chris was in his study sitting at his desk, blankly looking through the glass at the tall trees that shaded his front yard. His eyes were following the soft sun rays and the harmoniously swaying branches. The golden sunshine seemed a little too shy to penetrate the office window.

Indeed, it was a lovely weekend morning. Chris was in very good spirits, ready for anything, even for a peculiar email that popped up on his computer screen.

He narrowed his eyes as he somehow recognized the familiar name that graced the email. He was sure he had seen it somewhere before.

"Wasn't that the same last name I once found in my sister's diary ages ago?" he asked himself.

He couldn't recall what took him to Ella's room that afternoon many years ago, but he remembered very well the look on her face when she spotted him with the open diary in his hands, staring at the man's picture he found tucked safely among the pages. The back of that picture had the same name as the email sender he received today. He could still picture the horrified expression on her face, which he never explained nor understood at that young age. All that mattered to the little boy was that his sister quickly relaxed, realizing he was just messing around like any ten-year-old would on a boring summer afternoon. She hugged him and kissed his cheeks.

Happy to have escaped the punishment of digging into his 'insane' sister's things, he disappeared with a big, mischievous grin on his face. Since that incident and for a reason he could not explain, that name was well embedded in his memory. It faded a little with time, but this email triggered it right back as if he had seen it just yesterday.

"Well, my dear sister, this day may have come," Chris said to himself clicking on the email.

He pushed his chair back and put his feet up the desk, gazing at a dark spot on the ceiling. Lost in his thoughts, he took a stroll down memory lane, way back in time, as far as he could remember.

He was born in England, on a beautiful, unusually sunny day, his mom told him, in one of London's hospitals. He was a big lump of pink flesh with a hint of brown hair on top, and the cutest little face anyone could imagine. His baby fist found its way into his mouth, sucking on as if milk would burst out of the tiny fingers. Indeed, the newborn was hungry after enduring the long, tiring labor. He was so adorable during his first struggle on this earth. His dad and big sister, who welcomed him into the world, surrounded his little crib while Mom was exhausted, trying to get a well-deserved rest. He was blessed with such a loving environment.

Chris smiled when he pictured himself as a baby; he must have been an easy one to handle and soothe. All he probably needed was a good feed, a full stomach, and voila, he would quiet down into deep sleep and Mom would rest. He put his hands on his tummy and said, "I know the feeling very well" before bursting into giggles.

Time passed by, and he was soon ready for school. His first day was not an easy one, he was told. He thought it was picnic time when Mommy and sister buckled him up in the back seat with a small lunch box full of yummy snacks. He was only two years old then, but he was ready to rock the world. His sister introduced him to his beautiful smiling teacher, who took him by hand to show him the place. He was very excited, roaming the small classroom and chatting with his newly made friends. He was so cute trying to share his packed goodies with everyone. All was happy and everything seemed to be going well just as it was supposed to until little Chris found out that Mom and sister had left. He cried like never before, calling to them to come back. The teachers tried to calm down stubborn little Chris for quite some time until Ella had to turn back and stay with him for the rest of the day.

Chris did not remember much of his first day at school, only bits and pieces, but always enjoyed Ella speaking about it. Indeed, Chris always carried this stubbornness in him, and secretly, he was proud of it, although he would never admit it to anyone.

His first-grade teacher was Mrs. Fleming, an older lady. He thought she was the nicest person on the planet, just like a grandma would be, kind and big-hearted. Chris had never met his actual grandparents; his mom told him they passed away long before he was born.

The early years of elementary school passed smoothly. Chris loved going to school in Ella's mini car. She insisted on driving him and spending every morning with her little brother, while most students went by bus. He enjoyed the songs she played for him; they sang along on the way to school. Chris smiled and started humming, 'The wheels on the bus go round and round' his favorite childhood rhythm while his hands drew circles in the air.

At school, Ella often volunteered to help in his classroom. It was always a happy day when she was in. The kids enjoyed the college student's games and stories as they gathered in the front parlor. Little

Chris always stationed himself in front of the fireplace, hypnotized by the beautiful hues of yellow and orange. It still fascinated him to this day.

These fond memories of his early years in London always brought a smile on his face and cheered him up. Chris changed position; he put his feet down again and stretched his back all the way, cracking his knuckles.

Soon, it was time to move on. It was the end of third grade when his mom and dad announced they were moving to a new home, in a new city, in a whole new country, far away from London. His father was promoted to a senior position in his company, and he was needed to manage their main branch in Sydney.

Chris was nervous. He felt his stomach full of butterflies fluttering, almost hearing the noises they made. It was the first time he experienced such sensation, a first of many. Indeed, he learned with time that these 'butterflies' would always keep him company through some rainy days.

Meanwhile, his sister was very excited about the move and she almost pushed for it. She was then twenty-something years old, had finished university, and was working. The move meant that she would meet new people and experience a new way of life. She kept reassuring her dearest little brother that everything would be fine, for they would be together, and that was what mattered the most. She helped him pack his favorite toy car and action figure. And didn't forget to tuck in a small collection of his favorite bedtime storybooks she read to him every night.

Ella was right. He adjusted fairly quickly in this new city, Sydney. While his mother and father were busy establishing the new home and work, Ella and Chris were discovering their new surroundings. She took him sightseeing and visited playgrounds together. They enjoyed a few weeks of pure fun time while Ella was still unemployed, and schools were in-between terms. It was so amazing for Chris to experience the winter in the summer months. The climate in Australia was the opposite of London and was one of the many things that Chris adjusted to rather easily. People there had their distinctive accent and way of pronouncing words and Chris was a fast learner. He enjoyed talking like the locals. He didn't remember when he stopped using his West London accent; it just happened naturally and gradually.

Time passed by in a blink. Soon, Ella had met a nice gentleman at work. They fell in love and got married. They chose to live nearby for a while, in the same neighborhood, and Chris enjoyed having two homes instead of one.

Soon after, he graduated high school, attended the first two years of university in Sydney, and then transferred to Malaysia where Ella and Michael had moved the year before. The couple were both approaching their 40th birthdays and decided they wanted a new adventure in their life.

The east had its charm that attracted the couple first, then young Chris to follow.

Michael, Ella's husband, was a tall, brown-haired, green-eyed gentleman, and he looked so much like an older version of Chris. It was as if only Chris's big brown eyes set them apart. Ella was a petite blond lady getting her beautiful looks from their mother, and her smaller stature from their father. The couple were both attractive in their way and were a perfect match for each other. They were kind and loving, and he enjoyed spending time at their home where he was always welcomed.

His mom and dad did not mind his move at all; they were probably expecting it. Ella was ecstatic to have Chris around again as she missed his laughter, fun, and gentleness. Besides, she thought it would be a good opportunity for Chris to experience life in a new environment while she and Michael lived there. Ella always had Chris's best interest at heart. So it worked well for everyone. Yet, his 'butterflies' would still visit him whenever he thought of his parents' advancing age. Mom and Dad were in their sixties then; he could sense them growing frail, and knew they would soon need someone constantly closer to them, a lot closer than the long flight he or Ella needed to cross over to the southern continent.

All in all, things went well, up until the day his father called with gloomy news. He had cancer, and his condition was not looking good. His cancer had spread like a creature sneaking up around his body quietly until it fully captured its prey, and then announced itself arrogantly and loudly with pain, fatigue, and lots of panic.

Chris, without a second thought, rushed over to be with his parents. The ten-hour flight felt endless. He still remembered his agony, and restlessness onboard. He could not forget the extraordinary and frightening loneliness he felt during that flight, for his sister and husband were to follow in the next one. Once again, he had only the 'butterflies' keeping him company.

Chris felt like his heart had been ripped from his body upon glancing at his father on the hospital bed. He realized how gravely ill he was. His eyes brimmed with tears to see how fragile and pale he looked. The once strong and energetic man was now lying helplessly, fighting to grasp every breath. It was clear his dear father's time on this earth was nearing its end.

The mother and her son hugged for a long while outside the hospital room. They cried and cried till there were no more tears to shed. The doctors explained his father's very serious condition. His mind was wandering, unable to concentrate. He was searching for a miracle, a miracle only a loving son believed existed. He refused the doctors' heartless and cruel advice to stop medical interference and wait for his demise. He was appalled by their lack of compassion as they tried to convince the family of the useless struggle.

He knew there must be something that could be done to halt the mercilessly expanding evil in his father's body. Finally, and with a last drop of sympathy, one of the doctors suggested a bone marrow transplant, a complicated procedure, and a very difficult one. To find a matching donor was a whole ordeal in itself. Chris followed the glimmer of hope.

There was no time to be wasted looking for donors. So, without any delays, Chris and Ella went through a series of physical and blood tests to determine their eligibility to donate their bone marrow. That sharp laboratory smell, the stench of sickness and mortality, still lingers in his head to this day. He still remembered the ice-cold air, and the careful approach of the nurse carrying the needles lying on the tray like fallen soldiers next to each other and sharply pricking his vein, thirsty for the red liquid that had in it all the answers to Father's good health. The God-given magic potion.

Chris felt content doing this. He wanted to give back the gift of life to his ailing father and pull him out of death that was fast approaching. He would do anything to see him strong and healthy again.

A few days later, while still waiting for the results, Chris's father lost his battle. It was a sad afternoon. The birds stopped singing, the sun hid behind the clouds, the lush green trees ceased to dance with the breeze, and all the butterflies left the blossoming flowers in the fields and took a place in Chris's stomach. As if life had changed direction, and the whole universe was declaring that his dear father had started his eternal journey in a different dimension, beyond the reach of his beloved. He passed away before anything could be done.

Sitting in his office, Chris realized that he needed some tissues to wipe the flow of tears on his face. No matter how far back it happened, he would always cry when he remembered the day his father bid his last farewell.

He wiped his tears and put his attention black on the screen in front of him.

"Dear Chris," he started reading. "I hope this finds you well.

"My name is Nehma Ouroogh. I am Turkish and live and work in Istanbul. I am contacting you regarding an important matter that has recently come to my attention. I understand if you find this upsetting and do not wish to contact me back, but I believe I have a duty to share this.

"I was recently traveling on business in the USA, and I came across an advertisement for DNA testing. I have always wanted to learn more about my ancestry origins and family tree, so I decided to take the test. I received the results in six weeks, and I created a profile on the company's site. Your name was listed as being a first cousin to me.

"I am contacting you because I know all of my uncles, aunts, and cousins. I am keen to understand how and if you are related to me. If this is too much of an intrusion, I completely understand. If you don't wish to connect, please ignore this email.

Wishing you well,
Nehma"

Nehma captured Chris's attention fairly easily.

He got excited. He remembered what made him take that same test years back, just after his father's passing. His family had broken apart. He had to stay with his mother in Sydney for a while to help her wrap up the family home and finish her affairs to move back to England, while Ella and her husband left for their home in Malaysia for work. They had become separated again.

He felt so lonely, so trapped within, and no matter where he turned, he saw grief and darkness. He wanted to know more of who he was, his identity, his ancestry, his own body, and the diseases he inherited, illnesses that he was prone to. He thought he could fight off any malfunction in his body early on before it manifested and spare his loved ones any suffering. DNA testing was his small window of hope. He thought he could get all his questions answered with just a little sample of saliva in a small testing tube.

Undoubtedly, his DNA test result was very detailed and broad. It revealed to him all the information he wanted to know and more. Through the test, he could see a clear mix of genes that seemed to him a little awkward: Eastern European, a little Middle Eastern, and some Italian ancestry, in addition to Scandinavian, and some Western European. It looked like his ancestors came from all over.

It fascinated him how his blood could carry prints of so many different people. His big brown eyes were practical evidence of his ancestors' reality. He always wondered about his eyes and brown hair. Indeed, he stood out with his looks among two blond ladies and the gray-haired man in his family. Alas, his curious inquiries about these looks never received any attention from his parents.

Chris enthusiastically opened his profile page on the lab website. It had been a while and he almost forgot about it. He smiled upon seeing the updated information. Nehma's name was added recently to his relatives. She was on top of the list of the little number of distant cousins he had. Nehma was the closest relation of them all. She was categorized as a first cousin, just as she said in her email. The accuracy of the test stated 'very high.'

While the thrilling news was sinking in, Chris thought of calling his mother and Ella to ask if they knew anything of a Turkish relative. However, he decided to investigate a little more by himself. He recalled the time he tried to persuade both his mother and Ella to do the test along with him, but they were indifferent. Neither did they show any excitement when he brought in the results. He thought then that both ladies were a little too old to fully grasp the potentials of DNA testing. "Too old, eh? I think not," Chris said to himself.

He wrote back to Nehma, thanking her for contacting him. He told her how delighted and pleasantly surprised he was to see that he had a cousin that far away from England, and how he would like to know more details of how they were related. He also told her his parents' names, as well as his sister's. They were the only family he had; there were no uncles, aunts, or cousins.

The more he wrote, the more scenarios bombarded his head with possibilities. One after the other. A cousin meant there was an uncle or an aunt somewhere in Turkey. That translated into a brother or sister to his late father or his mother. It was such a strange feeling to suddenly discover that his parents had family across the lands, families they never mentioned in the past.

Chris was agitated, his hands trembled a little. What else had his parents possibly hidden from the two siblings? Why were the relatives never mentioned as they were growing up? Did they know of these relatives? Or did his sister know? Whose picture was that in her diary that matched this lady's last name? It couldn't be just a coincidence. Many, many questions went through his head. And as confusing as the whole situation was, Chris was determined to follow up on this story. Stubbornness had always been his trait. It was time to put it to good use.

He needed to clear up his mind, so he left the house and walked through the garden, to get some fresh air. Amused by the flocks of migrating geese and the perfect V they formed in the clear blue sky, he decided to stay outdoors a little longer. Deeply immersed in his thoughts, he walked and walked through the narrow trail road, never minding the time. He knew in his heart that Nehma's news meant a great deal of change into his somewhat dull daily routine.

What started as exciting news for Chris had a whole new perspective by the end of the day. Some shadowy schemes found their way into his thoughts like an unwanted guest who desired to be entertained. And when the worst of them all, the possibility of adoption trespassed his mind, he fearfully waved it off without a second thought. Could he be adopted?

Why hadn't his parents ever spoken about their Turkish siblings? How could it be that they had family in Turkey? So many things seemed out of place to him. His thoughts zoomed by trying to make sense of it all. He tried brushing the whole possibility of adoption from his mind. He tried to laugh it off. Maybe there were things he did not know; perhaps deeply buried family secrets. However, at the back of his mind, he knew deep inside that he had to face reality sooner or later. If he was going to delve into his family history and investigate further, some secrets would eventually spill out. He did not quite know how this new revelation would map out and where it would take him. But he was ready to discover!

Finally, when the hues of dusk appeared on the horizon and he went back indoors. He still had to finish off sending that email to Nehma.

He ended it by expressing how important it was for him to keep in touch, and to learn more about the members of her family, and his. He felt a little strange to say that; his hands tingled when he typed it.

Gradually, with greater communication, the two new cousins became friends. They exchanged childhood stories, family photos, and discussed life experiences like any two persons starting a friendship. Chris for sure had some resemblance to one of the cousins, as cousins often did. Naturally, a sense of belonging to Nehma's family was increasing as they got closer. It was hard to believe they only met a few weeks ago, and only virtually, not even in person.

Nehma, too, was intrigued by the discovery. She started her little investigation quietly. Inquiring of the aunt and uncle's whereabouts in the yesteryears. Her mother was an only child so she couldn't find many answers with her maternal side of the family. Therefore, she concentrated all her efforts on her paternal aunt and two uncles.

Being biologically first cousins had many possible explanations. Chris could have been fathered by one of her two uncles, or only aunt, which meant that one of his parents related to her by blood.

Nehma did not dwell at all on the prospect of her only aunt being Chris's biological mother – the idea was repulsive to her. Even as open-minded as she was, she could not think of her lovely aunt giving birth to a child and abandoning it. She resolved to look into this only if all other paths took her to a dead end.

The whole thing seemed complicated and confusing. Nehma had to start a process of elimination. She quickly dismissed any of Chris's parents being the offspring of her grandparents, as their looks were undoubtedly completely different. It relieved her, even more, to know how close in age to her grandparents they were. That made it impossible to be biologically born to them. She slowly concluded that Chris might have been adopted, and was not raised by his biological parents, but she needed to find out why and how, and who was his real father.

She just needed some sort of positive confirmation, so she kept working on connecting the dots.

Meanwhile, the more Chris knew about his newly found relatives, the closer he wanted to be to them. The warmth of a big family was alluring and he always wished for one during his childhood. Nehma obliged all of Chris's curiosities. She understood very well how he felt, so she helped to familiarize him with her culture as much as she could. Although her sudden burst of questions and inquiries of the past caused a little stir in the family, she was cleverly prepared with the perfect explanation. Working on creating a family tree got the elders excited, and all her questions were answered.

On the other hand, back in England, Chris tried to get some clues from his mother but was always given short-sentenced answers with no elaboration. The avoidance of any dwelling into details of her pregnancy with him was obvious. Chris's questions were starting to cause his elderly mother emotional pain. He did not want to pressure her any further, for he loved and cared for her too dearly to do so. The confusion in her eyes broke his heart. He began to get more convinced of the possibilities of being adopted. His heart sank just thinking about it.

He was sure the missing information of his birth in London would get him closer to his biological relatives, unfortunately, at the same time, he knew they would draw him farther away from his beloved mother.

Ella was on the other side of the globe, so far away to be able to open his heart and talk to her about his findings. She had always been his refuge in difficult times, but not this time. He hoped that somehow his older sister had the magic explanation for all of it, as she always did in the past. But he was alone in the midst of all this chaos, and surprisingly, he grew a little envious of his sister. Ella looked a lot like their mother. The biological resemblance of the two was clear; there was no doubt they were a mother and a daughter. However, he was the odd-looking one, the ugly duckling that didn't belong. They say "the eyes have it all", but his eyes had the brown color among a family of blue eyes. He was a tall man among a delicately-built sister and parents. Adding to the dilemma was the big age gap between himself and Ella. Altogether, things made a lot more sense to him now. He decided to resort to silence until he got all the answers. The seed of anger and confusion about his identity was growing in him.

Christmas time was approaching. London got cold and dreary. Chris was suffocating. He needed to escape for a while.

The two cousins agreed it was time to meet in person. And no other place would be more suitable than enchanting Istanbul in the fall.

Chris hesitantly called Ella by phone to announce his trip.

"Hey sis, how are you?" he tried to sound as cheerful as he could.

"I'm good. Where have you been the past few weeks? You disappeared on me! I missed you. What are you up to?"

"A few things came up actually. I will tell you later," he said without any elaboration.

"Would love to hear about them. We are so much looking forward to our gathering at Christmas," Ella said.

"Yeah, same here. But listen, there is something I needed to tell you."

"Of course, what is it?"

"Well, I'm leaving London for a few days. Just wanted to let you know in case you spoke to Mom."

"Oh, that's amazing. Where to?"

"Turkey."

"…What business you have there?"

"Nothing really, just a few loose ends."

"Hmm, hope you enjoy it. I heard Turkey is a beautiful country. You have to tell me all about it when you are back."

"For sure I will. Please say hello to Michael."

"I will. Please take care."

It didn't take long for Ella to sense the changed tone in Chris's voice. She could not pinpoint what exactly was going on. But her mother was quick to convey her concerns over Chris's constant inquiries. Her heart sank. She flew to London immediately.

The two siblings missed each other by a few hours. He was heading east to Istanbul embarking on a new journey, while she headed west to London. For the first time in the brother and sister's lives, their fates went in opposite directions. Their paths separated.

"First time in Turkey?" the passenger next to him asked with a smile.

"Yes, the first time here for so many things," Chris said while peeking through the cabin window. He looked at this legendary ancient city that bridged Europe and Asia. The east and the west. He wasn't sure to which he belonged at that very moment.

The sapphire color of the sea was enchanting from above. While splitting the ancient city into two, the Bosphorus was about to split Chris's destiny as well.

The scenery of the golden sun reflecting on its surface was mesmerizing. It bounced back in all directions in a breathtaking array of lights. Chris's mood lifted. He was feeling rather at ease again.

Luckily, his flight arrived in the early afternoon, otherwise, infamous Istanbul traffic would have been a nightmare. His taxi driver was very experienced. He took every possible route to get him to his hotel in the most comfortable manner. He was driving through the maze of streets, easily deciphering its codes like a pro.

His hotel was in the Sultanahmet district, the old part of Istanbul. Chris chose to stay in the heart of the hustle and bustle of the old city to enjoy Istanbul's true spirit. He wanted to meet people, have conversations with the locals, and eat their authentic food. He wished to taste the true Turkish experience. After all, he had Turkish blood running in his veins, and he was about to meet his blood family.

November was a good month to visit Istanbul without the crowds of tourists – it was the same beautiful city, but a little quieter. Roses were still in bloom and the sun was still shining, spreading its warmth in the cool autumn afternoon. He checked into his hotel room, freshened up quickly, and went for a stroll in the famous Istanbul old city.

He had a couple of hours before he went back for his appointment with Nehma.

It was truly a walk-through time. Chris felt as if he had crossed a time-traveling gate or something of that sort. He found himself face to face with the legendary Blue Mosque that stood with all its glory and exquisite beauty. The magnificent building held within it a very rich history, while its walls were telling its visitors the tales of the majestic Ottoman Empire.

He took a stroll through the garden surrounding the mosque, then found himself a seat next to an old man feeding the pigeons.

"Merhaba," he greeted the old man with a smile.

"Merhaba," the old man smiled back.

"Güzel bir gün," the old man continued. He could not tell Chris was a tourist. Chris laughed, "I can't speak Turkish, I only know a few words."

The old man laughed and offered some of the bird feed he was holding. Chris took it with gratitude.

As the two men threw the seeds, the pigeons gathered around them, enjoying the generous feast. While feeding birds was never welcomed in London, he learned that in Turkey it was considered an act of goodwill, and everyone including tourists were welcome to practice. It was an exotic experience, and for sure a good omen for Chris.

It was approaching sunset when he turned back, heading for his hotel.

He changed his clothes into a warmer attire and went down to the lobby where Nehma and Chris agreed to meet. There she was, sitting with crossed legs, looking into her phone. He immediately recognized her from the pictures. Upon seeing him, her face brightened up with a familiar smile – it looked like his own. She stood up and hugged him with a loving embrace. She stared at him for a few seconds, and said laughing, "You can surely pass as my brother." She was a tall and thin lady, fair-complexioned, with beautiful big brown eyes, and short hair. Nehma was about his age, or a few years older, probably in her late thirties. She had a vibrant and open personality, and she was very excited to meet him.

Nehma suggested going to the modern part of Istanbul's Taksim Square and the Istiklal Avenue. There was a famous authentic restaurant she wanted to invite him there for his first dinner in Turkey, hoping he was a meat-eater, she said with a laugh. "In Turkey, you will miss a lot of tasty food if you don't eat meat," she teased while putting on her seat belt.

The night was falling; the air became a lot colder, and the beautiful colors of Istanbul street lights were captivating. The two cousins walked along the Istiklal Avenue passing by beautiful historic buildings, art galleries, and lots and lots of boutiques. It was a very different scene from the old town for sure. They chatted about their childhoods and their parents.

He shared more photos of Ella and her husband, and his parents in their younger years, while Nehma brought pictures of her three children and husband.

At the end of the avenue, they climbed down a flight of stairs, where there was Zubeyir Restaurant right at the corner. The aroma of grilled meat was filling the air, which surely made any passerby drool over the delectable scent. Chris was so hungry by then that he devoured everything Nehma ordered. The kebabs were out of this world, like nothing he had ever tasted before. They both laughed at the speed he emptied the dishes and knew they needed a good walk to burn off some of that food before bedtime. They took a stroll toward Taksim Square, got a cup of hot tea to warm up, and separated for the night, to see each other again the next day. He was invited to her home to meet the family, her husband, kids, parents, and uncles.

He was exhausted when he reached his hotel room. He threw himself in the armchair in front of the window, gazing into the void, reflecting. A flow of overwhelming feelings engulfed his whole being. There he was in a foreign country, visiting for the first time in his life to look for a biological father he had no idea existed a few months back. He had a good life and a happy family. Why was he messing all that and stirring up the past? He loved the father who raised him. Did he need to meet this blood father he knew nothing about, who abandoned him, to say the least, or perhaps did not even know of his existence altogether? Was he able to feel any love toward a stranger? What if he was not wanted? Was it wise to go through with the plan of meeting Nehma's family?

Up till that moment, he was excited, going with the flow, but in the next few days, his whole life was about to change; the life as he knew it was about to become a melody of the past. The night fell quiet; his thoughts became vague and he slowly drifted into slumber.

The sound of the *azaan* startled him out of his deep sleep the next morning. He couldn't tell the time when he opened the curtains. The sunshine greeted him with a warm strike of light. It was yet another beautiful, sunny day. He loved sunny days ever since his mother told him he was born on one. He smiled a half-smile.

He had a few hours to spend in town before his dinner appointment. He wanted to distract himself, so he decided to visit the Hagia Sophia museum nearby, and the old Souk to get a few gifts for his mom, Ella, and some friends back in London. He did not want to think much at this point; he just wanted to pass the time.

By 5 o'clock he was heading to Nehma's house following the directions on his GPS. The driver knew the residential area very well. He dropped him off right in front of their door. Chris stood there for a moment knowing that behind this door lay the rest of his future; one of his real parents was in there. There was no turning back now. He came this far, he just needed to go in and embrace the unknown.

Nehma and her husband came outside to greet him. Her husband seemed as nice and vibrant as his wife, and Chris felt at home. They took him inside and introduced him to Nehma's parents and the rest of the family. It was a full house. The two uncles and the aunt were all there and were looking forward to meeting Nehma's new English friend. She told them so much about him, careful not to mention anything about the discovered blood relation.

It was a warm welcome, and the English fluency of the guests made it so much easier to enjoy the evening. There were lots of laughter, lots of storytelling, and past recollections. The family opened up to Chris very easily; he did not feel a stranger to them, and with his familiar looks, he fit right in. That was precisely what Nehma and Chris hoped for. The needle in the heaps of straw they were searching for seemed a lot easier to find than they thought.

When things quieted down after dinner, Uncle Emir, the youngest of the three brothers, brought Chris a warm cup of tea and sat next to him.

"My dear Chris, I want you to know that I left a piece of my heart with one of your kin back in the day," Uncle Emir said abruptly.

Chris was startled. He looked at Uncle Emir with astonishment, then he laughed, he thought he was joking.

"I had a few friends from the UK. We were such a close group of students in college," Uncle Emir continued nostalgically. He told Chris about his five wonderful years he spent in Germany while studying mechanical engineering.

"They were the best years of my life," Chris thought he saw a tear escaping the uncle's eyes. Chris listened attentively. He was glad Uncle Emir warmed up to him. It was his chance to know more about his past and the possibility of being his biological father. He didn't know where to begin, but for sure, getting closer to the uncle was a good start.

"So, are you still in contact with your college friends?" Chris inquired.

"I wish," he said with sorrow. "All contact was lost a long time ago, although I tried numerous times," he continued regretfully. "When Nehma told us about her English friend, it was all very exciting to me... brought back all my memories and hopes."

"With the social media nowadays, it might be easier to reconnect you if you remember their names. Have you tried Facebook?" Chris suggested earnestly.

"Oh, I haven't. I'm not a big social media man. I have no time and not sure what it is about."

"I can help you if you want," Chris offered to help as he wanted to get closer to the uncle.

"Oh, that will be very kind of you, but I don't want to trouble you."

"No trouble at all, it will be my pleasure," Chris said with a reassuring smile.

The uncle's face brightened up. His mustache widened as he smiled. He looked sincerely very happy about the offer. He had no idea how to use Facebook, although he knew his wife did, yet he would not ask her, neither did he want to ask his son for any help.

That evening, before Chris excused himself to leave, Uncle Emir wrote down a few names on a piece of paper and handed it to him with a wistful stare. Chris was a little taken by how tenderly Uncle Emir looked at him. *It must have meant a great deal for him to find these friends*, Chris thought to himself. He tucked the paper in his pocket and promised to start the search soon.

That evening, he called Ella to chat. He was pleasantly surprised to find her in London with their mother. He told both ladies how much he missed them. And how he wished they were with him enjoying Istanbul together.

Chris stayed up late; no sleep found its way to his eyes that night. His brain was buzzing, analyzing every conversation he had earlier with Nehma's family, hoping to get a clue to which of the two uncles was his biological father.

He got along with the aunt and both uncles. They were all very kind and sweet. But Uncle Emir had this look in his eyes that Chris could not explain; the eagerness and fragility he showed that evening made him for sure stand out among the rest. It made Chris warm up to him.

He needed to find out before he left back to England in a couple of days. He couldn't leave matters hanging, for his mind was about to burst with anticipation.

He finally dozed off at dawn and surrendered to slumber. All sorts of dreams followed him to the twilight. Ella and his parents, and Nehma and her family were all there in a mish-mash of events.

It was very hard to wake up in the morning; Chris was exhausted. Staying up late took its toll on him. Then, he suddenly remembered the paper Uncle Emir handed him. He got up and took it out of his pocket, unfolded it, and was ready to start the search online when his eyes caught the first name. He gasped in disbelief, his hands shaking. There was his sister Ella's Christian name, Ellen Ann Green, staring back at him.

The earth went in circles around him; he started sweating. He did not expect such a shocking surprise. *Why was Ella's name on the list?* Chris wondered. Then he remembered that Uncle Emir had mentioned a lady he had been madly in love with while he was in England. Ella's name was the only female name on the list. Was she his lost love interest? Chris's mind whirled as he thought about the shocking possibility. He began to shiver and gasp for air as his eyes moved in all directions, thinking of the possibilities of this discovery.

Chris felt like a ship in the middle of a storm. He didn't know what to make of this find. Nehma's uncle and his sister may have been lovers. Immediately, he thought that she must have been the English girl he left his heart with a long time ago. If so, Uncle Emir was the man in the picture his sister was keeping safe and protecting. "One day, someday, one day, someday, one day some…" Ella's words echoed in his ears again and again.

Chris got very anxious.

He desperately needed to talk to Nehma. He called her to calm himself down. He was still shaking.

"I think we may have found a breakthrough."

"What do you mean? How?"

"Your Uncle Emir is searching for my sister. He asked me last night if I could help him find his friend. And I found out this morning that it's my sister he is looking for. I don't know exactly the extent of their relationship, but it is clear they were in love and the picture in Ella's diary was his."

"Oh, dear! This is an amazing development, Chris… Do you think Uncle Emir is your…?"

Chris went quiet. It was the only explanation, the only logical conclusion. But how? What about Ella?

The uncle was desperately trying to find an old friend, and she turned out to be his sister; what were the odds of something like this happening? The passion of Uncle Emir in looking for his English friend surely meant a whole greater deal than just looking for an old love. "He is looking for his child," Chris said loudly while he was still on the phone with Nehma.

"His child," he repeated.

"Chris, are you okay..."

"Please forgive me, Nehma, I can't think clearly, I will call you later."

"Of course, please take care."

"Thank you."

There was still a missing link and he was determined to find it. How did he end up being his parents' child? Could it be that he was Ella's child? Why did she not admit to it? What had happened? Did the uncle give up his son to his girlfriend's parents to adopt? But why Ella? And why her parents? It seemed so bizarre, even if they loved each other.

"What if..."

"No, no, it can't be, no, no, no," Chris started shaking his head right and left. "No, no..."

Then in a pivotal moment, a moment meant only for great revelations, this insane thought made perfect sense. He had his childhood memories flash right before his eyes. Ella was in every single one of them. His sister's love and extraordinary care for him throughout, her constant support for all the battles little Chris endured. She was his anchor, the wings that kept him safe all these years. She had always been so much more than just a sister, but he never noticed... a mother, yes, she was his mother. That was the missing piece of the puzzle. The piece held all the beautiful details, and happy endings.

Chris burst into tears like a small child, covering his face with his hands, and he sobbed with all his might. He needed Ella by his side at that moment. He needed his mother. There was still that ion of doubt that he had gotten it all wrong but his heart, his instinct was telling him that she was indeed his mother.

It took him a long while to calm down; two prayers and a change of color on the horizon to be precise. Just before sunset, he called Nehma again. He was unusually quiet; it was the calm after the storm. He discussed his findings and conclusion. Nehma was ecstatic.

Chris paced his room back and forth, thinking how to proceed next. He knew he had to confirm his findings first with Uncle Emir. He called and asked to see him urgently. He was nervous as he dialed the number on the phone, but excited to hear Uncle Emir on the other side of the line. It was no longer a voice of a stranger, rather a voice of a dear one.

"Urgently? Is it related to the search of the names? Did you already find them?" Uncle Emir could not hide his excitement.

"Yes," Chris didn't want to say much, but he was very happy to feel the excitement in Uncle Emir's voice. "But there is this another private matter we have to talk about. It has to do with Ella... Ellen. We have to clarify a few things."

There was a moment of silence. "Ella? Haven't heard that nickname for so long," he said with a sigh. "Of course, shall we meet in an hour?"

"Perfect," Chris replied.

Uncle Emir gave him a name of a nice quiet cafe to meet at. He couldn't wait to hear what Chris had to say.

Chris did not notice how cold the evening had become. He left without a jacket.

The cafe was not far away, so he walked. He needed to quiet this roller coaster of emotions before he saw his 'father.'

He was not sure of Uncle Emir's reaction to his findings, but deep inside, he knew it would be good news. He had many questions to ask him, many *hows, whens,* and *whys*.

By the time Chris had arrived at the cafe, he was shivering and his nose was running.

There was a small fireplace inside. He always loved fireplaces. Chris sat in his favorite position opposite the fire in the quiet corner and ordered a hot tea till Uncle Emir arrived.

Uncle Emir entered the cafe quietly. He was greeted by the hostess like a well-known guest. He took off his coat and looked around for Chris. A wide smile bloomed across his face when he saw him sitting, warming his hands against the fireplace.

Chris stood up to greet him with a handshake. Uncle Emir hugged Chris affectionately, showing his warm and welcoming personality. The two men sat down and stared at each other.

Uncle Emir finally broke the silence.

"Thank you for taking the time to help me find my friend. I wish I used this Facebook a long time ago," he said with a grin.

He continued, "But how did you know her nickname?"

Chris smiled, and hesitantly said, "Actually, I did not find Ella through Facebook."

"Oh?" Uncle Emir asked.

"Well, Ella is my sister," Chris said studying his father's facial expressions.

"Good gracious God," Uncle Emir gasped. His face turned a little pale and he stared at Chris with disbelief.

"I need you to tell me why you were looking for her," Chris continued after Uncle Emir quietened down.

He took a deep breath and said, "Before I say anything, my dear Chris, would you be so kind to tell how she and her son are? Where are they living now? I beg you to tell me more about the two. I looked so long for them, and I will explain everything to you in a moment," he said eagerly.

"Well, Ella has been living with her husband in Malaysia for the past 10 years. And her..." Chris desperately wanted to say 'son' but couldn't utter the word.

"And? How about the son?" Uncle Emir asked eagerly.

"Well, that is really what I needed to talk to you about..." Chris became visibly nervous.

Uncle Emir tried to compose himself, "Of course, Chris, I'm listening."

"I don't know how to start this. But only a few weeks back, I discovered... Nehma discovered, that we are related by blood. You see, Nehma did this DNA test and it showed that she and I are first cousins. And that is why I am here in Turkey. I wanted to find out who."

"Oh, that's why Nehma was asking everyone all those questions," Uncle Emir said, not paying attention to what Chris had just stated.

Chris continued, "Yes, but..."

"Yes?" Uncle Emir asked with a quizzical expression sprawled across her face.

"The DNA test specified that I am a first cousin to her. We narrowed it down to yourself and Uncle Selim."

Uncle Emir's expressions changed. He was trying to understand the shocking flood of information that was pouring out of Chris's mouth.

"What was the nature of your relationship? I'm assuming..." Chris hesitated.

"But you just said Ella was your sister..." Uncle Emir stammered.

"Yes, but Ella has no children. There is only me, her much younger brother," Chris replied watching Uncle Emir closely.

Uncle Emir was speechless. He stared at Chris with wide-open eyes, absorbing the meaning of what he said. And then looked at him as if seeing him for the first time.

"You are... my son," Uncle Emir gasped.

He held his hand and, with very obvious joy, he started muttering Turkish words. Chris laughed. Uncle Emir then quickly stood up and hugged him with all his might, and then sat down while still holding

Chris's hand. He stared at him studying his features as tears rolled down his cheeks.

"You don't know for how long I looked for you, for both of you, but she disappeared. She took you and disappeared," Uncle Emir said with some sadness.

It was very emotional between the two men, but Uncle Emir needed to explain a whole lot of things to Chris:

"We were two young adults in love. We got engaged after Ella got pregnant with you and we were planning to get married before your birth. Then my father got sick. I had to leave and head back to Turkey for a while, and she went back to London to give birth to you shortly after. She sent me a few pictures of you that I still have and cherish dearly. After my father passed away, I was left with no means of financial support. When I came to visit you and Ella in London, she was finishing her university there and decided not to go back to Germany. She wanted to stay by her family while I had to go back to finish my last year. All circumstances had changed for both of us. We got cold feet and postponed marriage plans till we both got financially comfortable. I promised her to visit often, but I visited you one more time and then I stopped. The distance between us was not kind to our relationship. We both drifted apart. Honestly, we were so young and immature. I regret many decisions I made then, and I had to live with the pain they caused."

Chris was nodding his head but did not speak. He was absorbing this information, allowing Uncle Emir to finish his explanation. He desperately wanted to know all the details.

"I started working after college, and I must confess, that neglecting both of you was a big mistake. And I've paid a hefty price for it. By the time I was on my feet and was able to support a family, a few years later, Ella had disappeared from London. No one knew where she was. I am sure she never forgave me for abandoning you."

"We left for Australia when I was eight," Chris said.

"Australia? That far away? I wonder if you had your names changed as well. We called you Adam at your birth. I had no idea your grandparents adopted you," Uncle Emir said.

"My birth name is Christopher Adam Anderson, and I'm known as Chris."

Chris poured his heart out to his father. He told him about his parents, childhood, and upbringing as Ella's little brother. His college and his travels. He tried to squeeze his life story in those last hours of the evening. They talked and talked until it got too late, and the cafe was empty except for the two.

They stood up and left, with Uncle Emir's arms wrapped around Chris's shoulders.

The cold air hit them hard when they opened the cafe door. Uncle Emir noticed that Chris did not have a jacket on, so he took off his own and wrapped it around Chris's shoulders with fatherly affection.

"Here, put this on, it will keep you warm." Chris smiled and took it with gratitude.

It was indeed a different feeling of warmth. The father and son were beginning to bond in an evening to be remembered for many years to come.

The next morning, Chris woke up with a fever. He was so weak, he could barely open his eyes.

He remembered his evening and his heart danced with bliss. Despite the fever making him feel so exhausted, he could not help but smile.

Chris reached for his phone on his bedside table to find multiple missed calls from Nehma. He called her back to quickly brief her as he was not able to speak for too long.

"Please stay warm," she urged him. "I'll pass by in the afternoon to check on you."

"I will, thank you." Then he went back to bed. He had no strength, the fever had stripped him out of his last drop of energy.

Chris slept for the entire day, waking up to pounding on his door. He dragged himself wearily out of bed and opened the door to see Nehma with his father.

"You got us worried. We tried calling you numerous times. What happened? You look awful," Nehma said.

"I don't know. I just went to sleep. What time is it?"

"It's 5pm," Nehma said, as they all went inside. She opened the curtains, and half of the window to freshen up the room. She carried a layered lunch box with her. She brought some soup and light food as she expected that Chris did not eat anything yet.

He was pampered by the two like a small child and frankly, he loved the attention.

They ordered some soothing chamomile tea from room service and stayed and chatted with him. It helped him out of his weariness.

"Are you still flying back tomorrow? Can't you extend your stay a little longer?" asked Uncle Emir wistfully.

"I wish! I have to be back. There is an unfinished business I need to take care of," Chris said.

"But I promise to arrange another meet up soon," he added lovingly. His eyes twinkled.

"I would very much love so," he said. "You know, I can't let you run away from me now that I have found you." Everyone laughed.

Then Nehma and Uncle Emir helped him pack his bag, made sure he had everything he needed for the night, gave him a warm goodbye hug, and wished him safe travels. They took their leave and left.

When the taxi stopped in front of his parents' home in London, Chris panicked a little. He knew he would not be able to escape Ella's questioning. She could easily sense any change in him. She had always read him like an open book. But he had enough time to organize his thoughts during his flight; he decided to break the news to her, the sooner the better.

He put his hand on his stomach to quiet down the fluttering, took a deep breath, and went inside.

"I'm home," he yelled as he was getting in.

"You're back," Ella shrieked with excitement. She gave him a big warm hug, and took him by the hand, and said, "Come now, tell us all about this trip." Chris kissed both ladies and sat down.

"It is great to see you in London, Ella. What brought you all the way here at this time? How's Michael?"

"He misses you very much... We both do. I thought to stay with Mom while you were away."

"I'm glad she came... I would have felt very lonely without her," Mom said in agreement with Ella.

Chris looked at the two ladies and smiled. Something had changed between them. They were no longer a sister and a mother to him, but rather, a mother and a grandmother, and he had no regrets whatsoever.

This trip to Turkey did not gain him only a father, but a loving mother and a grandmother. He was so thankful for these gifts; he finally felt complete.

"Come now, let me show you what I brought you from the 'enchanting east,' from the 'heart of Istanbul's grand bazaar,'" he said.

The ladies laughed at his theatrical tone.

He gave his mother a colorful warm shawl that could brighten up any dull winter day in London and gave Ella a set of beautiful teacups with oriental motives.

The ladies were very happy with their gifts, but the Turkish delight stole the scene when he pulled it out of his carry-on bag. Indeed, it was a perfect dessert for afternoon teatime.

Ella and Chris went to the kitchen to prepare small sandwiches and brew the hot beverage.

"I'm really happy to see you, Ella," he said looking at her tenderly.

She gazed back, sensing the difference in his tone of speech, just as he predicted.

"Won't you tell me what took you to Turkey?" she asked while spreading some mustard on the bread.

"Well, I met a gentleman in Istanbul," Chris said hesitantly, his voice breaking. He wasn't sure he could say his name.

"Who was he?" Ella asked.

Chris took a big gulp and breathed in deeply. He had made up his mind to reveal all. It was a perfect time and he built enough courage to finally say, "I saw Mr. Emir Ouroojh."

Ella froze in place, dropped whatever was held in her hand and stared at him with wide eyes. She was utterly stunned.

"I know now," he said softly.

Ella covered her face and started to cry. She was completely speechless. Except for the sobbing, nothing else could be heard from her. She cried out the silence of all the years she had kept this secret buried deep inside.

The heavyweight had been lifted off her shoulders finally. She was relieved from the burden she carried for too long.

Chris's eyes welled up with tears at witnessing his sister's emotional breakdown. He hugged her with all the passion of a child longing for motherly affection. He tried to calm her down.

"It's alright now, Ella... it's alright, Mama," he said lovingly, uncovering her face and wiping her tears off. "All will be fine. We are together, and that is what matters most."

She looked at him with red swollen eyes and smiled. That was exactly what she used to tell him when he faced a difficult time.

She hugged him back for a long time. She could finally rest her head on her son's shoulder and weep the past away.

"I must tell you why..." she said raising her head.

He placed his hand on her lips, shushing her. "You were only being human, right?" He smiled. "You can tell me later. Anyways, I'm hungry, whatever happened to these sandwiches? Let's not keep Mom waiting."

The Twitch

By Banu Alptekin

Here I stand in front of the United Nations General Assembly as I make my speech. This is not the first time I am talking to a large audience, however, this time I feel deep excitement. My heart is beating extremely quickly. I feel my heartbeat intensely as if it is creating such a loud noise that people around me can hear it. Luckily, I have worn my dark-colored suit and nobody will notice my intense perspiration.

This speech is extremely important for me as I have worked so hard for it. I have participated in many discussions and have contributed to the establishment of a working group about the rights of disabled people, and it is now time to announce the actual application of the international treaty of disabled people's rights within the United Nation organization itself. It is such a big achievement for me.

When I look around the conference hall, I see many curious eyes from delegates all around the world. They try to see my mechanical arm, and my mechanical leg hidden behind the desk. It took some time for me to finally come to terms with my situation, but I am now used to have those types of glances. Disabilities always receive attention and pity. Even in the people who treat disabled people as normal, you can see the pity hidden in their eyes.

I was not disabled all my life, In fact, I was born as a healthy baby. My mother was beautiful, at least to me, like all children see their mothers. She was a strong, resilient, well-educated working woman. She had a long career in the foreign ministry. She was a talented writer as well which enabled her to have a parallel career as a columnist in one of the major daily journals. She was so hard-working, responsible, and disciplined. At the same time, she was so warm-hearted and caring toward me and my little brother. You may ask where my father is in this picture – well, my father was brave enough to marry a strong personality like my mother, however, he could not handle the responsibility of raising his children.

Therefore, they eventually divorced decently. Neither my brother nor I spent time with my father. I am not able to quite identify if this situation hurt us or psychologically damaged us. On the other hand, we were enveloped with such an intense and compassionate love from my mother and this created very strong bonds between the three of us. My father was a distant audience to our life. He was happy, we were happy. We are still happy, even though numerous incidents happened in between. Those incidents have tested our resilience, our joy for living, and the strength of our relationship as a family.

One of the most eventful periods of my life started when I fell in love at first sight with Michael. I met Michael when I was in high school. He was the drama teacher and I was his student. Until that day, I was busy with my own life; studying hard, spending time with friends, helping my mother and my brother as a responsible daughter and sister. With this packed agenda, I did not have time to focus on boys, nor did I believe in love itself. But as I learned later, 'Never engage in huge oaths'! Michael entered the class with his curled long hair tied at the back. He was wearing a gingham shirt and ragged jeans. His passion for his work could be seen right in his luminous eyes. He was very enthusiastic about what he was doing. His performance on the stage was so impressive that people were thrilled during the rehearsals. When I first saw him, my heart started beating like a symphony of a thousand drums as if it would jump out of my chest. My hands were moist with perspiration and shaking so badly that I wanted to hide them somewhere; they could not be seen. As I was trying to hide my admiration, I noticed his transient glance at me.

"Can this miracle be reciprocal?" I asked myself. Yes, it was. And it became a reality very fast. Indeed it was an impossible dream coming true. Our insistent glances at each other went on for a few days. Then one day, at the end of the class, he approached me and asked to have coffee together. What a miraculous moment it was! I jumped at the invitation which was the beginning of our great love.

We were an incredibly compatible couple, sharing similar tastes, joys, and ambitions. We had a wonderful year courting. By our first anniversary, Michael received a job offer from Germany that could not be rejected both content and money-wise. He had to go while I was put in a very bad situation where I had to convince my mother about following him to Germany. I fervently tried to convince her that I would complete my education in Germany and would not, in any circumstance, step back from any of my life's ambitions. My mother was a warrior and she brought me up as a warrior as well. We had long, challenging discussions. My mother was a rational woman. She listed all the possible drawbacks and tried to convince me not to go. I listened to her very carefully, however, being under the influence of love and being loved, I insisted on the dignity of love. I reminded her of my courage and effort to live my way. As a last attempt at changing my mind, she tried to use my brother to convince me, but it did not work either.

Finally, drowning in the deep waters of love, I faced all the objections and I followed Michael to Germany. I was so happy although my whole life was different. Our life in Germany was like a dream. Michael was happy with his job, actualizing himself in his artwork. I started my university studies in journalism. I was studying in English but also learning German at the same time. I found a dancing course where I was performing regularly and that was helping me to get involved in and understand Michael's world more closely. We were both very busy but we were madly in love. We had created a nice, warm house where we cooked, drank, and laughed all the time with our friends. We were such a joyful couple. Our magical relationship was an object of envy for the people surrounding us. We were mainly socializing with Michael's friends. From time to time, I felt alone, but also, I was having a great time making new friends, socializing, learning about different cultures and lifestyles, and, most importantly, knowing Michael better. Those were wonderful days for me.

Both Michael and I were a friendly couple and had many friends. However, one particular friend, Victor, held a special place in our hearts. Victor was Michael's best friend. They knew each other since their childhood. They had grown up in the same neighborhood, had gone to the same school, and always shared the deepest secrets of their youth. When Michael first introduced me to Victor, he was kind but a little surprised to meet me. Slowly, he started to warm up to me. He was a very honest, open person, sharing with me all his thoughts. One day, he told me something that caught me off-guard. He said: "Dear Jasmine, you are so young and naive, I can see the love and ambition in your eyes. I have known Michael for a long time. He is charming. I am concerned about the age difference you have and I'm afraid you will be disappointed at some point." Although I was a little surprised at his words, I chose to not focus too much on his concerns at all. I brushed his thoughts aside as just an opinion. He did not understand the extent of our love! Brimming with hope and positivity for the future, I was ready to embark on a fulfilling life for eternity with Michael. Destiny, though, had other things in mind. With time, unfortunately, I realized Victor was right.

One day. Michael came home with a very pale face. I tried to talk to him but he was so upset that he started crying. Michael had discovered something terrible that day. It was revealed to him that Victor had pancreatic cancer. Victor's illness had been a real shock for Michael. However, he recovered from the shock quickly and gained acceptance of Victor's condition. He could cope with his inner turmoil better and became a real support for Victor. He took him to several specialist doctors around the country and even in other countries. When he realized that Victor was suffering from a later stage of cancer, he started supporting him during his treatment process. He was offering him all the plans that he had on his wish list. I felt very sorry for Victor and grateful to Michael that he was doing this for his friend. Michael was extending an incredible level of support to his ailing friend. Michael's selflessness made me admire and love him even more.

One day, Victor suddenly called and said he would be coming to visit us. He was living in another city two hours by train from our home. He informed us that he was in the middle of his vigorous cancer treatment and wanted to have a break. Needless to say, we were both happy to have him visit us but once he arrived, we realized how hard it would be on us. The visit was tough. We knew that he was at a late stage of his illness and the inevitable ending was approaching. Even he knew this fact and he was sad, hopeless, tired, and even dazed from time to time. Despite his weak health, he insisted to come and see us. We then realized that he was coming to bid farewell to us, especially to Michael.

We both wanted to cheer him up. We had wonderful dinners around the city in beautiful restaurants and visited art galleries with beautiful exhibitions. We bought wonderful wines; we had great wine and cheese nights at home. I also let them spend time alone as two old and best friends. Soon, time drifted by and the ten days of the visit were over. It was time to go. I insisted on accompanying Victor to the train station as Michael was too emotionally-devastated to do so. Michael and Victor had a difficult separation, both crying with a deep silence. They knew that it would probably be their last interaction.

Soon, Victor and I took the taxi and arrived at the train station. Unfortunately, we were late and it was almost time for the train to leave. I was worried that Victor would miss the train so I asked him to hurry up and get onto the train, while I got the ticket from the ticketing office. Soon, I got the ticket and started running toward the platform. Victor was in the last wagon, at the door, waiting for me. As I hurried toward the train, it started gaining speed. I began to move as fast as I could. My legs were shaking and I began panting heavily. I felt a strange ache in my heart as I rushed against time. I was racing against the train and I almost caught it. At that very moment, I suddenly felt my feet stumbling. I could not understand what was happening. My mind was in disarray. I tried to race but the race was over. The train had mercilessly swallowed me.

It was a very strange moment. The ground glided underneath my feet. I was in the air, like a bird flying around the train. This scene that seemed to be out of a movie, ended in an instant as I was packed between the platform and the cold steel body of the wagon in just less than a second. My mind was in deep chaos with different thoughts flying in my head, "What's happening to me? I don't want to die. Did I lose any limbs?" My mind began to wander beyond the present. I thought of my upcoming dance exams. I thought about what I would do. I did not want to be bedridden… I was immensely scared. So many strange thoughts were coming into my mind probably because I was in shock. My body was so hot that I was strangely not feeling the pain.

Suddenly I started shouting as I started feeling terrible pain. That was the same moment when I saw my arm away from my body and my leg badly crushed. I wish I could lose my consciousness at that very moment. But instead, I was aware of all the things going on around me. People were screaming and crying out. Some were frozen with astonishment. Railway officers were running around. I guess somebody had called the ambulance as I saw them running with a stretcher through the platform. Everything happened so quickly, they were almost shocked that I was conscious and asking questions.

"Where is my bag?"

"I need to call my husband!"

"Do you think I will survive?"

A doctor was there tending to me. I whispered to him, "Do you think you can save my hurt parts?" He was devastated. He was in such unease that his voice could be hardly heard.

"I'm afraid not!" It was a short and sharp answer.

"Then save what is left!" That was my last sentence and I don't remember what followed. I passed out.

When I opened my eyes, I was alone in a room. The walls were all white, as was everything else in the room. A total silence dominated the space around me. My body was heavy as lead. I wanted to ask for water, but I could not move my lips. I wanted to move, but I couldn't. At that very moment, I remembered the accident. I remembered my conscious state with thoughts flying in my mind and then how it turned to be a state of panic when I started feeling horrible pain. There was blood everywhere. The desire to go back to sleep defeated my thirst for water and I closed my eyes.

I don't know how long I slept. Then I woke up and tried to reopen my eyes. When I finally did, I was in the same room. I was not alone this time; my mother was there. Her face was dark and her eyes were puffy. She looked tired and resilient at the same time. I remembered that she was not supposed to visit us before Christmas. As she had come to be with me, I understood that the accident must have hurt me very seriously. Then suddenly, I thought of Michael. My eyes darted around, looking for Michael but didn't find him. *Where is he?* I wondered. Too many thoughts were flitting in my mind and suddenly, a feeling of intense lethargy descended upon me. I felt tired and was unable to voice out my thoughts or call out to Michael. I slowly drifted off to sleep. I could feel my mother holding my hand and I felt secure and loved; it helped lessen my pain.

After a few hours, I woke up again. I asked for water and my mother was as fast as light. She gave me the glass, held my hand, and did not say anything. She was in tears, which was extremely rare; my mother hardly cried or showed her emotions. My situation must have been devastating for her. I felt this urge to comfort her.

I said, "Whatever has happened to me, I will survive. I will fight for life, Mommy. I love you so much. I am grateful that I have you as my mother. We will do this together…" Her tears were increasing and she was holding my hand harder. I think she was sad but proud of me at the same time.

"The accident has been terrible," she murmured.

"I know, I saw my arm ripped apart from my body and my leg that was badly crushed. Did I lose them both?" I could not hear her voice but could only see her nodding her head. I couldn't help but wonder why this had happened to me instead of someone else.

Suddenly, I remembered Michael again. "Where is Michael?" I asked.

"You have been in a coma for one month without opening your eyes and in an unconscious state. Nobody could get close to you in the intensive care. When you got better, they transferred you to a normal room." She did not answer my question about Michael. I knew he was devastated because of Victor. Moreover, his work schedule was very busy with several projects. Most importantly, he was preparing to go on a tour in a month.

"Where is Michael?" I asked the second time.

"My dear, he came a few times while you were in the intensive care unit. Then he left for the tour." That last sentence was like a knife stabbing my heart. He was so caring towards his friend Victor at all times. But now that his wife had a terrible accident and was hurt very badly, he was gone. I felt so angry that if he was in the room, I would have hit him. I wanted to shout at him and ask why.

Instead, I was in silent tears. I could not ask more. I wanted to rest. I needed him so much to be with me. Getting over this trauma could have been much easier with him. My mother did not mention his name or this topic to not bother me. I was thankful to her. She was a rational person and she wanted to raise me to be the same. She always explained the opportunities and good sides of situations, as well as the risks and possible negativities. After mentioning her thoughts, she would let us decide and supported us all the way through. This approach helped me and my brother to be confident and responsible adults.

A sudden unease disturbed me deeply. I wanted to see myself. But how? There were no mirrors around. I was so afraid about what I was going to see; however, I was very curious as well. I asked for a mirror. My mother was pale. She said she would get one from the nurse and came back in a few minutes with a hand mirror. I could see my face now. I knew half of my body was lost and the overall look of my body was deplorable. I took the mirror from my mother. I waited a few minutes to collect my courage and turned it to my face. It was a real shock. My beautiful long hair was all gone. My face was full of scars. My head was taped. My skin was faded. I was like a ghost. I felt a deep sense of fear and sadness.

After a few hours of sleep, I woke up to the door knocking; my doctor came in. I found the strength to ask him about my recovery process. He kindly asked me if I was ready to hear. I nodded my head. He explained how the accident took my left arm and leg. He said I had two major operations to get my system back to normal. He also said that I would need to have two more operations. In the meantime, as my body recovered, I would start the physiotherapy sessions. The whole convalescence would take more than a year and would require serious commitment and courage. His sentences were short but to-the-point, explaining the process. He was telling them so sharply and matter-of-factly like they were so easy to handle like a piece of cake. He said he had seen my potential during the coma stage as my body had fought very strongly. He would expect a similar response during this whole recovery process. I was silent, trying to swallow my new reality. It lasted a few minutes. I then realized that I needed to make a choice. Either I would let go of everything and become a miserable disabled person, or I was going to fight my destiny and I would go after my ambitions and aims under any conditions.

I chose the second option. I knew that my choice was going to be very painful and difficult. If there was a chance that I could survive and enjoy life, then I had to be courageous to fight through this. My head was full of all these 'have to, must be' sentences that were easy to pronounce but also very hard to put in action. I knew there would be times when I would writhe in pain and be very depressed.

Just then, I began to think of Michael again. He hadn't even called me. I felt deserted and uncared for. Where was he when I truly needed him? Our memories together were coming to my mind with all the promises we made to each other and all the dreams we had shared. I realized they were only for the good times. Now that I was in the middle of this hurdle, Michael was not around. My mind told me to wait for him and that he would come but my intuition said that I had lost him forever. He should have been here with me at this devastating point in my life. But he wasn't.

I resolved to find my way with the help of my mother and my brother. I would not hope or depend on him.

The two operations that the doctor had mentioned were very difficult and hard to survive. The operations took more than 10 hours each and my body was devastated after each of them. My body was combatting to survive, however, my soul was in tatters. I was trying to justify Michael's absence in my mind with rational reasons like he may not be as strong as I am. This just did not make sense for long as I remembered his devotion to Victor. I even blamed Victor for being so selfish and not coming to see me.

But I tried not to think about them too much. I was focused on improving my health. The physiotherapy sessions started after four months of struggle. My mother and I became like the staff in the hospital. All the doctors, nurses, and hospital attendants were now our friends. They were providing incredible support to us and they were impressed by our patience and endeavor. We had many visitors who were coming to see me and my mother. My brother was taking turns with my mother to enable her to have moments of rest for her.

As the hospital became my new home, my mother went to our actual house to handle some of my things. There was still no news of Michael. Whenever I asked about him, my mother would evade answering my questions. By then, I knew that something was very wrong and Michael did not want me. He wasn't going to come back. My heart ached at that thought but by then I had faced so many challenges that I became immune to the pain of possibly losing him. I asked my mother to help me out with things. I knew that I needed to redesign my life. To begin the new chapter in my life, I needed to close the old chapter. For the closure, I needed my mother's help again.

She went to the house to collect my books, personal documents, and a few objects that were special to me. She gave away all my clothes to charities as I needed to renew my wardrobe to suit the new me. All the furniture was left there in the house Michael and I had shared. My mother did not tell me much about Michael. She had learned that Victor had passed away and that Michael was in a deep depression. My mother also did mention that Michael had asked about my situation and she had briefed him on what was happening. He was not able to talk as he kept crying all the time and apologizing for not being strong to fight with me on this tough journey. He said he did not have the courage even to see me in such a state. What could I say to this? *What if the same accident happened to Michael? What would I do?* I was helpless and clueless to answer those questions.

I preferred to utilize the little courage and energy I had to recover and continue to live. Indeed, the closure of the old chapter happened when I collected my critical staff and distributed the rest. I felt relieved. My rehabilitation process was still tough but I was stronger every day. I started planning about how to complete my education. I lost a complete year and a half. My registration to the school was suspended with the accident. I had checked with the doctors and after their approval, I had sent an email to my school to inquire if I could start back in the fall term. I needed to recover and complete a year of the course before getting my bachelor's degree. I needed to work hard. Ironically, focusing on work would be easy as my new physical condition did not let me move around much. I had to be at one place. I did set a target for myself, to finish school in one and a half years and apply to the graduate program at the same time. My topic on the postgraduate study was chosen as International Relations. I decided to concentrate my work more on the human rights issues concerning minorities, refugees, children, women, and especially disabled people.

Time went by as it often does. Soon, my hospital days were almost over. I got used to mechanical body parts and was comfortable moving around with them. As I got stronger and stronger every day, I could see the happiness in my mother's eyes. She was back to her old days as an energetic and resilient individual. She was proud of me. I was proud of myself! It was hard for me to say that I was proud of myself as I wasn't used to appreciating myself. However, the two years in rehabilitation taught many things to all of us. We had very difficult times when our emotional states were vulnerable. However, going through so much taught us to lift each other through our pain. Eventually, we overcame the burden.

Soon, my mother rented a one-bedroom apartment for me. It was very close to the institution I was attending. She has decorated it with minimal furniture that would be easy to maintain by a disabled student who had tough targets to meet in life. She never asked me to come back home. Instead, she encouraged me all the time to run after my ambitions. Her approach was a real inspiration for me.

Finally, the day to leave the hospital came. Everybody was so excited including all the management team, even the cleaners. They asked me to give a farewell speech, after which they showered me with huge applause. To be honest, though, I was astonished, even scared going out into the real world. And I decided to confess my feelings fully. "I would not be able to do this without your unending support. Every one of you carried me gently and decisively through this tough journey. Words are not enough to express my gratitude. Thank you all from the deepest corner of my heart…" Everybody was crying. They were sad but proud at the same time. They told me that they had never seen such a strong, decisive, resilient patient who was able to fight and to recover through such a difficult treatment. Later, they informed me that they had written a thesis about my recovery process. I was so proud of myself when I heard this news and I realized how unusual and extraordinary my survival battle was.

I started going back to school. My mother arranged for a lady to help me with the housework as I was concentrating on completing my school. She was a nice lady handling everything within two hours every day. So I was easily able to concentrate on my studies when I came back from school. I was not fast as I used to be but somehow I got used to what I could do. Also, I learned to listen to my body. I would lie down as soon as I felt the need to rest. I was handling things well and therefore, I was doing great in most of the courses. There were a few I was struggling with. I felt my personality had changed as I was more humble and ready to ask for help from the teachers. They were very helpful and flexible. With this continuous support, I was able to hit my target to finish school in one and a half years.

In the meantime, I was completing out the correspondence course with the London School of Economics for my graduate studies. They were very much interested in having me in their program. They invited me for a face-to-face interview. It was a new challenge for me. I would be flying to London alone with my new physical condition. Strangely, I was not afraid. I knew I could handle it after all the challenges I had overcome. The flight was easy. As I was at peace with my state, I asked for a wheelchair and that helped me a lot. I had a wonderful flight and I was full of energy and motivation for my interview.

When I reached the venue of the interview, the interviewers were very cordial and helpful. They did not force me up until the time they asked what happened to me and how I had managed to survive. When I started explaining what had happened to me, I remembered the full story. I was alienated from my case. I was explaining it as if it was someone else's reality. I guess they were impressed by my equanimity. They told me that I was accepted to the graduate program right after the oral examination. I was so happy, I called my mother to give the good news. My brother was with her as well. We had an initial celebration on the phone. Then it was time for me to fly back home to complete my final exams and responsibilities. On the flight, I found time to rethink my speech during the examination. It was easy to tell but hard to live. I was still questioning Michael's vulnerability and unfaithfulness. I think that questioning will be with me as long as I breathe. The tears started flowing from my eyes. I was strong enough to follow my ambitions, however, my desperate wish for a faithful relationship would last forever.

Time zoomed by so quickly and finally, it was time for my graduation ceremony. My mother and my brother were there in their seats, looking at me with joyful eyes. Soon, the Dean announced my name to collect my diploma. I was walking slowly with my mechanical leg. Everybody was clapping and cheering as I was approaching the stage. I could see my mother and my brother in tears. I was in tears, too. It was such an incredible moment. The moments when I was lying hopelessly in the hospital bed came to my mind. I remember the horrible pain. Receiving this diploma was such an achievement for me and my family. It was a testament to the fact that I could survive a huge accident, an enormous betrayal, yet be triumphant.

I walked slowly towards the Dean with my head held high. She was smiling. I responded with a similar smile. It was time to be proud of myself and not feel sad in any way. I had accomplished the first part of my aim. I received my diploma with enormous applause. We celebrated my graduation together with my mother and brother. They were so proud of me and I was so grateful to be with them. Our celebration was rewarded with yet another good news. I received a written positive response from the London School of Economics. I was accepted into their Graduate Program with a full scholarship!

After starting the graduate program, I have been blessed with a flexible schedule that allowed me to do my academic work as well as fieldwork. I attended several international research projects that have enabled me to travel to several countries like Iraq, Afghanistan, Syria, Egypt, Jordan, and Yemen. I was able to witness such testing lives that I was more forgiving to my own experience. During those international researches, I had correspondence with the United Nations (UN). The opportunity enabled me to network effectively and I had ready employment right after my graduation.

Due to my work with the UN, it was soon time for me to move to New York. My mother was again by my side to support me. She was my angel. We decided to have a holiday before I started my job at the Human Rights commissariat of the United Nations organization. I marveled at the transformation in my life; from my vulnerable days at the hospital to the days where I was employed by one of the most influential organizations in the world! That was a wonderful present for all the effort, struggle, patience, and endurance.

Mom and I decided on Hawaii as our travel destination. The weather was hot and sunny. The sea was light blue with wonderful fishes. Our hotel was situated on the coast and the beach was mesmerizing. We spent time lying on the beach, chatting, reading, walking (slowly, because of my mechanical body parts). It was the first time we were relaxing and resting after a very long time. We had wonderful food, drinks, and fun. The week flew by quickly. After Hawaii, we had a full week in New York with my brother joining us. We visited museums, saw musicals, and we went to wonderful restaurants. Life was showing its positive aspects to us after very tough periods. We had long walks in Central Park. Then, my brother had to go back. My mother was again supporting me to settle in. We found a nice apartment close to the office. We furnished it nicely and here I was, ready to go as far as I could go!

Soon, my mother got back home. I was very excited about my new independence and responsibility. Here I was in the United Nations, at a position where I could influence big communities. How could I have ever imagined such a state of life while I was lying down in my bed in the hospital after the accident? It was such a difficult time that I could survive but as time passed I was only remembering the goods things. The support of my family and the hospital staff. My struggle in dealing with Michael's betrayal and the strong desire to survive.

After all those years, I was finally realizing a human being's power to do anything, to adapt to any situation, and to survive. Maybe I was exceptional with my strengths and my family bonds. But I now had the chance to spread this spirit to the masses. I was so excited and grateful at the same time.

Soon, I started working at the head office. I was involved in tough fieldwork. I was courageous and brave enough to travel again to the most dangerous geographies of the world like Afghanistan and Iraq. I was a woman and disabled. Many people reacted toward and resisted my courage. As time passed, people who were opposing me understood that it was their prejudice. I was handling all the travel and hard work. What truly drove me was the fact that I was touching so many lives and creating a positive impact in this world. However, long-distance travel was tiring for me. So in between the projects, I requested jobs at the central offices.

I stayed a couple of years in Geneva where I was the project manager at the global public relations and strategic communication department. It had given me a different perspective about the protocol that has to be followed in any organization or project. Moving between cities was easier for me now. While undertaking this position, I was alone and I could handle everything by myself. My mother came just after I had settled and we just had a few days off at the Alps. She was so happy spending time with me and I was feeling the same. It was spring and nature was awakening. There were colorful flowers everywhere. The air was so warm and fresh. We had wonderful walks, fruitful chats, and I was ready again for my new responsibility. During this holiday, I received good news about my brother. He was getting married to his girlfriend. They had been together for more than three years. They had the time to know each other for a long time. And now they were getting married. I was so happy to hear this news. The wedding was planned to be at the end of summer. Therefore, I had to arrange my holiday not to miss the ceremony. My mother was so excited. It was hard for a mother to separate from her son. However, luckily, this time the bride was a person she had approved.

During one of the walks, my mother and I started discussing my situation with Michael. It was a strange moment for me as I had not thought of him for a very long time. We had officially divorced two years after the accident. Michael did not object. I did not ask for anything, not an allowance nor an indemnity. I only asked to keep his surname. It was an emotional decision that reminded me of the dignity of the love we have lived through in the beginning. He loved me a lot and I loved him back. Keeping the surname was a symbol for me to remember this wonderful beginning although the ending might not have been ideal.

But I do not blame anyone for this ending. Nobody's guilty of this ending. Life is such a challenge itself that throws surprises at you. These trials remind you that you need to struggle and survive if you have the courage, energy, and support. I explained all this to my mother with all my honesty and openness. I guess she had doubts about me keeping his surname but she has understood very well my rationale behind this decision. She was in all tears listening to me quietly. I let her cry and I cried myself, too. I still question my patience and my destiny. I think that will never end.

The new position in Geneva enabled me to be more exposed to senior levels of bureaucracy. Also, I learned to manage the relationships at those levels. After two years at the position, I started to miss the fieldwork. I felt I rested enough so I asked for a position in the field projects. The authorities suggested that I work on disabled rights. That was a huge topic, having many implications globally. I decided to learn sign language. It was a new world opening in front of my eyes. I was a disabled person. And I was able to communicate with another huge group of disabled persons who were having difficulties in their lives on a large scale.

Hence, I created several projects involving the hearing impaired. Disabled people's rights were acknowledged only in the western and highly developed countries. However, in several countries, the disabled were humiliated, even ignored. I decided to create awareness under the organization of the United Nations. We were having deep discussions around what was happening globally about the rights of disabled people. However, the organization itself was conflicting with what it was doing in terms of staffing and managing disabled people. Due to this observation, I started several discussions. As a result of those discussions, a working committee was established. Members of the committee were gathered from different departments. After a few meetings, people realized how they were depriving disabled people of opportunities. Therefore, with my lobbying and support, the committee created an internal procedure on how to manage disabled people.

Often, my thoughts wander back to the day when I gave my speech. With the applause at the end, I felt proud of myself and wanted to celebrate my persistence. I have never stopped after the accident. Although I had lost half of my body, my workload had almost tripled. I was lucky keeping my ambition to serve all people who are in need. I was thinking about carrying my courage and ambition to a further level. How could I do it? Thoughts zoomed in my mind. I had always been in an influential global organization where I could create huge projects. I was mainly involved in the design phase of those projects and not much in contact with the final implementation. The next stage could be for me to be closer to people. I considered politics to be an option for that. I was afraid at the same time. My observation about the political world was that it was dominated mostly by men. I was a woman, and more so a disabled woman. It could be a real challenge for me. My body and health conditions could not let me handle the dynamics. This hesitation could only be solved by discussing the topic with my mother. I needed her rational but compassionate approach. We were planning to meet for the Christmas holiday. So I decided to wait until she would come, to have a face-to-face conversation.

Days passed by so quickly. Soon, I was together with my mother again with our nice wines and meals. She told me what had happened in the last four months that we had not seen each other. We laughed, cried, and had a great time. All of a sudden, total silence prevailed. She was looking at me with curious eyes and she asked me what I had in mind.

"I know these glances, your mind is confused and you are struggling in your soul, am I right?" Yes, she was as always. I was so happy and lucky to have her as my mother.

I started explaining my plans about carrying my efforts to the next level. She listened very carefully. She tried to understand my motives, my concerns, and my targets. She let me speak for more than an hour as she listened patiently. I could not understand what she was thinking or feeling. She was like a therapist letting me explain what was happening deep inside my soul. I was tired. I stopped talking after some time.

It was her turn to respond. I felt our conversation would be different this time. She started by congratulating me for all that I had done up till that day, starting from the accident, through my education, my struggle with Michael, and my passionate work life.

"You were wonderful handling all this. I tried to be next to you during this journey but it was your effort and your ambition to live. I am so grateful that you are alive and you have accomplished so many things." I felt there was an objection coming and I was ready to listen to her reasoning. "I have never imposed my opinion on you. I have always respected your decisions and supported you all the way through. This time I will react differently. I don't want you to enter the harsh world of politics." She was so sharp for the first time in my life. "Your body is tired and you need to take things slowly." I intended to object. Then, I stopped myself. She was right, I did not need to hear more. I was tired although I never confessed. My body needed a more relaxed pace. I was so busy thinking about my ambitions that I forgot to hear my body's voice. I put her to silence by touching her lips. She was puzzled. She was accustomed to explaining her reasoning in great detail. However, this time I did not let her speak.

"I am relieved, Mom. I feel a fire inside my body and I try to keep it burning as if I would die if I stop and that frustrates me. You are so right. I never let myself flow with things. I have kept on fighting for years and I can confess now that I am tired. I needed to hear it from you. Thank you so much." This battle was over and I did my best and became the winner with my vigorous stand!

Believe and Do Not Question

By L. Toma

Mold was deeply embedded in the wall and the ceiling, creating galaxy-like patterns. I had been staring at my surroundings for hours, thinking of the stories this feared organism could tell, of the people they witnessed being locked in the cell, breathing in the dangerous fungi cells. I am sure most of them had done more exciting things than I did. Then again, what could be more exciting than trying to reveal the truth?

When I packed my bags for my trip to Paris, I didn't think I would end up here. I had so much faith in what I had to do, a strong belief that had been driving me for years.

I am sure most people would hate being in this cell: the wretched smell, the lack of colors, the bars, the other people who might be here, and the agonizing claustrophobic feeling – all of it would make most people afraid. I am not afraid. Not anymore. I used to be when I was younger, though.

The physical prison is the easiest to deal with. It's the mental one that is the hardest. I learned this lesson from a very young age. I've never consciously thought about my past, assembling the puzzle pieces to reveal a clear picture, to find explanations. It scares me.

Just then, a chair scratched the floor tiles loudly as one of the policemen got up from his desk. He was holding some printouts in his hand. His absence revealed to me the screen of his laptop. I recognized myself in the picture next to the headline: *AMERICAN TOURIST ARRESTED IN PARIS FOR DISTURBING THE PEACE.*

Underneath, in smaller letters, the following words were inscribed:

James Patterson got into a physical altercation with the Louvre Museum security while trying to access what he declared was "the tomb of Mary Magdalene."

I hesitated about reading further. Seldom did anyone have anything positive to say about me and I doubt that the author of this article would be the first to break that pattern. However, the mold galaxies were starting to lose their appeal, so I decided that reading the article would be less of torture than continuing to stare at the walls.

Yesterday, an American citizen named James Patterson was arrested at 9:46 pm, Paris time, for disturbing public peace. Two police units arrived at the Louvre Museum after being called regarding an incident involving a man claiming that he has the right to see the tomb of Mary Magdalene. "He first came to the museum around noon," declared Karim Vidal, the security officer at Louvre Museum. "I remember him because he was wearing a tweed jacket. I thought this is was strange, given how high the temperature is. He initially seemed just to be walking around, but then he started approaching tourists. I thought he was asking for information, but the people he was talking to seemed rather annoyed or bothered by him, so I approached him and redirected him to the ticket office or the information desk. He looked blankly at me, barely registering what I was saying. After insisting on getting a response, he showed me his online confirmation for the ticket, so I redirected him to the relevant counter."

But James Patterson would soon return to the entrance hall a couple of hours later. This time, he decided to stand in line with the other tourists at the ticketing office. Once we reached the counter, he displayed aggressive behavior towards Sophie Menot, the junior ticketing officer on duty.

"I was about to welcome him to the museum when he cut me off and asked me to see the special exhibition. I asked which one of them, and he replied: the one in the basement. I was rather surprised, but I explained there was no exhibition in the basement. He seemed not to care about my explanation, and he became more and more agitated. After several exchanges, he smashed his fist on my counter, yelling that he demands to see the tomb of Mary Magdalene. Karim, our security officer, was already by his side to escort him outside. I was taken aback by the incident, but I decided to focus on the current customers and thought that was the end of it."

Unfortunately, Ms. Menot was wrong in her assumption. At around 9:30 pm, shortly before closing time, James Patterson appeared again, this time with a copy of "The Da Vinci Code" in his hand, reading the final pages out loud. He stormed into the museum, trying to get past the security guards. Once they tried to restrict his access, he became violent and used the book as an assault weapon, hitting one of the security officers in the head with the book. No one was considerably injured, but the incident made waves on both sides of the Atlantic. While James Patterson is in the custody of the French police and his mental condition is being assessed by a professional psychiatrist, many have chosen to resume criticizing Dan Brown for writing the book in the first place. While "The Da Vinci Code" was a certified bestseller, success was at times shadowed by negative feedback and even lawsuits.

Dan Brown didn't make any statements, but Tom Hanks was asked, during an interview promoting "The Simpsons Movie," in which he gives voice to his character, what he thought about the incident: "I am sorry to hear this happened. Sometimes, fiction can become larger than life, but I don't think Dan Brown is to be blamed. It is obvious there are other circumstances around this incident and the discussion is not black and white."

That was all that I could see. The article ran longer, but someone would need to scroll down for me. I doubted that anyone would like to indulge the man who was under 'psychiatric assessment.' I wondered what the outcome of this morning's hearing would be. It was a matter of time until I would find out.

Of course, I did not reveal my story truly and fully. By now, I was aware that everyone's minds were under a cloud of ignorance. I responded to questions briefly and according to the expected pattern.

"Have you consumed any drugs?"

"Yes."

But not actually. We like to believe things that follow our predetermined thoughts. The cognitive dissonance would be too hard to take on for anyone, even a trained professional.

Our mind has a way of putting things in categories. For example, we would like to believe all children have a happy time before growing up. What more can you do than spend your time playing, going to school, and watching TV? The truth is – oh, how I loved the truth – that most children have a miserable time growing up. At least where I come from. The world doesn't want to know about the miseries. Such children are statistics used by politicians in speeches to promote their agendas. They are objects of pity for fancy people to sponsor at a charity's gala.

The paradox is that as a child growing up in a difficult place you don't realize that being miserable is not the norm. Until you get glimpses into the outside. Until you understand that there is another way things should be like. One of the things I knew was not usual was not having a TV. I grew up without a T.V. The only house in the neighborhood. 10% more miserable than everyone else. Although, T.V. was a privilege for even some of the kids who had one. They had to be allowed to watch it. And between a drunken father and an absent mother, who is there to give permission?

I used to read books instead. I got them from people who would throw away their books or pile them up to burn them during the winter. Or we would get books from the fancy charities. One way or another, books were finding their way into my life.

It is much easier to watch TV in a disturbed home. It's loud, it covers the screaming or the crying or the sound of a palm hitting the flesh. With books, it takes focus. You have to find a way for the characters and the story to come alive in your head.

I remember the first time a book came to life. I had been reading a book every two days, practicing with allowing the stories to take over my mind, my little room. But it never really worked for me. Until I got my hands on *Moby Dick*. While reading this book, I was on that boat. I was hearing the sea during a storm and the sound of the waves smashing against the boat, drowning my every thought and the world around me. The call of Captain Ahab, the whaling sound of Moby Dick… they were so loud in my head that I didn't hear the sirens.

A social worker was with the family next door, someone sent from school. The neighbor had complained about us telling them that her neighbor's kid (who was me) bruised too easily – and that she heard Mom screaming. So she called the police. When they arrived, the social worker came inside the house, probably to comfort my mother. She came up to my room, startling me. I nearly screamed. It wouldn't have mattered anyway. She wouldn't have known the reason why. She would have assumed it was because of all the trauma. The social worker was so young, you could see she meant well, but that she didn't understand where she was. She was kind and nice, and she stayed with me while everyone went to the police station. She told me she also read Moby Dick and that she loved it. I didn't say a word. The waves were still pounding in my head.

Mom never pressed charges against Dad. She faulted the young woman for calling the police. Dad never forgot the humiliation of having to go to the police station, of being told that what he was doing was wrong. You don't tell a man like that he is wrong. His self-righteousness was blinding him and controlling his actions. He had justice and force on his side.

I continued to explore different worlds and to remove myself from the day-to-day routine. I was now reading a book every day. I had to read. I needed to read. I was there in the room with Madame Bovary when she was crying, I swung the ax together with Raskolnikov, I had all of these amazing experiences. I didn't do anything except reading.

According to reports, 12.4% of kids in poor areas do not go to college (and only 41.3% finish a Bachelor's degree or higher). It is said to be seven times more likely for a child from a neighborhood such as the one I grew up in to drop out from high-school and college. Rich people were eight times more likely to graduate from college. At that time, I had no idea about the sentence that was awaiting me without having done anything wrong, except being born in the wrong place. Little did I know that I was going to be one of the inmates of our fate who escaped the gloomy verdict.

When you read the way I did, you learned a lot of things. My classmates were completely disinterested in what was going on in school. By the time I finished middle school, it was pretty clear who belonged in which gang, who would overdose in two years, and who was already having sex for money.

But I was a recluse. I would go home and read. Never in public, never on the bus, just at home. Kids around me thought I was a weirdo, and with that tag, came to a couple of beatings and curse words thrown at me regularly. In time, my classmates decided they had bigger fish to fry, so they administered me a minimum of torture, just so I would remember where my place was. I was fully aware of my status in our little twisted society, so I kept my head down. I knew that if I were to read in plain sight, the beatings would become much worse. Even the trips to the library happened in a very stealthy manner.

The moment when my life would take a different course came out of nowhere. One day, in a physics class, our old and – some believed, senile – the teacher was talking about gravity and Newton's law. No one, absolutely not one single mind or soul, was paying attention to what he was saying in the classroom. They were making bets about when he was going to die and whether it would happen during class. They were coming to class just to make sure they had the right information, otherwise, they were not connected to what he was saying. Except me. Well, partially me. I was reading the *Lord of The Rings* at the time, so in my head, I was strategizing the defense of Minas Tirith with Gandalf. I must have said something out loud because the teacher turned to me instantly. Someone was paying attention – in his class! We spent the next hour talking about which side – the humans or the orcs – were more advantaged on the battlefield. We started drawing and making calculations about things being thrown at or from the towers. For me, it was good fun.

The next day, when I was stepping on the school grounds, the headmistress was in the yard. When she saw me, she waved at me. Oh, no, I thought.

But I didn't get into trouble. I achieved a B in physics. I never got above C- in Physics, while 80% of the class was failing. The headmistress wanted to know what I said in class. I think she wanted confirmation that the old man was losing his mind. I told her what had happened. I almost replicated my entire conversation with the physics teacher word by word. I told her I read. It was the first time anyone knew what I was doing with my life. Her eyes were tired and she was always sad, but the moment I started listing all the books I had read, I felt a saw a ray of light in her eyes. She encouraged me to use what I read to participate in class. ALL the classes. And so I did.

I was never an A student. But the fact that I was doing a bit more than the rest, that I was coming sober to school and acknowledging the presence of teachers, opened doors for me. Teachers were encouraging. I was at least trying to do my homework and study for my classes, but I was there, I was present, I was saying interesting things. My B grades allowed the counselor to be able to push for me to get a sort-of scholarship (it was a charity program) to do some courses.

At this point in my life, I wanted to get away as far as possible from home and be by myself and just read. I was aware that I had to make a living, too. I wanted to have a simple job, where working with others was not involved or kept to a bare minimum, maybe do some work from home.

The answer came to me when I was browsing the brochures the counselor had given me. One of the courses being offered was for computer programming. Writing lines of code to build websites, apps, and games. I signed up for the course, focused, did the work, and got a certificate that allowed me to leave my family behind, pack my books, and move to the city. I got a job and I was taking evening classes at a community college. I was breaking the seal on my designated fate.

Coding was not as solitary as I wished it to be. At first, the people around me had come to understand I did great work and that I reached better results when I was left to my own devices.

I was now experiencing the normal: small house, a good paycheck, paying taxes, like any regular citizen. But my existence was not regular. I spent every waking moment reading, devouring worlds like the character in *Guardians of the Galaxy*. Yes, I experimented now with comic books, graphic novels, poems. Everything fiction, every world new, every character coming to life for me.

Similar to what happened in school, I started building communication bridges with the people around me using examples from the books that I was reading. As because I did not discriminate based on genres or authors, there was something I could say that was relatable to the passions and interests of my colleagues. I knew who was enchanted by the world of *Twilight* – mostly female colleagues – and who was a fan of Asimov's science fiction worlds.

My advanced skills in coding, together with the connections I could create with the information and emotions I brought back from the worlds I was visiting daily, allowed me to be noticed. In a positive way. I would be invited to lunch or movies by colleagues. I was no longer invisible and I no longer had to hide.

I continued reading as much as I used to. However, I felt the sensations were not as strong as they used to be. I kept a copy of *Moby Dick* which I would turn to from time to time to read again. Somehow, it felt that

Captain Ahab's commands were escaping me, that the sound of the waves was not as powerful as before. Where did it all go? Could it be that the crashing of the waves against the boat was stronger than my mother's screams but less powerful than the sound of laughter shared with colleagues?

I decided that if that were true, the tradeoff was worth it. I began to hang out with my colleagues more and more and to get more involved in my work. I even received a promotion and got to be engaged in a major project, having to coordinate a team of young programmers. I was beating the odds and the statistics. I felt that my past was where it belonged, in the dark corner of a time gone by.

Until March 2003. I was sitting at my desk debugging a software error when one of the account managers stopped by my desk. She was there to check the status of the website we had to finish in a couple of days. I could see she was holding a book. When I asked what was the title was, she immediately showed me the cover: *The Da Vinci Code*, by Dan Brown. Mona Lisa's eyes, framed by the title and the name of the author, were staring back straight at me. I immediately felt a connection, similar to the sound of the waves in *Moby Dick* crashing into my ears. I swallowed hard. My colleague was going on and on about how the book was fantastic, easy-to-read, and that it was causing waves. I interrupted her. I didn't want to hear what the book was about *from her*. I wanted to experience it *myself.* She must have thought I was rude because she immediately walked away. By that time, I had learned the social codes and I was becoming better at applying them, so I knew that the right thing would have been to follow her and apologize. However, I decided not to. The eyes from the cover were haunting me. I had to finish my work as fast as possible and go to the nearest bookstore.

In less than a couple of hours, I was running from my office building to the mall across the street. I remembered there was a bookstore there. Once inside, I realized what my colleague was saying. The book, *The Da Vinci Code*, had a stand of its own. The promotional efforts signaled this was the book of the moment. I bought a copy and went straight home.

No experience was more real or fantastic for me than meeting Robert Langdon. I envied him; the discoveries he made were colossal. The things he had done and the great lengths people went to hide his monumental work from us impressed me and frustrated me at the same time. I read the book in one go. I was in France, then in Great Britain. I ran and dodged bullets and felt the disks of the Cryptex turning under my trembling hands to reveal a hidden clue. It was a revelation similar to the first reading of *Moby Dick* and other books from when I was younger. But this time, there was no screaming to cover. There was no solitude to disperse. This book was indeed the ultimate experience. Its world was revealing to me in ways no other had done before. It became my truth.

The people around me were more interested in the controversy it generated rather than the enlightening content. It seemed that the Catholic Church was against it – how could they accept that Jesus had a child with Mary Magdalene – and many claimed that there were too many historical and scientific inaccuracies.

I read the books which supported the facts and the ones which tried to dismantle the theories in *The Da Vinci Code*. But no voice was louder in my head than that of Robert Langdon. He was not an ordinary person. I wished I had had a teacher like him in my school. I read his other adventures, but the one that remained close to my heart was *The Da Vinci Code*.

The conversations that I was having with Robert Langdon while reading the book made me want to meet him. I tried to track him down, but the few Robert Langdons I found were not connected to the topic or Harvard. Most of them were very angry when I reached out to them. It seemed that I wasn't the only one trying to get a hold of the professor, which meant that maybe there was a cover-up. Indeed, after drawing all the connections and the symbols onto a wall in my room, I came to see not only the truth but also the mechanisms in which it was being kept hidden.

Between 2003 and 2006, I read *The Da Vinci Code* 257 times. The experience became clearer and more tangible with every single reading. When the book was adapted into a movie, my colleagues decided to go and watch it for our weekly movie night.

I couldn't shake off a nasty feeling that evening. Meeting with my colleagues in front of the cinema felt like getting on the bus with the bullies in my school. In the first five minutes of our gathering, they were already making fun of Tom Hanks's hair, of the plot, of how 'lame' the movie was going to be. Once the movie started, every second was painful. They were ruining the experience for me. They were laughing. For them, it was just a 'stupid movie.' For me, it was pure truth put on a widescreen. Inside, I was screaming. I wanted to leave, I wanted to flush out their words, their reactions. It was not easy for me to drown out their voices, as I didn't have a book and I wasn't used to watching movies. I did try to focus, to remember the words from the book. I knew the characters' lines by heart by now.

However, that wasn't helpful enough. Once we were outside, I couldn't take it. I lashed out at them. At first, they were taken aback and someone even apologized for talking during the movie. I told them what I thought. I revealed my beliefs, that the book and the movie were renderings of the truth. They were staring at me blankly. Then one of them started laughing. He thought I was joking. The others followed suit. They assumed I was making a weird joke.

Even though the verdict of being weird had been assigned to me a long time ago, some took advantage of what I said that night at the cinema and decided to make jokes and fun of me. High-school never ends and bullies are everywhere. My colleagues would not abuse me physically, but they were mocking me and attacking the truth. I began to retreat again and to cover their verbal and mental abuse with the wisdom of Robert Langdon's words.

I bought the DVD once it was released. Although movies had never managed to capture my attention, especially those inspired by books – how could anyone achieve a successful rendition of my world? – this adaptation captured the most inner images. It felt like the projector was connected to my mind.

The ending is the most magical moment. After all the adventures, Robert Langdon is enjoying a moment of peace in his hotel room at the Ritz. In the background, a French voice is reporting the news. Professor Langdon is shaving. A simple, rewarding experience, after all, that he has been through. A drop of blood falls in the sink and as it rushes towards the hole in the sink, and it forms a line. The professor looks pensively at it. The wheels in his head have started to turn at this point. He rushes to the bed, where he opens his book, Symbols of the Lost Sacred Feminine. He flicks through the pages, settling on a page with the map of the bloodline. He whispers the words "rose line". His blue eyes flicker as he starts to figure out where he must go – lines beneath the rose. He knows at that moment where he needs to go. He must follow the Blood Line. He rushes from the Ritz Hotel through the streets of Paris. He follows the Arago signs and he arrives where his adventure began: at the Louvre Museum, where the two pyramids meet. He finally understands the poem that Sauniere left for him:

Adorned in masters' loving art, She lies.
The blade and chalice guarding o'er Her gates. She rests at last beneath the starry skies.

He is aware of the greatness of the moment he is living, so he kneels. The camera follows the gaze of Professor Langdon and is transported underneath the visible layers of the museum to reveal the tomb. Her tomb. The book does not describe it, but the movie offers a revelation. It's the most beautiful real thing I have ever seen.

That is when my focus shifted. I was so fascinated by Professor Langdon, I was oblivious to the core of the mystery. She was entitled to my full attention. The tomb should have been the real focus from the start. Professor Langdon was only the channel that guided us to the real truth. I had to see it, be humbled by its greatness and its beauty.

Most probably, the idea of coming to Paris must have been in my head ever since I read the book for the first time. But seeing the movie, understanding the mystery at a greater level, the power of the truth, transformed the thought into motivation. Then, after I had seen the movie for the fifth time, motivation became action.

I realized that I wanted to see it, to see Her, to kneel at the tomb and say that She was acknowledged. Just because She was being kept hidden from the world, ignored and misunderstood, she was not alone. Some people knew about Her and cared about Her. I started imagining that moment over and over in my head.

I began planning my trip. I would have loved to go as soon as possible, but I hardly ever took a day off, and I didn't want to create any gossip in the office. I resumed organizing my trip during the two weeks of summer, in August, when our company had official time off. My colleagues were talking about their travel plans and I briefly mentioned I was going to Paris. Everyone became excited at that moment. They started telling me about the restaurants and escargots and the Eiffel Tower. Someone did mention the Louvre, but only to tell me that the Mona Lisa is a disappointment because the room where it is placed becomes so crowded that you only get to glance at her for one second. Another colleague suggested that going to Paris in August is a drag; too many tourists, too hot, too overwhelming.

The word 'crowd' got my attention. Indeed, I would love to visit the museum when there were not a lot of people around. I was still drafting my plan to get inside the tomb. I was planning to pretend I was a student of Museology and request, through an official letter, that I would be allowed to intern or study the museum for the two weeks I was away. I drafted the letter but never received a response. I became angry. Then, I realized that the word *crowd* never left my mind. Why was it so important? I struggled for a while to get the meaning.

The answer came to me one day of work. We were discussing code, in general, and how some members of the developer community would like to keep resources open, share their work and be available for the world. One of my colleagues was already working on a project with developers from all over the world, developing a piece of software that would help several NGOs to manage their volunteers better and, consequently, to provide more help to the people in need.

"People need help. People need knowledge. That is the only way we are going to move forward," he explained, championing the idea to work – openly – for the greater good.

I realized then that my endeavor was extremely selfish. I was only aiming for myself to see the tomb. I was allowing only myself to have that experience. I had been alone all my life, but finally, I had something that I could share with the world. The power of the written word, the truth, the discovery of the hidden and forgotten things. I knew what I had to do. For the first time in my life, it wasn't only about me anymore.

I didn't know how things would unravel. I wondered what Robert Langdon would do. Going back to him for inspiration was a good idea. He was a man who functioned on intuition. I would do the same. Go on an adventure and follow my heart.

I had never traveled before. Where I grew up, people didn't have those dreams, and if they did, their destination was always L.A. or New York. As Americans, our travels are usually hemmed by the confines of the continent. You don't say you want to go to Paris, because you don't even know Paris exists.

People get excited about being on a plane or visiting a country where they speak another language. Simple things. I was there for greater things, so I didn't let the food or language distract me.

On the plane, I re-read *The Da Vinci Code*, for the 258th time. When I landed, there was a big ad for a telecom company with the image of the Louvre. I didn't know what the copy said, but I knew it was a sign, a clue left to me to confirm my mission.

It was already half past 10 pm when I finally picked up my luggage and I went straight to the hotel. Although I took time off from work for two weeks, I wasn't planning to stay for the entire time in Paris. Centering my existence around books and limiting the other existential experiences to a minimum meant that I had gathered a nice, comfortable sum in my savings account which allowed me to book a standard room at the Ritz Hotel in Paris – the same where Robert Langdon stayed – for three nights, airplane economy tickets, and a tweed jacket, similar to the one the professor wore in the books and movie. I kept this piece of clothing in perfect condition and I was aiming to wear it the following day. I couldn't stay in the hotel room, there was a magnetic pull that drew me outside. The city had become illuminated. I had studied the map diligently and I let my steps take me to the Louvre Museum. I arrived in front of it, but I didn't dare cross the street. I swallowed hard and I allowed myself to feel Her presence. *Tomorrow*, I thought. *Tomorrow would be the day.*

Tomorrow, you will be covered in the light of this city, instead of facing only the dark of a dusty basement.

I woke up early in the morning. I played the DVD of the movie on my laptop. I watched the final scene with teary eyes. By the time the end credits rolled, my tweed jacket was on and I was ready to go.

In the metro, I started reading the book again. I had to be prepared. The city was indeed very crowded and hot. I made my way to the museum entrance. I had already bought the tickets online. It was safer that way. Once I reached the pyramid, I could feel everyone's eyes oriented toward the sky. They were so excited about the architectural wonders. My eyes were looking at the ground, my heart at what was beneath it. I had decided to get there around noon to gather information. My big moment was planned for the evening. In the meantime, I took the escalators down to the entrance hall. There were so many people there, from all over the world, speaking languages I had never heard before in my life. Nevertheless, I knew that my message would get to them.

I saw a couple of guides holding banners with the words *The Da Vinci Code Tour* written on them. How marvelous! A thought sparked in my head. What if I was underestimating everyone? What if they already knew about the truth? What if I was misjudging them as everyone else had been misjudging me my entire life? What if they had already seen Her and they could point me in the right direction?

I approached a couple of tourists to ask if they knew the way to the tomb. Many were polite enough to show me the printed maps of the museums and make suggestions of things to see, but neither could point to the right way to the tomb I was looking for. After pressing them on with additional questions, some started laughing, while others simply walked away. It was becoming clear they had no idea. After a couple of failed interactions, a security officer approached me. He was telling me about different counters which offered me more information, useful and relevant. The basic social skills that I had learned alerted me that I had to comply. For now. I showed him my online confirmation and he seemed relieved. I was allowed to continue my visit inside the museum.

I was angry by now. I decided to take a brief tour of the museum, to see Da Vinci's work, the Egyptian, Greek, French, English, German – you name it – works of art. I couldn't focus. The paintings and sculptures passed me by like a landscape seen from a fast-moving train. Nothing could capture my attention or fascinate me as much as Her tomb. The moment of truth was fast approaching, it was getting later in the afternoon now. I went back to the entrance hall. Groups of tourists, couples, excited visitors, kids – these were all people whose lives I was about to impact. I looked at them. Would they believe me?

I went around for a bit and decided to get a bottle of water. I had to have a strong voice. I rested for a while then opened my book. I flicked the pages to the end. I read the final words: *For a moment, he thought he heard a woman's voice… the wisdom of the ages… whispering up from the chasms of the earth. Wisdom of ages.* Wise people. Would we all become wiser that day? The thought crossed my mind that maybe someone from the staff knew about the tomb. Maybe, they would join me in my mission of revealing the truth and sharing the information they had with the rest of us. I orderly joined a queue. The ticketing officers were smiling and politely offering help to the visitors. Although the line was long, they and their systems seemed effective enough for me to advance fast enough until I was face to face with the ticketing officer. She smiled at me, asking me which type of ticket I wanted. I said I wanted to see the tomb. She went on and on about the different areas, just as the other tourists had responded earlier. I asked her again about visiting the tomb, the one which was in the basement. She explained the basement is a deposit and there is nothing to be visited. She went on and on about temporary exhibitions. Somehow, her voice resembled my mother's, during those moments when she couldn't stop talking. For the first time, I understood the depth from which my father's anger ignited and the energy pulsed through my arm and I landed my fist on the counter. I screamed at her, demanding to see the tomb. She had the same scared look on her face as my mother. She didn't say a word. The security officer was immediately by my side and grabbed my arms and removed me from the spot. Everyone was looking at me and the ticketing officer was in shock. The security officer was much stronger than me, so he removed me quite easily outside of the museum. He firmly instructed me to leave and not to come back.

I was shaking while I crossed the street towards the Tuileries Garden. I was failing. I was completely failing at my mission. I couldn't defend the truth, I couldn't see Her. I sat on a bench until the night set in. The garden was peaceful. I opened the book again. I couldn't see the letters, but I knew what was written by heart. So I started reading the final pages. With every word, the magnetic pull of Her tomb was growing. Tears filled my eyes. I couldn't abandon Her. I couldn't abandon Her as others abandoned me. She deserved better. I stood up, arranged my jacket, and walked toward the museum again. I was standing in front of the pyramid. Inside myself, there was a storm. The shuttering noise of the waves in Moby Dick, the hit of the ax from *Crime and Punishment*, and all of the noises they were trying to suppress took over me. I kneeled and I found my voice, I started reciting the poem with a loud voice:

Adorned in masters' loving art, she lies.
The blade and chalice guarding o'er Her gates. She rests at last beneath
the starry skies.

This alerted some of the people around me, I could feel their stare on me. Not one of them made any gestures. I got up and I went for the entrance. There were people in line, but I went past them. They were expressing frustration in different languages, but I moved on. After all, I was doing this for them. I was once again at the entrance hall.

I raised the book, and I started reading out loud the final paragraphs of the book:

A miniature pyramid. Only three feet tall. The only structure in this colossal complex that had been built on a small scale.
Langdon's manuscript, while discussing the Louvre's elaborate collection of goddess art, had made passing note of this modest pyramid. "The miniature structure itself protrudes up through the floor as though it were the tip of an iceberg – the apex, of an enormous, pyramidical vault, submerged below like a hidden chamber."

My voice was loud and echoed through the chamber. The same security officer who threw me out earlier was approaching me. I started taking steps toward the entrance and continued reading:
Illuminated in the soft lights of the deserted entresol, the two pyramids pointed at one another, their bodies perfectly aligned, their tips almost touching.
The Chalice above. The Blade below.
The blade and chalice guarding o'er Her gates.

"Sir, you need to stop."
He tried to grab my hands, my book, but this time I was stronger. The truth was giving me the necessary strength. I continued reading.

Langdon heard Marie Chauvel's words. One day it will dawn on you. He was standing beneath the ancient Rose Line, surrounded by the work of masters. What better place for Sauniere to keep watch?

A second security guy joined him. They were both trying to hold me. They stopped my advancing, but they couldn't stop my reading. They couldn't silence me.

Now, at last, he sensed he understood the true meaning of the Grand Master's verse. Raising his eyes to heaven, he gazed upward through the glass to a glorious, star-filled night.

They tried to take away the book, but I refused to give in. I used the book to defend myself. It didn't matter, I knew the words and they were guiding me.

She rests at last beneath the starry skies.
Like the murmurs of spirits in the darkness, forgotten words echoed.
The quest for the Holy Grail is the quest to kneel before the bones of Mary Magdalene. A journey to pray at the feet of the outcast one. With a sudden upwelling of reverence, Robert Langdon fell to his knees.

"Why aren't you all falling to your knees?" I screamed.

I believe one of the security officers screamed at a colleague to call the police. I kept moving and using my book to defend myself.

For a moment, he thought he heard a woman's voice… the wisdom of the ages… whispering up from the chasms of the earth.

The police arrived eventually and dragged me out of the museum. "She rests at last beneath the starry skies. We should be allowed to see Her," I continued, shouting until I was dragged in the car and brought her to the police station.

After the formalities of taking my fingerprints and my picture, checking my documents, a police officer came to speak with me. I was silent. I didn't see Her, I didn't get to marvel at Her beauty. I never experienced sadness such as this. And I didn't have a book at hand to block out the questions asked by the officer.

It seemed that he had given up. He left the room. He returned a couple of minutes later with a colleague. I only heard the word *psychiatrist.* My minimum social skills breached through the sadness and alerted me about the dangers of this conversation. I couldn't remember the statistics, but they weren't on my side: most of the people from where I came from ended up in jail. I had figured out by now that I was in serious trouble and I would be losing my job unless I could come up with a reasonable explanation. The truth was not sought after. An explanation was needed though. And it came straight from the words of the psychiatrist: as soon as she mentioned the word *drugs*, I jumped at the opportunity. My memory was fuzzy, but I could extract a passage from a book I had read about the paranoid reactions created by smoking marijuana. I fabricated a story about a dealer who approached me the evening before and provided a basic description of his features.

I was taken to a room where blood samples were taken. After spending a couple of hours in the cell, morning came and brought with it an audience before a judge. I made enough noise to be granted an urgent hearing. There was someone from the American Embassy there, together with a lawyer assigned by the court. The entire incident must have been seen as an embarrassment for the country, with which they wanted to deal as fast as they could. I looked apologetic and declared how sorry I was and the whole thing was over very soon.

Since then, I have been spending my time in the cell, studying the patterns that the mold created on the wall. I took the time to process how I got here. I didn't plan this whole trip properly. I didn't consider… I didn't realize that I should have started with the beginning. I had to start with Da Vinci, of course. I had to go to Italy. I decided to give my journey a new, extended purpose. I decided that once I was out of here, my journey would become greater in Italy. I would find the right clues and the right people who would help me to finish my quest. Then, I would return to Paris and see Her. To complete the journey I started with the book and the movie. The new resolution brightened my spirit and dispersed the way everyone else looked and laughed at me.

A couple of hours later, a policeman came to explain that I was free to go, that I needed to pay a fine, and that I needed to report for community service hours once I was back home in the United States. I nodded and went through all of the procedures and left the police station. *Onwards*, I thought. *Once a journey begins, it must not end until its purpose has been achieved*, I thought to myself.

Paris, Gare De Lyon, A Couple of Hours Later…

Cadence takes her seat at the ticketing office in Gare de Lyon. Her shift is about to begin. She has been working at Gare de Lyon for nearly twenty years. Her children would tease her that she would be replaced by the machines in the stations, or by robots who could do her job faster and for free. She would brush these thoughts away with a smile. Passengers were still coming to the counter to buy their tickets. She is a courteous and helpful person. She will keep her job. She values the job because it had been her rescue from a life lived in the dangerous suburbs of Paris. It allowed her to move to a nicer part of the city and to meet a man who agreed to marry her and love her. Indeed, he divorced her, but she was better off without him. He didn't understand her. He didn't believe her when she shared the experience she had when reading books. She loved and will always love books. She has a new one in her purse every single day.

Passengers line up and she helps them one by one. It's incredible how she is the facilitator of all of their journeys and adventures. There is one young man in line who immediately draws her attention. He is young and skinny and he is wearing a tweed jacket. *In this heat! How can he do it?* He seems so familiar. Where does she know him from? A couple more passengers make their way to the counter before the young man is in front of her. She gasps. She knows who he is. He is the man who made the scene at the Louvre Museum, the American who is on the front page of every newspaper in Paris. He wants a ticket to Florence. But why? She is intrigued. How could he have been released from jail so soon?

She decides to be helpful and cheerful as she usually is. As she presents him the options for the timing and the routes, she makes the connections and the thought occurs to her that he is going to Florence because of Da Vinci. He is continuing his journey because he believes. She stares at him and for a moment, she doesn't know how to proceed. The tickets are being printed. What to say? What to do? She feels this is a moment she will look back on in the future and reprimand herself if she didn't do the right thing.

As she passes him the train tickets, she looks into his eyes and whispers: *She rests at last beneath the starry skies.*

Amel

By Shetha Hijazi

Allah does not charge a soul except [with that within] its capacity. It will have [the consequence of] what [good] it has gained, and it will bear [the consequence of] what [evil] it has earned.

"Our Lord, do not impose blame upon us if we have forgotten or erred. Our Lord, and lay not upon us a burden like that which You laid upon those before us. Our Lord, and burden us not with that which we cannot bear. And pardon us, and forgive us, and have mercy upon us. You are our protector, so give us victory over the disbelieving people."

Surah Al Baqarah, Verse 286

The first thing I heard when I opened my eyes was a strange clicking sound. *Where am I?* There was a bright light above me that was so intense that it felt like the sun was right above me. The strong stench of alcohol started to seep through my nostrils and at one point, I felt lightheaded and dizzy. I could hear scurried footsteps all around me, but everything looked so bright and blurry that I couldn't quite see who was walking around me.

Suddenly, I heard different voices coming from everywhere at once, as well as sounds of metal *clinking and clanking*. I tried moving my arms and head, but every part of my limbs felt heavy and stiff. I started blinking my eyes repeatedly until I could see everything clearly around me. The walls were painted white and there were shiny stainless-steel cupboards all around me. The stainless steel was so clean that I could see a blurry reflection of me lying on a surgical bed. Inside some of the glass cupboards, I could see small bottles of medication, syringes, white clothes, and dark blue blankets.

I slowly moved my eyes upwards, and I noticed there was a colorful image on top of me and it was a beautiful image of a waterfall in the middle of a jungle with beautiful and exotic flowers surrounding it. I lifted my head slowly to see what was going on, and I saw so many nurses and doctors running in and out of my room to the next room and preparing surgical instruments that were going to be used for surgery. "Hello there, my dear!" I heard a gentle voice as I saw an old woman's face suddenly appear in front of the waterfall image. The facial lines that were deeply etched on her face told me that she was around 70 years old. She held my hand gently and told me in a sweet and kind voice, "I am the anesthetist. We will insert the anesthesia now into your IV and you will fall asleep. So, goodnight and sweet dreams."

Suddenly, a large group of nurses came from behind the doctor and surrounded me. They removed my patient's robe from under the large blue blanket that was covering me and quickly covered me with warm heated blankets. I turned my head and looked at that beautiful image above me of the waterfall as the anesthetist started to inject me with anesthesia. Before my eyes completely closed and everything went pitch black, there was a sharp and icy blow of air drifting through my bones from my feet and climbing its way to my legs. I tried to move my body left and right, but my body was limb and heavy from the anesthesia injection.

I looked down to see why my body was feeling this chill, and that is when I saw a dark, shadow-like figure with long arms stretched out from its sides, creeping its way towards me, filling its coldness and darkness in every part of my bones. As it moved closer to me, my heart was racing so quickly that I felt as if it was going to beat out of my chest. I was gripped with tremendous fear so I closed my eyes tightly, reciting Qur'anic verses for protection in my head. I fervently murmured the verses from the Quran so my heart would calm down and the dark figure would leave me, but it didn't work. Soon, an icy chill went through my neck, and could feel the hairs on the back of my head stand up straight. *Just go away! Why won't you leave me alone? What do you want?*

After several moments, I opened my right eye halfway to see where the figure was, and that's when I saw the dark, faceless figure looking straight at me, its bony fingers brushing against my cheeks as the creature breathed shallowly against my face. It felt like an ice-cold air was hitting my delicate and sensitive face. The black figure started coming near my left ear and I could feel its chilly, nippy breath brushing across my skin, sending chills across my body. It whispered, in a dark and eerie voice, "See you soon," as its cold fingers moved from my cheeks to my heart. As its fingers lay on my chest, my heartbeat slowed down, and my body felt colder and colder. When I looked at my left hand, I could see the flesh turn from pink to bluish-purple, almost as if death was taking over my body.

That's when I realized that it was Death lying above me, waiting for my last breath to exit my lips. It was waiting anxiously to take my soul as its property in his cold, bare hands as if I was its salvation.

*****

"Ouch!" I yelped as I bit the right side of my tongue while having my lunch. The bite was so hard that the pain of the bite numbed my tongue for a moment. Without hesitation, I dropped my cutlery while eating and jumped out of the chair, and hastened toward the mirror that was placed above the sink in the dining room. As I stood in front of the mirror, I opened my mouth widely felt inside my mouth. Thankfully, there was no sign of any unusual marking due to the bite, so I thought I should check if there was any bleeding. I opened the tap and turned the handle towards the cold water, allowing the water to run for a while until it turned ice cold. *I hope it's not bleeding!* I checked to see if the water had become warm. I placed both of my hands under the water and scooped up some of it. I started rinsing my mouth with the cold water for a while and it felt satisfying; the coolness of the water started to relax my tongue and numb the pain.

After a few seconds, I spat out the water toward the sink and checked if there was any blood, but the water was clear. Thank God! I felt great relief knowing that there was nothing wrong. After I washed my hands with soap, I walked back to the dining table and continued eating my lunch. *Thank God, it's not bleeding but what a bite that was! Maybe I should massage it with olive oil or rinse my mouth with salt water to prevent from any bacteria forming in that area.*

"Ameera! Ameera! Are you home?" Suddenly, I heard my mom yell from upstairs. Her calls made me jump out of my chair.

"Yeah, Mama! I'm having lunch!" I answered her loudly, as I was sitting on the colorful dining table, trying to have a quiet and peaceful lunch. *Should I tell her I bit my tongue? I don't think so... I mean, my tongue feels fine now and there was nothing there, so why cause her to panic?* All of a sudden, I could hear my mom's feet descending the stairs and scampering toward the kitchen door.

"Hi, habibti! Oh, I see you're having your lunch... Good! I'm going to make tea for myself than finish my packing," she informed me in a distressed voice. I nodded my head to let her know that I had heard her. As she was preparing her tea, a heavy and uneasy feeling started to form in my gut, saying that I should tell her about the tongue incident. However, at the same time, I heard a voice in my head saying not to trouble her and that it wasn't something to worry about as I had already checked my tongue myself. I ignored my gut feeling and watched my mom prepare her daily afternoon milk tea from across the room. She was wearing a long, silk pink robe that had images of flying cranes around it and different geisha women. Her thick brown hair was let down and flowing past her shoulders. I then watched her walk toward a small bread box that was placed on the counter by the water cooler. With a mischievous smile, she pulled out a few slices of sweet bread and eagerly munched on them.

Watching mom's innocence was like watching some sort of peaceful and beautiful art form in motion. The simple things in life brought her such joy. It was the only thing that gave me peace for the day. Watching her enjoy something so simple made me feel like I should start appreciating the little things that life had to offer me.

"Hey, honey, would you like some dessert? I bought your favorite Ben & Jerry's chocolate fudge brownie ice cream," she asked me with a squeal of joy in her voice like she wanted me to join in her little mischievous plan.

"No, Mama, I am okay. Thanks!" I replied with a sigh, as I picked up my plate and stood up, and walked to the sink in the kitchen.

******

Since I was a little kid, I never told my parents and the people I cared about how I was truly feeling. I would always lie to them when they asked how I was doing, as I always believed that telling your problems to others makes you their burden. I remembered when I used to be bullied at school for having a foreign mother. Girls from my class would call me offensive names and insult my mother and her nationality, and that angered me so much. I would feel my blood boil and every muscle of my body would tense up from the amount of anger. My nose would flare up and I would breathe hard. However, instead of attacking back, I would just ignore them and tell myself that karma would handle them.

As a kid, my parents brought me up to be humble and strong. They often told me that when someone hurts me, we should not hurt them back, but instead, pray for them to change and to forgive them. However, I would often wonder how long I had to do that; a body and mind can only handle a certain limit of pain, and beyond that, it will fall apart.

As a result of my upbringing, I hid my anger and frustration, and sadness inside of me and never showed it to my parents; I always wanted them to believe that their little girl was a tough fighter. However, that gave an advantage to the people who would bully me and walk all over me. There were times where I wanted it all to end. Sometimes I would have thoughts of hurting myself, just to release the emotions I felt inside. At the same time, I fought such negative feelings and urges by remembering what my religion taught me. In Islam, it is believed that Muslims will go to hellfire if they take their own lives. Therefore, I would often remind myself that if I hurt myself, I will end up in a terrible place like hell. Even so, I often wondered how I could avoid putting myself in a situation that

255

would propel me to hurt myself! So, for 19 years, I kept my issues and emotions hidden inside of me. I secretly believed that I was the weakest person in the whole world. I suppressed my internal feelings and never fought back. What type of human being wouldn't fight back and stand up for herself? Only weaklings get pushed and shoved around, and that is how I always saw myself: a weakling who would not fight for herself nor stand up for herself, but rather depend on others to fight her battles.

******

A few weeks after the tongue incident, everything was normal until the end of December.

One day, I woke up and felt like there was a huge and hard lump between the back of my mouth and my sternum. I thought it could be from the dryness of the air in my room, so I swallowed my spit to dampen the area, but I felt tremendous difficulty swallowing my spit. It felt slightly painful, like a rough rock trying to be pushed down my throat. I got off my bed and dragged my tired body towards my bathroom I got ready and left the house to go to university.

******

"Ameera, you don't look so well? Are you okay? Do you need to see the nurse?" my guidance counselor, Mrs. Joanna, whispered at me, in a low and concerned voice. "You don't look well." I nodded my head and told her I was okay and that I just had a sore throat, but I wasn't. Something was very wrong. Recently, I had been experiencing excruciating pain at the back of my throat up to the back of my ear. It was so painful that I couldn't eat nor sleep. The pain felt like there was a nail being pushed into the skin and through the back of my neck, repeatedly being pulled backward and forward. This torturous pain would start from morning until night, non-stop, resulting in sleepless nights. I also noticed that I had started losing weight and feeling very weak and dizzy; I couldn't eat properly due to the difficulty in swallowing my food.

Later that day, I went home after finishing university, weakness, and tiredness taking over my body. *I just want to sleep and not wake up! When will this sore throat go away? It has been weeks now!* I got off the bus and dragged my lethargic body toward the entrance of my house with heavy footsteps. I felt like the whole world was on my back, and I was walking around with it. *I wish Mama was here so she could look after me and make me feel better*. As I knocked at the wooden door of the front house, I saw a blurry, dark figure appearing through the stained glass on the wooden door, and saw it grow bigger and bigger as the figure came closer to the door. *Clink! Click! Clink! Click!* I could hear the keys rattle from the other side of the door, while the blurred figure tried unlocking the door for me. Finally, the door was pulled open for me, and there stood my maid on the other side of the door, grabbing my handbag and laptop before I walked in.

"Your father wants to see you. He's waiting for you in the dining room," my maid informed me in a low voice.

"What does he want? I am really tired and I don't want to talk to anyone nor see anyone now," I replied in annoyance, as I just wanted to be alone in my room and peace.

"I don't know, but he said it's very important that he talks to you once you arrive," the maid replied with fear in her voice, like a small child afraid to be caught in trouble with her father.

I walked toward the dining room where my father was sitting, stomping my feet at every step, from the annoyance and frustration due to my lack of sleep and the pain in my mouth. I could hear the news from the television in the dining room, getting louder and louder, as I walk closer to the dining room. My father was a strict man built on morals and values. He always believed that he had the upper hand on important decisions relating to his family. He hated people that disrespected him and his decisions, as it made him very angry, which then resulted in him having high blood pressure. So, when the maid told me that he wanted to speak to me, I knew that I should not disrespect his order, as I didn't want to increase his blood pressure and get mad.

My father was sitting at the dining table, his droopy brown eyes looking downward at his phone, while the news was on the television in the background. He had a look of confusion and anxiety on his face like he just got bad news. I walked toward him with heaviness in my heart, for I could never know what to expect from him when he calls to see me.

"Salaam, Baba," I greeted my father as I kissed his forehead. "The maid told me that you wanted to talk to me," I continued with worry in my heart.

"Yes, Ameera… your guidance counselor called your mother and informed her that you have been dozing off during class and that you don't look well. So, your mama called me and told me… are you okay? Should I be worried?" he asked me with nervousness in his voice.

"Yeah, *Baba,* I am okay… I just have a sore throat that's causing pain in my throat… that's all," I replied.

"Hmm… For how long did you have this sore throat? And how come you never told me?" asked my father in a voice filled with anger now as well as slight concern.

I gulped in fear and replied, "I had it for a couple of weeks, Baba... I didn't want to tell you as I know you are busy and I didn't want to trouble you over something so small."

He continued looking at his mobile in silence, and this made my heart pound faster and faster, leaving an uneasy feeling in my stomach. Ever since I was a little girl, I always had a fear toward my father, as he was very strict with me, especially since I was his only daughter. I always remembered that one of my fears toward him was his silence, as no one could ever tell what he was thinking about. After a long and awkward silence, he told me to go get ready as he would be taking me to the hospital to get checked up.

During that particular week, I visited around seven doctors. Each of them gave me various diagnoses and medication regarding my health issue, but nothing worked. I even extracted one of my wisdom teeth, as the dentist I visited in Sharjah believed that the tooth was compressing a nerve resulting in my severe earache, but even that wasn't the solution to the problem. After weeks of frustration, my aunt told my father about a renowned dentist in Abu Dhabi named Dr. Mahmoud who might help me with my situation. My father called up his clinic and booked an appointment to see him, as he was getting nervous and frustrated with all the misdiagnoses we were receiving from other doctors.

During this time, my mother cut her business trip short, as she was getting nervous also about my health, and she wanted to be next to me and make sure I was okay. I was glad that she came back soon, as I was missing her and a female presence at home. Although Baba was at home, I still felt lonely, as I didn't have anyone to talk to, and talking to my father caused fear and nervousness in me.

******

The day finally arrived when my family and I would know what ailment I had exactly. So far, it had been a roller coaster ride for us, so when the day came to see the doctor in Abu Dhabi, we felt a sigh of relief. We wanted this issue to end, especially me. The drive was a long but relieving one. My family members and I sat together in the car, listening to our favorite music and talking about the events that were going on in each of our lives. It was in moments like these that I truly found happiness. I always loved going on long family drives, as it was the only time we truly got to enjoy each other's company. Baba would tease Mama, and then to cheer her up, he would take her hand in his and kiss it gently like she was his queen. I would then catch a glimpse of Mama blushing like a little girl getting an innocent kiss from the little boy she had a crush on.

258

Baba would then sing her a famous Arabic love song from his favorite Lebanese singer, Fairouz, the one that he played for Mama when they first met and fell in love.

Looking at them from the backseat, I always prayed and wished that I would also get a chance to experience the love they had for each other. Their love was like a romantic movie being played in front of me. It gave me a sense of peace, and joy to just look at them together, enjoying being together and cherishing the moment they were in. To me, they were my definition of true love.

After an hour and fifteen-minute drive, we finally arrived at the clinic. My father parked his car and we all got out of the car. All of a sudden, as I stood in front of the clinic, I felt like someone grabbed my stomach and squeezed it. Then, I felt like there were butterflies in my stomach – not the happy types that you get when you are in love, but rather the ones that make you feel like your stomach is sinking. As I walked toward the door of the clinic, my feet felt heavier and heavier with every step.

I pushed the glass door open and walked into the clinic. There was a reception desk at the end of the hallway and a waiting area behind it, filled with white, square-shaped leather chairs and a glass table in the middle with newspapers piled on top of it. We walked toward the reception, where there was a young woman dressed in a smart casual, black suit and white blouse sitting at the desk. She had shoulder-length black hair that was neatly blown and styled, in a wavy style. She greeted us with a gentle smile and welcomed us to the clinic as soon as she saw us. We told her that we had an appointment and she told us to wait in the waiting area. So, we sat in the waiting area and waited for my name to be called. After a few minutes, the receptionist came to my father and asked for my details so they could open a file for me in their system.

As my father was filling out the form with my details, my mom and I nervously sat in the waiting area. As a little kid, I never liked going to hospitals and visiting doctors, as they gave me a sense of uneasiness and discomfort. The aura of the place would always leave me feeling depressed as I watched ill patients going in and out of their rooms, looking like lifeless bodies that lost all hope in their lives. It was like walking through a deserted abandoned that was filled with the voices of the spirits that suffered within the walls.

"Ameera, the doctor is ready to see you," announced a nurse who was standing by the stairs next to the reception desk. I stood up and anxiously walked towards what waited for me on the other side of those stairs. As I reached the entrance of the doctor's room, the nurse knocked at the wooden door and opened it. Standing behind the door was an old, short, gray-haired man, wearing a doctor's coat, a small smile on his face. He had a face filled with wisdom and kindness.

"*Salaam*, Ameera! How are you feeling today? I heard you're having difficulty swallowing your food and have pain in the back of your mouth. Come, sit on the chair and let's take a look," said Dr. Mahmoud in his kind and gentle voice.

I walked to the dentist's chair sinking feeling still in my guts. The nurse placed a tissue-like sheet under my chin and turned on a lamp above me.

"So, Ameera, please open your mouth for me," the doctor told me in a muffled voice, as he sat behind my head. "Hmm... Okay, Ameera, you can close your mouth. Just wait outside while I talk to your parents," he said in a concerned voice that worried me. This made me nervous, why wouldn't he tell me what was wrong? *Is it serious? What do I have? Why won't he tell me? Why only my parents?* I nodded and walked out of the room. As I went down the stairs, a sense of heaviness and sadness came upon my body, like all the life in me just vanished, turning me into a corpse.

******

"Ameera! Hurry up! We have to board the plane soon!" my father called out in a loud voice as he walked towards the boarding lounge. After the doctor spoke to my parents, my parents came out with sadness in their eyes and fear on their faces, as if they just received horrible news. I asked them what the doctor said, but they wouldn't reply. I felt Since the day we left the dentist's office, I felt like there was a dark figure following me and creating this sense of fear and sadness in me. It was also creating a sense of heaviness that my parents knew what I had but they would not tell me. *If they are telling me that there is nothing wrong, then there isn't. They would never hide something from me or lie to me. Maybe I am just overreacting. The lack of sleep is probably just stressing me out and messing up my thoughts.*

The very next day, my father informed us that he and I would be taking a vacation to Germany for a short while, just so we could rest and relax. This made me feel uneasy, as my father would not just plan to travel overnight unexpectedly, and he would never travel without mom. It was unlike him to act like this suddenly. *Why would he choose to take us to Germany of all places? What is so special about it? Does Germany have to do with what my parents are hiding from me? Maybe I should just agree and go. Maybe he will tell me once we are there. And anyway, why refuse to travel for a change? I love to travel and I do need a nice and relaxing vacation from university stress*. I agreed to his request and he informed me that we would be leaving the next day. Why isn't Mom coming with us? We left for the airport very early in the morning.

"I'm coming, Baba!" I called back to my father as I pulled the luggage and ran toward the boarding lounge. *Did I send an email to my professors that I won't be attending class? Hmm... I will email them once I land in Germany and check into the hotel.*

The flight was six hours long. My mind began to wander once again about my condition. The pain in my throat was still there. I tried to stop my thoughts from wandering off. Luckily, I drifted off to sleep and, before I knew it, we had landed in Germany.

Soon, we found ourselves inside the airport. After the passport clearance, we headed to the luggage area. After collecting our baggage, we headed to grab the taxi to our hotel.

"Hurry up, Ameera," said my father in an agitated voice, as I helped him to carry the luggage and place it at the back of the taxi. "We are late!"

Late? What does he mean 'we are late!'? Where are we supposed to be going? Why is he getting all nervous and panicky?

We sat in the taxi and drove off to an unknown destination. Germany looked like a forgotten dystopian world, one you would see in sci-fi movies. The buildings were old and dull. The roads were filled with towering trees that looked like tall men standing in a line. They had long, skinny branches that looked like arms reaching out from their sides like they would come alive and grab at the passersby. They reminded me of a scary story my mom would tell me as a kid so I would listen to her orders. She told me about a scary creature called the boogeyman that lived in darkness and would kidnap kids who troubled their parents.

"I want you to take me here, please," my father instructed the driver, by pointing at his phone. I quickly turned my face from the window to see what he was pointing at, but all I saw was a large building. I couldn't make out anything else, as everything was written in German.

Maybe it's the address of the hotel. I will close my eyes and rest until we reach.

My eyelids felt heavy as I stared outside and watched the boogeyman follow me, an evil look in its bright red eyes.

"Ameera... Ameera... wake up! We have reached," my father said in a loud whisper.

I slowly opened my eyes and rubbed them. "Where are we, Baba?" I asked in a sleepy voice.

"We are at the hospital. *Yalla!* We need to see the doctor now! We are already late," my father replied.

Hospital? Why are we here? Did we already go to the hotel? How long did I sleep?

I got out of the taxi while my father paid the taxi driver. He informed me that he already dropped off the luggage at the hotel while I was asleep. I stood at the entrance of a tall building that was gray and filled with small windows. The building looked like one of those secret governmental buildings you would see in movies and TV shows. In front of the entrance, the name of the hospital was written on top of the sliding entrance doors, 'LMU Universtats Klinikum Grosshadern.' *This hospital doesn't look that scary, but it is quite huge!*

"Come on, Ameera! Let's go!" said my father as he grabbed my hand tightly and pulled me inside the gigantic building.

There was a large glass window cubicle with lime green and white office at the reception area of the hospital. A young blond lady was sitting at the reception. We walked up toward her and she greeted us with a smile and warmth on her face. My father asked her where Dr. Harreus' office was and we were surprised that she provided the location to his office in perfect English. We thanked her for the directions with a smile across our faces and walked toward the doctor's office. The walls inside the hospital were cream in color in certain sections, while others were gray or white. Everything was bright inside the hospital, as there were windows everywhere, which allowed the beautiful sunlight to come in and bring life to the building. I also noticed how everything was so clean and organized. The furniture and structure were well-maintained and looked brand new. Looking at all of this and the hospital, created fear and anxiety, as the size and look of the hospital intimidated me. We walked towards the hallway and reached our destination. My father told me to wait in the waiting area, while he would attend to all the formalities. As I sat and waited in the waiting room, thoughts kept entering my head of what the visit would be like. *Is the doctor nice and handsome? I hope he is! Will they finally tell me what I have? I hope they do… Why is Baba taking so long in there? I hope everything is okay.*

After signing some forms, we continued walking through the hospital. The atmosphere was creating a depressing feeling within me. The hospital was filled with patients in their gowns, pulling their I.V. stands next to them like ghosts walking aimlessly around and haunting the hospital. I tried smiling at them while passing by, but they just gave me looks of anger and sadness. There were empty hospital beds and wheelchairs laid out everywhere across the hallway. Doctors and nurses were walking up and down the hallways in a rush. Everything was moving so fast in that endless hallway that I felt I was running on a treadmill trying to keep up. *How long is it to the office? I feel like I have been walking for days!*

Soon, we reached the room with the words 'HNO Department – Prof. Dr. Harreus' written on it. I grabbed the door handle and opened the door. A sudden sense of sadness and fear filled my body. I saw a few old people sitting on chairs around the waiting room. Some came alone and some with their loved ones, but none of them were young like me. They all had a look of sadness in their eyes and fear on their face like they are going to a funeral or just came back from one. I took off my jacket and hung it on the cloak stand that was located on the left side of the office door. I walked across the waiting room into the doctor's secretary's office. The secretary was a tall, slim woman dressed up in an elegant top and trousers. I approached her and greeted her with a smile and informed her that I had an appointment. She asked for my name and told me to wait in the waiting room until a nurse called me. I sat down on one of the chairs, anxiety coursing through my body. *Why am I always getting this uneasy feeling? Since the bite incident, this feeling never left... Maybe I am just overthinking like I always do. Okay, Ameera, just calm down!*

Soon, I heard my name being called. I got up, slowly opening my eyes, and replied with a yes.

"The doctor is ready to see you," said the nurse.

I felt a heaviness on my shoulders and hollowness in my stomach as I walked toward the consultation room. *Don't be scared, Ameera. There is nothing wrong.* I could hear my heart pound faster and faster in my chest like it wanted to break free from my chest. Drops of sweat started to form on my temples and trickled down across the side of my face. My footsteps got heavier and heavier and I could feel the floor beneath me tremble. As we reached the door of the room, the nurse knocked against the door then opened it. I saw a young, well-built man standing behind the door.

He held out his hand, shook my trembling hand, and said, "Hello, Ameera! My name is Dr. Harreus and I am here to see what is troubling you." He had a charismatic smile across his face, and a twinkle in his eyes, that could make any girl melt for him. "Please sit on the medical examination chair as I examine and see what you have," he said in a gentle and kind voice, as he pointed toward the chair.

Suddenly, there was a knock at the door and my father walked in. I felt a sense of relief when I saw him, as I was scared for what was happening and I needed comfort.

"Sorry to disturb. I had an important call to attend. I am Ameera's father. Is she okay?" my father asked Dr. Harreus in a voice filled with fear and nervousness.

"Don't worry, Sir. I was just telling your daughter that I am going to examine inside her mouth to see the problem," replied Dr. Harreus, while he was preparing the instruments. "Now, Ameera, I want you to open your mouth wide for me," Dr. Harreus instructed me. I opened my mouth as wide as I could, even though I could feel the pull of my jaw muscle hitting the back of my ear and making the earache worse. I clenched my eyes tightly, as I could feel the unbearable pain of the earache hitting the bone at the back of my ear. I could feel the cold metal instrument touching my tongue and the side of it.

"Hmmm... I see you have an ulcer at the right side of your tongue, behind the base of it. Can you tell me how that happened?" Dr. Harreus asked me in a serious and concerned voice.

While I told Dr. Harreus about the incident, the heaviness in my stomach grew heavier and I felt nauseous. A bad feeling of fear, confusion, and nervousness started to overcome my body, like an evil spirit taking over its host. It was like an evil spirit creeping its way through my bloodstream; the roots of a tree spreading out under the ground to hold itself up. My father was standing beside the room door, his arms folded, his eyes and face filled with fear for his only daughter and her health. This was the first time I saw my father scared. It seemed the evil spirit had taken over another host.

"Ameera," said Dr. Harreus in a voice filled with sadness and regret. "I am sorry to inform you, but you have tongue cancer. Stage 4. We need to..."

Cancer? Did he just say cancer? How? I just bit my tongue! I never smoked nor drank! No one in my family ever had cancer! How did this happen? Everything around me froze and then crumbled down. The ground started to shake, as my body fell to the ground. All the life in me, just crumbled down. My heart started to beat so fast that I started to breathe hard. My body and hands started to tremble. *This must be just a nightmare! It's just a dream. It can't be true! This can't happen to me!* Tears started to run down my father's face. Seeing him in that vulnerable state and knowing I was the reason for his tears, ached my heart. My eyes started to tear up, but I tried my best to fight back the tears.

"I know it's difficult to process the news, especially when you are so young and have no history of alcohol consumption nor smoking. However, we do need to act fast before it spreads to your bloodstream," said the doctor in a sympathetic voice. "We need to operate on your tongue. We will be removing the affected area of the tongue and then reconstruct your tongue using your arm tissue, as it is the closest to the tongue muscle. Then we will take tissue from your thigh and fill up the arm tissue. We will also put a feeding pipe, as you will have difficulty swallowing after the operation. Also, we will insert a cannula, or breathing tube, in your neck. To keep the cancer from spreading, we will remove the affected lymph nodes from both sides of your neck and make you go through radiotherapy to be completely safe. Take the time you need to make the decision and we will start right away," said the doctor.

My body went numb. I couldn't feel my body nor any feelings. I was completely frozen. Thousands of thoughts went through my head. *Will I die? If I agree to the treatment, will I be able to have a normal life? Will I be able to talk later? Will I have a chance to be a wife and a mother? Why isn't mother here? I need her now more than ever! Is this some sort of punishment from God? Was I a bad daughter? Was I a bad Muslim?* Suddenly, something took over me, but this time, it wasn't something evil. It was something different, that I never experienced before, and there was no word to describe it.

This force-like power started to take control of me, and without hesitation, I blurted out, "When can we start the treatment?"

The doctor, with a look of shock and puzzlement, answered, "Umm… let me ask my secretary when I can squeeze you in the earliest. Are you sure you want to go through with the treatment? Don't you have any questions?"

Of course, I have a lot of questions! You just told me I have cancer! What will be the side effects of the treatment? Will I be completely be cured? How can an ulcer lead to cancer? Will I die if I refuse treatment? Will I experience pain? Oh my God! I can't breathe! My heart is pounding so fast! I feel so dizzy! I just want all of this to end...

"I know you must be thinking about how you got cancer. I am also confused and I don't know how… That is why I want to take extra care with your case," Dr. Harreus informed me in an assuring voice.

I looked at my father, hoping that he would help me with the decision. But his face went white and his eyes were bloodshot from crying, his body shaking with shock. Looking at that state of his, an unusual force took over my body and my mouth.

"I have no questions. I agree to the treatment," I said quietly.

After that life-changing and shocking visit to the doctor's office, he informed my father and me that the operation would take place the next day and that I would be admitted to the hospital the same day. From the time we left the doctor's office and got admitted to the hospital, my father was quiet all the way. As the nurse at the ward prepared me for admission and prepared my room, I saw my father walking up and down the corridor of the ward, frantically, on the phone, talking to my mother. He had a look of tiredness and sadness on his face. He kept wiping his tears, hiding his vulnerability from his family. This was one of the most painful visions a daughter could watch and endure, especially when she knows she's the reason for it.

When I was a kid, I was very naughty and mischievous. I would always throw tantrums and fight with my parents when I didn't get what I want. I remembered my mother telling me how I would just lay down on the supermarket floor and cry out hysterically if I didn't get the candy I wanted. When I became a teenager, I went through a rebellious phase where I would disobey my parent's orders. I would go out with friends and come home after curfew without informing my parents. I would cause problems at school by skipping class or creating pranks with my friends. So, when Dr. Harreus told me that he didn't know how I got cancer, I knew how. I got it by not being a good daughter to my parents, By not being a better person for myself.

I deserve this sickness. I wasn't a good daughter nor person. All I do is create problems and trouble everyone, so why did I agree in doing the treatment? Maybe I should just give up and die on the operation table. At least if I die, everyone will be happy without me.

My father walked into the room after a while, and he told me that his mother is going to take the next flight and come to be with me. I grabbed his hand gently while lying down in the hospital bed. I told him not to worry about me, and to be strong. I asked him if he and Mother knew about this, and he told me they did but didn't want to believe it. I asked him for his forgiveness, and he looked at me with confusion.

"Why do you need forgiveness, my dear?" he asked me.

"I am sorry for troubling you and for not being a better daughter to you and Mother. I know I was mischievous and made you and Mother worried. Maybe this is God's punishment for me because I troubled you and Mother a lot and never listened," I told him, with tears running down my face, and my voice breaking from sadness.

My father broke down in tears and kissed my hand and forehead and told me that I was no trouble to him nor Mother. He also told me that this is no punishment from God, but a test of faith in Him, and that He gave me this sickness because He loves me and He knows I am strong to handle it.

How am I strong? What type of love is this? How can you give someone this sickness and test their faith? This isn't the right way to test

266

faith! And why would God love me? I am a horrible person and daughter!
I don't deserve to live!

I just wanted to scream and break the large window in my room with the chair sitting on the corner of the room. I wanted to punch the mirror on top of the sink in my room, with my fist, just to release the anger and hatred I felt toward myself. My body and soul were filled with so much rage, that I started to breathe deeply just to calm down.

"Ameera, my dear, why don't you sleep and get enough rest? You will have a long day tomorrow," my father told me in a calm voice. I agreed to his request and he kissed my forehead and tucked me in bed. My heavy eyes started to close slowly and slowly until my room was filled with total darkness.

It was 7:00 am. I was woken up by the sound of the nurse walking into my room to prep me up for the operation. She was a big woman, with pixie cut hair and black rectangle framed glasses. Her name was Regina, according to her name tag. She had a motherly aura about her. I felt sudden comfort when I saw her like I knew she will take good care of me.

"Hello, my dear! Are you ready for the big day? Let me give you a small injection on your tush before I take you to the operation room," Nurse Regina informed me in a voice filled with positivity and excitement. I told my father to stand next to me and grab my hand, as I had a phobia of needles. I turned on my stomach and grabbed my father's hand tightly as the nurse injected me on my bottom.

"All done. Now let's take you to the operation room," Nurse Regina said. She unlocked the wheels of the bed and pushed me out of the room, towards the corridor of the ward. My father walked beside me with a look of nervousness on his face, not knowing if his daughter will come out of the surgery alive or not. I slowly started to feel lightheaded and sleepy, which I believed was the effect of the injection. As I saw the flashing bright lights from the corridors come across me, over my face, I slowly felt numb and fell asleep.

As I lay ready for the operation to commence, I wished for my beloved mother to be there. I did not want her to go through the sorrow of seeing her child in this state but, yet I needed my mother's presence for comfort. Just then, almost as if my prayers were immediately answered, the doctors informed me that my mom was here to see me. When I saw mom come in through the door, something broke inside of me. Her eyes were sunken with tears and she looked disheveled and traumatized. I guess seeing one's child in a state like mine was sheer devastation. She quickly hurried toward me and grabbed me. Tears began to flow effortlessly like the ocean.

"Mom," I murmured as I tried to hold back my tears. "Be strong, Mom. This is a test from God. Pray for me, Mom." My words did not seem to placate her as she sobbed relentlessly.

Soon, it was time for me to be wheeled into the operating room. They were going to get me ready for the great task which could alter my life forever. Mom squeezed my hands, even as the needles pricked me all over. She could not follow me inside and I could see that she did not want to leave me. Mom had always been my blanket of comfort. But this battle was mine to fight alone. Slowly, I let go of her hand and closed my tearing eyes as I entered the operating room.

My eyes started to open slowly, and my body and head felt so heavy. It felt like I had slept for a few minutes. In a dream, I saw myself waking up in my hospital room. No one was in the room; it was just me. Everything was quiet outside my room. So, I got off my bed and walked toward the door of my room, to see why it was so quiet outside. As I was walking, I felt heaviness all over my body, like something was pulling toward the ground, making it difficult for me to walk. I opened the door and peeped outside, but no one was in the corridor. The rooms of other patients were empty. The whole ward was empty and I was alone. I felt scared and confused, as I didn't know what was going on.

I shouted out loudly, "Hello? Is anybody here? Hello? Can anyone hear me?" No one answered. My heart started to pound faster and faster, as I ran frantically around the other wards, and hospital and my mind just kept spinning and spinning.

Where is everyone? Why isn't anyone answering me? Where is Father? Dr. Harreus? Nurse Regina? What is happening?

Suddenly, a small figure appeared at the end of the ward corridor. It was unclear who it was us, because of the sunlight appearing at the back of a small, dark figure. "Hello? Hi! What's your name? Are you alone? Do you know where everyone is?" I asked the small dark figure, but it didn't answer.

It slowly started to walk toward me, making its facial image clearer and visible. It was a small girl, probably six or seven years old. She had long, straight, dark brown hair, and the sweetest smile and innocence I had ever seen. For some strange reason, I didn't feel threatened toward this little girl. Instead, I felt calm and at peace when I saw her. I felt like I was in the presence of an angel.

She stood in front of me with a sweet smile across her sweet and innocent face and grabbed my hand with her small, soft hands wrapped around mine. "Come on, Ameera! We need to start moving! There is not enough time!" she said in a sweet, childlike voice.

"Moving? Where are we going? What do you mean by there is not enough time? Who are you, anyway?" I asked the little girl with confusion in my voice and mind.

The little girl just giggled and pulled me towards the corridor of the hospital. "I am going to take you to your parents. I thought maybe you would like to see them," said the little girl.

We walked together outside of the hospital and toward the hospital park. I saw Mother and Father sitting on a bench, crying loudly. "Mother! Father!" I yelled out and ran toward them, but they didn't hear me nor looked in my direction.

Why won't they look at me? Why won't they answer me? What's going on? I looked at mother and father in confusion, as to why won't hear me nor look at me. I felt a tiny hand slip through mine, and I turned and saw the little girl standing next to me.

"They can't hear nor see you. You are just a ghost," said the little girl.

"What do you mean I am a ghost?" I asked the little girl in confusion. "You are dead," she said and looked at me with sadness in her eyes.

Dead? Ghost? How? When? Were there complications during the surgery? How can I be dead? And when?

"There was a complication during the surgery, and instead of making your body fight, you decided to let your body give up. So, you died. You died giving up," said the little girl, with disappointment. "Because you chose to die instead of fight, you left your parents heartbroken and depressed. They loved you very much. They prayed hard for you. They have blamed themselves for your death ever since. They think they haven't been good parents to you, so that's why you chose to die," the little girl continued.

"That's not right! They are amazing parents! Why would I do that?" I told the girl, in shock. *I thought if I died, my parents will be at ease and not be troubled by me... but they aren't... instead, I caused them more pain and suffering... maybe I was wrong... maybe I should fight!*

"Now, we will go to your best friend, Maryam," said the little girl with joy in her face, and a twinkle in her eyes.

Everything went black, and I felt my body being pulled into a vacuum. Suddenly, I found myself standing in my World History class in university. The class was in session. I saw Maryam sitting at her desk in the third row. She was writing down in her notebook, while the professor was explaining the Ancient Egyptian religion. I slowly approached Maryam and felt a sense of happiness as I saw her. However, she looked different. She looked serious and responsible, which was unlike her. "Since you died, she became hard-working and studious. She became responsible. She became a better person," said the little girl.

So, Maryam looks to be doing better without me.

"She just got accepted for an internship at the Prime Minister's office. I heard it was her dream job," continued the little girl.

She finally got the internship she always dreamed of... and that was all because I wasn't in her life anymore... out of all of my friends, I believed she would be the only one who wanted me to stay alive... But it seems, she is better off without me... and who am I to stand in the way of her happiness...

Suddenly, I had a heavy and sinking feeling, filled with sadness and self-doubt. To find out just now that I could not only bring pain and sadness to my family if I died, but I could also destroy the happiness of the person I cared for the most. The one person who stood by me through all the rough times I had. Giving her the happiness she deserved shouldn't be taken away by a selfish person.

"Come on, Ameera," said the little girl, in a pleading voice. "We have just one last stop before the operation is over. After meeting all these important people in your life, you need to decide if you will fight through the operation and live, or give up and die from the operation. The choice is yours. Hopefully, the last person you will meet now will help you to choose," continued the little girl.

What?! Now I should choose whether I should live or die? And who is this last person? I just met the only three people I cared for and loved the most! There isn't anyone else! I just want all this nightmare to end! I just want to die and end all of this!

Suddenly, I found myself at my favorite beach, next to my home. It was a big and beautiful beach that I would often visit if I ever wanted to be alone and contemplate important things in my life. The beach always held a sentimental value for me. It was the place where my family and I would go to spend quality time together and share a few laughs. It was the only place that heard my cry and had tasted my tears. It was the only place that gave me peace, happiness, and calmness. I remembered that I would come to this beach after I had a bad day, and just walked on the white sand, barefoot. I would stand at the edge of the shoreline, close my eyes, and feel the sand seep through between my toes. I would also feel the coolness of the sea breeze brush upon my cheek and intertwine through my hair, like a male lover caressing his female lover after a long voyage at sea.

The squawking of the seagulls and the ocean waves filled my ears while I would feel the cool, ocean water touch my toes and then gently fill up to my ankle, and suddenly get pulled back to the ocean. This simplistic moment filled my mind and soul with peace and made me believe that there is always a good thing to enjoy right around the corner. My thoughts got interrupted suddenly when I saw a couple, far away from me, holding each other and their arms wrapped around each other as they watched the sunrise. I could hear them laughing and giggling from a distance as they walked down the shoreline, holding hands, and just enjoying the most beautiful scene that nature could offer us.

"So, where is this last person that is supposed to help me with my important decision?" I asked the little girl eagerly. The little girl pointed out toward the couple I was looking at and said, "That man over there is your husband and one true love, named Mohammed. He fell in love with you from the moment he saw you at an Ed Sheeran concert that you both attended with friends. You both got introduced through a common friend from the group. You both spoke all night and hung out. Soon, you both started to develop feelings for one another. Both of you realized that you have a lot of things in common, but what was strange is that you both felt that you knew each other for a long time. So, after three years of being together, he proposed to you and you got married in a month. Two years later, all your dreams came true," said the little girl, with a smile across her face and pure joy in her eyes.

Suddenly, I heard Mohammed call out from a distance, and looking in my direction, "Amal! Amal! Come on! We need to go!" as he waved his hand in the air.

Hmm... Who is this Amal that he is calling out for? There is no one here but me and the little girl... I looked behind me but there was no one.

"Coming, Baba!" I heard a childlike voice in my ear. I turned around to see a little girl run across the beach and toward the loving couple. *Oh my God! Was that...? It can't be! The little girl... Amal... is my daughter! She is my daughter! I finally became a wife and a mother! My dream finally came true! I experienced true love, married my soulmate, and had a beautiful daughter! Finally... I have hope...I have Amal. And she will be the true reason I will fight this battle and make sure I come out alive... She is my Amal.*

As I watched my dream come true in front of me and enjoyed every moment of it, I suddenly felt at peace.

"I will always be there with you, Mama," said a childlike voice in my ear. "I am very proud of you and I will be honored to have you as my mother. You are a strong woman and a fighter. You always told me to fight, be strong, have faith, be happy, and most importantly, never give

271

up. God loves you, Mama, and He chose you to have this cancer because He knows you are strong and you can fight it. Don't fail His test. On yourself. On the people that love you and on your dream. Don't fail on me, Mama. Don't be scared about how your life would be later because it will be beautiful. You live a long and healthy life after this, and see all of this as a dream. You will become a strong person. An independent and responsible person. You will make your family proud and you will know who your true friends are. I love you so much, Mama, and I can't wait to be held in your arms one day and see you and your father together. As my parents." As I heard this from Amal, tears flowed down my eyes, and pure love filled my soul and body. *I won't fail you, my baby. I will make sure I fight and make you proud of me as your mother.*

Thirteen hours later, I woke up at the ICU. Dr. Harreus informed me that all went well during surgery and that I fought like a warrior. Mother came just as they started the operation and she and Father never left my side. The doctor told me I would be in ICU for three days and two nights to make sure all my vital signs are good and for observation. My body felt very heavy and so did my tongue. I tried talking, but I couldn't. I could only hear the voice of myself in my head. I wanted to tell my mother and father about the dream. But, instead, I fell asleep, as I was looking forward to a night of good, long sleep, after all I had been through.

Five years have passed from the day of my surgery, and I am medically declared cancer-free. However, I still consider myself a cancer fighter. I completed 32 sessions of radiotherapy. I attended physiotherapy and speech therapy sessions for five months. I completed my first *Umrah* with my father as soon as I arrived back home after six months. I graduated from university and got my first job at a theme park, which I enjoy so much. I got my driving license on my first attempt after getting cured. I got awarded by Abu Dhabi Health Authority for being a cancer fighter. My circle of friends became small, but Maryam and I are still best friends. I became closer to my parents. I became closer to my faith. I became strong, confident, funny, independent and grateful for the second chance God gave me.

Although I still suffer from the effects of the treatment, such as short-term memory and difficulty in pronouncing certain words, I make sure to always stay positive and never let weakness take over me. I make sure to spread my story to as many people as I can, so they can also have an Amal in their lives. I wanted everyone who is going through cancer to know that they have an Amal. To know that they are fighters and this is all God's test to us and that we should try and ace it. Having cancer was once seen as a curse for me, but now I see it as a blessing. I see it that way because it made me a better person. It made me look at life in colors and enjoy every bit of it because not everyone gets a chance to survive death and become reborn. We are given one life, so we need to live it to the fullest and be grateful for all the people in our lives and what was given to us. Nothing and no one should be taken for granted. Also, we should learn to love ourselves first, before anyone, and to put ourselves first before anyone else. I became a new person. Thanks to the hope I have for my future. Thanks to my Amal.